Forgiving Mariela Camacho

by
AJ Sidransky

Berwick Court Publishing Co.
CHICAGO, IL

Berwick Court Publishing Company
Chicago, Illinois
http://www.berwickcourt.com

Sidransky, A. J.
  Forgiving Mariela Camacho / by AJ Sidransky.

  pages ; cm

  Issued also as an ebook.
  ISBN: 978-0-9909515-6-8

  1. Detectives--New York (State)--New York--Fiction. 2. Serial murderers--New York (State)--New York--Fiction. 3. Murder--Investigation--Fiction. 4. Drug dealers--Dominican Republic--Fiction. 5. Mystery fiction. I. Title.

PS3619.I37 F67 2015

813/.6   2015946176

OTHER WORKS BY A.J. SIDRANSKY

Forgiving Maximo Rothman

Stealing a Summer's Afternoon

For William, Mitch and Thom

If I had had just one of you for a friend, I would have been lucky enough.

Preface & Acknowledgments

THE GENESIS OF THIS BOOK lies in its predecessor, Forgiving Maximo Rothman. I had originally intended to include a fourth story line in that book that dealt with the Dominican immigrant experience. My teachers, publisher and editor all strongly suggested that I needed to shorten the story for narrative purposes. That story line, along with the many loose ends I left with respect to other characters, resulted in Forgiving Mariela Camacho.

Forgiving Mariela Camacho and Forgiving Maximo Rothman share many themes, including the immigrant experience. Over these past few years, as my relationships within the Dominican immigrant community here in Washington Heights have deepened, I have come to understand how all immigrant experiences are essentially the same. The desire for a better life for oneself and one's family, particularly one's children, is permanently handcuffed to a longing for home and a desire to feel at home.

I am the grandchild of immigrants. When I hear my Dominican friends talk about their lives and their experiences, it is as if I am listening to my grandparents speaking about theirs. The names, customs, foods and languages have changed, but the stories are the same.

Underlying everything else, Forgiving Mariela Camacho is a story about male friendship. Men have a hard time expressing themselves, especially to one another. Emotional honesty is viewed as weakness.

Those of us who have brothers are sometimes fortunate enough to have a relationship that provides us with someone to trust without fear of judgement or ridicule. For those of us who don't, we are sometimes lucky enough to find a friend who can step into those shoes.

I have been incredibly blessed to find three such friends. William, Mitch and Thom, you have made the difference in my life, and I thank you. You've been there when I needed someone to talk to, and always without judgment. I hope I have been as good a friend to you as well. This book is for you.

To Joel Kravet, my friend and client, you wanted to be in one of my books. You're here, sitting in your store on Amsterdam Avenue. Congratulations on what you've done for yourself. The Joel pictured here is history. No one will ever describe you as a "fat guy" again.

A special thanks to the force behind UptownCollective.com, Led Black, for all your efforts on my behalf and your generous dose of "Uptown Love."

To my editor, Dave Balson, and publisher, Matt Balson, my thanks for your continued support. To my publicist, Meryl Zegarek, and to the cover artist, Dan Swanson, thank you. To my wife and son, thanks for the love and support, and for the confidence you have in my ability to continue to discover who I am, even at this late stage in my life.

Lastly, as I said in the forward to Forgiving Maximo Rothman, I have tried to reach out to the concerns and hidden feelings of men. Like the lyrics of a good bachata, we are all really pretty soft at heart. We fall in love and get hurt, but rarely discuss it.

I hope I touch a few readers with this story. And for those of you who love Kurchenko and Gonzalvez, they'll be back in two years or so.

A J Sidransky

Prologue

MARIELA FELT THE STEEL BLADE slide across her neck. It didn't hurt, not at all. That made her smile. She liked that her face would look forever happy. The coldness of the blade was what struck her. A knife never felt like that in one's hand. Then she felt wet and realized it was her blood, warm against the place where the cold knife had been. It dripped down her neck, then reached her T-shirt, producing yet another sensation, a thick stickiness between her skin and the fabric. She wanted to sigh but couldn't.

She opened her eyes and looked around the room, realizing this was the last thing she would ever see. How sad, so far from the place she thought of as home and the people she loved. In the corner of the room, on top of the ebony dresser was a framed photograph of her daughter. Love welled up in her. She had done this for her and thanked God she was safe, far away from here. Her eyes closed slowly. She saw only blackness. The blade finished its job and, before she realized it, this world had slipped away.

Part I

Chapter
1

WASHINGTON HEIGHTS, NYC
3 JUNE 2010
4:15 P.M.

T OLYA WAS LOOKING AT THE clock when the call came.
He was a wreck these days. One would think that, with the
impending birth of his third child, he would have been an old hand
at waiting for the call. Every time the phone rang, he thought it was
Karin, which he knew in itself was ridiculous. He was a detective with
the New York City Police Department. There were a hundred reasons
his phone would ring for something other than his wife calling him to
tell him to meet her at Columbia Presbyterian. Nevertheless, he was
nervous, more so than usual. This pregnancy had not gone as smoothly
as the previous two. The doctor had said the baby might come early
so, though she wasn't due for another six weeks, Tolya was certain little
Oleg was on his way and that every call was that call from Karin.

He stared at the phone for two rings before he heard Pete from
behind him. "You gonna pick that up?"

Tolya reached over the desk and grabbed the phone. "Detective
Kurchenko," he said into the mouthpiece.

"You're up. Front and center with Gonzalvez, now," the duty officer said, then hung up before he could say OK.

Tolya was relieved. "Pete, come on," he said, taking his cell from atop the desk. He knelt and pulled open his bottom drawer and withdrew his gun, slipping it into the holster under his pant leg in one swift motion before turning for the door.

"Finally," Pete said. "It's been a slow day."

Tolya smiled at Pete. "For who?"

The super was waiting at the front door of the apartment building on Wadsworth Avenue between 190th and 191st streets. Tolya chuckled to himself. What real estate genius built a luxury apartment building in this location? He had read about it in the *Manhattan Times*, the neighborhood's free bilingual paper. The building had been conceived as a condominium before the market collapsed in 2008. The builder had been forced to rent the units rather than walk away from the building. At least there would be an elevator.

"You speak English?" Tolya asked the super.

"No," he replied.

"All yours."

"What's the story?" Pete asked in Spanish.

"There's a terrible odor coming from apartment 7F," the super replied. "The other tenants are complaining."

"Who lives there?" Pete asked.

"A woman," the super said.

"Did you try to get in?"

"Yeah, but no one answers and the chain lock is against the door. I didn't want to break it."

"So you called us." Pete sighed and explained to Tolya what the super had said.

"OK then, let's go up and break in."

Pete grinned. "I was hoping you'd say that."

The smell in the hallway was overwhelming. Tolya knew what it was before they unlocked the front door. Only a dead body smelled like that, and then only after a few days, and the last few had been warm.

He slipped his hand into the crack between the door and the frame, realizing immediately that there was no way his large mitts could unhinge the lock. He knew Pete's hands were even bigger than his. "Anyone there?" he called out. "Police."

There was no answer, though the neighbor from across the hall opened the door. A small woman in a blue and red bathrobe with her hair in curlers stepped out into the hallway, a handkerchief over her mouth and nose.

"I told him to call you yesterday," she said.

"Thank you, ma'am," Pete replied, smiling. "Now please go back into your apartment and let us do our job." He turned back toward Tolya. "What do you wanna do?"

"Shoulders, I think," Tolya said. Simultaneously, he and Pete rammed the door with their bodies, shoulders first. It took three attempts, but the chain did give way and, as the door opened, the smell intensified.

Light streamed into the apartment, the late-afternoon sun blazing through the uncovered windows. They were blinded at first. "Police," Tolya shouted out again. Still no response. Both he and Pete pulled their guns. As Tolya turned toward Pete to tell him he would lead, he saw the super cross himself and withdraw from the apartment.

They walked slowly down the narrow hallway into a small foyer that opened into a large living room. What they saw was inconceivable to both. In front of the window, silhouetted against the sun in the western sky, was a huge wooden frame. Suspended in the frame was a woman seated in a chair, her hands extended like Jesus on the cross. A kitchen knife dangled from her right wrist by a leather cord. Her body slumped forward but, by the volume of blood that covered her, it was obvious that her throat had been cut.

Tolya and Pete pulled handkerchiefs from their pockets and covered their mouths and noses. "Check the rest of the apartment," Tolya said through the handkerchief, lowering his gun. As Pete moved out of sight, Tolya moved toward the victim. He removed a pair of latex gloves from his back pocket and slipped them on, then gently lifted her head. Her face was contorted into a smile. Despite the heat, he shivered.

"All clear," Pete called out, coming back into the room. He walked toward Tolya and the dead woman, then stopped in his tracks. His eyes widened and his mouth opened, but at first nothing came out. Then he vomited and collapsed to his knees. He looked up at Tolya. "I know her," he said before passing out.

Karin cleared the last of her papers off her desk filing them in the appropriate folders in the cabinet behind her. She had been messy all her life but this job changed that. Managing museum exhibitions required more organization and neatness than police work had, at least on top of the desk.

She was particularly excited about this exhibition, as it was her first as a full-time employee of the Museum of Jewish Heritage. She had worked on it as a volunteer before she had decided to go back to work full time. She didn't want to go back to her job at NYPD Internal Affairs. She had been volunteering at the museum when a permanent position opened. She applied despite her lack of experience in museum management. It turned out her Spanish skills, coupled with her personal connection to the few living survivors of the Sosúa experiment, were more important than a fancy graduate degree. "Dominican Haven," an exhibition dedicated to the 854 Jewish refugees saved by the Dominican Republic during WWII, was set to open in a couple of weeks. She would be there, pregnant or otherwise, unless she was actually giving birth.

She looked at the clock 5:15. She was already late for their class. She had hoped that she and Tolya would finish their conversion course before the new baby came, but if Oleg came early, well, some things were beyond her control. She stopped and texted Rabbi Rothman to tell him she would be a little late, then turned on the small TV on her wall. She wanted to check the traffic before heading uptown. Tolya had insisted she begin driving to work a few weeks earlier. He didn't want her going into labor on the subway. The museum gladly supplied her with a parking space rather than lose her earlier than expected, especially with the show opening.

"Breaking News" flashed across the screen as it popped to life. She read the caption: "Unidentified woman found dead in locked apartment in Washington Heights." She recognized the curve in Wadsworth Avenue, then saw Tolya's familiar face.

Karin sat down at her desk, pulled out her phone and texted him, "What happened?"

Seconds later, she saw him reach into his pocket and check his phone. Then, seconds after that, her phone vibrated. "You wouldn't believe what we found. Tell you later. Can't make class. Please tell Shalom."

"OK," she texted back, then she called the babysitter and asked her to stay for an extra hour.

Pete sat dazed in the interrogation room at the precinct. Tolya and the captain sat opposite him. "Pete, tell us again, how did you know her?" Tolya said.

"I helped her come here," Pete said.

"Is she related to you?" Tolya asked.

"Not really. Sort of, a cousin, kinda," Pete replied, then thought for a moment. "She was the cousin of my cousin."

"How long has it been since you've seen her?" the captain asked.

"About ten years."

"Yet you recognized her?" the captain said.

Pete's mind raced back. He couldn't forget passion like that. "Yes," he said, nodding slightly.

"What was her name again?" the captain asked.

Pete swallowed hard. "Mariela Camacho."

"The woman's ID—or should I say, one of them, anyway—confirmed that," Tolya said. He took a plastic baggie with a Dominican passport out of a file and dropped it onto the table.

"How many did she have?" the captain asked, removing the

Dominican passport from the bag and flipping through it.

"Three," Tolya said. "One Dominican, one American and, get this, one Russian."

Pete shook his head. He couldn't believe what was happening. He'd been a cop a long time, but never had he expected to find a dead body—no, a mutilated dead body—of someone he knew at a crime scene. "I just can't digest this yet," he said.

"I understand," said the captain. "Maybe we should pick this up tomorrow. You can write out a statement, tell us what you knew of her. And I'll have to take you off the case."

"Of course," said Pete. He rubbed his shoulder where he had hit the heavy front door of the apartment earlier. "Tomorrow. That would be better. I can't do this now."

They all rose. The captain walked around the table and put his arm around Pete, the ever-increasing bulk of his stomach pushing Pete into the corner of the tiny room. "Gonzalvez," he said, "I'm sorry about this. Go home, kiss your wife and kids and get some rest. We'll sort this out."

"Thanks, Cap," Pete said, then looked at Tolya. He knew Tolya understood to stay back for a moment after the captain left.

The captain walked through the door and down the hallway. Tolya turned toward Pete. "What's up, hermano?" he asked.

"Let's go get a drink. I need to tell you a few things."

"Sure," replied Tolya. "I already told Karin I'd be late."

Karin walked quickly up the steps of the yeshiva on Bennett Avenue. Once in the vestibule, she made a quick left and headed up the stairs, holding the banister with her left hand, her right hand under her pregnant belly, supporting herself. She loved being pregnant but hated the last trimester. She was big and felt uncomfortable in her own body, like she took up too much space. She also couldn't wait for the little life inside her to wrap himself around her neck and breathe in her ear. She reached the second floor and stopped for a moment to steady herself then walked to Rabbi Rothman's study at the end of the hall.

She liked Rothman. He was a good and honest man and, although she knew she would never practice his severe, rigid brand of Judaism, both she and Tolya felt comfortable having him complete their conversions. Tolya, though, had bristled at the idea that he needed to be converted to begin with.

He was the genuine article, Rothman, a man who had come to his faith by choice rather than just acceptance. She knew his beliefs were a matter of conviction, not indoctrination. Also, she respected how he had embraced a friendship with Tolya, a friendship that had changed Tolya deeply after Tolya had arrested Rothman's wife for murdering Rothman's father. She admired his dignity, a quality she rarely found in people.

Karin knocked gently on Rothman's door, the old sign with his father-in-law's name still appended to it. He had died a broken man a few months earlier, never recovering from the tragedy of his daughter's actions.

"Come in."

She opened the door slowly and peeked in. "Good evening, Rabbi," she said. "Sorry for my lateness."

"Not a problem, Chava," Rothman said, using the Hebrew name she would soon adopt as her own. Chava, Eve, the first woman, the mother of mothers. "Where is Akiva?" Tolya picked that name because it had been his maternal grandfather's Hebrew name. As far as Tolya knew, he was the last member of the family who had had one. Tolya and his twin, Oleg, had been close to him as children, spending summers with him and their grandmother in Ukraine.

"He's caught up on a case, up on Wadsworth," she said, settling into the chair opposite Rothman's. "He asked me to send his apologies."

"Hmm," replied the rabbi. "I saw something earlier on the news. Seems it was a rather grisly scene."

"Yes."

"Well, let's get started then. Do you have any questions about what we discussed last week?"

Karin paused for a moment in thought. She did have questions, but she wasn't sure how to ask them. "Yes," she finally said.

"Then why are you hesitating?" said Rothman.

"Because I don't want to offend you," she replied.

Rothman leaned back in his chair and smiled. "Karin, nothing you say will offend me."

"Even if it offends the rules you live by?"

"You know me better than that. My rules are for me," he replied. "You may choose to live any way you want. I can only hope to guide you. What happens between you and HaShem is your business."

"OK then," Karin said, shifting herself slowly into the chair to relieve the pressure against her back. "I understand thoroughly the idea of rest on Shabbat, of separating the holy from the profane, but I can tell you with all honesty that we, my family, Tolya and me and the kids, we won't observe the Sabbath in the way you do. It's not practical for us. Yet, I want to build a construct within which my family will experience the Sabbath."

The rabbi smiled at her and placed his hands on the desk. "Chava," he said, "I am going to tell you a little story. But if you ever tell anyone I told you this story, I will deny it because, as a rabbi of such a traditional congregation, I would be run out of town for suggesting this to you."

"Go ahead." Karin laughed. "It's our little secret."

"Many years ago, before I became ba'al t'shuvah, I was going on my first trip to Israel and I had a pair of tefillin that had belonged to my father's grandfather. My father had carried them with him from Europe. I wanted to pray with them at the Western Wall in Jerusalem. You understand what tefillin are?"

"Yes," Karin answered. "The small boxes men wrap around their arms and forehead when praying. They contain a passage from the Torah."

"Very good." Rothman gave a broad smile. "I've successfully taught you something. Anyway, I had to have the tefillin checked to make sure the parchments inside the old boxes were still good. There was one shop on the Lower East Side where you could do this. I went to the shop and found a very old man with a very long beard and a yarmulke way too big for his head sitting on a low stool repairing religious articles. There was another man, not quite so old, in the shop as well. When I walked in I explained to the old man what I was seeking—to make certain that the tefillin were kosher—and before the old man answered me, the other man chided me for coming into the shop with my head uncovered. The old man, who had been silent till then, turned to the other man and told him to apologize to me for his rudeness. He said that, though I didn't wear a yarmulke on my head, it was clear I was wearing one in my heart."

Karin shifted again in the chair, then smiled. "So, Rabbi," she said, "are you suggesting that I can build a construct for Shabbat that might differ from the more traditional approach?"

"I have a very intuitive student," he replied.

"And I a very tolerant teacher."

"What are your plans for your first Shabbat?"

"I plan to have a family dinner where we will bless the wine, the challah and the children, and then for us to spend the evening together with the kids, no television. I have a special project planned for Tolya and the boys to do together."

"Excellent. Good luck with it. And let's talk again early next week."

Karin got up slowly from the chair. Shalom came around the desk to help her. "Chava," he said, "a question."

"Yes, Shalom, what?"

"Are you sure you want to do this?"

"Do what?"

"Convert."

"Yes. Why are you asking me that now?"

"We have an old custom that we must continue to ask at least three times before the conversion is undertaken to make sure the person's heart and mind are together in the decision."

"They are."

"And why are you doing this?"

"I want my children to understand this part of who they are and, at the same time, I want to be able to share this heritage with them. I can't do that if I don't become a part of it."

"And you accept, or should I say, you believe in our view of HaShem?"

"I believe there can be more than one interpretation of the same thing, and I am comfortable accepting this interpretation."

Shalom smiled. "Are you still planning on doing your conversion before the birth?"

"If possible, yes. The day after the pre-opening party."

Shalom raised an eyebrow. "And will Tolya be joining you?"

She smiled. "I'm not supposed to tell you, he wanted to tell you himself. But, yes. He decided you were right, that he should look at this more as a recommitment than an insult to his personal history."

Shalom smiled.

Pete downed the shot of Tequila without flinching, took a long swig of the beer and turned to the bartender. "Another, please."

"You sure that's a good idea?" Tolya said, sipping at his beer. "You've had three already."

"I'm fine, Tol. You might want to consider having a couple yourself before I tell you this story."

"I'm fine with the beer, thanks. You ready to enlighten me?"

"I will be in a moment," Pete replied. "Just let the tequila settle in a little first."

He picked up the fourth shot and downed it. The warmth of the liquor rose up from his stomach into his chest. The effect of the first three began to lighten his mind. The rush of the tequila reminded him of the warm breezes coming off the ocean in Samaná that summer, all those years ago. The tiny fishing village, the broad beach lined with palm trees, the tiny room facing the ocean where they had spent four days sleeping under mosquito nets, the windows open to catch the breeze and the sound of the surf. He looked Tolya directly in the eye. "OK," he said. "Let's get right down to it. We were lovers."

Tolya put the bottle of Corona down on the bar. He hesitated for a moment then said, "OK. I can't say I'm surprised."

Pete turned his head away. They were closer than brothers, but sometimes Tolya didn't know when to keep his comments to himself. Pete forgave him for that. He swallowed hard, remembering those moments so many years ago when he knew this woman, this woman who was now lying on a slab in the morgue at the coroner's office.

"Wait, I thought you said you were cousins," Tolya said.

Pete turned back toward Tolya. "I said we were cousins of cousins. No blood relation. But then, I don't suppose you Russians ever marry within the family. Let's see, didn't that neighbor of yours end up marrying…"

"OK, OK," Tolya replied, putting up his hands in surrender. "Point taken. Sorry. I shouldn't have said that."

"Enough said. Now, you wanna hear the story?"

"Yeah. And please, tell me everything."

Pete lifted the bottle of beer, took one more swig then began. "It was my first time back in Santo Domingo in about six, seven years. I had just become a citizen and finished school. I wanted to take a little break before I began on the force. I was going with Glynnis, but she was still in school so I went back to visit my family, my cousins, aunts, uncles, alone. It started out as innocent as could be."

Chapter 2

THE SUNLIGHT WAS AS BRILLIANT as Pete remembered it. The air felt warm and wet against his skin, all his memories rushing back at him at once. He walked down the ramp toward the doors. In the distance he could see a man with three young women and a younger man waving at him. The man was older than he remembered him to be, but he knew it was his uncle, his mother's youngest brother.

Tío Polito had been like a father and an older brother, protecting him and getting him into trouble at the same time. Without doubt, the younger man was Chicho, his amigo de alma. He recognized two of the women as his cousins, his uncle's daughters, but they were not the little girls he had left behind. He didn't recognize the other woman. She was a great beauty in that way only Caribbean women—no, only Dominican women—can be. Not perfect, but enticing.

"Pedrito," his uncle called to him. He felt himself smile, slung his bag over his shoulder and ran toward him. His uncle did the same, crossing the flimsy rope barrier meant to keep the tourists from being overrun by returning Dominicans and their families. They slammed into each

17

other and embraced for a long moment. Then something happened that Pete had never expected since the moment he had left this sad but beautiful place. He cried. The feeling of his uncle's arms around him brought him back to his childhood, to the closeness of those he loved, a familiarity so often missing in New York, where everyone chased the dollar. Here where there were no dollars, they smiled for each other, not for money.

"Tío," he said weakly through his tears.

"Why are you crying, Pedrito?" his uncle said, pushing Pete back and looking at him. "Diablo, you've grown up. You're bigger than me." He laughed, then pulled Pete to him and hugged him again.

Pete wiped his eyes and smiled. "Because I've missed you and I didn't realize how much." He slapped his uncle playfully on the head. "And yes, I'm bigger than you now, so you better watch out."

Chicho came up from behind Polito. "Hermano," he said, then grabbed Pete and pulled him close, hugging him tightly.

"Chicho, mi hermanito. I'd better watch out. Look how big you are. Like a bull."

Chicho laughed. "It's so good to see you, man."

"Pedro," the girls called out to him.

"They want to see you," Tío Polito said. "They've been talking about nothing else for days." He took Pete by the arm and led him through the crowd.

As they neared, the young women smiled. The taller one, slightly older, came toward him. From her dark hair and cinnamon-colored skin, he knew immediately it was Imelda. He embraced her. She kissed him gently on the cheek. "Do you still have all those dolls?" he said.

She laughed and poked him in the stomach. "Yes, I saved them for you. You'll be sleeping with them."

She released him and he reached out to her sister standing just behind her. She was shorter than Imelda, with the same cinnamon-colored skin but unmistakable from her blue eyes. "Brisas," he said, using the nickname he had given her as a child.

Katarina embraced him. "No one calls me that anymore," she said.

"They should," he replied. "You're still like a soft breeze."

She smiled. "I want you to call me that for as long as you're here."

Pete hugged Katarina close.

The third young woman stood behind her, perhaps three feet away, smiling at him. Somewhere, deep in his memory, her face was there.

"You don't remember me, do you?" she said.

"No," he replied, letting go of Katarina and straightening up. "I'm sorry."

Her beauty riveted him. Long black hair framed her perfect face, her cheekbones high and her lips full and red, black eyes deep and dark but ringed with a thin rim of gold, full of mystery, the color of her skin like coffee ice cream. She smiled, her perfect white teeth filling her face. "Soy Mariela," she said, shifting her eyes downward, then back to his. "Do you remember me now? I remember you."

Pete was surprised at how much had changed in the years since his mother had sent him his ticket to come to New York. The wooden, single-story house he had lived in with his uncle and his uncle's family after his mother emigrated was gone, replaced by a villa with modern baths and kitchen, running hot water, and lights that stayed on thanks to a private generator. There was a second story where the bedrooms were, all built around an interior courtyard. They sat in that courtyard at a long table, the heat from the barbecue warming the cool night air, enjoying the last of the desserts his aunt had made in his honor.

Chicho raised a glass. "One last toast to mi hermano. How much we've missed you. But it's like you were here with us yesterday. Bienvenidos compai."

Everyone raised their glasses and shouted, "Felizidades!"

Mariela sat opposite him. He stared at her all through dinner. He was captivated by her smile. It was seductive and innocent at the same time. "Would you like to show me that view now?" he asked her.

"Por supuesto," she said, rising gracefully from her chair, the sleekness of her body evident under the gauzy yellow fabric of her sleeveless dress. "We can stop at my room to get a sweater." She rubbed her shoulders to warm them.

Pete followed her slowly with both his legs and his eyes as she walked across the patio and up the stairs to the second floor. She turned left toward her room. He waited for her in the open-air corridor outside, peering over the banister into the courtyard below. He was proud of how well his uncle and aunt had done with the beauty shop and motorcycle repair they had opened in front of the house facing the street, hiding the tangible evidence of their prosperity behind it. He smiled, remembering the little outhouse that had stood where the barbecue pit was now.

"Ready," Mariela said, taking his hand and leading him toward the circular wrought iron staircase that led to the roof. He followed her up the stairs.

The sky opened above them, the brilliant light of the full moon illuminating the city. He could see the crests of the mountains to the north way off in the distance outlined by the reflection of the moonlight. The stars shone above much brighter than in New York. The sparse lights of the houses in the patios that filled the hillsides of Arroyo Hondo descended below them, twinkling, the sound of Salsa filling the air in every direction. He felt at home for the first time in many years. He had forgotten how much he loved this place, how much it was home to him.

"Qué lindo," Mariela said.

"Sí," Pete replied, turning toward her and repeating her phrase, "qué linda," changing the masculine to the feminine. She turned her head and smiled that smile again. He knew she understood his meaning. The "linda" was for her, not for the view. "I want to apologize," he continued.

"For what?" she said.

"For this afternoon, for not recognizing you."

She laughed then touched his arm. "How could you? It was so long ago, I was a little girl. We hardly knew each other."

He ran his fingers over her arm, then took her hand. "I'm sorry about your parents," he said.

"Thank you," she replied. "Thank God for your uncle and my aunt. They took me in when I had nowhere to go." She smiled, then chuckled. "My grandmothers were too afraid to take me in. I would have been left to the streets."

"How long ago was that?" Pete asked.

"Five years. I was 13."

Pete leaned in toward her and put his hand over hers. She moved in closer to him, their bodies nearly touching. His lips grazed hers, soft and warm.

"Mariela," Imelda called from below.

She pulled away from him, tossed her hair back and smoothed her dress. "Sí," she called back. "We're on the roof."

"Chicho and Freddy want to go dancing. Do you want to come?"

"Do you salsa?" Mariela asked Pete.

He smiled at her. "Sí, como un boricua."

"Vamos," she said, taking his hand and leading him down the circular stairs to the world below.

The beat of salsa pulsed through the club. Inside it was hot, steamy. Bodies moved in synchronized rhythm, lights flashed, the music impossibly loud. Pete turned Mariela on the dance floor, twice, three times. She was a good dancer and could keep up with him, better at salsa than most Dominican girls. Salsa, the current wave in Latin music, wasn't native to the island. He had learned from Puerto Rican girls in New York how to move to the beat of son, the Cuban grandparent of salsa. It was very sexy, and he could tell a lot about a woman by how she danced it. Mariela invited him with it. It was an interview for what might come later.

The DJ mixed to another cut, faster, more like a plena. He shouted, "Let's go outside for a drink."

She nodded and led him off the dance floor to the terrace on the second floor of the club. As he pushed open the glass door and held it for her, a rush of humid air hit his face.

"What would you like?" he asked her.

"Whatever you're having," she said, pushing her hair back over her shoulders.

His stomach tightened as he watched her fan herself lightly with her right hand, a thin film of perspiration making her skin glow. "I'm drinking whiskey."

"Well," she said, "in that case, I'll be drinking whiskey too."

They laughed. Pete turned toward the bartender. "A bottle of Black Label, please."

"Right away, señor. Did you want anything to mix with that?"

Pete looked at Mariela. "Orange juice, please," she said.

"And ice." He laid out two 5,000 peso bills on the top of the bar, took Mariela's hand in his, brought it to his lips, and then kissed it gently.

The bartender returned with the bottles and glasses. Pete poured the whiskey and added a splash of orange juice. He picked up his glass and tapped hers. "Salud," he said.

"Salud," she replied.

"Mariela," Pete said, fidgeting a bit, not sure where to look. He usually wasn't this nervous around women. "I'm glad we met again."

"So am I."

Awkwardness hung in the thick air for a moment. Pete chuckled to himself. He hadn't expected to fall in love his first night back. He caught her eye and smiled. "What are you studying in school?" he asked, trying to lighten the moment.

"Nursing," she said.

"That's very noble," he replied. He tapped her glass with his again.

Mariela laughed. "No, not really, but I'll be able to get a job, maybe even leave the country. There is little else a woman can do here, you know?"

"Do you want to leave the country?"

"Of course," she said. "Who doesn't? And besides, there are too many difficult memories for me here."

"I'm sure that's true."

"Sometimes this is a very ugly place," she said. "And at other times, it's the most beautiful place in the world."

"I understand that feeling completely. Our people are desperate to leave and then desperate to return."

She took a sip and touched his hand. "Enough about me," she said. "And you? Imelda told me you've just finished school."

"Yes," Pete replied. "Not college like you, Police Academy. I want to be a detective."

"Also admirable," she said. "I imagine the police are different in New York than here."

"What do you mean?"

She hesitated, took another long sip of her drink as if to fortify herself. "You know, the corruption."

"Yes," Pete replied, "it's better, or maybe it's just different. There's plenty of corruption there too."

"You know," Mariela said, "here, when the police don't want to solve a crime, they don't bother."

Pete moved closer to her. He was curious about the circumstances of her parent's deaths. "Can I ask what happened?"

She slid her hand into his, interlocking their fingers. "Sure," she said, "Why not? The police said it was a crime of passion, that my father had killed my mother and then himself after he found out that she was having an affair. In the barrio, they said my mother was a bruja and my father a drug dealer, and that the local gang killed them after they turned informant for the police. That's why my grandmothers wouldn't take me in. They said they would kill anyone who helped me because my parents were informants."

"What do you believe?" Pete asked.

Mariela looked off into the distance, across the club toward the dance floor inside. She moved her hips slightly with the music. Pete watched her as she prepared to answer him. She seemed far off for a moment. She turned toward him and sipped her drink again. "I believe the police killed them."

Chapter
3

TOLYA SAT BEHIND KARIN ON the bed, massaging her neck. "Stop fighting with your brother," he shouted to Max in the other bedroom.

"I love those big hands, mi amor," Karin purred. Her head fell forward, her hair covering her face. Another screech came from the boys' bedroom. This time it was Erno. Karin straightened up. "Nilda," she called out to the babysitter, "could you see what's going on with the boys?"

"Sí, señora," she heard Nilda say from the kitchen.

"Thanks." She turned toward Tolya and kissed him gently on the lips. "We're going to need a bigger apartment, amor, especially with this one on the way." She patted her stomach and got up from the bed. She took the brush from the top of the dresser and brushed out her hair. "I can't stop thinking about that crime scene, Tol, the way you described it. Why go through all that effort to kill yourself? How about pills?"

25

"Once a cop, always a cop." Tolya laughed. "I agree. What's wrong, getting bored at that museum job?" She stuck her tongue out at him in the mirror. He looked at Karin's reflection. He was as attracted to her now as he had been the first time he saw her. "That was my thought too," he continued, pulling up his pants. "But all the evidence points to suicide. First of all, there was a note. Second, the door was chain-locked from the inside. And third, the apartment was seven floors up with no fire escape, so…"

"So I guess it's a suicide then." She pulled up her dress over the baby bump and lifted her hair. "Could you zip me up please, Tol? How creepy that Pete knew her."

"What's suicide, Mommy?" Max said, striding into the room with Erno in tow.

Karin looked at Tolya. "Nothing for you to worry about, my sweet thing," she said, bending to kiss him on the forehead. "We're going to have to be more careful," she whispered in Tolya's ear.

"Yes we are." Tolya picked up Max in one arm and Erno in the other and kissed them both sloppily on their cheeks. "My good boys, stop fighting, you're brothers."

"Yuck," Max said, wiping off his cheek. Erno did the same, imitating Max.

"You dun't like vet Russian kisses?" Tolya said, donning a thick Russian accent.

"No," both boys said while forcing themselves from his arms.

"OK then, out of here with both of you," he said chasing them from the bedroom and laughing. He straightened up and moved toward Karin. He put his arms around her from the back, wrapping himself around her, patting her stomach gently. "Oleg," he said, putting on the accent again. "Vhen you are comink?"

"When he's ready," Karin replied, turning toward him. "You're a good father, Anatoly Kurchenko." She kissed him on the cheek. "Which is why you won't mind making our first family Shabbat ever tomorrow night."

"You're kidding, right?"

"Nope. Gotta go, I'm late for work."

"I'm starting to agree with Pete here, Cap," Tolya said. "On the surface, it looks like a suicide. But hell, why would someone go to all that trouble? It just doesn't sit well with me. I think it deserves a little more looking into."

"Detective Kurchenko," said the captain, reclining in his black leather chair, "why would we commit the resources of this otherwise resource-strapped precinct to the continued investigation of a suicide so apparent that it came with a note?"

"It's just a feeling I have, Cap," said Tolya.

"You're not just trying to humor your friend over here?"

"Damn, Captain," Pete said, jumping up and out of the chair. "This isn't about me, it's about the victim, and it's not 'cause I know... knew her either. Something's not right here. Nobody kills themselves that way."

The captain frowned and looked at Tolya and Pete over the rim of his reading glasses. "I tend to agree with both of you, but I've got all kinds of bullshit to contend with in terms of, what did that efficiency jackass call it?"

"Case triage," Tolya interjected.

"Case triage," repeated the captain. "And then there's the matter of your personal connection to the victim, Gonzalvez. You shouldn't even be on the case. And where's your statement?"

Pete looked over toward Tolya then the captain. "I can handle it. As a matter of fact, it would help me if we knew for sure."

The captain took in a deep breath then let it out slowly. "OK," he said finally. "The coroner's inquest won't be in for a couple, three days, so I can cover you for a short time. This isn't official. Stay on top of your other workload and you got the weekend to do some investigating. I'll probably have to close this out by Monday afternoon."

Pete smiled. "Thanks, Cap."

Tolya laid out the contents of the evidence bag on the gray steel table in the small interrogation room at the back end of the precinct. He surveyed it: suicide note, driver's license, checkbook and three passports. "You know," he said to Pete, "the weirdest thing is that Russian passport."

"I'd have to agree," Pete replied, turning it over in his hands. "And I'm a little intrigued by the various names she was using. The only place her real name appears is on the Dominican passport."

"Which hasn't been used in over ten years," said Tolya. "The last stamp on here is back into JFK in June 2001."

"From where?"

Tolya examined the passport's pages till he found a match for the entry stamp date. "Santo Domingo," he said. "Could you find anyone to verify she was there?"

"Not sure," Pete replied.

"How about your uncle and your cousins?" Tolya sensed Pete's hesitation.

"The girls are here. Been here since 1999."

"And your uncle?"

"Lost touch with him," Pete lied.

"You were so close."

"Shit happens."

Tolya didn't want to press Pete on his uncle. "Do you think you could find someone in Santo Domingo who might know something about this?"

"I'll try." He picked up the American passport. "Roberta Brusca," he said, staring down at the photo. "Why would she change her name?"

"Seems like the question we need to answer. Any stamps in there?"

Pete flipped through the passport's pages. It was well used. "She's been around. Paris a few times, London, Berlin, Madrid twice." He checked the entry and exit dates and wrote them on a slip of paper. "All short trips, no more than four days at any one place. And all in 1999 and 2000."

"What's the issuance date on the passport?" Tolya asked, leaning forward over the table.

"January 3, 1999. It expired last year."

Tolya picked up the Russian passport. "There's only one stamp in here. June 2005."

"What's her name there?"

"Roberta Grushkina."

"So what the fuck happened?" Pete said.

"Our opening is a little over a week away," Karin said to her staff assembled in her office. "Is everything in place?"

Lacey, her administrative assistant, spoke first. "The majority of the responses to the opening are in. We've had just over 200 accept. We haven't heard anything back from approximately eighty more invitees."

"How many total in attendance are we expecting with those 200?"

"Approximately 430," replied Lacey. "More than we expected. A much higher percentage than usual."

Karin sat back in her chair. She placed a hand over her stomach, rubbing it gently. "We're approaching that all-important 500 mark when the auditorium becomes too small."

"Don't worry about that too much," said Miriam Stein, director of exhibitions for the museum and Karin's immediate superior, sitting on the couch to the left of Karin's desk. "Experience tells us that approximately 15 percent of the respondents who say they're coming won't show. And as to the eighty or so who haven't replied, it's unlikely they will be accepting the invitation this late. Remember it's June as well. Graduations, weddings…"

Karin swiveled the chair in Miriam's direction. She smiled. "Under normal circumstances, I'm sure you're right. My concern is that we might get a slightly different response from our Dominican guests. Dominicans are very relaxed. They may accept the invitation for two guests and show up with four or not bother to accept and just show up. It's a cultural thing. And I don't want anyone turned away at the door."

"Of course not," said Miriam.

"She's right," said Dionelis, the museum's event planner. "As Dominicans, Karin and I can attest to this."

"Well," Miriam said, getting up from the couch, "then make sure we have more than enough folding chairs on hand for the back of the auditorium and plenty of food. I think this is progressing perfectly. Sorry all, I've got to leave now. We have a trustee's meeting this morning and those always run long."

"Enjoy, and thanks for all your help," Karin said. "Are there any problem areas?"

Dionelis raised her hand. "There might be one."

"What is it?" asked Karin.

"It concerns the hotel arrangements for the out-of-town guests."

"I thought everything was settled on that months ago. They're staying at the new Andaz Hotel on Wall Street, aren't they?"

"Yes they are," Dionelis said. "The problem is that we underestimated the number of rooms we reserved and I didn't catch it till yesterday."

"How many rooms? Did you check with the hotel?"

"We're short four rooms. And yes, I checked with them, they are fully booked. Some kind of event that has to do with the Ground Zero site."

Karin thought for a moment. "That's always touchy. I'll have Miriam call them. Leave me the name and number of your contact at the hotel. If worse comes to worst, we'll put them up elsewhere and provide limo services."

"Do we have enough left in the budget for that, Karin?" asked Lacey.

"If not, we'll have to find it. One last question, is everything set for the banquet the night before the opening?"

"Yes," replied Dionelis with a smile. "And I got them to agree to holding it in the biergarten for us instead of the small ballroom if the weather is good."

"Excellent," said Karin. "I'll be there with this baby in me or hanging around my neck."

Tolya stared at the frame of the suicide machine. "You OK, Pete?" he asked.

"Yeah," Pete growled. Tolya turned to face him. He was seated in a desk chair facing the frame. "Did we ask for the videos from the front door and the elevator security cameras yet?"

"I did. They're here in the basement. Why?" Tolya answered.

"Someone had to bring the 2x4's in through the front and up the elevator."

Tolya felt tight in his throat. He knew this was too much for Pete. They had been partners for about eight years, but he'd never seen anything affect Pete like this. It was evident from what Pete had told him that he once had deep feelings for this woman. "I told the super we would be by in the morning to look at them."

"Yep," Pete said in the same low growl, "yep. You want the bedroom or the living room?"

"Let's do it together," Tolya said.

Pete got up from the chair. Tolya followed him into the bedroom. "You take the closet," Pete said. "I'll take the dresser and under the bed."

"OK," replied Tolya. He watched Pete out of the corner of his eye as he opened the door and began sifting through the contents of the closet. The clothing ran from conservative gray suits to expensive red and black cocktail dresses, one smaller and sexier than the next. The clothes gave him no clue of her life. He chuckled to himself; the variety of clothing was no different than what he would find in Karin's closet. She could be a Wall Street executive or a prostitute for all he knew. "Anything yet?" he asked Pete.

"Nope."

Tolya reached up toward the shelf at the top of the closet to pull himself up a little. He turned and surveyed the room, looking for a chair or something to stand on to get a better view. He pulled over a folding chair from the corner of the room. The shelf was half empty and dusty. He removed the few boxes sitting there. Two of them contained shoes, one had some papers in it, and the other two were empty. He sorted through the papers. A lease for the apartment, some old credit cards and bills addressed to Roberta Brusca with expired dates.

"Tol."

"What you got?"

Pete looked up at him, his face expressionless. He held up a dusty creased photograph. "It was under the bed. She has a daughter."

"How do you know it's her daughter?"

Pete held up the photo and turned it around. "It says 'Mommy and me' on the back, and that's definitely Mariela."

Tolya stepped off the chair and took the picture from Pete's hand. It was her for sure. She was smiling and hugging a young girl of about 6 in front of her. The date stamp on the side of the photo said July 2009. "Did you notice the date?" he asked.

"Yep," Pete said, getting off his knees and sitting on the bed. "Not quite a year, so where's the kid?"

"That's a good question. Maybe that buys us some time with the captain. Missing kid." Tolya handed the photo back to Pete. "Wait a second, I wanna check something." He took one of the boxes from the closet shelf and removed the lease. "April 28, 2010," he said.

"What's that?" Pete asked.

"The lease for this apartment, one bedroom, one bed, no kid's stuff. Doesn't look like the kid lived here with her. And she just moved in a little over a month ago."

"No," Pete turned the photo over in his hands again. "But it's a start." Pete smiled for the first time in two days.

The captain looked at the picture. "And this proves this wasn't a suicide?"

"It means something, Cap," said Pete. In his heart, he knew Mariela would never have left her child without a mother. She herself had lost her parents at a young age. No way.

"I don't see that it changes anything," the captain continued, "but as I said earlier, you've got till Monday night to pursue this and then it's likely the whole incident will be ruled a suicide. Case closed."

"What about a missing child report?" Tolya said.

The captain sat back in his chair and shook his head. "We don't even know that she's missing."

"She's not here," Pete said.

"Perhaps she's with her father," the captain replied, "or another relative."

"Jesus, Captain," Pete said. "Give me a fucking break."

Tolya slumped into the chair.

"We've got till Monday night, right?" Pete said, pacing nervously.

"Yes," the captain repeated. "Now go make your statement."

Pete took a bite out of the Cuban sandwich before answering Tolya's question. "I think it was after she came here, I ran into her when I visited my cousins. She was living with them for a while." Pete watched Tolya's expression as he scribbled a version of his answer onto the new witness statement form. "What you so irritated about?" he asked.

"You and this form. You know I hate these forms, there's no room to write anything. And I'm pissed as shit with you."

"Why?" Pete leaned back in the chair, wedging himself in between the floor and the wall.

"You're not being honest with me. For starters, you were in love with this girl. What the hell happened? And second, what the hell happened between you and your uncle?"

Pete rested his head on his forearms. The weight of the memories exhausted him. He didn't want to remember any of this. He had put it behind him long ago, or so he thought. Now he felt the pain again like the hurt had happened yesterday. He lifted his head. "OK, put down the pencil. I'm gonna tell you everything, the rest of what happened."

Chapter
4

PETE CARESSED MARIELA'S CHEEK, THEN kissed her gently on the lips. The scent of her body mingled with the scent of guayaba coming from the blooms on the bush outside the cottage. "Te amo," he whispered in her ear.

"Y te adoro," she replied then kissed him hard, her tongue plunging deeply into his mouth. "Again," she said.

"Mi amor," he murmured rolling on top of her. A cool breeze drifted through the open window and the mosquito netting over the bed, caressing his back. He had never felt this way for any woman or with any woman, not even Glynnis. He'd made a decision about that as well. Though he loved her and he knew he'd break her heart, he was going to break it off with her and bring Mariela to New York. He couldn't live without her.

"Sí, otra vez," she purred.

"Cómo, otra vez?" he said, laughing a little and kissing her on the neck, suspending his body over hers. He heard the sound of the waves

35

lapping gently at the shore outside the window mixing with the cawing of parrots and the laughter of children farther down the beach.

"Make love to me again," she whispered in his ear, flicking her tongue gently against it.

He kissed her slowly and passionately and rubbed himself against her. He could feel her wetness against his skin.

"Ay, papi," she said. "Te quiero mucho."

"I know," he whispered to her, then moved off of her.

"Where are you going?" she asked. She lifted herself on one arm, exposing her breasts.

Pete stuck his head out of the window, looking up and down the beach. He grabbed the two terry cloth robes draped over the small dining table near the front door and tossed one to Mariela. "Put this on, follow me."

"For what?" She giggled.

"Tú sabe, there is a saying in this country. If you take a woman to the beach, you must make love to her in the sea."

Mariela tossed her head back and laughed, her hair falling behind her. Pete loved her even more when she was like this, a mischievous smile brightening her face. She jumped out of the bed, grabbed the robe, threw it over her shoulders and followed him out the door and down to the beach.

Playa Bonita in Las Terrenas on the Samaná Peninsula, a long curving stretch of fine white sand lined with palm trees, was empty save for three young children playing near the boat dock at the very end. Both Pete and Mariela dropped their robes and ran into the turquoise water. It felt cool and refreshing against the warm humid air. They quickly dove under the surface and swam out about twenty-five feet, where it was deep enough to cover them to their shoulders.

Pete took Mariela in his arms and kissed her deeply. Her lips were salty from the seawater. She wrapped her legs around him. The tepid water enveloped them like a blanket as she leaned against him, arching her back and letting out a low moan. He nibbled on her neck as he made love to her, his feet in the soft sand, the currents moving around them, the only sounds the lapping of the waves, the rustling of the palms and their own guttural moans.

Pete opened his eyes to the sky. A black wide-winged bird flew overhead, the sound of its call sharpening the moment. He looked deeply into Mariela's eyes as he felt her near orgasm. His knees nearly buckled at the climax, both of them sliding off of each other into the warm liquid sea.

She reached for him and wrapped her legs around him again, her silky skin electric against his. "Te amo," she said barely audibly.

"And I you," he said. They floated where they had made love, catching their breath. The children playing on the beach ran toward a hut at the opposite end, a small dog following them and barking.

Mariela ran her hands through Pete's wet hair, slicking it back against his head. "I want to have your children."

"Many," he answered. He leaned back and paddled gently toward the shore, carrying her with him. The beach was empty now. They reached the point where they could lie in the surf, covered by the gentle waves. "I want to marry you," he said. "You make me so happy. I can't live without you."

Mariela sat up and stared at the horizon. She said nothing for a long moment then turned to Pete, a sad smile on her face.

"Do you want to marry me?" he asked.

"What about Glynnis?" she said.

He took her hand and kissed her gently. "I decided days ago. I'll tell her when I get back. I'll come back here at Christmas and we can marry then."

The drive back to the capital was long and slow along narrow back roads that had more potholes than tarmac. They drove over the mountains toward the southern coast, the air cooler and crisper as they reached the summit of the Cordillera Central. They stopped for lunch at a tiny restaurant just off the side of the road on a cliff overlooking a verdant valley below. Goatherds and their flocks ambled through the clearings.

At a small table under a palapa, they had a simple meal of stewed chicken served with rice, red beans and avocado. As they ate, a middle-aged man in a wheelchair wheeled himself into the palapa. He had no legs. The man called out to the proprietress. A moment later, she appeared with a steel guitar. He took the guitar in his hands and began to play a slow, mournful tune of lost love.

"Bachata," Mariela said. "It's becoming very popular."

The lyrics touched Pete's heart more than she could know. He would soon break Glynnis's heart the way the songwriter's heart had been broken. He would tell her his heart belonged to someone else. Someone he was destined to love, who he had found again by pure accident.

They sat next to each other, sipping coffee and staring out over the valley below in silence. He took her hand and smiled at her. He had never felt as calm as he did at that moment. She smiled back. "What are you thinking?" he asked her.

"Did you mean what you said earlier? Do you really want to marry me?"

He squeezed her hand. "More than anything in the world."

"How long will I have to wait here for you?"

"Six months, perhaps a year."

"You'll find someone else," she whispered, her eyes cast toward her lap. "Or you'll go back to Glynnis."

He gently touched her chin, turning her head toward him. "Nunca," he said. "Nunca jamas. Never ever will I love like this again." He pulled her into a kiss.

"Bravo," the legless guitarist called out before he began to play again, this time a slow ballad of eternal love.

It was dark by the time they arrived at Polito's house. The humid night air enveloped the dim light of the streetlamps. The streets were nearly deserted. They parked his uncle's car in the corner of the driveway in front of the locked gate. Mariela took her keys from her small canvass bag and unlocked it.

"Hola," Pete called out as they walked through the darkened rooms toward the courtyard in the back.

"Sobrino," he heard his uncle call out from the courtyard. "How was your trip? I wasn't expecting you till tomorrow."

They walked into the kitchen and saw the family sitting in the courtyard relaxing in the night air. "We missed you," he called to them, "so we came back a day early."

His aunt and uncle rose from their chairs to welcome them. Polito embraced him. Pete could smell the whiskey on his breath.

"Why so serious?" Polito asked Pete.

"Not serious at all," Pete said, releasing his uncle's embrace. He smiled. "See?"

"Let me look at you, both of you," his aunt said, taking Mariela by the hand and turning her around. "Sit down. I'll bring you something to eat."

Imelda reclined on the settee and Katarina slept, her head in Imelda's lap. "How was your trip?" she asked.

Mariela smiled and looked at Pete. "Muy romántico."

Polito laughed. "Coño, nephew, what have you done to this girl?"

Pete looked at Mariela. "Should we tell them?"

Mariela said nothing. The blush in her skin was evidence enough.

"Tell us what?" Polito said and sat up in the wicker chair, suddenly very serious.

Henrietta came back into the courtyard. She surveyed the scene, wiping her hands on the flowered apron she had tied around her waist. "What's wrong?" she asked.

"Nothing's wrong," Pete said. "We're engaged." Pete watched his uncle's expression with a policeman's eyes. He was hiding something behind his smile. He caught the quick glance Polito shot at his wife. Pete's eyes moved undetectably toward his aunt.

Henrietta raised one eyebrow and mouthed the words "no ahora" to Polito before her face broke into a broad smile. "Chévere," she screamed, opening her arms and embracing Mariela.

Imelda woke Katarina with the news. "I'm so jealous," she said to Pete. "I thought you were mine, amor."

He laughed and kissed her. "I'll always be yours."

"Polito," his aunt said. "This calls for a celebration. The colmado is still open. I'm going to get some more whiskey."

"It's too late, Henrietta," Polito said. "I don't want you going out alone."

"Go with her, Pedro," Mariela said.

Pete caught the look Polito shot Henrietta. "Ta bien," she mouthed to Polito, then took Pete's hand and walked toward the front of the house. "Put on some music and call the family," she shouted back as she and Pete walked through the heavy, wrought iron front gate. "Leave it unlocked," she said to him. "We'll be right back."

They walked the twenty feet down the driveway to the street and turned left toward the colmado. It was then that Pete saw the two men slouching in the big black car with the windows down. Their movements were catlike. In less than a moment, he saw the machine guns rise out of their laps through the windows. It was surreal to him and didn't register at first. The sound of the gunfire was ear-shattering. Flashes of light came out of the gun barrels as the bullets whizzed by his head. His aunt was standing between him and the gunmen.

The first volley threw her back on top of him, knocking him to the ground as the bullets hit her. He quickly flipped himself over, covering her with his body and reaching for his gun, which wasn't there. Why would it be? He was on vacation. Before he could get to his knees, the big black Cadillac had pulled into the street and sped away.

His uncle, his cousins and Mariela came running from the house. The neighbors hung from the windows facing the street. Mariela screamed and collapsed to her knees. Polito picked up Henrietta in his arms, her blood staining his white linen shirt and slacks. "Are you shot?" he screamed at Pete.

Pete stopped for a moment to consider the question. "No," he replied.

"Get the car. I have to get her to a doctor immediately or she'll bleed to death."

Pete sat in the waiting room of a private clinic in Cristo Rey. He held Imelda's hand in his left hand and Mariela's in his right. Katarina sat on the couch next to Polito, weeping silently. They had been there for over three hours. The doctor appeared in the doorway separating the waiting room from the hallway leading to the examination rooms. He motioned for Polito to follow him. Pete's eyes followed his uncle as he rose from the couch and walked through the doorway, closing the door behind him.

Pete wasn't sure what was going on. Polito had had him drive to a private clinic, not a hospital. He said the hospital would ask too many questions, would contact the National Police. Pete asked him why he didn't want the police called in and his uncle just laughed. "You don't understand this country," he said. "You were too young when you left and you've been away too long."

Katarina's weeping became more audible. Pete let go of Imelda and Mariela's hands and walked to the couch to comfort her. They remained like that until his uncle returned to the waiting room.

"She'll live," Polito said, closing the heavy metal door quietly behind him. "But she's lost a lot of blood and will require additional transfusions. She's going to be here for a few weeks." The three girls ran to embrace him, all of them crying. Pete noticed the look on Mariela's face, an expression that said she'd been through this before. Polito hugged the girls and kissed each one.

"Tío," Pete said, "should we stay the night here to make sure she's OK?"

"No," said Polito. "You take the girls home. I'll stay with her. You come pick me up in the morning."

Pete looked at him. "Can I speak to you for a moment in private?"

"Not now," Polito replied, hugging the girls again. "In the morning, when you pick me up."

Pete lifted his eyebrow. "OK then," he said to the girls. "It's late, let's go."

"Vamos," Polito said, getting into the car. His face looked drawn and tired. He still had on the blood-stained clothes from the night before.

Pete left the gear shift in park. "What's going on here, uncle?"

"What are you talking about?"

Pete grasped the steering wheel tightly, his knuckles stretching the skin of his hand. "Drive-by shootings, private clinics, no hospitals, no police report. What are you hiding?"

Polito sighed heavily. He put his hand over Pete's. "Drive, mijo. I'm tired, but I'll tell you everything."

Pete shifted the car into drive and pulled out into the morning traffic. Though he had been born here, he was a boy when he left and his memories were incomplete. He was really a product of the streets of Washington Heights in Upper Manhattan, but this foray back to Santo Domingo had opened his eyes. Now he understood Washington Heights as well. "Tío, why are you afraid of the police?" he said, dodging the traffic along Avenida Nicolas de Ovando.

"Pedrito, when you left we were very poor. Now we are, how should I say, very comfortable. How do you think we got that way?"

"The motorcycle repair and the beauty salon," Pete replied.

Polito chuckled. "Mijo, think about it."

Pete smiled to himself through his anger and concern. He still loved it when his uncle called him mijo.

"This is a poor country. How much money can we make fixing scooters and dying hair? And everyone else here does the same thing. You can get your motorcycle repaired and your hair dyed on every corner in the capital."

"Tío, what are you telling me?"

"The businesses are a front."

Pete watched the traffic with one eye and focused the other on his uncle. "For what?"

Polito hesitated. "Drogas. It's the only way out of poverty in this country. There are no jobs, no chances, only the drugs."

"So what are you saying?" Pete asked. He couldn't bring himself to believe his uncle, this man who had cared for him, defended him, raised him when his father had abandoned them and when his mother went to New York to find a new life for all of them, could be a criminal.

"I'm telling you the truth. I'm saying we're involved in the drug trade because we had no choice. I had to feed my children."

"I can't believe that," Pete said, slapping the wheel with the palm of his hand. The car swerved into the opposing lane. Polito grabbed the wheel and righted the car's direction. "Pull over," he said. "I'll drive."

"No," Pete shouted at him. He thought his heart would explode through his chest. The car swerved again.

"Pull over, damn it," his uncle shouted, "before you kill us both."

Pete slowed the car and pulled over just before the intersection of Avenida del Zoologico and Paseo de los Reyos Catolicos under the hillside slums of La Augustina. Dozens of teenage boys and young men milled around shoeless and shirtless. There was no work here. There was no way to feed your children. Polito got out of the car and walked around to the driver's side. The young men stared at them as they exchanged positions. Polito nodded almost imperceptibly to one group standing around a small open fire.

"You know them?" Pete asked, getting into the passenger's seat.

"They know me, they know who I am," Polito said, putting the car in drive and pulling back into the street.

"So how do you do this?" Pete asked.

"We act as a transfer point and as couriers."

Pete looked at his uncle but remained silent.

"The cocaine comes in from Columbia hidden in shipping containers in the seat cushions of used motor scooters and motorcycles sent here to be reconditioned and resold. When we get the bikes, we remove the cocaine packets from the cushions and hire the mules to bring the product into the United States."

"The mules?" Pete asked.

"Sí, we recruit young women through the beauty shop. They swallow a number of packets of cocaine and we send them on short trips to the United States. We pay them well for this. It's all rather simple."

"And last night's shooting?"

"Was meant for me."

"Who? Rivals?"

"No," Polito said. "The National Police. They're corrupt. How do you think we get away with this?"

"Why are they after you?"

"They wanted a bigger piece or they would help my competitors against me. And I said no."

"So they'll kill you."

"Yes, the same way they did Mariela's parents."

Pete tried to respond but no words escaped his mouth.

"He was my partner," Polito said. "And the only reason she's alive is because I protect her. She saw something, Pedrito, and they know it. She can identify the killer, which is why you can't marry her. If she tries to leave here or I'm not there to protect her, they'll kill both of you."

"I'm not afraid of them," Pete said.

"You should be. Now do you understand why no police and no hospital?" Polito pulled the car into the driveway in front of the house.

"Uncle, please, you have to let us help you. We can get you to the States. You can testify against them, inform on them, the Americans will help you."

Polito leaned back in the seat and laughed. "For what, mijo? So I can go to los Estados Unidos and change my name and hide and bag groceries in some slum? Here I am a man of means. I'll take my chances. Come, let's go in the house. It's not so safe here right now."

Pete opened the passenger door and got out of the car. Chicho and Freddie were standing in the entryway of the house, their pistols showing conspicuously. They opened the heavy front gate.

"I'm going to clean myself up," Polito said and disappeared up the stairs to the bedrooms.

Pete walked toward the courtyard. Mariela was sitting in the kitchen peeling garlic. "How is she?" she asked.

"I'm not sure. I didn't see her. The same, I think." He took Mariela's hand. "We need to talk," he said.

The phone rang, its bell shrill against the silence in the house. Mariela rose to answer it. "Pronto," she said into the phone then held it out for Pete. "It's for you, it's Glynnis."

Pete took the phone. "Hey."

"You don't sound very happy," Glynnis replied, a world away.

"Just tired, it's been a long night," Pete said. He looked over at Mariela and knew how deeply in love with her he was. He didn't care what his uncle said or anyone else for that matter. He would take her away from this nightmare. "Glynnis," he said into the receiver, "we need to talk."

"First I have to tell you something, amor," she said. "I have great news."

"You got the job with Macy's?"

"No, amor, I'm pregnant."

Chapter 5

WASHINGTON HEIGHTS, NYC
4 JUNE 2010
4:00 P.M.

PETE LOWERED HIS HEAD INTO his hands. "And that's the story."

"That's a lot of story," Tolya replied. "Who knows? Maybe this all has something to do with her parent's murder all these years later."

Pete stood up. "I gotta get out of here, man. This was just all too intense."

"Go home," Tolya said. "I gotta get out of here too. Tonight is our first family Sabbath and I have to conduct it."

Pete checked his cell phone and his gun. "You gotta be kidding. She's taking this whole thing a little too seriously."

"Yep."

"Well, good luck with that rabbi," Pete said.

They clasped hands and embraced. "Thanks. I'll meet you at the Caridad tomorrow morning at 8 to pick up on this. We need to go through those videos."

"Make it 9."

"Why?"

"I got a date."

"Jeez."

"Give me a break, man. I need to relax."

Tolya watched Pete amble his large frame out of their tiny office and down the hall to the front exit of the precinct. He began closing down his computer, then changed his mind, opened his browser and typed "Interpol" into Google. On the Interpol website, he found the Interpol Data Exchange page. When it asked him to log in, he clicked on the button for registration, created a screen name and a password, and continued. The next page asked for his affiliation and personal information, which he supplied. Verification took a nanosecond and he was in.

Tolya typed the term "suicide machine" into the search bar. No results appeared on the screen. He clicked on "information request," provided a full description of what he was looking for and attached a photo from the crime scene, then pressed send. A message came back instantly: "Thank you for your request. Interpol Data Exchange will respond within 48 hours."

Tolya looked at his watch, 4:35, time enough to stop at the liquor store and then surprise Max and Erno in the park.

Karin sat in the green room at NBC studios. She considered herself lucky to have gotten the station to do more than a cursory report on the exhibition. She had contacted a reporter, a woman she knew from her days as a detective, and asked her if she could arrange for the local news to do an in-depth story on the exhibition.

The reporter was more than happy to help. They agreed to an interview with her that would appear on the *Visiones* segment on Sunday Today in NY, plus coverage of the VIP opening before the show opened to the general public.

Karin wore her best black pregnancy suit for the occasion. She laughed to herself. She couldn't wait till she could wear her regular clothes again. Though she had wanted a girl, this would be her last child. She loved her children, but she was ready for new challenges. She looked down at her wrist and ran her fingers over her silver and jade bracelet. Erno Hierron had given it to her shortly before he died. It had belonged to his wife, Ava. He had had it made for her when they lived in the Dominican Republic in Sosúa.

A voice broke her concentration. "Ms. Reyes is ready for you now," the young woman said.

"Excellent," Karin replied, pushing herself up with the help of the writing desk next to the high-backed chair she had chosen over the low couch. "Just a moment."

The young woman smiled at her. "Do you need help?" she asked, not moving from her perch in the doorway.

"No," replied Karin, righting herself. "I've got it. Thanks." She followed the young woman out of the door, down the hall and into the studio.

Meredith Reyes smiled and extended a hand toward Karin. "Mimi didn't tell me you were, well, this pregnant."

"Yes, I'm due in about three weeks or so," Karin said. "And truth is, I spoke with Mimi on the phone. She hasn't seen me in a while, so she didn't know herself."

"Will you be comfortable on those stools?" Meredith asked, pointing toward two stools on the soundstage in front of the *Visiones* set. "I could change the interview venue, though that might take us a few minutes."

"No," Karin said, flashing a look at the clock on the wall opposite her. It was already 4:30 and she wanted to be home by 6 for her first family Shabbat. "I think I can handle it."

"Great," Meredith said. "Then follow me and let's get started."

They walked the few yards to the stools. Two technicians followed them, one to set up Meredith's microphones and the other to set up Karin's. "How exciting," Karin said. "I've never been on TV before."

"Don't be nervous," Reyes said. "It's nothing really. Just make believe we're sitting in your office and chatting. That's how we do this, very chatty, you know, like we're old friends."

"Yeah," Karin said, "I've noticed that feel on other segments. I'll do my best."

"Light and sound check, please," Meredith called out to the

technicians then turned back toward Karin. "So we want to do a segment of approximately five minutes. I've got a series of questions for you here. Would you like to look at them?"

"Sure," Karin replied. She perused the paper while the technician finished placing the microphone under the lip of her neckline.

"Test please," the technician called out.

Karin looked at Meredith. "Say your name a couple of times," Meredith said.

"Karin Martinez-Kurchenko," she said twice.

"Good," the sound technician called out from the booth. "Now check Meredith."

Karin continued to study the questions, formulating answers while the technicians finished the sound and light tests.

"OK," the technician called out, "In five, four, three…"

Meredith turned toward the cameras. "Hola, and welcome to Visiones," she said and smiled broadly. "I'm Meredith Reyes, your host. Today we are very honored to have with us Karin Martinez-Kurchenko, chief curator for an exciting new exhibition, Dominican Haven, opening in two weeks at the Museum of Jewish Heritage. Karin, could you tell us a little about the exhibition?"

The camera shifted slightly toward Karin. She smiled and looked in its direction, the bright lights making it hard to see. "Certainly, Meredith," she said. "We've been working on this project for some time now, and are very excited to bring a little-known part of history to the people of New York and the world. Dominican Haven is a story of friendship and tolerance between two very diverse communities that began in the Dominican Republic."

"Well, please tell us," Meredith said.

"In July 1938, at the Evian Conference, in an attempt to help the European Jewish communities threatened by the Nazis, the Dominican Republic—the only country in the world to do so, I might add—offered to take up to 100,000 refugees as settlers. The initial destination for the first groups of these refugees was a defunct banana plantation on the north coast of the Dominican Republic known as Sosúa. Now, while the number of refugees never reached 100,000, in the period between 1939 and 1941, 854 refugees came to the Dominican Republic and settled in Sosúa, escaping certain death at the hands of the Nazis. They built a farm and dairy, becoming the main supplier of dairy products to the people of the Dominican Republic for decades."

"Really?" said Meredith, looking directly into Karin's eyes and smiling incredulously, "I'm Dominican and I've never heard anything about this."

Karin felt suddenly more at ease. She clasped her hands in her lap. She leaned forward toward Meredith slightly and said, "So am I and I had never heard of it either."

"How did you learn of it?" Meredith asked.

"Well," continued Karin, "my husband, Anatoly, is a detective with the New York City Police Department. I used to work there myself, and he solved a case that involved a former settler who died under mysterious circumstances some years ago here in New York, in Washington Heights, where we live."

"How interesting."

"Yes, and when I learned of it, I became determined to bring this story to the world."

"So you contacted the Museum?"

"Well, the short answer, and I know we're pressed for time, is yes. I worked on this project first as a volunteer, then as an employee of the museum."

"What would you like people to learn from this story?" Meredith asked her.

"Tolerance," Karin said. "It's really a beautiful story about how two groups of very poor, very oppressed people came together in very difficult times and helped one another to heal and to prosper."

"When does the show open?"

"June 17. We'll be having a special event that night to kick it off. The show opens to the public on June 20, which is also Father's Day."

"And it looks like you'll be giving your husband, what did you say his name was?"

"Anatoly, he's Russian."

"You'll be giving Anatoly the ultimate father's day present?" Meredith said, pointing toward Karin's stomach.

"Yes." Karin laughed. "Hopefully not that day!"

Pete drove the car down to the end of Dyckman Street and parked in the lot of the defunct bar that once served as a drug supermarket for the neighborhood. He looked out over the Hudson toward the Palisades on the Jersey side, then glanced over at the clock on the dashboard. It said 5:10 in pale green numbers. He was early. Perhaps he should have told Tolya and the captain everything.

He leaned back into the seat and waited. He hadn't spoken to his uncle in almost ten years. Though he hated him for what he'd done to the family, he still loved him. How could you not love someone who had been a father to you when you had no father, who had taught you to be a man?

He remembered that last time he saw Polito in Santo Domingo, when he had made the deal with him. "Turn yourself in, turn state's evidence against the corrupt police," Pete had said to him. "The FBI would get the girls safely out of the country." Polito had agreed, his daughters and Mariela were more important than his freedom. It was the other part that was more difficult for Polito. He knew he would never see them again. What other choice did Pete have? He was a cop and his uncle was a criminal, but the girls, they had done nothing wrong.

His cell rang. "Dime lo," he said.

"I'm coming down Dyckman now," the voice replied.

"I'm in the black mustang," Pete said. "Park next to me."

The call disconnected. Pete checked his gun in the holster at his hip. A black BMW sedan with Jersey plates and blacked-out windows pulled up next to him. The driver's side window rolled down. A muscular man with a modified Mohawk turned toward him and smiled broadly, his white teeth filling his face.

"Qué lo que, pana," came the voice. The face had changed a little, older, blockier, perhaps fattened by steroids and alcohol but unmistakably Chicho.

"Qué lo que," Pete said. They got out of the cars and embraced.

"How many years has it been?" Chicho asked.

"I'm not sure," Pete replied. "Too many for brothers. You look good man. You spending some time in the gym?"

Chicho stepped back and flexed then laughed. Despite the tough exterior, Pete saw the same gentleness in his eyes that he had when they were boys in Santo Domingo. "A little bit," Chicho said, "not as much as when I was inside. You know then, you don't got much else to do."

"True," Pete said. He took a toothpick from inside his jacket pocket and stuck it into his mouth.

Chicho leaned back against the trunk of his Mercedes and crossed his arms. "Panito, I was surprised to hear from you. How did you get my number?"

"I called Freddie."

"Claro," Chicho said. "La verdad, I never thought we'd speak to each other again unless it was with me on one side of the bars and you on the other. What can I do for you?"

Pete leaned against the corner of the back of the mustang. He picked his teeth for a moment. He looked at Chicho. "I need a favor," he said.

"Well, if only for old times' sake. What?"

"I need to speak to Polito."

Chicho laughed. "Pana, that's not gonna be so easy."

Tolya took the elevator in the subway station up to Ft. Washington Avenue and walked stealthily into Bennett Park. He wanted to surprise Erno and Max in the playground. He climbed the few steps from the street into the park, crossing the bronze band that outlined the original Fort Washington built during the Revolutionary War. He was still amazed at how Americans rarely noticed their own history. Almost no one ever mentioned that the park had been an important Revolutionary War site.

He stood near the benches and surveyed the playground. He spotted Nilda sitting near the swings with the other nannies while Max and Erno played in the sand with plastic trucks. He walked toward the gate and let himself in. Nilda waved at him. He put his finger over his mouth. She smiled and tilted her head in the direction of the boys.

Tolya crept silently toward them. Their heads were down, diligently loading sand into plastic dump trucks and making sounds they thought would go with excavation. A day at the playground wasn't relaxation for little boys, it was work. He slid down in between them, grabbing both by the shoulders and making monster growls startling them.

"Daddy," they both screamed, wrestling him to the ground. He could easily have pried them off. Instead he let them pin him down. He continued making monster sounds, the boys laughing uncontrollably. Five years on, he still couldn't believe how much he loved being a father. How natural he was at it, just as Pete had told him he would be.

"Roar," he growled one more time, then sat up and took one boy in each arm and kissed them both on the tops of their heads. They hugged him back. "OK, boys," he said. "Let's get our stuff together. We have to go home. Your mother has a special surprise for us."

"No," they both whined, looking back and forth between Tolya and Nilda.

Nilda walked over to help him. "OK," she said, "is time to go." They looked up at her briefly, stood up and brushed off their clothes.

Tolya was amazed at the control she had over them. "They never give up that easy with me."

She smiled. "That's why I'm the nanny."

They collected the boys' things and put them in the back of the stroller. "Nilda, you can go home from here," Tolya said. "I can get them back OK."

"Thanks," she said, then kissed the boys and walked off toward 181st Street.

Tolya put Erno into the stroller, took Max by the hand and led them out of the park up Pinehurst Avenue toward 187th Street. He breathed the warm evening air deeply into his lungs. He was worried about Pete and the investigation. He could see the toll it was taking on Pete, but that would have to wait till tomorrow. Tonight was for Karin and the boys.

"Where are we going, Daddy?" Max asked.

"To the bakery and to buy flowers," Tolya said.

"Why?" Max asked.

He questioned everything. There were days when Tolya was

exhausted by it. He had to explain everything to him. But then, he didn't want his sons to be afraid of him the way he and Oleg had been of their father, afraid to ask him almost anything. "Well," Tolya replied, "for two reasons."

"What are they?" Max interrupted.

"Give me a chance and I'll tell you," Tolya said.

"OK, Daddy, I'll give you a chance. It's your turn."

"Thank you," Tolya said. He squeezed Max's hand gently. "First of all, we're going to the bakery to buy cookies for your mother because she loves those cookies and I like to make her happy, and we have to buy a challah."

"What's a challah," Max said.

"It's a special bread for the Sabbath."

"What's a Sabbath?" Max said without missing a beat.

"Well, that's more complicated."

"What's complicated?"

Tolya laughed to himself. It was like an endless loop. "I'll explain it to you when we get home."

"OK," said Max.

"Daddy?" Erno said.

"Yes?"

"What's complicated?"

"My life." Tolya laughed. "I'll explain it to both of you when we get home. Now let's pick out some flowers for your mother."

Karin looked across the table at Tolya, the flames of the Sabbath candles framing his face. She was happy, no, delighted. She had pulled it all off, candle lighting, prayer over the wine, prayer over the bread, blessing of the children, dinner. Thank god for online transliteration, because neither she nor Tolya would have been able to do any of this reading the Hebrew alphabet. Tolya smiled at her across the table, shoving another forkful of bowtie noodles with kasha into his mouth.

"I'm a lucky man," Tolya said through the mouthful.

"Oh really, why's that?" Karin asked, sipping water from her goblet.

"I'm married to a sexy Latina who can make kasha better than my Russian mother."

"Why are you laughing, Mommy?" Max asked.

"Because I'm happy, my darling."

"Why are you happy?" he continued with his endless stream of questions.

"Because I have a wonderful family and I love you all and that makes me happy. And we're having our first family Sabbath."

"I'm happy too, Mommy," Max said.

"Me too," said Erno, attempting to spear the bowtie noodle with his fork, which was too big for his hand to begin with.

"Can I go play in my room now?" Max asked.

"No, we have more to do," said Karin.

"And what would that be?" Tolya asked.

"Yeah, and what would that be?" Max repeated.

"Well," Karin said, "remember I explained to you earlier how the Sabbath, Shabbat, separates the days of the week when we work hard from the days when we relax and enjoy the things we like to do best?"

"Yes," said Erno. He lifted himself off his booster seat and down to the floor, then crawled on Tolya's lap.

"She was asking me," said Max.

"I was asking both of you," Karin said, picking up Max, placing him on her lap and caressing his head. "Well tonight we're going to do something that we enjoy doing to help us relax so we make the Shabbat special."

"Like TV?" Max said.

"Yeah, Mommy, like the Yankees?" Tolya said.

"Maybe later for the Yankees. First we'll do something without TV."

"Like what?" Max asked.

"Like a whole new project."

Max turned his head and looked at her. She peered into his blue eyes, the color of the summer sky on a cloudless day. She smiled both inside and out. Her kids were the best thing that had ever happened to her. They were the first thing, well maybe with the exception of Tolya, that made her put something before herself. "There's a big box in the living room. Why don't you take Daddy in there and open it?"

The kids jumped off their laps and ran into the living room.

"What did you do?" Tolya asked her.

She simply smiled and said, "They'll need help."

Tolya rose from his place at the table and kissed her softly on the lips. He lingered for a moment and kissed her again, hard. "More of that later," he said and headed for the living room. She watched him as he walked away. All these years and three kids later, she still loved the way his hips moved when he walked. She followed him down the two steps into the living room and walked to the black leather couch. By the time she had lowered herself into its corner, the wrapping was off the box.

"The trains, it's the trains we saw at that big toy store downtown," Max screamed.

Erno just screeched.

"Yes," Karin said as they climbed on top of her.

"Careful," said Tolya. "I don't want you to crush Oleg before he gets here."

"Thank you, Mommy," both boys said, hugging her and kissing her.

"Yes, thank you, Mommy," Tolya said. He walked across the living room and kissed her softly on the lips.

"You'll enjoy doing this with them," she said. "You may have forgotten but I haven't. You love to build things."

"I do," he replied as he sat down on the floor and tore open the top of the box with his bare fingers.

Karin watched them as they set the pieces in little piles and Tolya explained to them how the tracks would work. Nothing could have been more relaxing for her than to watch this. She understood now what Rabbi Rothman had meant, that Shabbat was as much a state of mind as it was a set of rules.

Pete dropped Liza at the entrance of her building, then waited for her to get into the front vestibule before driving down the block to Broadway. He made a quick right and a left, pulled into an empty space on 185th Street reserved for members of the precinct, then walked down the hill and back down Broadway to 180th Street and took a right. Halfway down the block, he pulled out his keys, walked up the five stairs to the entrance of his building and took the one flight up to his apartment in double steps. He tiptoed into the apartment, dropping his keys on the little table by the door, then unstrapped his pistol and checked the safety, stowing it on top of the armoire in the foyer. With four kids, he wasn't taking any chances. He checked Pete Jr.'s room. Junior was in bed and asleep, unusual for 2:45 on a Friday night. Then he looked in on the girls. Resting comfortably. Last, he looked in on Jeremy. At 12, he was Pete's heart. It wasn't that he had a favorite. It was just something, a connection he never had with Junior or the girls that made this one special. Or maybe it was just that when Jeremy came it was an accident, and he knew there wouldn't be another one.

He'd lived in this apartment since he had come to the United States. It had been his mother's. His brothers had moved away, first to other apartments in the neighborhood, then to Jersey and Long Island and Pennsylvania. He was the youngest. He stayed to keep an eye on his mother. Then Glynnis became pregnant and they got married and she moved in. After his mother died, they remained. It was close to the precinct and he loved the neighborhood. Glynnis had wanted a house, but he didn't want to live out there, in America. He liked it here in Washington Heights with his own people. He still felt more Dominican than American.

Pete walked quietly into the bedroom. Glynnis was asleep in the big bed on the far side near the window. He slipped off his clothes and folded them on the chair next to the closet. He stood there in his underwear, looking at Glynnis. He still loved her. How could you not love someone you'd shared a life and a lifetime with? Someone you'd had four kids with, who put up with all your bullshit and forgave all your imperfections?

Then the guilt started to creep in. He didn't know why he did what he did. He could never stop himself, girlfriend after girlfriend, always looking for something and never finding it. Glynnis was a good woman, and she deserved better than him. He walked down the hall to the bathroom, closing the door as quietly as possible. He brushed his teeth and washed up, then stared at himself for a long moment. He was going to give up Liza. He would tell her next time he saw her, after the weekend. He needed to change. He had to change.

Pete went into the living room and sat down at his desk in front of the computer. He turned it on to provide some light. The living room was too close to the kid's bedrooms to turn on the lamps. He didn't want to wake anyone. He needed this time to himself.

He reached into the bottom drawer on the right side of the desk and pulled out his mother's Spanish language Pentecostal Bible. He opened the back cover and took a folded piece of paper with the blue and red edgings of an old airmail envelope from the book. He held the paper for a moment, then placed it under his nose imagining the scent he hoped it would have, the scent of Mariela's skin. He sensed it in his mind though he knew it wasn't there, that it was only in his memory.

After a moment, he unfolded the paper. He hadn't looked at it in many years. He knew he should have thrown it away years ago but he couldn't. He'd never spoken of it to anyone. Pete stared at the fading ink for a few minutes before silently reading the lyrical Spanish words, "Mi amor, mi vida, mi corazón…"

> My darling, my life, my heart. How can I tell you this while my heart is breaking? I love you more than anything in this world. I will never love anyone or anything the way I love you. But I cannot marry you, my darling. Do not come back. I could never live with myself for what I would do to Glynnis if you left her like this. She is carrying your child. I know you love her. You loved her before we found each other. What happened between us was beautiful. It was magic, but it was an accident. I will never forget the passion in your kiss and the love in your eyes. Thank you for teaching me the true meaning of love. I'm sorry, mi amor. I will always love you.
>
> Mariela

Pete felt a lump in his throat. "Is this why I do the things I do?"

Chapter

6

WASHINGTON HEIGHTS, NYC
5 JUNE 2010
9:00 A.M.

T OLYA SIPPED HIS COFFEE AND perused the paper while waiting for Pete. He was, as usual, late. Habitually prompt, Tolya had found this trait irritating for many years. As he got to know Pete and then other Dominicans, including Karin, he had come to accept it as a cultural thing. Now he found it both endearing and a little comical.

The waitress approached him again. "Are you sure," she said in a combination of English and Spanish, "that you don't want something to eat while you wait for your friend?"

"No," he said and smiled broadly. "Just a little water, please."

He tipped his head back to drain the remaining liquid from the cup. As he peered over the edge of the paper, he spotted Pete running across the street. Pete pulled at the glass door forcefully to counter the air lock it created in the vestibule, then pulled the inner door open and crossed the dining room in three large steps to where Tolya was seated.

"Nice of you to come," Tolya said, smiling.

"Fuck you," Pete said, sitting down and rubbing his eyes. "Man, am I tired."

"What time you come in?"

"Late."

"How's Liza?"

"Good, irritating, you know. What's with the interrogation? Didn't we do enough of that yesterday?"

"And we're likely to do a lot more today. Calm down, I'm just fucking with you."

Pete's shoulders slumped and his face relaxed. "I know, brother, I'm just really stressed out from all this. She was an important part of my life. I gotta figure out who did this to her. No way she did that to herself."

The waitress returned with two cups of steaming Dominican coffee. "What you like?" she asked them.

"Mangu," Pete said, "con tres golpes."

"The same for me," Tolya added.

"Bien," the waitress replied then ran off into the kitchen.

"Where do you want to start?" Pete asked.

"The security cameras."

"The super expecting us?"

"Yeah, I had the precinct call yesterday evening. Here's the warrant."

Pete took the papers and slid them into his back pocket. "And then what?"

Tolya hesitated for a minute.

"What?" Pete said.

"I think we need to interview your cousins."

Pete pulled his arms in toward his chest and took a deep breath. "I haven't told them yet. And the body is still in the morgue. There's the whole question of what to do with her, a funeral. I have to think about that before I tell them."

"I understand," said Tolya.

The waitress arrived with two large plates heaped with mangu, eggs, salami, fried cheese and pickled onions. "Algo más?" she asked.

"Nada más," Pete said.

It had taken many years for Tolya to develop a taste for boiled, mashed green plantains. Karin had taught him to love it. Pete had added the fried salami to the plate. "Dig in," he said to Pete.

"Not hungry anymore," Pete replied.

Tolya pressed the super's buzzer at the front door of the building at 209 Wadsworth Ave. A crackly voice came through in Spanish. "What she say?" Tolya asked.

"She said it's Saturday and he's not home."

Tolya sighed. "OK. Hold up your badge to the camera." He pushed the buzzer again, leaning on it heavily, both he and Pete holding up their badges. He didn't let up on the buzzer till he heard it buzz back and could enter the building. Before the outer door slammed shut and he could press the interior button, the buzzer on the interior door sounded. Pete pushed the door open and held it for Tolya. They took a left into the stairway and ran down the one flight to the basement. The super's apartment was at the end of the hall at the back of the building.

The door opened before Pete could knock. A small woman in her 50s stood in the doorway, her hands on her hips. "He's not here. What do you want?" she said in Spanish. "And I don't know where he is, he never came home last night."

"We need to review the building's security camera files," Pete replied in Spanish.

"You have to come back Monday," she said, beginning to close the door.

Pete grabbed the door with his hand. "I don't think so," he said. "This is a suspected murder investigation now."

"The machines with the recordings are in the office downtown."

"I have a warrant," Pete said holding up the official paper. "Your husband told us the recordings are here."

"Coño," the woman said. Tolya knew the Dominican term for "damn."

She grabbed the keys from the hook next to the door and led them down to the small office at the front end of the basement. She opened the door and pointed toward the recording equipment. "OK?" she said.

"Sí, gracias," said Tolya. She turned and stomped down the hall, slamming the door to her apartment behind her.

Pete pulled the one chair from behind the desk and put it in front of the screen. "You wanna sit?" he asked Tolya.

"Nah, you go ahead. I'll find something else. Get the recordings working."

Tolya walked down the hall to the laundry room. He found an old bar stool and carried it to the super's office. Pete had the surveillance files open on the screen. "What date do you want to start with?" he asked Tolya.

Tolya calculated in his head. They found the body on Thursday. It had to have been there a couple of days. The neighbor had been complaining about the smell for at least a day. That would put them back to Tuesday. "Sunday, let's start looking at Sunday, in the late evening. That would be May 30."

Pete punched in May 30, 2010, 10 p.m. "Got it."

Reviewing the recordings was slow-going. After an hour they took a break. Tolya mostly stood, as the backless stool was brutal to sit on for more than about five minutes at a time.

Pete stared relentlessly at the screen, fast-forwarding the recording until a shadowy figure appeared, then slowing it down to catch a glimpse of the phantom entering the building. He was looking for something specific, a lumber delivery, the posts and beams that created the mechanism that ended Mariela's life. As the hour on the video became late, later than a commercial delivery would occur, he increased the speed.

"Pete," Tolya said, putting his hand on Pete's shoulder, "look."

"What?" Pete said. "Sorry, I missed that, I was yawning."

"Run that back about twenty seconds."

"There's nothing there, Tolya, look at the time. It's the middle of the night."

"Go back," Tolya said. "Just humor me."

Pete ran the recording back.

"There, stop it now," Tolya said.

"Shit," Pete mumbled. There on the screen were three men carrying 2x4's and metal joists and bags of other equipment. They pulled out a set of keys and opened the front door to the building. "Look at the time, 2:20 a.m. Monday May 31, 2010. Who the hell makes a delivery at that hour? And they had keys."

Tolya squinted at the screen for a moment, then straightened up quickly. "We're gonna find out right now. Come on." He turned and sprinting down the hallway, up the stairs and out into the street.

"What you looking for, pana?" Pete shouted. He followed Tolya up the stairs and out of the building.

Tolya pointed toward the light pole at the curve in Wadsworth Avenue that led around to West 192nd Street. "There," he said. "Suspended under the streetlamp, that's a city security camera. We gotta go back to the stationhouse now."

Tolya typed his badge number and password into the sign-in boxes on the NYPD intranet. He clicked on the navigational button for surveillance cams then typed in the location of the cam he was seeking. In a nanosecond, the corner of Wadsworth Avenue in front of the building where Mariela had died came into view. He clicked on the archives button. Another box came up asking for the approximate date and time.

"May 31, 2:20 a.m.," Pete said.

"Great," Tolya said as he typed in the information. Pete's hands were on his shoulders. "Calm down, big boy, you're squeezing a little too hard there, man."

"Sorry."

In a long moment, the image of that night only a few days before appeared on the screen. There in front of their eyes was a panel truck with its rear door open and three men unloading wood beams and posts, along with the other items they would need to build the death trap that had taken Mariela's life.

"I told you," Pete said. "Shit, with the door rolled up, you can't see the name of the company that owns the truck."

"But you can see the license plate." Tolya pressed pause on the replay, then zoomed into the license plate. He jotted down the fuzzy numbers and letters. New York plate VSA510.

"Rewind it."

"OK," Tolya said. The screen appeared empty again at 2:15. A few seconds later, the panel truck pulled up. On the back door was stenciled the name Rockaway Lumber and Building Supplies. "Brilliant, hermano. I should have thought of that myself."

"That's why we're a team."

The trip to East Rockaway was tense and long. There was a good amount of traffic to the airport and the beaches that tied them up on the Grand Central Parkway and then on the Van Wyck. Tolya looked over at Pete. His hands were clenched into fists as if he was ready to punch the first guy he'd see when he got out of the car. "You OK there, partner?"

"Yeah, I'm OK," Pete said, staring straight ahead. "Just can't stand this traffic."

"You wanna take the streets instead?"

"Nah, won't save any time. You know we have to go back to the videos. The killer is probably on there with Mariela, entering the building."

"Yeah, I think so, I left instructions at the precinct. They're sending someone over this afternoon to continue reviewing the videos"

"OK," said Pete.

Tolya turned on the radio to La Mega, the Spanish language station. He noticed Pete's hands tapping the rhythm of the merengue against his thigh. "You wanna talk about it?"

"Talk about what?"

"What you're really thinking?"

Pete continued to stare straight ahead. Tolya thought it best to back off. The traffic opened up a little as they passed Kennedy Airport and swung around onto Rockaway Blvd.

"You ever wonder why I can't keep my dick in my pants, brotherman?" Pete said.

Tolya didn't know what to say. He wanted to help Pete, but this wasn't a place he wanted to go. He never judged Pete for his philandering. He knew what was in Pete's heart and how much he loved Glynnis and his kids. Some guys just needed more and it wasn't his place to judge that. "You wanna tell me, hermano? Whatever you wanna say, I'm here to listen."

"I realized it last night. It's because of Mariela." He reached into his jeans and pulled a piece of paper out of his back pocket. "This is the letter she sent me breaking it off. No one other than me has ever looked at it. No human eyes except mine, and now yours."

Tolya hesitated. "You want me to read it?"

"You can't," Pete said. "It's in Spanish." They both laughed. Tolya was glad for that, as it cut the tension between them. "You'd think by now you would have picked some up."

"Karin tells me that all the time."

"I'll translate it for you," Pete said and began reading, first in Spanish and then translating each phrase into English. Though the sound of his own voice was in his ears, the sound of Mariela's was in his mind. A couple of times, his voice caught in his throat. When he finished, he stopped for a moment then turned to Tolya and said, "You see, I've been looking for her ever since."

"Do you love Glynnis?"

"Yes I do, but this was different. Did you ever love anyone like that? So deeply that when you're apart it hurts?"

Tolya nodded his head slightly. He bit his lip gently. "Yep, Karin."

"You don't know how lucky you are, brother," Pete said.

"I do know. Every day." Tolya slowed the car and followed the fork in the road to the right toward the Rockaways just before the Atlantic Beach Bridge. "Pete, why didn't you go after her?"

Pete smiled and hesitated a moment. "How many years we know each other, Tol?"

"Long time. I stopped counting."

"And you ain't figured that out yet?"

"It's that Latino thing."

"Yep," Pete replied. "We don't run after a woman. And you know, I was here, she was there, Glynnis was pregnant, I was a kid, and man was I overwhelmed."

"Claro," Tolya said.

Pete's cell phone pinged. He clicked on the text icon and read Chicho's text: "Tío Umbrella tonight VIP section 2:30"

"Glynnis?" Tolya asked.

"Yep," Pete lied.

They pulled up in front of Rockaway Lumber and Building Supplies. There was a spot at the end of the block. Tolya didn't like the idea of the car being boxed in, just in case of trouble. He backed out onto Beach Channel Drive and saw another spot half a block down. He pulled up and backed into the space, completing the parallel park in two moves. He slipped his NYPD ID card on top of the dashboard. "Tranqui," he said to Pete, using the Dominican term for "keep calm" he'd learned from him.

"Tranqui," Pete replied.

Rockaway Lumber and Building Supplies occupied a dilapidated, one-story building of wood construction with a corrugated metal roof. It was little more than a shack. It fronted the street for about thirty feet and extended back another 100 feet into the block on the corner along Beach Channel Drive and Beach 48th Street. Next to it was a vacant lot enclosed by a chain-link fence with a locked gate. Inside sat the delivery truck they had seen on the surveillance tapes. A fat, mangy dog slept in the shadow next to the truck.

As they entered the darkened building they removed their sunglasses. A tall, thin, unshaven man stood behind the counter. He appeared to be in his mid-40s. He wore a sweatshirt with the sleeves cut off, revealing large garish tattoos on both of his skinny arms.

"Is the owner here?" Tolya asked.

"Why?" the tattooed man responded, crossing his arms against his chest.

"We need to speak to him."

"You can speak to me."

Tolya thought for a moment that he recognized the accent. "Russkiy?" he asked

"No, Shqiptare, Albanian."

"OK, well," said Pete, taking a step closer to the counter. "You made a delivery of some goods to a building in upper Manhattan a few days ago. We'd like some information about that."

The tattooed man chuckled then turned and picked up a clipboard. "That's private business. We don't release information about deliveries."

"No?" said Pete.

Before Tolya could stop him he jumped over the counter and grabbed the tattooed man by his shirt and held him up against the shelves behind the counter. Pete's biceps bulged through the short sleeves of his T-shirt. The man was no match for Pete. "You'll tell me whatever I wanna know, you piece of shit."

Tolya pulled out his badge. "We're cops," he said. "This is a murder investigation." He grabbed Pete's shoulders. "Yo, hermano, put him down."

Pete resisted at first. "No, I kinda like him up here."

"Pete, please."

Pete lowered the tattooed man to the floor, who then backed away about ten feet. The tattooed man bent toward the right and reached for something under his pant leg. Tolya pulled his gun. "Hands up now!" he shouted. Pete pulled his gun as well, the barrel targeted at the Albanian's forehead.

"All right, OK," the tattooed man said, raising his hands over his head. The knife he had pulled from behind his calf fell to the floor, the mother-of-pearl hilt shattering. "OK, please," his accent thickening, "vat you vanna know? Pleez put don da guns."

Tolya lowered his gun first. "Cover me," he said, then approached the man and frisked him. "He's clean."

"OK," Pete said, lowering his weapon. "Sit down," he growled, pointing to the rickety old chair at the end of the counter.

"OK, OK," the tattooed man, said again. "What you wanna know?"

"For starters, who the fuck owns this place?" Pete said.

"My cousin."

"Yeah, right you're all cousins."

"Pete, let me, please."

Pete grunted then backed off. Tolya approached the tattooed man.

"Tell me everything you know about that delivery."

"It was strange, weird," the Albanian began.

"In what way?"

"These two guys came in that day, Russians like you, one very young and the other not so much, about your age."

"Thanks," Tolya said.

"They ordered all this stuff and then I asked them where they needed it sent and they told me they wanted to take the truck and deliver it themselves. I started to laugh, I told them they were crazy, we couldn't do that, and then they grabbed me just like your friend over there did."

"Fuck you, you piece of shit."

"Pete," Tolya said, turning toward him and gesturing to him to calm down.

"They told me they were friends of my cousin and he said it was fine, so I said OK, let me call him, and my cousin told me to do whatever they asked."

"Write your cousin's name and number here," Tolya said, taking a small notebook from his back pocket and handing it to the Albanian. "Here's a pen."

The tattooed man hesitated, then groaned. He mumbled something in Albanian.

"What you say?" Pete said.

"I said he's gonna get really pissed at me and I'm gonna get my assed kicked again, one way or the other."

"I suggest you do as I asked," Tolya said, gesturing toward the pad, "or I'm gonna let my friend over here have some fun with you."

"You can't do that, man, you're cops. I could report you."

Tolya moved closer to him and bent so that his face was inches from the Albanian's. He hesitated for a moment while the Albanian's breathing became shallow. He could smell garlic and onions on his breath. "Really? Who's gonna know? We're off duty. We were never here. This investigation is still unofficial. There's no one else here. There could have been a burglary."

The tattooed man took the pen from Tolya's hand. "All right. Here's my cousin's name and number. He lives over in Hewlett Harbor."

"Good choice," Pete said from behind Tolya.

"Damn," Pete mumbled. "That's crazy shit, can you run that again please?"

"Sure," said the junior detective, Olivia Peña. She played back the section of video of 209 Wadsworth she had copied that afternoon. At 6:23 p.m. on June 1, a woman entered the building with what appeared to be a man. He was holding her by the back of her upper arm, pushing her through the door. He had on a black ski cap, despite the fact that it was June. It was impossible to tell anything about him, other than that he was taller than the woman. A long-sleeve black shirt covered his arms and he wore gloves. Only his ears appeared visible, peeking out from the cap. They appeared to be large and one appeared to be split at the top, some kind of old scar. By their color on the video, he appeared to be white.

"Well, at least we know what time they came in," said Pete. "That establishes a timeline."

"If it's them," said Tolya,

"If it's not, maybe we got something else to investigate."

"Yeah right. I think it's time we break for tonight."

Chapter
7

TOLYA POURED KARIN A FRESH glass of wine then refilled his own. "So the doctor said it's OK to have wine now?"

"Yes, a little. Thank you," Karin said. "Finish the story about what happened today."

"This case is getting crazier all the time. This whole thing about the delivery indicates something is very wrong here. And that guy coming into the building dressed like a burglar."

"Agreed."

"You miss this stuff, don't you?"

"No," Karin said, taking another sip of the wine, "not really. I'm just trying to seem like an interested wife. And I'm worried about Pete."

Tolya laughed and sat back. "Really? OK. I'm worried about Pete too, but let's talk about something else. I need to get this out of my mind for a little while. How's the run up to the exhibition going?"

"Excuse me," the waiter said, "are you ready to order now?"

"Sí," Karin said. "We'll take the tortilla español, the stuffed dates,

73

the chorizo and the camarones ajillo. Is that OK, or you want anything else?"

"I'd like the jamon iberico?"

"Got it," said the waiter.

"So, how's it going? Well, pretty well, but I think we're going to have a last-minute funding problem. We're over budget and we've got some hotel and transportation issues."

"Can Miriam increase your budget?"

"She's trying. She's not sure, which could present a huge problem, and then the whole thing doesn't reflect well on me, as it's my first exhibition and you are judged on how well you manage it."

"Which means coming in on budget."

"Or close to it. Remember, I had to go back to the board for an increase in the budget once already, and now, with two weeks to go…"

Tolya reached out for her hand. His large fingers enveloped her small delicate ones. "They love you, Karin. It won't matter."

"I hope not. I like this job, Tol. I like this whole career. I'd like to continue doing this."

"I don't think you have anything to worry about."

Karin sighed. "I hope you're right. Here comes the food."

The waiter placed the first three plates on the table: jamon iberico, tortilla español and shrimp in garlic sauce. Karin peered up at him and smiled. "Gracias," she said, forcing her tongue in between her front teeth to create the lisp for which the Castilian pronunciation is famous. She took the large serving spoon and placed three shrimp on Tolya's plate. "What are you smirking about?" she asked.

"I love when you put on that Madrileño accent." He handed the wood plank server to her with the thin slices of ham laid out on it.

She smiled back. "When in Rome. I don't like the way they turn up their nose at my accent, so…"

Tolya savored the shrimp. He took a piece of bread from the basket tore it in half and dipped it into the sauce. "Really good."

"I need to discuss something with you, Tol," Karin said in between bites of the ham. "I didn't have a chance yesterday."

"What?"

"Rabbi Shalom and the conversion ceremony."

Tolya took another slice of ham and popped it in his mouth. He chuckled. "That again?"

"He asked if you would be joining me at the mikvah."

"And you said?"

"Yes."

Tolya put down the fork and sighed. "I don't know, Karin. I know I said yes last week, but it still bothers me."

"I want us to do this as a family. The boys have to go too, so please..."

"It's such a slap in the face of who I am, who my parents were."

She reached a hand across the table to his. "I know, but for us, now..."

He laughed. "For us now... seriously? I never asked you to do this. I was shocked when you told me you were going to convert. It was never important to me."

"True," she replied. "And I know this is painful for you, but it's really about the kids, about who they are."

"They're only half Jewish. To be honest, according to most of these religious fanatics, they're only a quarter Jewish. According to them, my mother wasn't Jewish enough. I don't know why this is so important to you."

"It has a lot to do with the exhibition. It's changed me. I'm Dominican and you're Jewish and I've learned that our cultures have more in common than they are different. I want our kids to know what our peoples did for each other and to feel they belong to both."

"And Christmas, you're willing to give up Christmas?"

"A difficult price to pay, but we'll figure that out too."

"And next I suppose you'll want them to have religious educations and bar mitzvahs."

"Probably," she said. "Let's just get through the conversion first. So what are you going to do?"

Tolya put his hands in the air. "OK, I surrender." Tolya sighed. No matter what this woman asked of him, he couldn't say no. "I'll discuss it with Shalom this week when I see him."

"You're seeing him?"

"Yeah, Monday. Lunchtime, about his wife's parole."

"OK," Karin said. She speared a large portion of the tortilla español and put it on Tolya's plate.

"Thanks," Tolya said, "and by the way, this was a really inappropriate meal for a discussion about converting to Judaism."

Karin looked at the ham and the shrimp and laughed. "True, I should have done it last night over the kasha varnishkes."

Pete pulled up to Club Umbrella, got out of the car and handed the keys to the valet. He checked his watch, 2:25 a.m. He felt a knot in his stomach at the thought of seeing Polito. As angry as he was over all the bad shit and unhappiness Polito had caused, he still loved him. He was still the man who had raised him.

Pete walked up to the door. The bouncer frisked him. He had left his gun in the trunk. When the bouncer felt his wallet in his pocket, he asked him to remove it. He opened the fold to reveal his badge. The bouncer nodded once. Pete entered the room.

The club was large and dark, the music ear-splitting. Omega El Fuerte blasted through the haze of smoke from the hookahs, the king of Mambo Urbano, a new kind of merengue—the old beat but with a hip-hop style. Dancers crowded the floor. The room swayed with them. Pete laughed to himself. No one could dance merengue like Dominicanas. They were all dressed in miniskirts with high heels, the sexiest women in the world and they knew it.

Pete walked up to a hostess in a tiny black skirt and a lime green tube top. "Where is the VIP section?"

She pointed toward the back of the club, an area even darker than the dance floor with a velvet rope and two big goons in front of it.

"Gracias," he said. He took his phone out of his pocket and texted Chicho. "I'm here."

A few seconds later, Chicho appeared at the velvet rope. Pete walked toward him. Chicho gestured to the two giants to open the rope and let Pete in. Pete smiled at each of them and entered the restricted zone. He clasped Chicho's hand and they hugged. "Follow me," Chicho said.

As they retreated into the bowels of the back of the club, the volume of the music receded. Pete could hear Chicho now. "Sit down over there," he said, pointing toward a red leather banquet. "Pour yourself a drink. I'll be right back."

Pete took a large glass from the tray on the table and filled it with ice. He poured from the bottle of Johnnie Walker Double Black. He had never seen Double Black anywhere but at the airport. He took a long swig from his drink, the sweetish amber liquid warming his throat. He closed his eyes and leaned back into the settee very tired. It had been a long day. At this point, he was running on adrenaline. He had one single purpose now: to catch and kill whoever had done this to Mariela.

He caught himself falling asleep when he felt a hand on his shoulder. He opened his eyes. Chicho was standing in front of him, smiling broadly. "Pedrito, wake up man, stay with us, the night is young."

"Yeah, for you. I'm running on no sleep for the last two days."

Chicho tipped his head back and to the right. Pete's eyes followed him. Polito stood in the shadows behind Chicho. He was thicker and older and grayer than Pete remembered, and wore a beard, but it was definitely Polito.

Pete stood up. Polito walked toward him. He wasn't sure what to do. It had been more than ten years. He never thought he would see him again, not after that day he turned him over to the DEA and the DEA sent him into witness protection. Polito extended his hand. Pete hesitated a moment, then took it. Polito tightened his grip on Pete's hand and pulled him close. Pete wanted to pull away but couldn't. Polito embraced him. Pete embraced him back. That familiar feeling from his childhood was still there. For a moment, time felt as if it had stopped. Polito whispered in his ear, "I'm sorry, sobrino, for everything. Dios mio, how good it is to see you, how I've missed you."

Pete's mind snapped and he pulled himself away. "Bullshit, Polito, you should have thought about that long before you destroyed the family."

Polito backed away from him. He leaned against the counter along the top of the banquet. He sighed. "I see you've poured yourself a drink. So what is it you want? It wasn't to make peace with me, though I'd hoped."

Pete took another swig of the Scotch, downing about half of the glass. "Nope, not even close."

Polito pulled up a chair and turned it around and sat down facing Pete. "What can I do for you, then? I'm jeopardizing myself just seeing you."

Pete laughed. "Yeah, right. So, where you been living large while your daughters are struggling in Washington Heights?"

"You know I can't tell you that, sobrino."

"Don't call me that."

"OK, Pedrito"

"Or that either."

Polito hesitated. He turned his drink in his hands, staring into the glass. "What would you prefer? Detective?"

"That works just fine."

"So, what can I do for you... detective?"

"You can help me to find someone."

"Who?"

"The man who killed Mariela."

Polito's mouth opened then closed. Nothing came out. Pete watched his face. It registered only shock. He glanced to Chicho. He sat down at the edge of another banquet, his hand over his open mouth.

"When? How?" Polito said finally.

"Oh c'mon, uncle. You didn't react like this when you found out your wife was dead."

Polito hesitated a moment. Anger crossed his face. He breathed deeply, his breath catching in his throat. "Pedrito, please. That's not true, you know that. You have to believe me."

"Why should I?" Pete said, standing up.

Polito stiffened again. He moved toward Pete, his fists clenched. He pulled back his arm. "You son of a bitch." He lunged at Pete.

Chicho grabbed him. "Wow, jefe, calm down." Two goons appeared out of nowhere. One helped Chicho restrain Polito the other held Pete back.

"Let the fuck go of me," Polito shouted.

"Tranquillo, jefe," Chicho said, still restraining him.

Polito relaxed. "OK, 'ta bien. Let go of me."

Chicho released his hold on Polito. "Juancho, please ask my son-of-a-bitch, ungrateful nephew to take a seat. I have a few things to say to him."

"The fuck you do," Pete said.

"Sit down," Polito shouted.

Pete turned to leave. Chicho and Juancho pulled their guns. "I said, sit the fuck down," Polito repeated calmly. Pete sat back down on the banquet. "Pour the detective another drink, please."

Juancho picked up Pete's glass and refilled it with ice, then poured the Scotch to the rim. "Disfruta, amigo," he said grinning.

Polito paced the room for several moments, then sat back down directly in front of Pete. "You think I didn't mourn my wife, you asshole? What do you know? I cry every night. I was in shock. They sliced her up like a piece of cattle and threatened to do the same to my daughters and Mariela. Why would I have turned state's evidence? I knew I'd never see my kids again. I did it to save their lives. You can hate me if you want. I don't give a shit. I've lost everyone and everything. I live in something like a prison. Now, tell me what the fuck happened to Mariela."

Pete hung his head for a moment. Maybe he'd been wrong to hate Polito so much. He never understood why Polito got involved with drug dealers to begin with. Yeah, they were poor, but so was he and that's not how they were raised. That's not how Polito raised him. He'd hated him for so long. Now he didn't know what to feel. "She was murdered. Her throat was cut. My partner and I found her."

"Mi madre."

"It was made to look like a suicide."

"Ay, dios mío," Polito said, then crossed himself.

"We knew from the first moment, it was no suicide. No one cuts their own throat." Pete stared at Polito. "I gotta know for certain who it was. Your people, because of her parents, they didn't?"

"No, Pedrito, I swear."

Pete took a long breath. "OK, then I gotta know this. I know you're still working from the inside. You keep your ears to the ground?"

Polito leaned back and crossed his arms. "Why do you think that?"

Pete raised an eyebrow and nodded his head toward Chicho and his henchman.

Polito shrugged. "OK, well maybe I do a little reconnaissance."

"Then look at this and tell me if you know this name." Pete handed Polito the piece of paper he and Tolya had gotten from the Albanian man.

"Hassan Leka," Polito said. "Sure I know him, small-time Albanian hood. He made some money in real estate in the Bronx, then of course thought drugs would be a better way to earn a living. He's not your man though."

"What do you mean?"

"I have to tell you something. I saw Mariela about seven years ago, at a strip club in Midtown. Leka operated that club. I was shocked to see her on the pole. At first I wasn't sure it was her, then I asked to see her for a private lap dance. When she came into the VIP room and saw me, she turned to leave."

"What did she say?"

"She apologized. I asked her how she got involved with a place like that. She told me she needed the money and had met a man who was a part owner of the club. She said the money was good and he protected her."

"What is his name?"

"I don't remember."

Pete's heart missed a beat. "Have you ever met this man?"

"No. But I did a little reconnaissance at the time, and what I learned from the Albanians was that he's mysterious and very dangerous. He's one of their investors."

Pete pulled into a lot at the end of Dyckman Street in front of the abandoned bar where he had met Chicho twenty-four hours earlier. He was exhausted but couldn't go home yet. He needed to think about what had just happened. Seeing Polito brought back everything. It seemed like another life, that day when he was in the locker room at the 20th precinct on the Upper West Side getting out of his uniform, his shift over.

Chapter
8

UPPER WEST SIDE, NYC
15 DECEMBER 1998
5:00 P.M.

P ETE SAT DOWN ON THE bench in the locker room, dead
tired. He'd been on the beat all day and it was cold. He hated the
cold. He pondered whether he should head home or go to the library
on Amsterdam and 82nd Street to study for his detective's exam. He'd
failed once already.

He was hungry and he knew Glynnis, or more likely her sister,
would have plenty of food on the stove, but the kids would be running
around the house and he wouldn't get shit done studying. On the other
hand, if he went to the library, he'd get no dinner and Glynnis would
be pissed off when he got home. She was already pissed off and he was
pretty sure she knew about Juana as well. Hiding a girlfriend was a
talent he hadn't fully developed yet.

"Pete," he heard from behind the door of the locker room. "Captain
Grossbart wants to see you."

"OK," he replied. "Give me a minute. Let me put my street clothes
on." He pulled up his jeans and tucked in his shirt, then slipped on his

hi-tops, leaving them untied. He left the locker room and walked down the hall to Captain Grossbart's office. There were two men in dark suits sitting on the couch opposite the captain's desk. One was thin and blond and the other was dark-skinned and extremely muscular. He had the build of a bull, obvious even under his suit jacket.

"Officer Gonzalvez," the captain said. "Please sit down." He pointed to a folding chair that had been placed next to the captain's desk. "May I introduce agents Macomber and Velez of the DEA?"

The two suits rose and extended their hands. He knew immediately which one was which. The blond guy was taller than he first appeared. Instinctively, he realized this had to have something to do with Polito. "Nice to meet you, but I'm not sure how I can help you," he said.

"Officer Gonzalvez, do you have a relative by the name of Hipolito Guzman?" Macomber asked.

"Yes."

"What is his relationship to you?"

Pete hesitated for a moment. "He's my uncle, my mother's youngest brother. I haven't seen or spoken to him in many years."

Velez bent forward and whispered something into Macomber's ear. "Do you know where he is at the present time?"

"No," Pete replied.

"When was the last time you saw him?" Velez asked.

"Around the time I finished my term at the police academy. So, that would be, like, middle of 1992."

"Do you know what your, um, uncle does for a living, officer?"

"He owns a motorcycle repair shop in Santo Domingo." Pete did his best to keep his body relaxed.

"Actually, officer," said Macomber, "that, and his wife's beauty salon, are a cover for a narcotics business."

Pete looked back and forth between the captain and the agents. He figured at this point, the less he said, the better.

Macomber looked at Velez, then continued. "Last night, he walked into our offices in Santo Domingo and offered to turn state's evidence against the organization he works for. He believes they murdered his wife and he wants to bring them down."

"My aunt is dead?" Pete said.

"We're not sure about that yet, though it appears she is missing. He says he'll talk, but only to you."

The flight to Santo Domingo was short but tense. Pete sat between Macomber and Velez. He felt like a prisoner being escorted to jail. The two agents said very little to him on the three-hour trip, save to review what they wanted him to do and say to Polito when they arrived.

Escorted by the DEA, Pete bypassed customs. A black Cadillac SUV picked them up and took them directly to the DEA offices in an inconspicuous, single-story ochre building near the American embassy. Velez took Pete to a small, dark room in the back of the building. The hurricane blinds were drawn on the outside of the windows. A small, through-the-wall A/C unit hummed under the sill. "Sit down, make yourself comfortable," Velez said, then left the room.

Pete sat down on the worn, brown leather sofa and looked around. The room was filled with non-descript old office furniture—a desk, a couple of chairs, a filing cabinet, a plastic plant in the corner. The only adornment on the walls was a framed photo of President Clinton. After a few minutes, a woman entered carrying a tray with ice and bottles of water and soda. She smiled at him. She looked Dominican and wore a dark blue skirt and jacket with the DEA insignia sewn into the pocket over her left breast. He smiled back and thanked her. She left without speaking a word to him.

A few minutes later, the door opened and Macomber and Velez entered with Polito in cuffs. He was older, thicker, worn down. Not at all the man Pete remembered.

Pete didn't know what to do. He'd had very little contact with his uncle in the six years since he'd visited him—a few words by phone at Christmas to placate his mother. She had asked many times what had happened between them when he was in Santo Domingo. They had been so close. He made excuses or refused to discuss it. If she knew what Polito was doing, she would have cut herself off from him. Pete was a cop and his uncle was a drug dealer. He couldn't condone it and wouldn't compromise himself.

"Hola, sobrino," Polito said in a low voice.

"Tío," was all Pete could get out of his throat.

Velez unlocked the cuffs. "Why don't you take some time to get re-acquainted?"

"Thanks," said Polito. Velez and Macomber left the room.

"Polito, what the fuck happened?" Pete said, his hands balled into fists at his side.

"Pedrito," Polito whispered, "ten cuidado, the room is bugged."

"Of course it is," Pete replied. He began pacing around the room. "Why did you bring me into this?"

"I'm sorry, Pedro, I need your help. I can't do this anymore. You're an American citizen, and you're a cop. I figured they might trust me more if you were involved."

Pete shook his head and scowled. "It's always about you, isn't it? What about me? My career?"

Polito lowered himself onto the couch. "Pedrito, this time it's not about me, it's about the girls."

"What the fuck are you talking about?"

Polito began to cry silently, tears escaping his eyes and trickling down his cheeks. He made no effort to wipe them away. "Tía Henrietta is dead. The girls are next. That son of a bitch in the Policía Nacional is going to kill them to get my share of the business, then he's going to kill me. I don't give a shit if he kills me, but I gotta cut a deal to save the girls. They have to go to the U.S. When I came in here last night, I tried to make a deal to get the girls out, but they saw no reason to help them. They said it was only for me. That's when I told them about you."

Pete stopped pacing and sat down on the couch. "First tell me what happened."

"Ay, sobrino, I did so many bad things."

"Yep, that's true."

"I have to tell you something though first. You might as well know everything." He hesitated and looked down for a moment. "You remember Alberto and Juliana, Mariela's father and mother?"

"Sí."

"I was responsible for their murders."

Pete moved to the other end of the couch. He held his hands up toward Polito as if to stop him. "Ay, uncle. Why do you tell me this now? He was your best friend. How could you do that?"

Polito rose from the couch and began to pace. He stared at the floor as he spoke. "Alberto and I, we were starving with the motorcycle shop. The kids were starving. They had no shoes. We knew this guy. You led me to him to begin with."

"Me?"

"Yes. He used to ride around on a motorcycle. The big guy with the ridiculous sunglasses?"

"Double X?"

"Yes. He thought he was Eric Estrada, the way he rode around on that thing."

"You hated that guy, you nearly killed him once."

"Yeah, but you know how things are down here. You get nice with people, even people you don't like. Anyway, one day he came to us to fix his motorcycle and he tells us how we can make some money with him, how he's with the National Police now and he's working with this Columbian to transit cocaine through Santo Domingo to the United States. So we figure, OK, we need the money."

"When was this?"

"Like, around June '86, just after your mother sent for you. So we start by helping him with the scooters coming in from Columbia with the coke hidden in the bikes. It goes great. We start making money. Then one day he tells us we can make a lot more if we can provide mules to bring the bags into the states. So Aunt Henrietta, she hears us talking and she says she can talk to some of the girls in the shop, they need the money. And the next thing we know, we're building a new house. Pedrito, it was like a dream."

"But what happened to Alberto and Juliana?"

"One night, Double X comes to see me in the new house and tells me there are too many people involved—it's not safe, too many mouths, and the profits are cut up too many times. I asked him what he meant. He told me we needed to shave the payroll. He told me to get rid of Alberto."

"What did you say?"

"First I told him no. Then he laughed. I remember it like it just happened. He took his knife out of his holster on his hip and he played with it for few minutes. Then he looked at me and he said, 'Get rid of Alberto and Juliana.' I said no. He walked over to me and put the knife next to my hand and said, 'Alberto is like a pinky, you don't really need it.' I told him we were like brothers. He told me to get rid of Alberto or something might happen to my daughters on the way to school someday."

"What did you say to him?"

"I stood up and put my face in his. I told him I would kill him first. He grabbed me and flipped me over, then slammed the knife into the back of my hand." Polito rubbed the scar on the back of his right hand.

"I thought that was from a fishing accident."

"That's what I told everyone. I had no choice. I sent two men to kill them. I had to save my family."

"And that's why you took in Mariela?"

"Yes. And you see, sobrino, I always knew some day he would come back for me. And that's what happened. He tried once before. You remember when you were here that time? But I threatened to turn him in. He was still vulnerable then. Now he's very strong. Only the Americans can take him down. So you see? I got to save the girls because he'll kill them. You gotta convince them to take my girls out of here."

Pete hung his head between his legs. "Ay, Tío, all this for what? A big house? Money?"

"You'll never understand, Pedrito. You got to go to America."

Pete sat in the bare interrogation room with Velez and Macomber, his palms down on the gray metal table. The gentle tap of the rain against the window was the only sound in the room.

"Pete," Macomber said, finally removing his forefingers from in front of his mouth. "Why should we believe anything your uncle is telling us?"

"Because he's lost everything and has terrible guilt about what he's done."

"Again," Macomber said, "why should we believe him?"

"For God's sake," Pete said, rubbing his eyes with his hands. "They killed his wife. They forced him to kill his best friend—and I can tell you they were like brothers since childhood—and he is certain they'll kill his daughters."

"You know he's asking for witness protection in the United States?"

"Yes, for himself and the girls."

"No," said Velez, "just for himself. He just wants passports for his daughters. He disappears into America, new name, new life. And he's made some expensive requests for the information he wants to give us."

"What?" Pete said. "What are you talking about?"

"Your uncle sees himself as an important informant with a substantial lifestyle. He has to give up that lifestyle if he becomes our witness. He wants to continue living in the style to which he is accustomed."

"Jesus, he is some piece of work. Look, I'm not gonna try to justify him. He may be my uncle, but that doesn't mean I approve of anything he's done. The girls will be in danger in the States under their own names."

"One would think," said Macomber.

"Agent Macomber…"

"Pete, please call me Tad."

"You gotta try to help me. If nothing else, I gotta get the girls out of here. I don't give a shit if Polito rots in jail for the rest of his life."

"OK then," said Macomber. "Here's what we want."

"I can't give them that information," Polito said.

"You're gonna have to, Tío."

"I don't gotta do nothing, sobrino. Double X is a big fish. They should be happy with that."

"That's not enough for them. They want his connection in the Ministry of Transportation and the name of the kingpin in Columbia."

"Pedrito, the guy in the Ministry is so high up, he can sign orders. They can't touch him. And the guy in Columbia, they won't even find him. He's living in a palace in the jungle. He's got guards all around the place and his own helicopters and shit. When they took me there, I was scared to death. If I give him up, there's no protection program on the planet good enough to keep me alive."

"Sure there is, it's called maximum security prison in the U.S."

Polito stood up. "Whoa, whoa, just a minute. I'm not going to prison. I made that clear to them. They gotta give me a new life and a new identity. I gotta live like I live now."

"Yeah, but without the girls," Pete said. He was ready to punch Polito. He rose from the chair and grabbed him by the shirt, holding him up against the wall. "You think you're just gonna abandon them? If your drug friends don't finish them off, the streets will."

"Wait, wait," Polito said, trying to push Pete back. "You don't understand."

Pete dropped him and then screamed, "What don't I understand? They gonna get in the way of your new life? You got una chamaca to replace Henrietta ready to go?"

"No, please," Polito said. He sat down on the couch and began to weep. "They need to get away from me. They need new lives. I know I'll never see them again. That's OK, because if I do this and these bastards ever find me and they are with me, they are dead."

Pete stood over Polito and put his hand on his shoulder. "Then you gotta tell them what they wanna know, Tío."

Pete handed the pile of papers to Velez. "It's all here."

"OK, let's see," Velez said as he reviewed the documents. "His confession to trafficking drugs, his confession to the murder of Alberto and Juliana Camacho, his accusation against Felix Martinez, also known as 'Double X,' his statement against Minister Ernesto Molina and his naming of Carlo Albino as the kingpin behind the whole operation."

"And what about his plea bargain?" asked Macomber.

"The federal attorney is still working on that," Velez replied.

Macomber looked at Pete. "He'll agree to plead guilty to everything," Pete said, "and accept a five-year jail term with a new identity and maximum security. When he gets out, he goes on the payroll. The girls get new identities and passports now."

Macomber shook his head. "I guess it's worth it, considering what he's given us here." Macomber pulled a folder from under his briefcase. He withdrew three blue United States passports. "These are yours as soon as he signs the plea bargain. Go get your cousins and bring them here."

Chicho came for Pete in a beat up old van at 5:00 the next morning. He was his uncle's chief henchman and bodyguard and, as such, was the only one who knew where the girls were hiding.

Pete yawned and smiled. They had been kids together. Slept in the same room together, sometimes the same bed. They got into trouble together, had their first woman together. Chicho motioned to get into the car. He grabbed Pete and pulled him toward him. "Hermano, que vaina?"

"Mala vaina," Pete replied. "Let's go get the girls."

Chicho pulled into the street and made a circuitous route around Santo Domingo. Pete knew he was making sure no one was following them. He pulled a CD from the pile next to his seat and slid it into the CD player. Raulin Rosendo. Chicho chuckled. "Remember those nights, pana?"

"Who could forget?" Mostly he remembered his nights with Mariela, how beautiful she was. How she moved on the dance floor and under the sheets. "Where are they?" Pete asked.

"With my grandmother in Santa Clarita de las Hermanas."

Pete looked at Chicho, furrowing his brow.

"So remote, even you don't know where it is." He laughed that same laugh he'd had since childhood. He threw his head back and screamed his happiness, overruling the gravity of the situation. "It's up a little mountain road behind La Vega on the way to Santiago. We can't even take the van. We have to hike it. My grandmother is there. She'll never leave. I kept them safe."

Pete grinned. The one thing he knew for sure was that Polito trusted Chicho completely.

Chicho parked the car behind his aunt's house just off the main road north of La Vega. Pete breathed in the clear morning air. He looked north at the mountains in the direction of Santiago. How beautiful was his country. He felt free here, like he could breathe. All the years in New York melted away. He was here and Mariela was nearby.

"This way," Chicho said, pointing toward the dirt path that led into the hills. They walked in silence for about twenty minutes when the path became steeper. The silence was comforting, nothing but the crunch of the leaves underfoot and the birds chirping and rustling through the trees. As they ascended the small mountain to the village, the air became even cooler. Soon there were the signs of human habitation, the sounds of chickens and pigs and of people calling out to one another. They came around a turn in the path and entered a small clearing. A dark-skinned man waved at Chicho, calling his name.

"Juan," Chicho called back. "Qué lo que?"

"Todo bien, tranqui."

The shorthand of Dominican Spanish made Pete smile. This is where he came from and, under it all, who he still was. "He looks happy," Pete said.

"He is happy," Chicho replied. "He doesn't know anything else and he doesn't want to."

"How much farther?"

"Three minutes, Americano."

They walked up through another bend in the path and then suddenly, from behind an outcropping of rocks and up a few man-made steps, appeared a small village. The huts were of wood with thatch roofs. Pete remembered visiting places like this as a child. Even then, people from the cities viewed this life as quaint, a thing of the past.

"Katarina," Chicho called out.

A tall, thin woman in a long cotton dress walked out of the house at the very top of the hill carrying a pail. It had been six years. She was a grown woman now. She waved at them and turned and said something to the people in the house. As he neared the steps, Imelda walked out, helping an old woman through the doorway. Behind them stood Mariela. She was more beautiful than he remembered.

"Nieto," creaked the old woman, reaching out for Chicho. He bent and kissed her on the forehead.

"Hola, mi amor," said Mariela. Chicho walked behind his grandmother and took Mariela by the waist, then kissed her on the mouth.

Pete walked next to Mariela in the forest behind the house. He longed to touch her but didn't. She too kept her distance. They stood looking over the bluff into the mountain meadow below them. A goatherd tended his flock there.

"It's beautiful here, no?"

"Yes," Pete replied. "Do you spend a lot of time here?"

"Yes. I come here a lot with Chicho. He loves it here and we help his grandmother as much as we can."

"Who takes care of her the rest of the time?"

"Her neighbors mostly. She has a younger sister who lives in the village."

"Younger?" Pete said, laughing.

"Well you can imagine."

Pete took Mariela's hand. "How long?"

"You mean Chicho?"

"Yes."

"About two years, on and off."

Pete let go of her hand. "Because of me?"

"No, amor," Mariela said, stepping back slightly. "I was lonely and heartbroken but it just happened. He was very sweet about it."

"I'm sure."

Mariela took Pete's hand and led him to a wooden bench overlooking the valley below. "He didn't want you to know because he didn't want to hurt you."

Pete smiled to himself. He couldn't hate Chicho for this. He understood how he felt. "Why doesn't he marry you?"

"It's not him. He keeps asking, I keep saying no."

"Why?"

"I'm not sure," Mariela said. She looked directly into Pete's eyes. "Maybe I still love you."

He took both her hands in his. "I do still love you."

"Don't say that, Pedrito, please." She withdrew her hands.

"All these years later, Mariela, and still I love you."

"But you have Glynnis."

"But I wanted you. And now you're coming to the U.S."

"Pedro, don't say it and don't even think it."

"Why?"

"Because if you do I won't come. I can't take you away from your family."

"Mariela…"

"No, shhh, mi amor. Close your eyes."

He did as she asked. She kissed him gently and sensually on the lips. He felt the same electricity as that first time on Polito's roof. He opened his eyes and then his mouth to speak. She put her finger to his lips.

"Say nothing. Each of us has our own destiny. That kiss is what we will always have. You will be here in my heart forever."

She turned and walked down the hill. He stayed for a few minutes, his heart breaking again. "Chicho," he heard her call out. "When are we leaving?"

The scene in the basement of the DEA headquarters was difficult at best. Polito had to tell Imelda, Katarina and Mariela that Henrietta was dead. Her body had been found in pieces in a dump at the foot of the slums that sit on the hillsides of La Augustina.

No, they couldn't go to the funeral. Henrietta's sisters would take care of it. They would leave today for New York. No, they wouldn't see their father ever again. He couldn't tell them where he was going. The crying turned to weeping when Velez came and cuffed Polito. They said their goodbyes and then he was led from the room. Macomber took them to the airport. He turned them over to DEA agents there. They would head to a safe house. In a few months, Pete could come to see them once their new identities had been secured.

Pete waited for Macomber and Velez to return. They would fly out on the red-eye for New York together. First he would be debriefed. His head was spinning when they entered the room.

"How are you?" Macomber asked.

"I've got a bad headache. You got anything?"

Velez took a bottle of Advil from his briefcase and tossed it to Pete. He popped two in his mouth and washed them down with the remaining Scotch in his glass.

"First of all," said Macomber, "we'd like to thank you for a job well done."

"I didn't do anything," Pete said his hands still over his eyes.

"Oh yes you did, detective."

Pete sat up. "I'm not a detective."

"You are now, Pete," Velez said. "You've been made detective for what you did for us. Congratulations, here are your promotion papers." He handed Pete a manila envelope. Pete opened it, a letter of commendation and a letter promoting him to detective inside. Pete stared at the documents.

"Thanks," he said. "Could I have a few minutes alone?

"Sure," said Macomber. "Be in the garage with your stuff in a half hour."

Pete sat down on the worn brown leather sofa, put his head in his hands and wept.

Part II

Chapter
9

I AM AN EARLY RISER. I always have been. I especially like the late spring. It reminds me of the White Nights in Russia when I was a boy. I prepare myself a tea in the Russian manner, in a glass with a sterling silver carrier sweetened with cherry preserves. We smuggled these carriers out with us when we left. What a job my father did of that. We looked to all the world like penniless refugees. He was a very smart man, my father, though he would later learn that I was smarter than him.

I took my tea with a small roll of brown bread. I have them flown in from Moscow a couple of times a week. You Americans have terrible bread. I went out to my garden. It's small but I love it. I find serenity there. My darling wife had it created for me. She brought in this tiny Japanese man to design it. He was very talented, but I couldn't understand a word he said. Now I have this beautiful space, this beautiful place that's all mine that brings me peace. I need peace.

I haven't had a lot of peace. Mostly I have had unhappiness. Except in those moments when I take complete control, when I finish my task, then I am happy.

There was only one problem with the garden. The seats were too small, like the Japanese man. I am a big man I needed a big seat, so after it was done I had a big lounge chair made for me and I had it set up under the shade of the Japanese Maple. Then I realized I needed a big wide-screen TV to watch the news and world affairs, especially in my Russia, my beloved Russia. Soon I had the TV and the satellite dish, and I could watch whatever I liked in my own little Japanese garden in my backyard in Brooklyn. My wife said it was garish. I said, "What is garish?"

She said, "A fancy English word you should know."

And so that is how I found myself watching *Visiones* on Channel 4 this morning, eating my little roll and sipping at my Russian tea. *Visiones*, ha ha, these Latinos, they think they should have their own TV shows. Who cares for their so-called culture anyway? Their women are attractive—I know, I married one—and they know how to treat a man and to make love, but they have no culture, they're half-breeds. And imagine my surprise when I began watching this comedy that the subject would be not only Latinos but also Jews, Jews who escaped from Hitler and went to the Dominican Republic. Imagine those pale, chubby German Jews struggling in the jungles.

A shame Hitler didn't finish them off. But that was our fault because, at that time, we were defending them, saving them even. Then later, when we had the chance, we could have finished them off ourselves. But no, the world wasn't going to stand by and let us perpetrate a second Holocaust, cultural or otherwise. Even the mighty Soviet Union couldn't get away with that.

And so it was with my good luck. And the truth is that, while I've had little peace, I've had much good luck. I saw there before my eyes the embodiment of Madame Kurchenko in the guise of a very attractive, though too dark-skinned for my taste, Latina.

What was it Shakespeare said about a name? Was it "A rose by any other name would smell as sweet"? So much is in a name, so much in that name, Kurchenko. I remember it well, though I was just a boy.

Perhaps I remember it so well because there were two of them, twins. So it was then, everything in stereo, they surrounded you all the time. By their quick wit and good grades and their athletic abilities and, worst of all, by that father of theirs, always the darling of the Party till he asked to emigrate. Why didn't they just let them go along with the rest of the Jews? Who needed them anyway? They were sneaky and untrustworthy and I know because I was forced to live among them for many years. The worst years, the years when we were poor, our wealth hidden for our final escape, the years after my deformity. I will never get used to that. It's made me crazy and it's because of them that I am that way now.

There she sat, the enticing, exotic Madame Kurchenko on the Latino news program. How fortunate for me because now I knew where to find her. One hour later, I was downstairs in my basement office filled with excitement researching Kurchenko on my computer. I had to make sure it was the same Kurchenko, the right Kurchenko.

This Internet is a wonderful thing. I don't know how we lived without it before we had it. Everything is there that you could possibly want to know. And there was everything about Anatoly Kurchenko, all the way back to 1977 when he came here from my beloved Soviet Union. The miserable brother had died in the Arctic. There had been a huge public outcry, demonstrations in New York, Washington, Los Angeles, Paris, London, Tel Aviv. Oh, how I hate Tel Aviv—hot, humid, full of Jews. Our time there was terrible.

Finally, the Soviet government had agreed to release them, a humanitarian action they called it. They were to go to Israel, but Kurchenko and Begin didn't see the world the same way. Funny, once a communist always a communist, and Kurchenko couldn't stomach the right wing Premier. But enough of ancient history. They came to America. After the floodgates opened, they receded into relative obscurity. The world forgot about them along with the rest of the Refuseniks. Then a few years ago, he appears in the papers again. Kurchenko broke a politically sensitive case. A young Dominican boy accused of murdering an old Holocaust survivor. He was in all the papers. He had it easy, my dear Tolya. Not like us. For us it was torture.

Chapter 10

TOLYA AND PETE PULLED UP to the address in Hewlett Harbor the Albanian had given them. The black wrought iron gate was locked. In the middle of the gate was an enormous crest bearing the Albanian eagle painted in red and gold. A camera was perched on the top of the gate. To the left was a buzzer and intercom system.

Tolya got out of the car and pressed the buzzer. He held his badge up to the camera at the same time. A few seconds later, the gate swung open. He got back into the car.

"That was easier than I expected," said Pete.

They proceeded slowly up a curved driveway about 100 feet. As they came out of the curve, a two-story stone house appeared through the dense trees. It was designed to look like a fortress, with crenellated towers on two sides to as if to mimic a Central-European castle.

The heavy double wooden door opened before they reached it. They flashed their badges again. A short, bald, very muscular man stood in the doorway. He was covered with tattoos, attempting to look ominous in his wife-beater. "You know," he said, "I could file a complaint for what you did to my cousin and my store yesterday."

"But you won't." Tolya looked around the large foyer. It was encased in white marble, as garish as the front gates and the exterior of the house.

"Why wouldn't I?" the short muscular man asked.

"Because we might start investigating your various businesses, and who knows what we might find? Besides, yesterday's visit was off-the-record like we told your cousin. Unofficial, so we were never there."

"Of course."

Tolya held out his hand. "Nice to meet you, Mr. Leka. I hope I pronounced that correctly."

"You did."

"I'm Detective Kurchenko. This is my partner, Detective Gonzalvez."

"A pleasure. Now, what can I do for you?"

"We'd like some information about a delivery that was made from your store to a building in Washington Heights last week," said Tolya.

"I'm afraid I have the same response my cousin gave you, we don't give out information about our business transactions."

"Mr. Leka," Tolya said, "did your cousin inform you that our inquiry is part of a murder investigation?"

"He did."

"Then do you want to be questioned at the precinct as an accessory to murder or could we have a friendly, private conversation here?" Pete said.

Leka sighed and grimaced. "I'm going to get screwed here one way or another so I suppose we should speak off-the-record now. Could we do that?"

Pete smiled at Tolya.

"We can," Tolya said.

"I don't want to be involved in this," Leka added.

"We will certainly keep your cooperation in mind as we continue our investigation," Pete said.

"All right then, follow me."

Tolya and Pete followed Leka down the marble-tiled hallway. He led them into a dark, paneled room that faced the garden in the rear of the house. Leka walked around a very large wooden desk and sat down behind it in an oversized leather chair that made him look childlike by its size. "Please make yourselves comfortable," he said, pointing at the equally large leather chairs facing the desk.

Tolya took the chair to the right, Pete the chair to the left. Leka touched a button on the desk and music filtered into the room, a lilting, sad ballad in a language Tolya didn't understand. He assumed it was Albanian. "You have a lovely home," he said.

"Thank you, yes. America has been good to us. We came here with nothing. I started as a handyman in an apartment building in the Bronx. Now I own that building."

"And by the looks of things, a few more too," said Pete.

"Which is why I would like to keep my name out of this," Leka said.

"Understood," said Tolya. He looked around the room. On the corner of the credenza behind the desk he noticed the Glock sitting in a crystal ashtray. He lifted the index finger of his left hand and tilted his head toward Pete. Pete's gaze shifted toward the gun. He nodded slightly without looking at Tolya. "Mr. Leka, who ordered the materials and why did they drive your truck to the location?"

"The answer to the second part should be obvious to you now," Leka said. "The answer to the first part is a little more involved." He leaned forward placing his elbows on the desk. "I got a call from a cousin of mine who is in the nightclub business. He asked me to do a favor for one of the investors, a Russian like you."

Tolya smiled. "Does my accent betray me?"

"No, but your name does."

Tolya smiled. "And this Russian's name?"

"Gruschkin."

"Do you know him?"

"Not well, though I have met him. But I wanted to help out my cousin. He began to give me the order and I told him stop, call the store and give it there and let them know where to deliver it. Then he stopped me and said no, I had to take the order and fill it, and some of Gruschkin's men would come by to pick up the stuff but needed our truck to deliver it. I told him this is crazy and he said he knew that, but he needed to keep the guy happy. So I wanted to help him out. Family, you know."

"Did you get paid for the goods?" Pete asked.

"I told you, family, no. It was a favor."

"Do you know where this Gruschkin can be found?"

"No."

"Can you ask your cousin?"

"He won't tell me anything about him. He's his investor. Private stuff. Why don't you ask him?"

Tolya looked at Pete then turned back toward Leka. "Perhaps we will. Please send me his contact information. Here's my card. OK then, that's it for now. If we need to speak to you again, where can we reach you?"

Leka took his business card from the crystal holder on his desk and wrote a number on the back. "This is my private cell. Leave a message and I will call you back. I doubt there is more I can do for you."

Tolya got up and extended a hand to Leka. Pete did the same. "We can let ourselves out." They walked back down the long hall toward the front of the house.

Once outside, Pete came even with Tolya. "So, we go after the cousin now?"

"No, Pete, let's wait on that. We don't want the suspect getting wind that we are on his trail. He could try to leave the country."

"Good point." Pete nodded his head slightly as he opened the passenger-side door to the car. "And this guy, we might need him again. By now he's dialing his lawyer, then he'll call his cousin. Let him think we can be nice guys. He already saw what we did yesterday."

Pete and Tolya sat nervously on the couch in Imelda's apartment. Katarina called from the kitchen. "What's so important that you had to see us right away?"

"I'm going to explain when you get in here."

"What are they doing in there?" Tolya asked.

"Making us something to eat, pariguayo."

Imelda came into the living room carrying a tray of sandwiches.

Katarina followed her with a pitcher of iced tea flavored with pineapple rinds.

"First explain to me why I needed to get the kids out of the house. Carlos wasn't too pleased about this. He works nights. He sleeps on Sundays. Try the pernil."

"You remember this drink?" Katarina said, pouring out the tea into tall glasses. "My mother used to make this."

"I remember, Brisas," Pete said.

Katarina smiled. "I still love when you call me that. I think of a different life. It was so long ago. Why don't we see more of you, Pedrito?"

Pete shrugged his shoulders, his mouth full. The pernil was warm and soft, the bread rich and soothing. "I'm just busy. Work, you know. This is delicious."

"Thank you. Is that true? Is he so busy?" Imelda said, looking at Tolya.

"I'm not getting involved in this," he said, taking a sip of the tea.

"Good decision," Pete said. "You cook like your mother."

Imelda looked at Katarina. "God rest her," she said, both she and Katarina crossing themselves. "OK, so spill it."

Pete popped the last quarter of the sandwich into his mouth. He chewed and swallowed, then took a deep breath, rubbing his eyes with the butt of the palm of his hands. "Did you see that story on the news a few days ago about the woman found dead in the new building up on Wadsworth Avenue?"

"Yes," Imelda said.

"Well, Tolya and me, we were the attending officers."

"So? There's dead bodies found around this neighborhood all the time and you're cops," said Katarina.

Pete took a deep breath. "It was Mariela."

Both Imelda and Katarina crossed themselves again. "Dios mio," said Katarina. Imelda reached for her hand. "Are you sure?"

"Yes," replied Tolya.

Imelda began to cry. Pete got up from the couch and walked behind her, putting his hands on her shoulders. Katarina put her hand on top of his. "I feel so bad. We should have kept an eye on her," she said.

Pete took his hands from Imelda's shoulders and hugged Katarina. "No, Brisas, I should have kept an eye on her."

"No one could help her," Imelda said through her tears. "She wouldn't let us. I begged her to stay with us. She didn't want to, she said she needed to start a new life. We tried to keep in touch with her, but she never returned our calls."

Pete released Katarina. He bent on one knee in front of Imelda and wrapped his arms around her. "Forgive me," he said.

"For what? This isn't your fault."

"I feel like it's all my fault." He felt the tears well up in his eyes. Tolya clearing his throat broke Pete's concentration. He let go of Imelda and got to his feet. "We're going to need to take statements from both of you," Pete said.

Chapter
11

BAY RIDGE, BROOKLYN, NYC
6 JUNE 2010
11:45 PM

LYING HERE IN MY BED, I am unable to sleep. It was so many years ago and so many lifetimes. That day when my father walked into our apartment and told us we would have to leave. It was in 1990. "Go where?" I said. "This insanity can't last forever. The party will be back in power soon enough."

"You idiot," he bellowed, then hit me on the side of my head with his open hand. He continued screaming at me as I fell backward. My mother came to help me up from the floor. "What don't you understand? The party is over. Never coming back. And I was a KGB agent. Do you understand what that means? If I get caught for what I've done, I'll go to prison. That's to say nothing of what will happen to you if they ever find out what I covered up that you did."

"What? What? What did he do?" my mother said.

"Shut up, woman," my father shouted, threatening her with his hand.

I winced. "Yes, Father," I said. "Where will we go?"

He outlined his plans for us. I was astounded by the brilliance of it. We would go to Israel.

"But we are not Jews," I said.

"We will assume new identities," he said. He slipped his hand into the inside pocket of his greatcoat, then withdrew five Soviet internal passports and threw them on the table. They were perfect except for the missing photos of the holders. "Then we will apply to emigrate."

"Father, applicants for emigration are routinely punished. You know that. It was your job," I said.

He rose from his chair with his hand extended to strike me again. My mother held him back. He sighed heavily. "Do you think I am an idiot like you?" he asked, looking directly at me. "I have information you don't have. Our government is preparing to let the Jews leave. The government of Israel and their friends in America, England, France etc. are willing to pay a handsome sum for a change in our policy. The ransom will remain a secret."

"How many?" my mother asked.

"Millions, if they want to go," my father replied.

"But Vitaly, they know your face and ours," my mother said.

"We will change our faces and anything else that might give us away." And that was the beginning.

My father shook me up when he mentioned that little incident in front of my mother. I didn't want her to know. It didn't happen all that often. I usually get enough satisfaction, enough happiness out of my work to keep me fulfilled for a long time. I'm like one of those lizards that eats only once a year. I enjoy the feast then I bask in the memory of it for many months.

I remember the first time, though I've matured since then. The first time was crude, bloody, without finesse. But it filled me with happiness. The look in her eyes as she watched herself in the mirror, the life streaming out of her. She opened her mouth to scream but nothing came out. Of course not, I had helped her to silence herself.

I was naïve though, uneducated, unsophisticated. I hadn't planned well. I'd given no thought as to what to do with the body. So I wrapped it in a plastic tarpaulin and hid it in the storage room in the basement of our building in Moscow behind the waste pipes. It was winter, but in a few days despite the cold—that room was very cold—she started to stink.

The building manager contacted my father. He knew he was a KGB man. When he came to the door, I quietly walked off to my room and stayed there. When my father returned, he walked calmly into my room and closed the door.

"For your mother's sake, I am not going to shout nor am I going to kill you," he said. "You are like me, you have my tastes but you lack my self-control."

"What are you talking about, Father?" I asked him.

"I found your handiwork. That girl, I've seen you with her?"

"What girl, Father?"

"The one I found dead, her throat cut, in the basement."

I stammered, not knowing what to say. I was only 23 years old.

"You're the son of a KGB colonel. You are under constant surveillance. I review your files regularly. I've seen you with her, walking in the park near the University. I must say she was pretty, too pretty for you."

"Thank you, Father."

"Why did you do this?"

My body contorted, my arms wrapping around myself, turning my head to avoid his gaze. "It was a game, it started as a game. How close we could get with the knife, then one day I began to press a little harder and there was a little blood and I was filled with excitement."

"She didn't mind?"

"No, she liked the danger of it. Afterward, we would make love. It was fantastic. Then I decided I would guide her hand, and the next thing I knew I, she, we, had cut her throat. The blood was everywhere. I did my best to clean it up. I burned my clothes. I hid her body. I didn't know what else to do."

My father sat down on the edge of my bed. "Nicolai," he said. "This time I will take care of it. If you ever do this again, I will let the police find you."

Chapter
12

"I'M REALLY SORRY I COULDN'T help you with this," Miriam said.

Karin took a deep breath. "That's going to be a problem. I don't want to blame Dionelis. She's done a great job."

Miriam leaned in closer to Karin and lowered her voice. She didn't want Lacey, who was seated at her desk just outside Karin's office, to overhear. "This is a strange, stab-you-in-the-back kind of world you've entered," she said. "The museum board will be watching how you handle this. There are people on that board who were against your hire to begin with. If she screwed up the guest reservations, then lay the blame on her. There's no blue wall of silence here."

"I understand," said Karin. "But I've got to figure out what to do without throwing Dionelis or anyone else under the bus."

"I admire you for that, young lady."

"Thanks. Do you admire me enough to get me a little extra money out of your budget to cover the additional hotel and transportation costs?"

"Not a chance, and as I said, there are members of the board who are watching you. You're already over budget and coming in on or very near budget is the key to your position being made permanent."

"I understand," Karin replied.

Miriam got up from the chair. "Good luck, keep me posted," she said, leaving Karin's office.

Karin leaned back into her chair and rubbed her belly. Oleg was moving around all morning as if he needed more room. She knew Miriam was right. Her provisional appointment had been difficult and hard won. Miriam had fought for her for several reasons. Mostly, she was impressed by Karin's dedication to bringing the story of Sosúa to public light. While she loved this job, she clearly chaffed at the culture of the museum world. The camaraderie of the police department was lacking and, unlike the PD, no one covered for you in this world if they thought the blame might otherwise fall on them. Regardless, she wouldn't blame Dionelis. Perhaps the museum world needed a little changing.

"Lacey, come in please, as soon as you can," she called out.

"Be right there."

A moment later Lacey came through the door, clipboard in hand. "Yes, Madame Director?"

"Miriam wasn't able to resolve the problem with the hotel."

"That's not good,"

"No it's not. Explain to me again how this happened?"

"Dionelis simply miscounted the responses requesting lodging and gave the wrong final count to the hotel."

"How can we fix this?"

"I can get some rooms at a discount up at the Marriot in Midtown, which is really inconvenient, but then we have to supply car service, which will be expensive. One couple in particular, they are quite old, in their late 80s, we need to get them rooms down here."

"The problem is the money. I'm sure we don't have it left in the budget."

"Well, I was thinking about that," Lacey said. "Here, look at this." She handed Karin the clipboard. "Take a look at the third column, the fifth line down. I've highlighted it."

"What's that from?"

"That's the refund we got from the caterer for that event last year that you oversaw as a volunteer."

"The one about Jewish Policemen and the Shomrim Society?"

"Yes."

"Refresh my memory. Why did we get a refund?"

"They were supposed to provide six types of pass-around hors d'oeuvres and they only brought four. They claimed it was the same amount of total pieces, but I pointed out that they gave us much cheaper items than we chose so we got a refund."

Karin smiled. "You are a marvel. How did you even remember that?"

Lacey sat up straight in the chair. "That's my job."

"Do you think it's enough?"

"It will have to be."

"Can we transfer the funds to this event?"

"Yes, you can do it because it was in your budget items," she said, moving around the desk to Karin's computer. "I'll show you how."

Tolya took his gun from the holster, checked the safety and put it in the back of the top drawer of his desk. He took his cell phone from his coat pocket and placed it on the top of the desk, then turned on his computer. He watched as it booted up. A few seconds later, it asked for his ID and password. He typed both and hit enter. A moment later, his email program opened.

The new emails were mostly routine items from the precinct. Farther down the page toward the bottom, he saw a red check next to a new message. It was from Interpol. He clicked open and began reading.

Dear Detective Kurchenko,

We have searched our files and found the following items, both embedded and attached, which relate to your request. Wood structures such as the one in the photo you sent to us have been found

before in Tel Aviv and Berlin some years
ago. The attached files give more details.
Should you need any more help, please
contact us again at your earliest conve-
nience.

    Very truly yours,

    Francoise Moulin

    Investigative Researcher, Paris Divi-
sion

"Suicide my ass," Tolya said out loud. He checked his watch. He had
to meet Shalom Rothman in twenty minutes.

Karin spent the morning reviewing the budget for the entire project
with Lacey. She saw a few places where she could cut some dollars. One
fewer security guard at the opening event, one fewer pass around at the
VIP party, plus the money Lacey had found would just about cover it.

Lacey knocked on her open door. "Karin?"

"Yes?"

"Can I come in a moment?"

"Of course, why are we whispering?"

"There's a man outside. He wants to see you?"

Karin's police background kicked into high gear. She leaned forward
over the desk. "Who is he?"

"He says his name is," Lacey looked at the business card, "Benjamin
Schneider." He said he saw you on TV yesterday morning and would
like to speak to you about the upcoming exhibition."

"Show him in."

Tolya set up the videoconference in the large interrogation room at
the rear of the precinct house. Shalom sat quietly at the end of the table,
his head as usual buried in a Talmudic text. He buzzed the captain on
the phone. "We will be starting in a few minutes."

"OK, coming in now," the captain replied.

Tolya turned to Shalom. "You're sure about this?"

Shalom looked up and closed the book quietly. He smiled at Tolya. "Completely. Why wouldn't I be?"

"Shalom, it's not every day that a man's wife kills his father with a prayerbook."

Shalom smiled. "No it's not. I've come to my peace about this. She was a good woman, Tolya, an 'aichet chayil,' a woman of valor. She will be again. HaShem forgives. He forgave my father and me and you and he will forgive her too. Now it's time for us to forgive her so she will forgive herself. And Baruch needs her."

"How is he?"

"He is as well as he ever will be. The school and HaShem have provided for him."

The screen lit up suddenly at about the same moment that the captain entered the room. "Hello?" came a voice from a room inside the large LED monitor.

"Detective Tolya Kurchenko here. Rabbi Rothman and Captain McClusky are with us."

"Great, I am Commissioner Waterfield and these are panel members Rose Cahill and Edward Turetsky."

"Are we ready to start?" Tolya asked.

"Yes," Waterfield replied. "We are assembled today to discuss the potential early parole of Rachel Rothman, convicted of involuntary manslaughter in the death of Max Redmond in November of 2005. Please note that Mrs. Rothman pled guilty to the crime and has served the mandatory portion of her sentence as a model inmate. She has attended regular counseling sessions and clearly has shown remorse in her recent personal statement attached herewith to her request for parole. Would either Rabbi Rothman or Detective Kurchenko like to make a statement before my co-members speak?"

Tolya glanced at Shalom. Shalom nudged his head from side to side. "I would like to say something, if I might," Tolya said.

"Go ahead, detective."

"In the five years since I broke this case, I have come to know Rabbi Rothman and his wife quite well."

"I understand you visit with Mrs. Rothman a few times a year," Rose Cahill said. "Sorry to interrupt."

"Yes I do. I have been personally changed by both of them. From them I have learned the value of forgiveness. It's not every day that a man is faced with the fact that his wife has killed his father. Most men would find it impossible to continue to remain married under such circumstances. In this case, from the first moment, Rabbi Rothman showed an ability to accept and understand his wife's actions despite their consequences."

"Detective," Cahill interrupted again, "this hearing is about Mrs. Rothman's parole, not the rabbi's."

"I'm getting to that. I believe it was the rabbi's genuine forgiveness that led Mrs. Rothman to the path of remorse and acceptance of her own actions that have changed her view of both herself and her beliefs that makes this early release possible and desirable."

"Could you expand on that, detective?" Waterfield said.

"Of course. The love and respect of her husband are the most important things Rachel has in this world. His forgiveness of her actions in a moment of great personal pain and passion has enabled her to begin to heal and even further to reach out to other inmates with her story and to help them come to personal peace with their own crimes."

"Yes, we read about this in the parole request," said Turetsky. "She has aided the in-prison social services network greatly by working with the other prisoners to come to understand themselves."

Tolya continued. "And I might add one more thing, she has even organized groups among the female prisoners to bring them back to observance of their own religious traditions. She has worked with the clergy in the prison across denominational lines despite her background and her former lack of contact and exposure to other religious groups. She is a changed woman."

"Rabbi, may I ask you something?" Commissioner Waterfield said.

"Of course," Shalom replied.

"Did you encourage her to do this? Was this your idea?"

"No, it was not. She asked me for my blessing after she began this project."

"Did she tell you how she came to this idea? This project?"

"She said that she realized that HaShem was the only judge. She had no right to judge my father and would regret her actions every day for the remainder of her life. She believed that the best way to show HaShem that she was remorseful was to help others come to peace with their crimes. I gave her my blessing."

"Rabbi, one more question."

"Yes."

"What do you want?"

"I want my wife back. I want to help her become whole again."

The tribunal huddled on the other side of the screen. Tolya looked at Shalom and smiled. "You are a remarkable man."

"Thank you, so are you."

"Gentleman, we will consider everything you have said and will review the entire situation and render a decision within the month."

"Thank you," Kurchenko and the captain said almost simultaneously. The screen went black.

"Baruch HaShem, she will be home soon," said Shalom.

"I hope so," said Tolya.

"I've gotta run," said the captain. He picked up his case files and exited the room.

"You have a few minutes, Tolya?"

"Sure, why?"

"I wanted to speak with you about Karin, and her progress…"

"And my conversion," said Tolya.

"In a word, yes."

Tolya leaned back into the chair. "Shalom, what do you expect me to say?"

"What do I expect you to say? What would you like to tell me?"

"What would I like to tell you? What would you like to hear?" Tolya put his head in his hands. "Aghhh, it's, like, too Jewish, answering a question with a question."

"I might suggest that Detective Jewish is Jewish enough, but…"

Tolya laughed. "OK, let's start again. You know how I feel about this. No one has the right to tell me whether I am an authentic Jew."

"You are one of the most Jewish people I know and you should take that as a compliment."

"I do."

"But I still think this has more to do with my father-in-law and that day in his study, all too long ago, than anything else."

"You may be right, he is a factor. But it also has to do with Oleg. He is on my mind so much lately with his namesake coming."

"I commend you for that decision, by the way. As we've discussed, a name is so powerful and this name will be in front of you every day now. Are you ready for that?"

"Yes, yes I am. I need him close by. He was like me. He was me. And he died because he was a Jew, at least according to the Soviet Union, yet not enough of a Jew for some of the Jews."

Shalom sighed. "I understand. My father was haunted by his brother's death all his life, as you are with Oleg's. I struggled with this so much when I was a boy. The Holocaust loomed so large and silent over us. How could we ever understand? And in my heart of hearts, I agree we don't determine who is a Jew. It's determined by the non-Jewish world at their whim. But the fact is, your wife made a decision to become a Jew, to become one of us. It is one thing to be born to this, another thing completely to choose it. Your mother was a living example of that."

"That's right, and she never converted."

"Tolya, I don't need to convert you. For me, you're Jewish enough. It's up to you. This reaffirmation of your heritage is more for your family, if you choose to do this. For Karin's sake and for her commitment, so that your children understand the great blessing of their history, do this as a family. Think of it as a reaffirmation of who you are, what your life has been about and what meaning your brother's death had for you and for the whole world."

Tolya stood up. He tried to speak but couldn't. He turned his head as a tear fell from his right eye. "You have no idea how much I miss him."

Shalom walked toward him. He put his hand on Tolya's shoulder. "Somehow I do."

The captain reviewed the documents from Interpol that Tolya had printed out. "That's astounding," he mumbled.

"See, I told you this was no suicide," said Pete.

"Something like this doesn't happen three times independently," the captain said.

"Which means we not only have a murder, we have a serial killer," said Tolya. The thought made his skin tingle and his stomach tie into a knot at the same time. It was his sickest, most secret desire to track and catch a serial killer.

"Yes," the captain mumbled, continuing to examine the photographs. "This has to be the work of one guy. There is no way more than one sick mind could come up with this idea independently."

"Unless somehow our guy found similar pics on the Internet and copied it," Pete said.

"I'd say unlikely." The captain reached behind him and retrieved a large manila envelope from the top of the credenza. It was already open. He pulled out a bound report.

"The coroner's report?" Pete asked.

"Yeah," he said, handing it to Pete.

"You've read it?" Tolya asked.

"Yes, the coroner is inconclusive on the cause of death. He acknowledges the suicide note but says the angle and depth of the cut to the throat would be impossible for anyone to execute without help."

"What about with the machine?" Tolya said.

"Even with it."

Pete looked up from the report. He breathed deeply. "So I guess it's officially a murder case now?"

"It will be shortly," the captain replied. "Get organized, all your warrants, etc. And let's make it quick, before this guy decides to do it again."

"So nice to meet you, Mr. Schneider."

"Please, call me Benjamin."

Karin observed how well dressed the gentleman was. She hesitated a moment, then said, "Benjamin. How can I help you?"

"The question is, how can I help you?" Schneider said, shifting in the chair opposite Karin and crossing his legs.

Karin leaned back a bit in her chair. "With all due respect, Benjamin, we've just met and I don't recall asking you for help?"

Schneider ran his index finger over his Panama hat. "I saw your presentation on television yesterday and I was very impressed."

The man had an unusual accent. It reminded her slightly of Tolya's when he became excited or angry and it came out. "Thank you, but I'm not sure by what."

"By your work, by the story you are bringing to the world. It's a very nice story."

"Thank you," Karin replied.

"I too am an immigrant, you see."

That would explain the accent. "From where?" she asked.

"Germany. East Germany"

"Really? When was the last time I heard anyone refer to East Germany?"

"Yes, I like to be specific. Most people don't have an understanding of what our lives were like there before the Wall fell. East Berlin, to be exact."

Karin leaned forward a bit and smiled again. "Mr. Schnei…"

"Benjamin"

"Benjamin, sorry. I don't mean to be rude, but I usually see people by appointment and I am in the middle of a crisis with our upcoming event."

"I'm sorry then to have bothered you. I'd better go," Schneider said. He rose from the chair then stopped himself. "Madame Kurchenko."

"Please, call me Karin. No one has ever called me Madame Kurchenko."

"OK, Karin, as I said, I too am an immigrant. Though I'm not Jewish, I came here to see if I could in some small way help with your exhibition. This country has been very good to me." He pulled a checkbook out of the inside pocket of his sport coat. "Would you accept a donation?"

"Please, Benjamin, that's very sweet of you. We usually don't take donations on the spot but sit down and let's discuss it. I'm always delighted to take a donation."

Pete parked the car on West 75th Street under the no parking sign and slipped the police vehicle identification onto the dashboard. He loved doing that, especially in this neighborhood. He'd handed out plenty of tickets here as a uniform to irate locals who believed their entire lives were an entitlement program. He was the law. He could park wherever he wanted. He followed Tolya up the block to number 115. A sign under the stoop read Berman Real Estate and Construction. Pete turned the handle on the wrought iron gate. "Open."

"Well, this isn't the Heights, hermano," Tolya said.

"True," Pete replied as he opened the wooden door into the basement office. A young woman in outdated clothing and a wig that gave her up for ultra-orthodox sat at the desk facing the door. "Can I help you?" she asked.

They held up their badges. "Is Mr. Berman in?"

"Sure, well, uh, what is this about? What should I tell him?"

"We need to speak to him about the body that was found a few days ago at his building at 209 Wadsworth Avenue."

The young woman got up quickly. She grabbed her handbag and disappeared down the hall.

"Why are they always so nervous?" Pete said.

"Ah ah, there now, Pedrito, let's be careful," Tolya replied. "Cultural awareness for all god's children by the NYPD."

"Fuck you," Pete whispered. He punched Tolya in the upper arm. They both laughed.

The young woman returned, nearly running down the hall. Her feet moved so silently under her long skirt that she appeared almost to be floating. "Follow me, please. Mr. Berman will see you in his office."

They found Berman at his desk nearly hidden behind the piles of paper on top of it. He was a man of about 50 in a white short-sleeve shirt and a short, wide, blue tie with close-cropped hair, a beard and side curls. On top of his head sat a very large black skullcap. He extended his hand to Pete and Tolya. "How can I help you, officers?"

"Actually, that's detectives," Tolya said.

"Sorry," Berman said, "my mistake, detectives."

"Tol, you ever gonna give that up?" Pete said.

"Nope," Tolya answered. "We're here about the body that was discovered at your building a few days ago."

"Yes, please sit down," Berman said, pointing at two chairs also piled high with files and papers. He got up from his chair and moved around the desk, then picked up the files on the chairs and placed them on the floor. "Please sit, can we get you something to drink? Chani, come in here."

Pete and Tolya both sat. "No thank you, nothing to drink," Pete said.

"Yes, Papa?" the young woman said, reappearing in the doorway.

"Bring some of that nice bottled water for the detectives. Or would you prefer Snapple?"

"Water's just fine," Tolya said. "Now, about the body."

"Yes," Berman said, reseating himself. "Just a terrible thing. A suicide, the super tells me. In all my years in the business, in all the years my family has been in the business, over fifty years, we've never had a suicide."

"Well, your record remains intact," Pete, replied. "It turns out it's not a suicide after all. It's a homicide."

Berman sat back in the chair, his mouth agape. "Really, wow, they said there was a note."

"There was, but it appears it was made to look like a suicide," Tolya said.

"How can we help you?"

The daughter reappeared with the waters and a bottle of Snapple Iced Tea on a silver tray. She put it on the corner of Berman's desk and left.

"We need whatever information you might have on the victim."

"Of course, anything you need."

"We have her lease. It was in the apartment. Did you keep a file on the lease application and background check? Also, if we could take the security recordings to the precinct it would be very helpful."

"Yes, my wife takes care of all of that. Sylvia," he called out.

A moment later, a shorter, older version of the daughter in an almost identical wig and pillbox hat entered the room. Berman spoke to her in Yiddish. Her right hand went to her mouth and her left hand steadied herself on the doorframe. She said something to Berman in Yiddish, then turned to Pete and Tolya. "Officers, we'll give you whatever we have."

Tolya opened his mouth. Before he could say anything Pete shot him a look and smiled. "Once a day is enough, Tol. That's all you get, detective." He turned back toward Mrs. Berman. "Thank you, ma'am."

"Just follow me."

"Excuse me, detectives," Berman said as they were leaving the room.

"Yes?" Pete replied.

"How long before we can get in there and clean things up? This is costing me a lot of money in lost rent."

"It's gonna be a while, Mr. Berman. It's a crime scene," Pete said. "Besides, I imagine she's paid up through the end of the month."

Chapter
13

WASHINGTON HEIGHTS, NYC
7 JUNE 2010
4:00 P.M.

TOLYA HANDED COPIES OF THE lease application and background information he and Pete got from the Bermans to the captain. "She applied for the apartment under the name Roberta Brusca. She claimed to be recently separated, which is why her reference for a previous landlord was seven years earlier."

"That's some fancy-ass address she was living at seven years ago," the captain said. "Did she give any information to the landlord about her estranged husband?"

"No," Pete said. "We asked the landlord about that. She said they asked her about it, but she didn't want him to know where she was living. It was an ugly divorce. She was afraid of him. The landlord's wife said they were going to reject her application, but she began to cry. They felt sorry for her."

"She also paid six months' rent in cash up front," Tolya added. "I'm sure that helped change their minds."

"I'm sure," mumbled the captain. "You boys gonna follow up on this immediately?"

"Yep. First we have to interview my cousins."

"What time is that at?"

"Now."

"Well, what are you waiting for?"

Pete showed Imelda and Katarina into the larger interrogation room at the rear of the precinct. "I'm sorry we have to do this here."

"That's all right, Pedrito," Imelda said.

Tolya smiled. "I might have to start calling you that permanently."

"I don't think so," Pete said.

"Can I get anyone something to drink before we start?" Tolya asked.

"No thank you," Katarina said.

"Nor for me either."

"OK. Let's get started," Tolya said. "If it's OK, I'm going to ask you some questions. Feel free to respond any way you want, either or both of you."

"When did you arrive in the United States?" Tolya began.

"December 22, 1998," Imelda said.

"Who did you arrive with?"

"My sister," Imelda said, turning toward Katarina.

"And Mariela Camacho," Katarina said.

"As I explained to you," Pete interjected, "they were brought here under the witness protection program."

"Right. Where did you go when you arrived?"

"First we were taken to a special facility for about a month," said Imelda.

"Where was that facility?"

"Omaha," said Katrina.

"In Nebraska," added Imelda. She took Katerina's hand.

"For our protection," added Katarina

"Then?" asked Tolya.

"We were moved to an apartment in Boston. We stayed there for about a year."

"Yes, about a year," Katarina confirmed.

"All of you together?" Pete asked.

"Yes. But we were very unhappy there," Imelda said. "Especially Mariela."

"Why?" Tolya asked.

"Because we didn't know anyone there. Everyone we knew was in New York. We wanted to come to New York, but we couldn't. They said it wasn't safe," Katarina said.

"But also we weren't allowed to contact anyone at that time," Imelda added. "Too dangerous."

Katarina looked at Imelda.

"Qué?" Imelda asked.

"Nada, sigue."

"Also Mariela was very unhappy because she missed Chicho. She kept trying to contact him even though we weren't allowed. The people in charge of us were very angry with her about it."

Pete tensed up at the mention of Chicho's name.

"Who's Chicho?" Tolya asked.

"An old family friend. He was my father's main henchman at that time. Pedro knew him," Imelda said, reaching for Pete's arm. "He was kind of Mariela's boyfriend at the time."

Tolya looked over at Pete. "I thought…"

"I'll fill you in later."

Tolya returned to questioning Imelda and Katarina. "When did you come to New York?"

"January 2000," Katarina said. "We went to live in a small apartment here in Washington Heights. It was good because we had family here, and there were lots of Dominicans so we felt at home."

"Hermana, there were plenty of Dominicanos in Boston."

"But it was different. In New York, we could move around more. And we had family here. In Boston, the police people were around us all the time."

"What prompted the move to New York?"

"The guy in Santo Domingo who killed our mother, he went to jail. The situation became safer for us. So we went to be closer to the family."

"I remember when you came," Pete said, a smile creeping up his face. "That little apartment on 185th Street."

"Did Mariela live with you?"

"Yes, for a little while," Imelda said. "She wanted to have her own place though. She wanted a new life."

"How long did she stay?"

Imelda looked at Katarina. She furrowed her brow. "About six months?'

"Sí," Katarina said. "About that. As soon as she saved enough money for school, she left."

"What kind of school did she go to?" Pete asked.

"She went to secretarial school and took English lessons."

"How did she pay for all these courses and an apartment?" Tolya asked.

Katarina looked at Imelda. Imelda nodded and made a face.

"She got a job at night."

"Doing what?" Pete asked.

Both Imelda and Katarina hesitated. "Exotic dancer," Imelda said finally. "We begged her not to. It was, you know, inappropriate. She said it was just for a short time, till she had enough money."

Pete leaned back into his chair, pushing it up on two legs, and let out his breath. "That explains the Albanian."

"Pete!" Tolya said.

"Sorry."

"The Albanian?" Imelda asked.

"We can't discuss it," Pete said. "Part of the investigation."

"Do you know where she worked?"

"No," Katarina, answered.

"How about where she lived?"

Imelda closed her eyes for a moment in thought. "At first, she took a room in a big shared apartment on the Upper West Side near Columbia University. We once went to visit her there. You remember that, Katarina?"

"Yes. She wouldn't let us up to the apartment. She said it was a mess because so many people lived there, but I think she was embarrassed by us."

"She was studying English," Imelda said. "And her accent was almost gone and she had changed her name. I don't think she wanted anyone to know she was Dominican."

"Do you remember the name she was using?" Tolya asked

"Roberta," Imelda said.

Bingo, Tolya thought. He glanced at Pete. Pete nodded almost imperceptibly. "How long did she live in the shared apartment?"

Imelda looked at Katarina again. "Do you remember?"

"Let me think. It was around the time that you got serious with Carlos because we called her to invite her to your engagement party but her number was disconnected. It must have been about six months."

"Did you have any contact with her again after that?"

Katarina laughed. "I did and it was by accident. It was less than a year later. I was walking to a job on the Upper West Side. I was working as a nanny and I saw her on Broadway near 82nd Street. First she didn't answer me when I called out to her, then when I came up to her and touched her on the shoulder from the back she turned."

"What was her reaction?" Pete asked.

"She seemed a little uncomfortable. I asked her if she hadn't heard me calling her name and she said she was going by Roberta now so she wasn't used to hearing Mariela anymore."

"Did you have any other conversation with her?"

"Yes. I asked her what she was doing and she told me she had gotten a job as a secretary. I asked her if she had given up the dancing. She said yes. I told her I was happy to hear that."

"Was that the last time you saw her?" Tolya said.

"Yes."

"And that would be around January 2002?"

"Yes."

Tolya glanced at Pete. "You have anything else you want to ask them at this time?"

"No," Pete replied.

"I want to thank you for your help," said Tolya. "We may have more questions. If we do, Pete or I will call you."

"No problem," Imelda said.

Pete rose from the chair and hugged both Imelda and Katarina. "Find this bastard," Katarina said.

"We will," Pete replied. "Wait here a minute, Tol, I want to walk them out."

"OK," Tolya replied.

Pete was back in less than five minutes. "We got a few minutes to go back to the crime scene?" he asked.

"Sure. Why?"

"I want to check something."

Pete stared at the living room. He paced around the room twice. "How the hell did he get out of here?"

"I don't know. I've been thinking about that myself. There's only one way out if the door is chained from the inside, the window."

Pete walked over to the windows. He slid the lower portion of the left window up. "Tolya, there's no fire escape. That's a long way down and it ends in the courtyard and there's no exit to the street from the courtyard."

"Then there's only one way out and that's up. Let me take a look."

Pete slid the screen upward. Tolya wedged his body through the window. He turned his head to look upward. He noticed several black scuffs against the light-colored brick. He turned his body to sit on the windowsill. "Pete, hold down my legs."

"OK, what do you see?"

"I'm not sure." He reached up to touch the scuffmark. "I can't reach it."

"What is it?"

"Scuffmarks. Looks like someone walked up the side of the building to the roof with some kind of suction thing on their shoes."

"You wanna stand up on the sill?"

"Bro, you crazy? You know I can't stand heights."

"OK then," said Pete. "Let me try." Tolya slipped back into the room and Pete wedged himself through the window. He hoisted himself on the sill, grasping onto the window frame edge. "Hold my legs," he said.

"OK," Tolya replied. He wrapped his arms around Pete's legs just above the knees.

"Not so close, big boy," he said.

"Fuck you. I don't want to lose my partner to a seven-floor fall. What do you see?"

"Same thing you did and I think you're right. Looks like he went out from here. So he's not only a ghost, he's the ghost of Spiderman. Help me in. We can send an evidence team later."

"So this guy just walked in and wrote a check for $10,000?" Tolya said. He took a bite of the chuleta smothered in cubano peppers.

"Yep. Nice to have money, no?"

"Tell me more about him."

Karin recognized it every time Tolya slipped into "detective mode," but she went along with it, harmless enough. "He's an immigrant like you."

"No one is like me," Tolya said, smiling, crossing his arms against his chest. "When did he come here?"

"1999."

"Where is he from?"

"East Germany."

Tolya sat up in the chair. He smiled. "East Germany? He said that?"

"Yes."

"Who says East Germany anymore?"

"He did. I guess he was trying to be specific."

"So he just pulled out his checkbook and wrote a check for $10,000? Boy, these ex-Komsomol types turn into rampant Capitalists real quick."

"Yep," Karin said. She took a sip of water. "I was a bit surprised, but you know these philanthropist types…"

"Oh, now he's a philanthropist…"

Karin kicked Tolya playfully under the table. "Yes, that's what you call people who make donations to museums. I've seen them do this with Miriam. They love the drama of it, pulling out the checkbook.

He said there was more if we needed it. And he owns a limousine company, which solves a huge problem for us in terms of getting the VIPs back and forth between the hotels and the museum."

"What did you say his name was again?"

"Tolya, please, what are you going to do, run a check on him?"

"Maybe."

Karin caught herself before letting the anger take over. Even after five years of marriage, the one thing she couldn't get used to was his macho. She had avoided Latin men for years; too bossy, too controlling. As much as she hated to admit it, he was the same way. Perhaps all men were. She loved him anyway, despite his smothering maleness. "I hate when you do this. I'm not a little girl."

"That's not it at all. I just don't trust East Germans."

They both laughed. Karin walked around the table. Tolya put up his arms in front of his face like a boxer. She slapped him lightly on the top of the head. "Schneider, Benjamin Schneider, you idiot." Karin sat down on his lap and kissed him. "You think you're so tough? I went to the same academy as you."

"You hear that boys?" Tolya shouted to the kids in the living room. They were playing with the new train set. "Your mother is a tough guy. She can take care of herself."

"What, Daddy?" Max shouted back.

"Nothing, darling, don't listen to your father's foolishness."

"OK, Mommy."

Tolya smiled. As irritating as he was, his smile made her all warm and tingly inside, it always did. She whispered in his ear, "I can't wait till I can make love to you again."

"Me either," he replied.

Pete knocked lightly on the door to the bedroom, then pushed it open slightly. Glynnis was standing by her closet, changing. After twenty years and four kids, she still looked good. "Can I come in?"

"Sure," she said, pulling the old, oversized baseball jersey over her head.

Pete sat down on the bed. "There's something I need to talk to you about."

She sighed. "Pedro, does it have to be now? I've got to get the kitchen cleaned up."

He reached over to her and took her hand, pulling her toward the bed. "Yes, please, sit down."

"OK," she replied.

"There is something I have to tell you that I should have told you years ago. Twenty years ago."

Glynnis got up from the bed. She looked toward the doorway. "That was a long time ago. Whatever it was then isn't important now. That was another lifetime."

"No, amor. Please, I have to tell you this to make things right because something has happened."

She sat down on the ottoman at the foot of the club chair opposite the bed. "I'm listening."

"You remember when we were just getting engaged and I went down to Santo Domingo to visit my uncle?"

"Yes."

"I had an affair."

Glynnis looked down and sighed again. A tear dropped from her eye onto the back of her left hand. "Pedro, why are you telling me this now?"

"Because…"

She stopped him. "First of all, I know. Second of all, what difference does it make all these years later?"

"It makes a difference because I love you and what I did was wrong and I want to ask you to forgive me. How did you know?"

She looked up at him. "Amor, Santo Domingo is a small place. My cousin saw your cousin. They had nothing else to do so they talked about it. They live on gossip. Why do you think I called you to tell you I was pregnant? I was going to surprise you when you got home."

"So you knew and you married me anyway."

Glynnis looked directly at him. The tears streamed down her face. He knew that all these years later the hurt was as sharp as it was the first day. "What else could I do? I was pregnant. My parents were furious.

And besides, I loved you then, the same as I do today."

"But do you forgive me?"

"I did, Pedro, and I do," Glynnis said through her tears. "But why bring this up now?"

"That apparent suicide we uncovered last week?"

"Yes."

"It was her, it was Mariela."

Glynnis put her hand to her mouth then crossed herself.

"And it turns out it's a murder." Pete lifted her from the ottoman. "I want you to know I'm sorry and that I didn't mean to hurt you."

She smiled weakly at him. "Does that mean you'll be giving up your present girlfriend too?"

Chapter 14

BAY RIDGE, BROOKLYN, NYC
8 JUNE 2010
1:00 A.M.

I HADN'T THOUGHT ABOUT OUR JOURNEY in many years. The excitement of my new project brought it back to me. My father had planned every detail with great care. First he had to provide us with our new identities. He had already found a family of Jews in the KGB files with similar ages and family structure to ours who had already left the country. All the ages were within two years of ours. They had two sons and a daughter. They had been born in Moscow. He pulled their files and took them home with him.

Next he had to destroy us.

We had a dacha in the countryside about two hours from Moscow. It was on a lake. It was lovely but very remote. Not even a phone line. He had a friend who worked in the city morgue for many years that now worked at one of the new private funeral homes. He brought him $20,000 American in a briefcase and the next night we took our car and picked up five bodies from the loading dock at the rear of the building on Peschanaya Street.

We drove to our dacha. I was very nervous and sick from the smell of the bodies and the chemicals they had been treated with. I had also never been in a car with five dead bodies before. When we arrived at the dacha, we dragged the bodies into the house through the slush. It was cold. You could see your breath, even inside.

The bodies were in bags. My father told me to unzip each one. They were naked, all of them. The young girl appeared close to my sister's age, about 16. She had beautiful breasts.

"Stop staring at her, you pervert," father called out to me from the other side of the room. He was attempting to light a fire in the huge fireplace. "Go into the bedrooms and bring clothes for each body. Sleeping clothes. We are going to put them in the beds."

I didn't question him. I knew I was better off to keep my mouth shut. I went into my sister's bedroom first, to her dresser. It was funny for me and exciting at the same time. She had beautiful lace underwear. I put my nose to it. It smelled faintly of her. Then I was ashamed. How could I do that? She was my sister. I grabbed socks and a shirt and an old pair of wool pants that I remembered she wore to bed in the winters. I went back into the living room.

"Dress her," my father said. He disappeared into his bedroom.

I lifted the young girl from the plastic body bag. Her skin was cold and smooth. I touched her nipple with the thumb and forefinger of my right hand. I felt myself become erect. I rubbed myself through my pants. I couldn't help myself. Then I felt my father's hand across the side of my head. "Get out of my way," he shouted. "Go into your room and get clothes for you and your brother."

"Yes, Father," I mumbled. "I'm sorry."

I watched him as he dressed each body. When he needed help lifting them or turning them, he would tell me. The feeling of these bodies repulsed me, they weren't beautiful the way the girl was. I kept my mouth shut. He talked while he worked. He explained to me what we were to do.

We carried the bodies into the bedrooms and set them on the beds under the sheets and blankets as if they were sleeping. Next we returned to the living room. He built up the fire so high that the flames were licking at the stone above the outside of the fireplace. He told me to go to the door and wait there with it open. He went into the kitchen and disconnected the gas line just enough that the cooking gas would leak into the air. He ran back toward the door, stopping to grab two items off the table, a picture of himself with the silver medal for wrestling in the all Soviet Games from 1964 and the silver medal in another frame. Boris Kurchenko had won the gold. "Quickly," he said, "get out of here."

We ran back to the car. He waved at me. "No, here, this car," he said pointing, to a small East German Trabant hidden in the bushes near the road.

"What about the Lada?" I said.

"It stays here. How else would we have gotten here?" He pulled the Trabant off to the end of the driveway near the road. It was after 1 a.m. We sat in the car and waited. After a few minutes, there was a flash of light and an explosion. "Excellent," he said. "Now we are dead. We can begin our new lives."

He started the engine and we drove back to Moscow. He pulled up to a building in a neighborhood far from ours. I didn't need to ask. I knew I would never see that huge, elegant apartment again. I followed him up the four flights of stairs to a small, cramped flat that smelled of cooking odors and inadequate toilet facilities. My mother, brother and sister were asleep in their beds.

Chapter 15

UPPER WEST SIDE, NYC
8 JUNE 2010
9:30 A.M.

TOLYA FOLLOWED PETE UP THE stairwell from the subway at Central Park West and 81st Street. "Slow down," he called out. "What's a matter, old man?" Pete called back at him without turning around.

Tolya surveyed the street, the Museum of Natural History to his left, the elegant pre-war apartment buildings of Central Park West lined up facing the Park on his right. Tourists everywhere.

This was a different New York than his New York. This was a New York of money and privilege, of dog walkers and doormen. Lives were private here. Everyone had secrets. The game was to keep those secrets to yourself while the servant class was watching you. He crossed the street to catch up with Pete. "What was the cross street on that address?" he asked.

"83rd Street."

The doorman stood silently in front of the entrance at 230 Central

Park West. He wore a dark gray uniform with red piping, a matching hat and white gloves. As Tolya and Pete slowed and approached the door, he shifted his gaze almost automatically. "Can I help you?" he said in a thick Irish brogue.

Pete pulled his badge. "NYPD," he said.

The doorman smiled, showing a mouth full of yellowed, uneven teeth. "Of course," he replied.

Tolya pulled a photo of Mariela from inside the folder he was carrying in his left hand. "Have you ever seen this woman?"

The doorman shook his head.

"How long have you been working here?" Pete asked.

"Just short of two years," the doorman said.

"Thanks," Pete said. "She lived here some years ago, about seven years ago or more. Do you know if any of the present doormen were here then?"

The doorman thought for a moment. "There is one for sure. His name is Damien. He comes on at four."

"Thanks," said Tolya, handing the doorman his card. They turned to leave. Tolya tapped Pete on the shoulder and held up his hand, then turned back toward the doorman. "One more question?"

"Whatever I can help you with."

"This a rental or a condo or a coop?"

"Condo."

"Mostly big apartments or small apartments?"

"Mostly studios and small one bedrooms," the doorman said. "The only big apartments are the ones in the front, facing the park. The side and rear units in all three wings are small."

"Thanks," Tolya said. He nodded toward Pete. They walked down 83rd Street. "Small apartment, fancy address." They headed toward Columbus Avenue. "That's a bad combination in this situation."

"I know what you're thinking, I'm thinking the same thing," Pete said. "I hope we're wrong."

"Me too, Pana."

"I don't know if I can handle that."

Karin decided to take an early lunch. The morning had been extremely taxing. She had expected the museum administration to react positively to a large donation, especially at a time when they sorely needed it. Instead, the Vice Chairperson for New Benefactors had blown a gasket. There were a thousand reasons why the museum shouldn't take an unsolicited donation of that size from an unknown contributor. The contributor had to be thoroughly vetted in line with all the regulations that emanated from the Patriot Act.

She had been roundly reprimanded by the Director of the Museum and the Vice Chairperson. Miriam had interceded as best she could. At the end of the call, the Director told her he was, in fact, not at all disturbed by her stroke of good luck, but that she did have to learn to play the organizational game better. She agreed, apologized, grabbed her bag and headed out to Battery Park to get some air. She had brought a yogurt from home.

Just past the entrance to the park was her favorite food truck, Sandwich Madness. The aromas coming from the truck drew her to it. What the hell, she had had a pretty miserable morning. Why not indulge just a little bit.

"Hello, Tron," she said as she came to the front of the line.

The face of the little Vietnamese man in the truck broke into a huge smile. "Miss Karin, Miss Karin, how you are? We no see you long time. Nguyen," he called out to the woman in the rear of the truck, "come here, look who here."

Karin felt lighter just by the reception. "It's good to see you too, Tron."

"You have baby soon," Nguyen said, reaching both hands through the window of the truck.

Karin took her hands and squeezed them. "Yes, very soon and I'm ready for him to come."

"Oh very good," Tron said. "Is a boy!"

Nguyen let go of Karin's grasp and put her hands on her stomach arching her back. "I have baby soon too. November."

Karin smiled. "They can play together."

Nguyen became very serious for a moment. She reached out to Karin again, taking her hand in hers. "I like that very much."

"Now what you want for lunch, Miss Karin?" Tron asked.

"What's good today?"

Tron leaned forward. "Everything good, but the short rib with the guacamole is the best. I make myself."

"I'll take that please, then. And a Thai iced tea."

Karin watched Tron as he made the sandwich with care and heart. She knew their story, how they had come to America with nothing. It had taken twenty years for Nguyen's grandmother to bring them, when she had escaped Vietnam in 1975 during the final days of the war. Her own daughter, Nguyen's mother, had died in Vietnam. She hadn't seen her granddaughter Nguyen since she was a baby.

They had worked in kitchens until they had enough money for a small coffee truck. Eventually, that truck bought a bigger truck and then finally this truck. All immigration stories were the same. All they wanted was a better life.

Tron handed her the sandwich and the iced tea. "Come by more, Miss Karin, please," said Nguyen.

"I promise and thanks," Karin said, taking the bag and walking off toward the monument at Castle Garden.

The first three dry cleaners between 83rd Street and 77th Street along Columbus yielded nothing. "You wanna try Amsterdam?" Pete said.

"Sure we gotta go back that way anyway. I wanna take the 1 back. I gotta make a stop on St. Nick to pick something up for Karin."

They walked about halfway down 78th Street in silence. Finally, Tolya said something. "Pete, what's the story with this Chicho guy that your cousin was talking about? I thought Mariela was your girlfriend."

"She was my girlfriend," Pete replied. "She was also Chicho's girlfriend after she broke it off with me."

"Do you know him?"

"Yeah, we were kids together. He was like a brother to me then."

"Did you know about this?"

"Yeah, kinda. I didn't know they were still an item after she left DR."

"Where's this guy now?"

Pete hesitated for a moment. He sighed. "Here."

"Here?"

"Yeah. And he's tied up with my uncle. I saw him last night"

Tolya stopped. "When were you gonna tell me that? Pete, he's a convicted felon. You can't be discussing a case with him."

"That's exactly why I didn't tell you. I knew you'd react this way."

Tolya took a deep breath. "OK. You know we're gonna have to talk to him. He could be a suspect."

Pete took his hands from his pockets. He held up his right hand. "Tol, there's no way he would have hurt her."

"Question is, does he know something?"

"I don't know, bro."

They began walking again. "And another thing, you didn't tell me you saw her here when she came here."

Pete stopped dead in his tracks. "Tol, give me a break here, she was living with my cousins. She broke my heart. I was married with kids. When I came around to their place, she would disappear." Pete let out a deep breath. "Let's talk about this later, back at the station," he said as they turned the corner of 78th Street onto Amsterdam Avenue. "There's another dry cleaner."

The sign over the shop read Apthorp Cleaners. Tolya opened the door slowly, jingling a small bell that hung from it. "Excuse me," he said.

A very large man with a shaved head sat behind the counter. He appeared to be sleeping. At the sound of the bell, his eyes opened. He smiled. "May I help you?"

Both Tolya and Pete flashed their badges. At the same moment, a woman some years younger than the man and as small as he was large walked out from behind the curtain that separated the rear of the store from the front. Tolya pulled the photo of Mariela from the folder. "Do either of you recognize this woman?"

The man took the photo. The woman looked at it over his shoulder. They looked at each other and then said, "Yes."

The woman smiled. "That's Roberta Brusca. She was our customer and we were friends." She took her hand from the photo. "I suppose if you're asking about her, that can't be good. Has something happened to her?"

Pete exchanged a glance with Tolya. They had been through scenes like this before. There was no telling how the woman would react when she found out the subject had been murdered.

"Yes," Pete said. "Something has, she was found dead last week."

The woman put her right hand on the counter then looked at her husband.

"I told you she would end up like this Deborah," he said. He got up from the stool for her to sit down.

"No, don't get up, Joel," she said. "I'm OK. I'll just pull the other stool in from the back."

"How long has it been since you've seen her?" Tolya asked.

The man thought for a moment. "More than five years, I think."

"Do you keep records of your transactions going back that far?"

"I'm afraid not."

The woman walked back in the room with a stool, which she placed next to her husband and sat down.

"How did you know her?" Pete asked.

"Well, she was a customer," Joel said.

"And then we, I mean she and I, not Joel, became friends. She liked to cook, as do I, and we took some cooking classes together in the evenings."

"What can you tell us about her?" Tolya asked.

Joel looked at Deborah. He raised his eyebrows. "You might as well tell them," she said.

"I don't like to talk about people's business," Joel said. "You tell them."

Deborah straightened her back and looked out the window. "Could you flip that sign on the door please that says closed? I don't want anyone to walk in while we are discussing this."

"Sure," Tolya said.

"When we met her, she was working as a receptionist in a large law firm downtown. She had gone to secretarial school, but she had to work her way up. She was very sweet and we liked her. She had no family, and we don't have any children so we kind of adopted her. Then all of a sudden, she started bringing in very expensive clothes. We didn't know what was going on with her, but we kind of suspected."

"Suspected what?" Pete asked.

"Well," Joel said. "You can tell a lot about a person by the clothes they wear, how much clothing they have and how often they have it cleaned. We suspected that she was working as more than a receptionist."

"What do you mean?" Tolya asked.

Joel looked at Deborah. Deborah nodded. He looked back at Tolya and Pete. "We thought she might be a high-end call girl. She moved to a very expensive building. She wore very expensive evening dresses and she had a lot of them. The quality of her perfume changed too. No more cheap stuff. You could smell the difference. Also, when a person works days, they don't drop off their dry cleaning at 2:00 or 3:00 in the afternoon."

"You said she moved?" Pete asked.

"Yes. She lived originally on 77th Street in a tiny studio in a five-story walk-up. Then suddenly, she was living at the Bolivar. That's some fancy building."

"You said you were friends. Did you ever actually discuss any of this with her?"

Deborah cleared her throat. "Well, I tried to bring it up a couple of times. I commented on the beautiful clothes and asked her where she was going every night. I made a joke out of it asked if I could come along. She said she was trying to find a husband, and you had to look for a rich one in the right places so she needed to dress the part."

"What did you say?" Pete asked.

"Nothing. I left it like that. What could I say? I didn't want to press her."

"Then one day," Joel said, "we realized we hadn't seen her in over a month so, when I sent the delivery guy to 230 Central Park West, I told him to ask after her. The doorman said she had moved out."

"Thanks for your help," Tolya said. "Here are our cards. If you can think of anything else, please call us."

"If we do, we most certainly will," Joel said.

As they exited the store, Pete turned the sign back to open.

"Madame Kurchenko," Schneider said.

Karin looked up from the remains of her sandwich. Benjamin Schneider stood in front of her in a blue pinstripe suit with a vest. His tie and handkerchief matched, a paisley pattern on a yellow background.

"Mr. Schneider, I mean, Benjamin, what a surprise. What are you doing in Battery Park? Please sit down and stop calling me that. Karin is fine."

"How are you today?"

Karin fumbled with the last crumbs of her sandwich. She rolled the crusts up in the paper the sandwich had been in, then stuffed that into the brown paper bag Tron had given her. She took a last sip of the Thai iced tea. "I'm OK. Actually, to tell you the truth, it's been a little difficult of a morning as a result of your donation."

Schneider smiled. "Really? Actually, I kind of knew that. My office received a call from the museum this morning. I turned it over to my attorney. Apparently, they wanted to make sure I am not a terrorist or affiliated with terrorism in any way. The times we live in. May I sit down?"

"Yes, of course. I'm so embarrassed,"

"Don't be. It's nothing really," Schneider said, sitting down on the bench next to Karin. "So, what brings you out of your office?"

"I needed some air after all the drama this morning."

"I see." He smiled as the moment became a little awkward. "When is the big day for your blessed event?"

"About four weeks, or it could be any time."

"And you continue to work?"

"Yes," Karin said. "At least until the show opens next week. Actually, I was meaning to call you this afternoon. Are you free next Thursday evening? We are having a special dinner for the donors at the Andaz Hotel."

"I'd love to come," Steinmann said. "I'll check my schedule and clear out whatever I might have already. What time?"

"It's at 7:30."

Karin heard Tron calling out her name. She turned to her left and saw him running toward her. "I'm so glad I found you. Nguyen wanted you to have this." He handed her a small, brilliant jade stone on a thin gold chain. "She say wear it till the baby come, it bring health and good luck."

"Thank you, Tron. Please tell Nguyen the same."

"I will," he said. He smiled toward Karin and Schneider and ran off in the direction of the truck.

"How sweet," Schneider said.

Karin looked at the stone in her hand. "Yes, they are. Very." Karin examined the necklace in her hand.

"May I help you with that?" Schneider said.

"Help me? Oh yes, of course." She handed the necklace to him and turned, pulling up her hair in the back.

He lowered the chain over her head and pulled it around toward the back, clipping the two ends together. "There. Let me see. Lovely."

A chill ran up her spine. It felt very strange being that intimate with any man other than Tolya. "Well, enough about me, Benjamin. What brings you down here again today? Don't you live in Brooklyn?"

"Yes I do. I had some business matters to attend to and then I wanted to see the new exhibit at the Museum of the American Indian."

Karin felt herself relax. "Really? You are an interesting man." Her cell phone rang. She decided to let the call go to voicemail. She was on lunch.

Tolya headed directly to his desk when they got back to the station house. He looked at his watch, 12:30. He tried Karin's cell. No answer. He tried her a second time, still no answer. He called her office.

"Office of special events planning," Lacey said, answering the phone.

"Lacey, it's Tolya. Is Karin there?"

"No, I haven't seen her."

"Did she go out for lunch?"

"I don't know. She had a meeting this morning with the director and hasn't been back."

Tolya sighed. "All right, please have her call me when she returns."

"Of course," Lacey said. "Have a nice day."

"Yeah, right," Tolya mumbled, hanging up the phone.

"Tolya, take a look at this," Pete said. He handed him a sheet of paper. "They found a partial print at the crime scene, on the hilt of the knife, and it's not Mariela's."

"But no match to anything in our databases."

"No."

Tolya thought for a moment. He reached toward the left side of the desk and grabbed a green folder. He scanned the Interpol report inside. "Look," he said to Pete. "The Israelis found a print on the wood post on their killing machine."

"Good afternoon, Mr. Taylor," the concierge of 2 Liberty Place said.

"Good afternoon. Do you have anything for me?"

"Yes, I have these receipts. I accepted your deliveries as per your instructions."

"You were able to execute the delivery with respect to my special request?"

"Of course, sir. Otherwise I wouldn't have accepted them. And thank you again for your generosity."

"Very good then. Everything is upstairs?"

"Yes. I hope you'll be very happy with your new apartment."

"I'm sure I will." He smiled, then walked silently through the marble lobby to the elevator. He pushed the call button. Within a second, the door of the elevator to his right opened. He entered and pressed 33. His ascent took less than twenty seconds. He stepped out of the elevator into the security foyer of his apartment, slipped the key into the heavy steel door and opened it. The view opened up in front of him, Upper New York Bay, the Statue of Liberty, Ellis Island, Battery Park at his feet. Just at the right corner of the window was the Museum of Jewish Heritage.

He walked into the bedroom. The bed was assembled just where he had instructed. Those delivery people from Macy's were very efficient. They had made the bed beautifully as well. Or perhaps that was the building staff. He would have to check with Jonathan. The house phone rang. He walked back out toward the front door to the entry area. "Yes?"

"Mr. Taylor. It's Jonathan, is everything as you expected?"

"Oh yes. And Jonathan, who was it that did such a good job on the bed? Macy's?"

"Oh no, sir, that was us. They just deliver."

"Thank you again."

"Nothing to thank us for, sir, that's why we're here. By the way, your other delivery is at the service dock. May I send them up?"

"Of course."

"They'll be coming up from the rear elevator behind the kitchen."

"Very good then. Send someone up to let them in. I'm going to take a bath."

"Very well, sir."

Taylor hung up the phone. He walked across the apartment through the bedroom to the bath, closed the door and locked it. He looked at himself in the mirror then turned on the shower. The jets came from eight directions. He removed the dark wig from his shaved head and rubbed it. He did not think he looked his 43 years. He slowly removed his clothing, first the suit jacket, vest, tie and shirt. He flexed in front of the mirror. What would his father think of him now? No longer skinny and weak. He removed his pants, then admired himself again, posing in front of the three-paneled mirror. He tested the water. Just right. He removed his underwear, looked at himself again, then covered his genitals with his hand. He didn't like to look at the scar. He hated the way he looked there now.

Taylor stepped into the shower, the warm water covering him from all sides. This shower alone was reason enough to pay the price he had for this apartment. But then, he knew once this project was done he would never use it again. He would have to leave the country. He had left too many breadcrumbs along the trail this time. He was tired of New York anyway. The idea of Rio or Buenos Aires excited him. As he soaped himself, he heard the deliverymen in the living room.

"Wow, check out this view," one of them said.

"This guy must be some kinda big shot."

Taylor laughed to himself. Yes, some kind of big shot. He felt himself get hard in his hand. If only they knew what kind. He laughed and leaned back against the marble tile of the shower stall. The cold felt good against his skin. It reminded him of Russia, of home. All cold things did.

Tolya dialed the number he found in the Interpol correspondence. The long tone sounded twice. "Shalom," said the woman's voice on the other end. "Shomrim l' Tel Aviv."

Tolya struggled to speak the few words of Hebrew he remembered from his limited religious training. All that came out was a muddle of English, Hebrew, Russian and Spanish.

"Shit," Pete said, laughing. "What was that?"

"I speak English," came the voice from the other side of the world.

"Yes, thanks. Sorry," said Tolya, slapping at Pete with his free hand. "I'm looking for Detective Ari ben Shimon. I know it's late, but is there some chance he is there?"

"Who is this?"

"Detective Anatoly Kurchenko with the New York City Police Department."

"Let me check," the woman said. Tolya waited on hold to the sound of Israeli rap music. "He's here, transferring you now."

"Halo?"

"Is this Detective ben Shimon? Do you speak English?"

"Yes and yes."

"My name is Anatoly Kurchenko. I am with the NYPD. I received some information from Interpol with your name and number."

"About?"

"Supposedly, suicide. But it didn't look like one."

There was silence on the other end of the phone for a moment. "Did it involve an intricate structure to slice a throat?" ben Shimon asked.

"Yes," said Tolya.

"Bivadai."

"What?"

"Of course. Can I ask you a question?" said the Israeli.

"Yes."

"Was the door locked from the inside?"

"Yes."

The line went silent for a moment again. "You know, I never thought it was a suicide either, but the victim was a poor Arab woman who worked as a prostitute and there was a note in badly written Hebrew. So no one cared, except my partner and me. We both knew that nobody could cut their own throat that way."

"I agree. One question for you."

"Yes?"

"You found a partial print. Did you match it?"

"Yes, but that only complicated matters. It belonged to a dead man."

"What?"

"You heard me right, a dead man. No one could account for that. The truth is that my superiors didn't want to be bothered with the death of a poor Arab prostitute so we accepted it as a suicide."

"Who was he, the print?"

"A Russian immigrant who arrived in 1991."

"How did he die?"

"A terrorist attack. Just prior to the discovery of the body. Perhaps a week earlier."

"Was the attack in Tel Aviv?"

"No, in the territories, in a religious settlement built by Chabad."

"Chabad?"

"You're not Jewish, detective? I thought from the name, the famous Refusenik."

Tolya smiled to himself, larger than life and larger than death, his father. "Yes, I am and he was my father, but I am neither religious nor political."

"I understand. Chabad, the Lubavitch Chasidim. The print belonged to a Russian immigrant who died with his family in an attack on the settlement at Ramat haDatim in 1995. The house was firebombed. The bodies were burned beyond recognition."

"Do you have any photos of these people?"

"We have immigration records. It's pointless. They were dead, the matched print is a fluke."

"Could I ask you to send me the print and whatever else you might have?"

"Bivadai."

"How did the Shabbat celebration go?" Shalom asked.

"Very well," Karin replied. "It felt good. I see now what you were saying about the separation of time."

"Were you able to extend that feeling into Saturday?"

"Well sadly, not exactly. I did with the boys, but Tolya had to work, big new case. That murder up on Wadsworth."

"I heard it was grisly. Perhaps with time he will come around to Shabbat. Have you decided anything about the timing of your conversion? By the way, did Tolya tell you we spoke about it?"

"No, he didn't. He's not a big talker, my husband, at least not about his feelings."

"True," said Shalom. "He's still reluctant to do this. I appealed to him as a father and husband."

"Thanks," Karin said. "To be truthful, I realized yesterday I can't do it right now. It will have to wait till after the Sosúa exhibition is over or after Oleg comes. You are coming Thursday evening?"

"Of course, I wouldn't miss it for anything. Chava, you understand there is no rush. If you wait till after the baby comes, I can take all of you to the mikvah together. But you have to do it before his bris."

"Thank you, rabbi, I understand and will try. I enjoyed today's lesson." She stood and began to extend her hand to him then drew it back. "I almost forgot, how did the hearing go?"

"Your husband spoke eloquently and I hope they will release her soon."

"I admire and envy your ability to forgive," Karin said. "It's something I have to try to emulate."

"You will. It comes with time." Shalom chuckled. "You know, Karin, most people when asked what they think is the most important thing in a successful marriage will answer compromise."

"Yes, I've heard that many times."

"What I've come to believe is that marriage is really about forgiveness—forgiving your spouse their shortcomings and forgiving yourself yours."

Chapter
16

UPPER WEST SIDE, NYC
8 JUNE 2010
8:00 P.M.

"ARE YOU DAMIEN?" TOLYA ASKED the doorman at 230 Central Park West.

The doorman smiled. He had a round face and blue eyes. Taller than both Pete and Tolya, he was built like a football player. "Yes."

They flashed their badges. Tolya pulled Mariela's picture from his folder. "Do you know her?"

Damien looked at the photo. He squinted for a moment, then laughed and nodded, still, chewing his gum. "My eyes aren't so good anymore, but yeah, I remember her. Her name was Roberta. She was a nice lady." He moved a little closer to Tolya and Pete and leaned toward them. "And you know, sometimes she would speak to me in Spanish 'cause she knew I'm Puerto Rican."

Pete switched to Spanish. "Did she ever tell you where she learned Spanish?"

"Nah, and she spoke it good too," he responded in English. "She sounded Dominican, like you, but she wasn't no Dominicana. Not in this building."

Pete stifled a smile.

"Do you know if she owned the apartment?" Tolya asked.

"No, she was renting it. That apartment is empty now. This is a condo, you know. The owners can do what they want. No board like a co-op."

"Yes, thanks for the real estate lesson." He moved a little closer to Damien. "Did she have a lot of, you know, boyfriends? Guests?"

Damien smiled sheepishly and covered his mouth. "Yeah, she did, but you know, she was very nice to us, you know what I mean? So we never said nothing. We would just ring her up and tell her that her guest was here and send him up when she said OK. And you know, she wasn't no cheap hooker. She never had more than one in a night and usually not more than two or three a week."

Pete felt a little sick. "Did she have a lot of repeats?"

"Oh yeah," the doorman said. "Regular customers, and they was generous too with us." Damien's demeanor changed suddenly. "Something happen to her?"

"We can't discuss it, man," Tolya said. "But thanks for your help. Listen, one more question."

"Whatever I can."

"Is that apartment still owned by the same owner as it was when she lived here?"

"I dunno."

"What apartment number?" Pete asked.

"14H."

"Thanks, man," Tolya said.

"I hope I didn't get her into any kind of trouble?" Damien said.

"Not at all," Tolya replied.

He and Pete walked down Central Park West back toward the C train entrance at 81st Street. "What was the name of that service we subscribed to for property ownership records?" Tolya asked.

Pete stared straight ahead. Tolya repeated his question, still no answer. "Pete," Tolya said, touching his forearm.

"Sorry," Pete said. "What did you say? I was thinking about something else."

Tolya hesitated for a moment. He didn't want to put Pete on the spot. He was a good cop, but Tolya also knew he was too close to the case. It was too deep inside him. "I asked you about that property ownership service we subscribe to. What's it called?"

"I don't remember," Pete said. "I've got it written down someplace on my desk. I'll check it first thing tomorrow morning."

"Where you heading?" Tolya asked.

"Uptown, home. You?"

"Me too." They entered the subway and flashed their badges again. The token booth clerk opened the emergency door for them. The platform was warm and it was only early June. "There is an uptown local train one stop away," announced the artificial voice on the P.A.

"What do you think of that new system they got?" Tolya asked Pete.

"It's stupid. It tells you the local is one stop away, but you don't know which local. Then you see the A fly by and you hope it's a C so you don't end up waiting on the platform at 125th street."

"I agree," Tolya said. "It's not for us though, it's more for the tourists."

"Seems like all of New York is for the tourists now."

"But where else you gonna go?"

Pete smiled. His eyes were far away. "Santo Domingo. Maybe we should take a trip down there for a little break when this is over."

"Oh, I'm sure Karin would love that."

They both laughed. "Thanks man," Pete said.

"For what?" Tolya replied.

"For doing this with me. For not going along with the captain to take me off the case. I always know that I can go all the way to the end with you."

"We're a team, right?"

"Always."

Pete waved at Tolya from halfway down the platform at 181st street. They lived at different ends. That was always the case with the Dominicans and the white population. Los blancos lived north of 181st street and west of Broadway. Los Dominicanos lived everywhere else.

He took the escalator up to 181st and Ft. Washington and walked down the hill toward Broadway. Instead of going home, he crossed Broadway and walked toward St. Nicholas Avenue. He looked at his watch. It was 9:00 on the head. He called Chicho earlier and asked him to meet him at 9:30 at the Mofongo House. He had a half hour and he knew Chicho would be late anyway. He texted Liza. He knew he had to take care of this and the sooner the better, before he changed his mind.

She was home. He texted her back that he would be over in five minutes, then took the two blocks to her place on 184th at a trot. She texted him back while he was on the way. Did he just think he could show up any time he wanted? He ignored it. He pressed the buzzer at the front door of her building and waited. He pressed it again then heard the buzz back. The buzzer for the interior door went off as the first one closed. He took the stairs, a little out of breath when he reached her apartment on the third floor. She was standing in the doorway in her red Chinese bathrobe, her breasts pretty much hanging out of her turquoise lace bra, her big brown nipples half exposed.

"Amor, what a surprise." She reached up to kiss him as he brushed past her through the doorway into the apartment.

He breathed in her scent. He loved it. For a moment his resolve faltered.

"Amor, what's up? What's wrong with you?"

He backed up a little to the other side of the dining table. "Liza, I have to tell you something."

"Qué?"

"It's over. I can't see you anymore."

She laughed. "OK, papi, not funny, come here. Take off those pants." She moved toward him, grabbing his trousers by the belt.

"No, no," he said, pulling away from her. "I'm serious, I'm sorry."

"What the fuck is this?" Liza said, pulling her robe around her.

"Baby, it's over. I can't do this, I can't do this to Glynnis anymore."

"Bulto," she screamed. "You've been doing this to Glynnis for twenty years, now all of a sudden you got morals?"

"I can't explain right now…"

"You're a lying bastard." She picked up her textbooks from the table and threw them at him. "Who is she? You found someone new? Una

Americana? Someone who fucks you better than me, bandolero?"

She came toward him and slapped him in the face. She was about to slap him again with her other hand when he grabbed her arms to restrain her. "Liza, stop, I don't want to hurt you."

"Oh no, you bastard?" she said through her teeth. "Well I'm gonna hurt you. When I find out who she is, not only am I gonna scratch her eyes out but I'm gonna tell your wife too."

Pete let her hands go. He stepped back and looked at her calmly. He hesitated for a moment, then said, "If you come near my family, I'll kill you. I told you the truth, and if you weren't the whore you are, not only would you have believed me, you might have asked me why."

Liza crumpled into the corner and began to cry. Pete moved toward her. He knew he had had gone too far. He never wanted to hurt her. In his way, he loved her, and breaking her heart was breaking his as well.

"Don't touch me. You call me a whore, you animal? You can't keep your dick in your pants long enough to zip your fly," she seethed, striking out toward him with her open hand.

"I'm sorry," he said. "I destroy everything I love."

"This guy found you in the park? That's not good. I don't like that at all."

"You don't like that? I'm in the middle of telling you about my day and you turn all daddy on me?"

Tolya sat down next to Karin. "Please, stop, listen to me for a moment."

"I'm tired of listening to you," she said. She pushed herself up from the couch. She intentionally kept her voice down so as not to wake the children. "And who the fuck do you think you are? You're telling me what to do?"

"Just be careful. Who knows who this guy is?"

"You're telling me to be careful? You think I can't take care of myself?"

Tolya reached out toward her. "C'mon, this is the hormones talking. Please..."

Karin froze. "You see, that's the whole problem. You don't respect me. You think because you're a man, you're more rational. Do you think I would endanger our child or myself? Am I just a poor judge of character? I'm sorry I ever told you about this."

Tolya moved away from her toward the other end of the couch. He knew she was beyond angry. "OK, you're right," he said. "I'm being irrational. I'm just concerned."

"About what?"

"I'm not sure. I just don't like the way this feels."

"Watch yourself here, Tolya."

"The guy sees you on TV at 6:00 in the morning on a Sunday. Then the next day, he shows up at your office and writes out a $10,000 check like it's nothing. And the day after that, you run into him in Battery Park. Sounds a little like a stalker to me."

Karin sat down on the edge of the black leather sofa. She hesitated for a moment. "OK, I see your point. I also think you are a paranoid cop, so here's what we're going to do. I'm going to give you his address and information, whatever I have, and you can run any check on him you want. Then, when you find out I'm right and he's nothing more than a nice man with a fat checkbook, you can apologize to me. And you can take me to the Palm for a lobster."

Pete walked into the Mofongo House. He scanned the bar for Chicho. No Chicho, late as expected. He walked back toward the booths at the rear of the restaurant. He would text him and wait there. As he passed the next to last booth he heard that familiar voice. "Pedrito el bandito." He turned. Chicho was seated with his back to the room in the corner of the booth. "What's so important that you gotta see me so fast?"

Pete smiled. When Chicho acted like a wise guy, the years melted away. It was like that with all his old boys. He was a kid again in Santo Domingo, haciendo travesura. And what was a cop, really, but a grown-up version of a bad boy? "We need to get real, hermano," Pete said, sliding into the opposite side of the red leather booth. "What you drinking?"

"Whiskey," Chicho said. He picked up the bottle of Black Label and poured a shot neat into an empty glass for Pete.

Pete swirled the amber liquid in the glass for a moment. He smiled and lifted it. "To the old days, hermanito."

They clinked glasses twice, once on each side, then downed the shot.

"Sí, to the old days," Chicho said. "Things were very simple then." He smiled and stared off into the dark room. "You know, you were my idol back then. The way you could handle yourself. Even then, you were a hit with the ladies—14 years old and you could talk them into bed. I only wanted to be you."

"You remember that woman, the one who lived in the patio behind your cousin's colmado?" Pete said.

"The older one?"

"Yeah, the one I took you to, to lose your cherry?"

Chicho laughed and poured another drink for them both. He lifted his glass to Pete again, Pete tapping the rim of his to Chicho's. "Salud," he said and downed the shot. "How could I forget, I was scared to death."

Pete smiled, his mind far off somewhere in the past. "I remember, brother, I remember." He hesitated for a moment. "I missed you when I got here. I had no friends. I didn't speak the language."

"And we were all jealous of you because you got to go to America."

"You were jealous?"

"Yeah, I missed you, but I was jealous. You always got the chances, with the girls, with everything. You got to live with Polito. He was so cool, not like my father. Polito was sharp. He was going places."

"Yeah, I see where he ended up."

"Hey, be careful with that. I ended up in the same place and I'm doing OK."

"Are you happy?'

"What's happy, man? We're here. We're alive. Lots of the guys from then didn't make it."

Pete pointed toward the bottle. "I'll take some ice this time."

"To Miguelito," Chicho said. He poured a bit of the whiskey on the floor under the table.

Pete raised his glass. "To Roberto."

Chicho looked at Pete. "So why'd you drag me out here tonight? I know it wasn't for a walk down memory lane."

"We gotta talk about Mariela."

"Mariela's dead. What we gonna talk about?"

"I wanna find her killer and I need your help."

"Man, what's the difference? She ain't coming back."

"She deserves that much."

"She don't deserve shit."

Pete was ready to dive across the table and choke Chicho. He stopped himself. "I know you had a thing with her, hermanito. How can you say that?"

Chicho laughed. "If only that was true. You have no idea how much I wanted that. How much I wanted her. It was all for show. I was like a puppy with her, your cousins used to make fun of me."

"They told me she was trying to contact you constantly when she came here."

"Pedrito, you are a cabron," Chicho said. "She was trying to contact me, but it wasn't about me. It was about you."

"But when we brought her out. When we went to your village in the campo, she told me…"

"She lied to you, hermano. I would have done anything for her, anything to have her. She used me as an excuse to push you away."

"Why?"

"Because she loved you. But she didn't want to break up your marriage and she didn't want to affect your career. She was the daughter of a drug dealer and she thought she was marked for murder."

Pete sat back in the booth. "You never had her then?"

"No."

"Did you ever see her here after you came over?"

"Yes, one time. By accident."

"Where?"

"You don't want to know."

Pete sighed. "I already know what she was doing."

"Then why you asking me?"

"I need to put the pieces of her life together so I understand what happened to her."

"She was dancing in a club on the West Side. I had just come over after I was released from prison. Your uncle helped me to come. We went out, a bunch of us, to this place over by 12th Avenue. There she was dancing on the pole. At first I wasn't sure. Her hair was lighter, she was in makeup. But then I saw her eyes, those deep, dark eyes like pools of water at night ringed by golden fire, and I knew."

"Did she recognize you?"

"After a while, yeah. I sent over a drink and she told the waitress to tell me, 'No, thank you.' I asked the waitress to ask her to meet me in one of the private VIP rooms and she finally agreed about an hour later."

"What did you say? What did she say?"

"I asked her what the fuck she was doing, and she said she was trying to make a living, that New York was expensive and that she was trying to get away from her life before. She told me she had cut herself off from everyone, changed her name."

"Did she say why?"

"No and I didn't ask. I was disgusted with her. But at the same time, I was still in love with her."

"Did she say anything else?"

"Yeah, she asked me not to tell anyone that I'd seen her and then she asked about you. I told her we had lost touch. I gave her my number in case she ever needed me."

Pete's stomach turned. "Chicho, man, I'm sorry, I never knew."

"Don't sweat it, man. It's over."

"What was the name of the club?"

"Gentleman's Quarter. It's long gone, but here's a news flash: It was owned by that same Albanian bastard you mentioned the other night to Polito."

Chapter
17

THE LIGHTS TWINKLING IN THE harbor and on Staten Island reminded me of the stars at night in the forest where our dacha had been. After our "disappearance," life became nearly intolerable. The party was finished. Gorbachev was on his way out. Our orderly, law-abiding society had descended into chaos. The streets weren't safe, especially at night. Inflation was rampant. Our money was worthless and the fingers were pointed at the former elite of the "People's Republic."

My father's plan had gone like clockwork. A few days after our evening of destruction, the KGB sent someone to look for him. At first they thought we might have defected. Then they found the dacha in ashes and the bodies burnt beyond recognition.

He was proclaimed a hero of the people, but then slowly, and in the spirit of the times, his crimes began to come out. Funds had disappeared under his watch. Valuable contraband that had been confiscated from the nation's traitors over decades had found its way to my father's care and disappeared as well. He had been instrumental in punishing Refuseniks and other counterrevolutionaries. He had been even better at extorting money from their foreign benefactors to permit them to leave the country. He was even better yet at diverting and hiding a portion of those funds for himself. After a few months, his image went from "Hero of the People" to the worst example of Soviet corruption. Whenever he saw these reports on our television, he laughed like a madman.

The day after we arrived in the new apartment, my father began to change us. First he dyed our hair dark brown so we would look more like Jews. We were blond, my brother and I, and my mother and sister had reddish-blond hair. No more. Now we were dark haired. My father shaved his head and grew a mustache, which he also dyed. Then he explained to us that we would have to gain twenty pounds each. The Jews were fat, he said. We needed to look like them. Then he took all of us to a criminal he knew and had our fingerprints changed just enough to distinguish us as someone other than who we were. That hurt a good deal.

We ate nothing but potatoes and black bread for the better part of a month, and lots of fatty meat. I didn't feel well from this diet. I became lethargic and my skin broke out. I had been thin all my life and now I felt the fat building up around my middle and I didn't like it. He changed our clothes as well. He told us we needed to look less fortunate. As a KGB agent, he had had access to better food, better clothes, better everything than other citizens of the Soviet Union. Now we would live like the masses.

I became bored quickly. I was unable to contact my friends. They thought we had died in the explosion at our dacha. I sat for hours playing chess with my brother. He was a dullard. We watched what passed for entertainment on Russian television. At the end of the first month, my father came to us. He was pleased with how things had gone so far. Now he, my brother and I would have to complete one more step before we could leave. We would need to be circumcised.

My brother dropped his head into his hands.

I looked at my father in horror. "You're joking, right?"

"When have I ever been known to joke?" my father asked.

He was correct. He was never a joker. Actually, he was always quite serious.

"You must understand. They mark themselves this way. When we get to Israel, we are entitled to citizenship but only if we can prove we are Jews. I have had forgeries made of the certificates they award themselves when they do this to their sons." He placed the papers on the table between us. They were covered with Hebrew printing. "They will ask for this. We can't take a chance that they won't ask to see the result."

My brother groaned. He rarely said anything, as he knew the result was usually a slap across the head with my father's huge hand. "I can't do this, Father." I grabbed my member through my pants. "You all go. I'll remain here."

He leaned over the table, his nose nearly touching mine. "You'll do no such thing. You don't exist here anymore. Tomorrow we will do this. I have arranged a doctor to do this for us in his offices. I paid him plenty. I won't let you jeopardize my escape. If you refuse, I will kill you, you know that. I don't kid around."

And so, the next day we went with him early in the morning to the office of the doctor. My brother went first, then me, then my father last to make sure we didn't try to leave. They gave us an injection in the spine first to numb us up, then some pills to calm us. Then, when I was in a half-sleep, I could feel the coldness of the steel blade slide across the foreskin of my penis, clipping it away and my former life with it forever.

My father gave us two months to heal from the surgery. By then, the situation in Moscow had become tenuous. One day in early April, he came in, threw the tickets and documents on the table and told us to pack. I was sick to my stomach. This life was bad enough, but to move to Israel was another thing entirely. I knew better than to challenge him again. He had made it clear what his response would be. The following morning, a Sunday, we left our hovel, door unlocked, and traveled by Metro to the offices of the Jewish Agency on Bolshoy Spasoglinishchevsky, each of us with two suitcases in hand. My father was smiling. Why wouldn't he be? The faces of my mother and sister showed fear. My brother? As always, he was blank, his eyes darting about, trying to process how the chaos around him would affect him.

We entered the lobby of the building. A hand-printed sign directed us to the offices of the immigration officials on the fourth floor. The lobby area in front of the elevators was packed with people—young, old, men, women—all in family groups. The elevators were full when they returned. Thank god it was a Sunday. No other offices were open, so the four elevators served only this mass of Jews waiting to leave for the past seventy years.

There was relative calm. We were all well-trained Soviet citizens in any event, and standing in line was the thing we did best. A tall, thin, unshaven man with a skullcap came toward us. He spoke to us in badly accented Russian. "May I see your documents, please?" he asked.

"Of course," my father said, removing them from the inside of his great coat. He handed them to the man, smiling. He looked back at each of us, the message in his eyes clear; say nothing, as he had directed us earlier.

"Mr. Portnoy? Yevgeny Portnoy?"

"Da?"

"You are emigrating with your wife and three children?"

"Da."

"Your children are all above the age of 18?"

"My sons, yes, my daughter is 17."

"Please take elevator 2 to the fourth floor and then wait on the line to the left."

"Da, and todah," my father said, using the Hebrew word for thank you.

The young man smiled. "Todah rabah, and welcome home."

We waited on that line for almost thirty minutes before we got into the elevator. Thirty seconds later, we got off at the fourth floor. We waited another thirty minutes to be processed for our exit. A young woman was in charge. She was obviously not Russian. She had the dark looks of the Middle East, though I suppose she could have been from one of our Central Asian Republics. I tried to make conversation with her. She responded only with a weak smile. My father scowled at me.

Eventually we reached the head of the line and were shown into a room. In front of us sat two men, one obviously a Russian. He had the fair hair and blue eyes of our race, the other, yet another swarthy, hairy, skinny Jew, this one without a skullcap. I felt like I was going to vomit. I began to sweat. I looked around the room for any means of escape. Sadly, my heart sank. I knew there was none and I knew that, if I tried to sneak off on our way out of the building, my father would prevent me from doing so. He was going to execute his plan and we were critical to that.

"Please, sit down," the swarthy Jew said in perfect Russian. "Welcome, this is your first step in your long journey home." He turned and addressed the blond-haired man in what I imagined could only be Hebrew. I was shocked. How could this be? This blond, blue-eyed man was also a Jew? Then I remembered. They come in all sizes, shapes and colors. I thought of the Kurchenko brothers, blond and blue-eyed like this one here.

The blond-haired man stood up. "Your documents, please?" he said in badly accented Russian. My father removed the visas and birth certificates from his folder and handed them to the man. He scanned them and turned to his swarthy companion. They mumbled to each other, the dark-haired man pointing to various spots on the papers.

My father stood up. He pulled some more papers from the folder. "These are our bris certificates," he said, waving them in front of the two men. "Do you want to see?"

The dark-haired man translated. The blond man laughed. He looked at my father. "Nyet," he said. "Save that for the rabbis at the airport in Israel," he added in broken Russian. He said something else in Hebrew, which the other man translated. "He is only interested in the ages of your children and whether they will be required to perform military service after your stay at the absorption center."

I stared out of the window at the flurry of snowflakes. I knew I would never see snow again.

The rest of our processing took another twelve hours. The flight time from Moscow to Tel Aviv was only three and a half hours. I expected it would be longer. I don't know why, it just seemed it should.

We arrived at night. The mood in the plane was one of elation and apprehension. As we approached the airport, you could see the lights of the many buildings in Tel Aviv. It was bigger than I imagined. There had been music playing at low volume all through the flight, mostly classical Russian composers, Tchaikovsky, Rachmaninoff. Occasionally a piece of Jewish-sounding music would come on—mournful, full of strings and horns. As we settled into the descent, the music changed to something I wasn't familiar with. My fellow émigrés, such as they were, smiled and began clapping and singing along with these folk songs. By the time we were approaching the landing strip for touch down, the music was at full volume, a mournful tune I would later learn was the Jewish national anthem, HaTikvah, the Hope.

As the wheels touched the runway, a shout went up and everyone clapped riotously. Many people were crying. I looked at my mother and my sister to my right, smiles frozen on their faces, and then turned to my left. Across the aisle, my father was singing and clapping with everyone else.

We stepped out into the desert night onto the tarmac, the air dusty and warm. No modern airport here. Across the runway was a small, low, open-air building. One could see the service desks of various airlines, their lights on and no attendants. It was after midnight and the airport was deserted, save for the brigades of bureaucrats and processors here to absorb us into our new lives.

What kind of place was this? My heart sank even further. Where would they send us, to some desolate desert outpost, fodder for their endless conflict with the Arabs? I had seen reports on our news services. This was a country of settlers, like the American Wild West 100 years ago. I was a modern, urban Soviet man. I wanted to return to my university, to all the pretty girls, to my hobby. I had had some success with that in the few months prior to our "deaths." My work had remained undetected, even from my father.

"Proceed to the large hanger, please," shouted a large man in a dark uniform. "Your luggage will be returned to you when you are finished with intake processing. Quickly, please, quickly." He shouted something else in Hebrew to a group of three men and a woman accompanying us. They walked alongside us, machine guns out and cocked, surveying the dark horizon while shepherding us into the hanger.

Our arrival was as tedious as our departure. More lines, more stamps. We were issued temporary passports and internal identity cards. Our Soviet passports were taken from us when we left Moscow. We were taken again as a family into a semi-private area. Two women sat at the desk this time.

"Welcome to Israel," the one on the left said. "You are the Portnoy family?"

"Ken," my father answered, using the Hebrew word for yes.

"You are all present?"

"Ken," my father said again.

"B'seder," the young woman to the right said. "I will call off your names and you will respond by saying 'hee'naini.' So you see, you have your first Hebrew lesson here with us, 'hee'naini' means 'here I am.'"

"Ken," my father said a third time. I laughed to myself. I could sense his nervousness. It was so unlike him, always so calm and in control. I on the other hand, though miserable, was resigned to my fate and was at peace with myself.

"Yevgeny Portnoy," called out the woman on the right.

"Hee'naini," my father answered then laughed loudly. "Not bad?" he said in Russian.

"Mitzuyan," the young woman responded, using what I would later learn was the Hebrew word for excellent.

"Olga Portnoy," the woman called out.

"Hee'… hee'nai," my mother said stumbling over the Hebrew.

"Boris Portnoy," she called out.

"Hee'naini," mumbled my brother.

"Raiza Portnoy."

My sister smiled. "Hee'naini," she said clearly.

The woman looked at me. "So you must be Nicholai Portnoy."

"Da," I said clearly and loudly in Russian.

The woman looked at me and smiled. "Hee'naini," she said. She had a short conversation in mumbled tones with the woman on the left, who then spoke to us.

"You have been assigned to an absorption center in B'nai Brak. You will stay there for approximately six weeks to study Hebrew and to be evaluated for work. After that time, you will move to an apartment. We will work with you to place you in an environment where you will be happy. I have a package for each one of you here with information in both Russian and Hebrew to help you with any questions you will have, and I am sure there will be many. In a moment, a photographer will come to take your pictures for your new Israeli passports, then a representative of the Chief Rabbinate will visit with you. After that, you will be taken to collect your bags and to the buses to take you to the absorption center. Do you have any questions?"

"Yes," my father said.

"What would that be?" the woman asked.

"I would like to change our family name to a Hebrew name."

She looked at our papers and was silent for a long moment. "Your name, Portnoy, in Hebrew that would be Hayat."

"Then Hayat it will be," said my father.

"I will inform the immigration official handling your papers."

They left us in the room. We waited what seemed like an eternity, the harsh fluorescent lights attracting moths, the flies buzzing around us. It seemed as if there were more flies in this small room than in all of Moscow. I could tell how tired my family was by the fact that they did not react at all to the conditions. They stared ahead of themselves in silence as if they were asleep with their eyes open. A young man and woman entered with a camera. They asked us one by one to stand against the blank wall at the rear of the room. They took several photos of each of us, thanked us in Hebrew, then left.

Some time later, three men entered, one very old in the traditional dress of the Orthodox Jew with a long beard and those ridiculous sidelocks, his teeth yellowed. His stained white shirt stretched over his protruding stomach. He wore a heavy woolen suit of bluish gray material. When he sat down behind the desk, he flipped up the back of the coat so as not to sit on it.

Two other, younger men, one of them tall and very thin, the other on his way to fat, accompanied him. They both wore skullcaps. The chubbier one was dressed in modern clothing. The tall, thin one in the same traditional garb as the old man. The thin one played with the wispy red hairs of his beard.

"Shalom," the one in modern dress said. He picked up the folder on the table and stared at the name on the front, then said, "Mishpacha Portnoy."

"We have changed it to Hayat," my father shouted back.

The same young man began to address us in Russian. "As you desire. I am from the Ministry of Religion. This gentleman next to me is Rabbi Krinsky, he is with the Chabad and this is his assistant. Are you familiar with Chabad?"

We looked at each other. For the first time, I saw confusion in my father's eyes. This was something he hadn't covered. Something he didn't know. I knew at that moment that I could break his hold over me, escape from him. He was unsure of how to respond. He only smiled. "Nyet," I said.

"They are the representatives of the Lubovitcher Chasidic movement. They are here to help us ascertain your status under the Law of Return and to speak to you about how they can help you once you get settled."

The old man said something in a language different than the Hebrew I had been hearing all day. It had a Germanic sound. He looked at my father, addressing him directly. My father maintained the smile frozen onto his face and said nothing. The younger man spoke to us in Russian again. "Mr. Portnoy, sorry, I mean Hayat, you don't speak any Yiddish then?"

"No," my father answered.

"Hm," the chubby young man said. "Many of your generation do. No matter. May I see your birth certificates please?"

"Of course," my father said. He pulled them from his folder and handed them to the young man. "Would you like to see these too?"

"Just the birth certificates please."

He examined the forged papers my father handed him with the rabbi, mumbling and scrutinizing at the same time. Finally he lifted his head. "You understand that under the Law of Return all Jews, from anywhere, have the right to claim Israeli citizenship upon their arrival in Eretz Israel?"

"Da," my father said.

"The rabbi would like to know your Hebrew name and the Hebrew name of your wife."

A current of electric shock went through my body. Perhaps this is where we would get caught. Perhaps we would be sent back. My father couldn't answer this question. I watched as he reacted, but much to my disappointment the sly, old, KGB agent reappeared in the room.

"Why?"

The chubby young man hesitated for a moment then smiled. "Mr. Portnoy, it's a simple question, we all have two names, the one we use in the street and the other we use in shul. The question is quite straight-forward."

My father chuckled then slouched into his chair his hands clasped around his knee, which was crossed over his other leg. "My parents and my grandparents were Communists and Party members since before the revolution. The same is true of my wife's family. We abandoned that custom long ago. We are Jews though, I assure you. Would we be here otherwise?"

"This question was not meant to offend you."

"But you have anyway."

I watched in horror as the chubby young man melted under my father's icy stare and intimidating smile.

"Perhaps this will help," my father said pulling the bris certificates from his folder.

The young man looked at them then passed them to the rabbi who examined them in great detail, then handed them back to chubby, mumbling.

"My apologies, Mr. Portnoy," chubby said. "Rabbi Krinsky assures me these are authentic. He said it's not uncommon for these to contain the common names of the parents and the child."

"Would you like to see the result?" my father asked.

Chubby blushed. "No, that won't be necessary," he said.

My stomach tied into a knot again. There had been no necessity to mutilate myself.

The tall, thin, young man with the scraggly red beard began speaking in Hebrew. Chubby translated. If we were interested in rediscovering our faith, the Chabad would help us to do that. We should register with them and they would visit with us before the Shabbat and before holidays to help us to learn to observe our faith. When we were finished with our stay at the absorption center they could help us to find a place in one of the growing religious communities in Judaea and Samaria. My father accepted their offer of help enthusiastically. He was delighted to be returning to the community of his ancestors. I wanted only to cry. I could see no way out.

Chapter 18

WASHINGTON HEIGHTS, NYC
9 JUNE 2010
8:30 A.M.

TOLYA AND PETE PULLED UP to the gate at Leka's house in Hewlett Harbor for the second time in less than a week. "You run the check on that guy who's been following Karin around before we left, Tol?" Pete said.

"I gave it to Peña to do. She'll have it back later today." He got out of the car and pressed the call button on the gate.

This time, it was Leka himself on the intercom. "You got a warrant?"

"No. I don't need a warrant to talk to you."

"Then get the hell out of here."

"I think you're gonna want to talk to us," Tolya said.

"Why?"

"Because we know you knew the victim. She was a dancer in one of your clubs."

The gates began to open slowly inward. By the time they arrived at the front door, Leka was standing there in workout shorts and lifting gloves, sweat covering his torso.

177

"You're pushing it," he said. "I'm not helping you any more than I already have."

Pete lunged at him, slamming him against the heavy wooden door. Barks and growling and the sound of paws scratching at wood came from the other side. "Who the fuck do you think you're talking to?" Pete said, one hand around Leka's neck the other on his gun cocked against the Albanian's head.

"I'll fucking kill you," Leka choked out, Pete's grasp tightening on his throat like a vise.

"Pete," Tolya screamed, trying to peel him off of Leka. They heard two guns cock behind them. Both turned to find two large men with their Magnums drawn and pointed in their direction.

"OK, OK," Pete said, releasing Leka, "tranquilo."

"Get the fuck off my property!"

"Not till we have a little discussion. Call off your goons," Tolya said.

"Fuck you," the Albanian said, rubbing his neck where Pete had grabbed him.

"Would you prefer we arrest you?"

"For what?" Leka screamed.

"How about prostitution and trafficking?" Pete said.

"What the fuck you talking about?"

"We know what you're doing in that club down on West Street. You bring in the girls illegally and they have to pay you back. They work it off."

Leka looked at the two security guards. He waved them off. They turned and walked off toward the garage at the end of the driveway. "Who told you that?"

"I got some connections inside," Pete said. "May we come in now?"

"Wait here," Leka replied. He cracked the door to the sound of barking, slipped in, then closed it. A long moment later, he opened the door. He turned silently and walked into the house. Pete and Tolya followed him back to his study, closing the door behind them as they entered.

"What do you want?" Leka asked.

"We know you used to own a club called Gentleman's Quarter over on 12th Ave."

"That was a long time ago and I only had a small piece."

"We wanna know who your investors were."

"Why?"

"Because one of them is a serial killer."

"Did Peña get any info on this Schneider guy?" Pete asked Tolya.

"Not a fuckin' thing. It's like he doesn't exist." Tolya shrugged. "Anyway, what was the name of that corporation that invested in the strip club?"

"Pobeda 1," Pete replied. "Look at this," Tolya said, pointing to the computer screen.

Pete scanned the screen. He followed Tolya's index finger as it moved slowly down the fifth column on the page. "Pobeda 4," he read aloud.

"I'd say the ownership behind the two is the same. Look at the mailing address. It's a P.O. Box in lower Manhattan."

Pete wrote the address down. "I'm calling the post office now."

Tolya stared at the screen. Pobeda, the Russian word for victory. Why? Victory over what? The phone rang, breaking his concentration. "Kurchenko."

"Detective," he heard the thickly accented voice say from the other end.

"Yes."

"This is detective ben Shimon in Tel Aviv."

"Yes, hello, good to hear from you. What have you got for me?"

"Did you receive the partial print?" said ben Shimon.

Tolya checked his inbox. He noticed the Hebrew lettering at the top. "Yes. Sorry. I haven't had a chance to check it. Email was the next thing on my list."

"I wanted to speak to you about something else. I remembered something about the case after we spoke so I went back and checked it."

"What was that?"

"About two years before we worked this case, we were on another case. The body of a young Filipina woman, a guest worker, was found with her throat cut in a vacant lot in a poor section of south Tel Aviv. The main suspect was named Hayat but our records indicate a different first name. So I checked the census and public records. It seems the suspect we questioned was the brother of the man identified by the print."

"I thought the last name was Portnoy."

"It was, they changed it when they emigrated. Very common to take a Hebrew last name. Often they continue to use both names."

"Did you solve the case?"

"No."

"Was the brother arrested?"

"No."

"Can you locate him?"

"I'm afraid he died in the same attack as our suspect."

"Very weird," said Tolya. "Do you remember anything unusual about him or the case?"

"Yes, he had the coldest eyes I've ever seen and they were of two different colors."

"Very unusual. Thank you, detective."

"Keep me posted, please. If I can help in any way…"

"Of course. Shalom for now," Tolya said, hanging up the phone.

Tolya clicked on the email links and brought up the information ben Shimon had sent him. He typed "terrorist attack Ramat haDatim 1995" into Google. In a nanosecond, the results were there in both English and Hebrew. He clicked on a link to a newspaper article in *The New York Times* first.

The attack occurred at a controversial settlement deep in the occupied West Bank. A local Arab farmer claimed the settlement had expanded onto his land. The expansion included his olive grove. He had no physical title to the land, but the court awarded him a monetary settlement. The local radicals threatened to burn the houses down. A few weeks later, at approximately 1 a.m., the residents of the settlement heard a series of loud explosions. They ran outside to find the house in the settlement next to the unfinished security fence ablaze. The house next to it caught fire as well. After the blaze was brought under control by army fire brigade units, the occupants of the first house were found dead in their beds, burned beyond recognition. The family had emigrated from the former Soviet Union. No names, no personal details. The Arab farmer maintained he had nothing to do with the attack, as did the local branches of Hezbollah, Hamas and Fatah.

Tolya went on to read an article in *The Jerusalem Post*. It was much more graphic and much more accusatory. An editorial appeared as well, asking how many more lives needed to be lost before the government would support the settler's security needs instead of fighting them at every step. The name of the family appeared in the article: Hayat, formerly Portnoy, recent emigrants from the Soviet Union. They had become active in the Chabad movement, returning to the practice of their faith after seventy years of anti-Semitic oppression. There was a photo of the terrorist site but none of the victims. Their names were listed and their ages.

"Chabad, Chabad," Tolya mumbled. "I'm gonna need some specialized help with this." He picked up his cell phone and searched for Shalom Rothman's number. The phone rang twice before Shalom picked up.

"Rabbi Rothman."

"Shalom, it's Tolya."

"How are you, detective?"

"Fine. I told you, it's OK to call me Tolya."

Shalom laughed. "I know how much you like to be referred to as detective."

Tolya chuckled as well. "I'm never going to live that down, am I?"

"No," Shalom said. "To what do I owe the honor?"

"I need some help. Do you have any connections with the Chabad?"

"Sure, why?"

"I need some information." Tolya explained to Shalom the details of the bizarre murder in Israel and its possible connection to the case on Wadsworth Avenue. "Can you find out if they have any information or, even better, photos of these people?"

"I'll call someone as soon as we get off. Tolya, what did you say the last name was again?"

"There are two. Portnoy and Hayat. They changed the name when they emigrated."

"That's an odd choice of a new name," Shalom said.

"Why?"

"Usually immigrants to Israel pick names like ben Ami, son of my people, or ben Barak, man of strength. Hayat means tailor in Hebrew. You know, like a guy who fixes suits."

"So does Portnoy in Russian," Tolya said.

"Well that makes sense now. See, detective, you've taught me something today."

"Glad to be of service, rabbi."

"And here's an interesting little piece of historical information for you, a former Russian yourself. A lot of Jewish Communists took Russian names after the revolution in 1917. Their name was probably Schneider or Schneiderman before. Schneider means tailor in Yiddish."

Tolya swallowed hard. It couldn't be more than a coincidence. Karin's new benefactor was named Schneider, but he was from Germany—East Germany, to be exact—not Israel or Russia, and he wasn't a Jew.

"Did you say Schneider, Shalom?"

"Yes, why?"

"No reason," Tolya replied. He took a deep breath. "Just very interesting."

"Will I be seeing you tomorrow night at your wife's event?"

"Yes, as long as she hasn't divorced me by then. See you." Tolya clicked off his cell phone. "Portnoy, Hayat, Schneider, all too weird," he mumbled.

"What did you say, Tolya?" Pete asked, returning to their office.

Tolya looked at Pete. "How did Natan Hayat, aka Portnoy, kill a young Arab prostitute, and so viciously, if he himself had already been murdered by Arab terrorists?" He decided to wait before telling Pete about the name thing. Even he realized it was reaching.

"Tol, what are you talking about?"

Tolya filled him in on what he had just learned.

"Hermano, that's a strange one. Can't be the same guy. Probably a screw up by their department."

"Bro, if there's one thing the Israeli's don't screw up, it's anything relating to crime or the military. So, what did you find?"

"The P.O. Box is registered to a law firm, Shorn & Robrich, located at 50 Broadway. The contact person for the box is one Lori Walsh."

"Do you think we should call or make a visit?" Tolya asked.

"A visit, definitely. Let's not give Lori a chance to slip out the back door."

The windows of Shorn & Robrich on the 33rd floor of 50 Broadway faced west. Pete and Tolya stood at the window. They watched silently as workers unfurled a banner across the parapet of a building several blocks away that read: 2 Liberty Place, Hi-Rise Luxury on the Edge of the Capital of the World. "Who do you think lives like that?" Tolya asked Pete.

"Not us, for sure."

"Detectives," said a voice from behind them.

"Yes," they both said.

"I'm Robert Shorn," a short, well-dressed man said, his hand extended to greet them.

"I'm Detective Kurchenko and this is Detective Gonzalvez."

"How can I help you?"

"We'd like to speak with an employee of yours, Lori Walsh."

"Yes, I know, the receptionist told me. I'm afraid Ms. Walsh is not available at the moment."

"What does Ms. Walsh do here?" Pete asked.

"Ms. Walsh is a paralegal in the corporate department of the firm."

"So, she's kind of a secretary then?" Tolya said.

"Let's say: more than a secretary, less than a lawyer," Shorn replied then looked at his watch. "Again, what is it you need to speak to her about?"

Tolya glanced at Pete and half smiled.

"Is this going to take some time?" the attorney asked.

"That depends on you," Pete replied.

Shorn walked to the head of the conference table and sat in the large black leather chair. "Again, gentleman, how can I help you?"

"We are conducting a murder investigation…"

"I can assure you, Ms. Walsh hasn't killed anyone."

"We didn't say she had," Tolya continued. "As I was saying, we are conducting a murder investigation and the trail of evidence has led us to a privately held corporation. Apparently, you are the registered agent for this corporation, or at least your firm is, and the person to whom inquiries are to be directed is Ms. Walsh."

"May I see those please?" Shorn asked, pointing to the papers Tolya held in his hand.

"Of course."

Shorn reached for the papers and examined them. "OK. So, what is it you'd like to know?"

"We just need to know the ownership behind these corporations."

"I can't divulge that information without getting permission from our client, detectives."

"I'm afraid ownership information isn't protected by privilege, Mr. Shorn. Here's a warrant for your files."

Shorn examined the warrant. He sighed. "Wait here for me, please." He got up from the leather chair and walked toward the door. "Shit," he mumbled under his breath.

Tolya pointed to the hastily drawn chart he had tacked to the bulletin board in the captain's office. "This umbrella corporation, Pobeda, which means 'victory' in Russian, is the sole owner of these other corporations, Pobeda 1 through 10. As you can see from what I've listed under each corporation, not all ten subcorps own assets at any given time, yet all have owned assets at one time or another. For the time being, we are interested in subcorps 1, 4, 7 and 8. Subcorp 1 was the investor in the gentleman's club on 12th Avenue. Subcorp 4 owns the apartment at the Bolivar. Subcorp 7 owns the investment in the strip club in Edgewater. Subcorp 8 is the only other with a current asset, a house in Bay Ridge, Brooklyn. Subcorp 10 was recently formed and has some pending activity."

"Do we know what it is?" the captain asked.

"I'm waiting to hear back from the State Attorney General's office."

"The lawyer wouldn't tell you anything?"

"Less than cooperative," Pete said.

"Who owns the parent corporation?" the captain asked.

Tolya slapped Mariela's Russian passport they found the first day of the investigation on the captain's desk. "Nicholai Gruschkin," he said. "The same name as we found in Mariela's Russian passport, Gruschkina."

"Who is this guy?" the captain asked.

"We don't know, but we're assuming he lives in that house in Bay Ridge. And that's the next stop."

Chapter
19

WASHINGTON HEIGHTS, NYC
9 JUNE 2010
5:30 P.M.

I WAS BOTH ELATED AND IRRITATED by the call from my attorney. Kurchenko circling. He was getting closer, only he didn't know to whom. I, on the other hand, had waited for this moment for years, for decades—since that day in the pool when his brother got lucky and, with one punch, knocked me off balance and my ear caught against the metal strip, gashing it. For years I wore my hair long, over the ears, to cover that up.

And then of course there was the matter of my father and his father, the one always a half step ahead of the other—in school, in sport, in the party. How could a stinking Jew always end up a half step ahead? But then I remember how happy my father was that day when he came home after supervising their exit. He inspected every item they intended to take with them. Anything he could deprive them of, he did. He laughed as he told us how the mother cried when he took the velvet piano cover away from them that her grandmother had embroidered. It meant nothing to us, so he left it in that fine apartment we abandoned after the fire in the dacha.

Ah, my father. I am so much like him, yet so different. I can scheme like him. I can be ruthless like him, only more so. I can be even more heartless. Yet I am capable of much more finesse and culture. He was a kulak, born in the fields. I, on the other hand, was privileged to be raised in the lap of Soviet luxury. I am the new Soviet man. Sadly, I may be the last.

I looked around the first floor of my house in Brooklyn and then stepped out toward the Japanese garden. I took a breath of the warm spring air. The sunlight streamed through the Japanese red maples onto the slate patio. I sat down for a moment in my large chair. I would miss the solemnity of this place and I knew I had best get out of here before Kurchenko and his partner showed up, as they certainly would. I lay back for a minute and closed my eyes to run through my plans one more time. I had a moment of déjà vu, back to those days so many years ago. What was it now, fifteen years, a little more, the last time I had planned something this intricate?

Our life had been very difficult. I had no choice but to adjust to it. After our six weeks in the absorption center, we were assigned an apartment in the south of Tel Aviv. The area was rundown and unsafe but cheap and peopled by many guest workers and poor Jews, mostly from North Africa.

The Moroccan boys taunted my sister. She had stopped dying her hair black. Her natural blond color had returned. At first, they tried to romance her and then, when her lack of interest became clear to them, they became more aggressive, frightening her. One night, I waited in the shadows after she returned from work in the factory she had been assigned to. As she passed, they called after her, vile insults and hand gestures.

I waited till the first two of the three had left, then I crept up behind the third as he smoked his cheap cigarette under the streetlamp. I brought my blade to his neck and held his arm behind his back. He struggled at first, so I cut him ever so slightly, enough to bring a drop of blood and a pulse to his neck. Then I told him in my broken Hebrew that if he bothered her again, I would find him in his bed and slice much deeper. He vomited on his shoes. She had no more problems after that.

I did though. The feel of the blade in my hand against his neck brought it all back for me. I felt myself become aroused each time I thought of it. I was gratified and horrified at the same time. How could that act with a man have the same effect on me as it did with a woman? I was not a homosexual. To the contrary, I hated homosexuals and their unnatural inclinations.

I determined to find myself a test case. I spied the neighborhood during the day. I considered my options. I could choose a poor Jewish girl, romance her, develop her trust, then make her disappear. That would be difficult in this society. The parents were in the middle of everything. I would have to get to know the family, and when their daughter ceased to return home, I would be the first they would point a finger at.

A foreign worker would be better, easier. And there was no shortage of them. The Zionist dream had, shall we say, matured. No longer did the Jewish people long for a normal society, where the police, the thief and the victim would all be Jewish, as we had been taught in the absorption center. No, rather, the Jewish people now longed to be Americans, middle-class Americans with suburban lives and hi-tech jobs. No one wanted their child to be a waitress or a bus driver. So, like their Arab archenemies, they imported labor from poor nations in Asia, Africa and Latin America to clean toilets and park cars. Our neighborhood was full of them.

I met Liya on the bus. She was tiny and demure. Her dark hair and brown skin could have passed her for a North African Jew, but the folds in her eyes belied her as East Asian. She spoke broken Hebrew, as did I. She lived in a room she rented from an old Jewish couple whose children had moved to the United States. She was alone here, adrift. She had escaped the wrath of her family when she ran away from the abusive husband they had married her off to at 14. She would never go back to Manila. She worked as a maid in the Sheraton at the northern end of Tel Aviv. Someday, somehow, she hoped to go to America.

For a few days, I would smile at her. At first, she averted her eyes from mine. After about a week, she smiled back. I continued to take the bus when I knew she would be on her way to work, but not every day. After another week or so, I spoke to her. "How are you today?" I asked.

"Tov me'od," she said. Hebrew for "very good." She smiled, then turned away.

A few days later, I tried to expand the conversation. I asked her name, where she was from. She smiled shyly and answered, "Liya, ani Filipina."

I avoided the bus for a couple of days. The next time I saw her, she smiled and spoke to me. "Shalom. Ma nishma?" she asked.

"Kol b'seder," I said and sat down next to her.

"Where are you from?" she asked me.

"Russia," I said. "My name is Nicholai." I refused to use Natan, the Hebrew name my father assigned to me. I waited to ask her the next question till we neared her stop. "Would you like to have a coffee with me sometime?"

She blushed, then smiled. "Yes," she said. She rose from her seat and left the bus. I waited two more days before riding with her again. She smiled broadly when she saw me. I asked her for her number and we made a date to meet the following day at Dizengoff Square in the center of the city.

From that day till the kill was two weeks. I gave her what she needed, an antidote to her loneliness. She opened up to me like a blooming flower. I would meet her after work, walk with her in the plazas and gardens of Tel Aviv. We would share an iced coffee and a pastry. She told me about her life, about the loneliness she thought at times would overtake her. She told me about the foreign men who would proposition her and the Israeli men who would bother her on the street. She told me how much she loved my blond hair and how she felt safe with me because I was so gentle with her. And then one day, on a quiet deserted street near the beach, I stopped in mid-step and kissed her gently on the lips. She sighed and kissed me back.

"Do you want to make love with me?" she asked.

"Yes," I whispered in her ear. "Come with me now."

She averted her eyes from mine and nodded. I took her hand and led her one block east to HaYarkon Street. I hailed a taxi and gave him my address.

"Where are we going?" she asked.

"There is a vacant apartment in my building," I said. "The door is open."

She kissed me again and snuggled closer to me in the back of the cab. I felt the old energy flow back into me. I felt alive for the first time since the night we burned the dacha.

I brought Liya to the vacant apartment every night for the next ten days. After the first night, I cleaned the place up a bit and brought a mattress and some pillows, which I left on the floor of the second bedroom. I put a padlock on the door, but no one seemed to notice. How unobservant these people are. Or perhaps they just don't care.

A few days into our affair, I introduced some playthings into our lovemaking—ropes and a small knife, which I held at her throat. She took to the role-playing quickly. I knew I didn't have much time. The apartment would be rented sooner or later. At the end of the first week, I drew blood from her neck as we made love, me holding her from behind. She winced at first, then moaned in ecstasy as she reached her climax, the cold steel against her neck, her warm, thick blood seeping out of the tiny cut. One week later as she reached climax, I plunged the blade into her neck, slicing her vocal cords on the first cut. I reached a level of orgasm I hadn't experienced in years.

Chapter
20

WASHINGTON HEIGHTS, NYC
9 JUNE 2010
6:30 P.M.

"TOL, TAKE IT EASY," PETE said. They were weaving in and out of traffic. "How many times you gonna try her?"

"Till she picks up. What's the difference?" Tolya said, his eyes staring straight ahead at the building traffic on the BQE heading toward Bay Ridge. "She just won't answer the phone. She's pissed off at me."

"For what?"

"About the guy who came out of nowhere and made the huge donation to the museum."

"Didn't you just have Peña run a check on him and nothing came up?"

"Yeah, nothing. Not one fucking thing. And there's no evidence that he even exists. This guy walked in out of nowhere and wrote a check to the museum for $10,000 after he saw Karin on TV and his name is Schneider."

"So?"

"His name is Schneider."

"And?"

"Remember I told you the murderer's name, it was Portnoy, they changed it to Hayat?"

"Yeah."

"Both those names mean the same thing: tailor. Schneider means tailor in Yiddish."

"Tol. I admit that's a weird coincidence but it's really stretching. And this guy isn't from Israel, is he?"

"No, he's German, or at least he says he is."

"Tol, you gotta calm down."

"I gotta calm down? You've been off the hook since the whole thing started."

"Yo, bro, be careful there. The victim was someone I was once in love with."

"Still in love with."

"Fuck you. Partner or no partner, don't ever fucking talk to me like that. If you weren't driving, I'd slug you."

"Want me to pull over?" Tolya said, swerving the car into the right lane and onto the shoulder then slamming on the brakes.

"You fucking crazy?" Pete screamed, balling his fists. Tolya turned toward him and grabbed his right arm. His face was red, veins bulging on his forehead. "OK, OK," Pete said. He could see how out of control Tolya was. "Tol, stop, I was wrong."

Tolya relaxed his grip on Pete. "Sorry, it's just…"

"I got it, bro. Look, the alleged perp in Tel Aviv was already dead when the girl was killed. They screwed up. You're building a story here that makes no sense. And also, she's an ex-cop, she can take care of herself."

"She's my wife," Tolya screamed. "I think the guy's a stalker, at best." Pete wanted to slug him? At moments like this, he wanted to slug Pete, but he held himself back. He couldn't hit him. He knew Pete had his back, always. And Karin's. "And she's an ex-cop? It's been a few years and now she's nine months pregnant."

"Wow, hermano, calm down. I didn't mean anything by it."

"That's my wife, and my child," he shouted, slamming his fist into the dashboard.

Pete put his hand on Tolya's forearm. "OK, OK. I got it, man, I understand. Tranqui. We'll get her on the phone. I'll try her myself."

Karin leaned over her desk, examining the final documents outlining the schedule for tomorrow's events. She was more comfortable standing than sitting at this point. Oleg was growing quickly and getting more uncomfortable every day. Her feet were a little swollen, but she would stand as long as she could. "Lindsay," she called out.

"Yes," Lindsay replied, sticking her head into the doorway.

"Did we make the final arrangements for transportation for tomorrow night?"

"I was waiting for you to tell me if you wanted to go with Triple 7 or if you were going to call Mr. Schneider and take him up on his offer for the four cars."

Karin stood up straight, stretching her back a bit to relieve the ache. "OK, decision time. Give me two minutes." Karin picked up her cell phone. Tolya's number was listed in unanswered calls seven times. She was still furious with him and going to make a point. She was no kid, no neophyte. He could take his macho bullshit and put it where the sun don't shine. Who did he think he was anyway? She'd risen higher and faster in the department than he had. And he knew damn well that today was the day before the opening. She didn't have time for his antics and paranoia.

She scanned her desk for Benjamin Schneider's card and punched his number into her phone. It rang twice before he picked up.

"Madame Kurchenko," came the deep, throaty, accented voice.

Karin laughed. "Hello, Benjamin. Please stop calling me that."

Schneider laughed. "It's my stiff German upbringing, I'm afraid. How are you?"

"Well, thank you."

"Can I be of some assistance or is this a social call?"

"I've decided to take you up on your offer of transportation for the guests." As Karin said this, the call waiting tone interrupted the conversation. "Benjamin, could you hold a moment please, I'm getting another call." She looked at the number and the caller ID. Pete. He had to be kidding. She wouldn't answer so he had Pete call her? She sent Pete's call to voicemail.

"Benjamin, sorry," she said.

"Nothing wrong, I hope?"

"No, not at all. We will need four cars at 5 p.m."

"No problem at all. Please have Lindsay send the address or addresses to my phone. I will make the arrangements personally."

"Yes."

"And the limo for you?"

"I've decided that would be a good idea too."

"I look forward to seeing you tomorrow night," Schneider said.

"As do I, you." Karin clicked off the phone. There was a message from Pete. She clicked to listen. It was in Spanish.

"What the hell did you just tell her?" Tolya asked, slamming his hand against the steering wheel this time.

"Hermano, calm down. It was just a little Dominicano a Dominicana, that's all. I was just giving her a little shit for not calling you back."

"That's not what I wanted you to do."

"Then what did you want?"

Tolya hesitated. "I'm not sure. I want her to stay away from that guy."

"Then tell her that when you get home. She's your wife, she's gotta listen to you."

"Shit, Pete, gimme a fucking break. How many years you know her? Longer than you know me. She doesn't listen to anyone unless she damn well feels like it."

"I know she's tough, man, but you love her and you gotta take this slow with her. She was always like that. No pushover."

"I know. I married her. I've been living with this shit for years. She doesn't defer to me like my mother did my father."

"Hermano, they never do, not the ones you get loco for. That's why we run after them."

"True, man." Tolya took a deep breath as he braked. The traffic slowed as they neared La Guardia Airport on the Grand Central Parkway. "You know, I love her more now than I did the first time I kissed her."

"I know what you mean, man." Pete stared off toward Flushing Bay. He bit his lip for a moment. "I had a love like that once."

Tolya slowed the car as the traffic slowed further. He turned toward Pete. Pete let out a long, slow sigh. "Tol, there's something I haven't told you."

"Pete, it's been a long day…"

"Tol, I didn't think it mattered till last night. It's something you gotta know. You remember that Christmas just after we became partners?"

Chapter
21

WASHINGTON HEIGHTS, NYC
23 DECEMBER 2002
6:30 P.M.

P ETE FELT FREE AND A little lonely at the same time. This was
the first Christmas in ten years he was without Glynnis and the
kids. She had been promising her grandparents in Santo Domingo she
would visit for the holidays for years. This year, her parents were going
with her sister and her sister's kids. Pete had planned to go with them,
but with a new partner, he couldn't take two weeks off.

He didn't know what to do with himself. He took the train down
to Rockefeller Center and walked around. He hadn't bought Glynnis
a present yet, but he felt like he had to get it before Christmas, even
though she was away. He walked down Sixth Avenue to Macy's. The
crowds were terrible but, in some way, he felt more alone than he had
in a decade. No one to go home to, nothing to take care of.

He entered Macy's at 35th Street and Broadway, dodged the women
with spray bottles of cologne and strolled slowly among the counters—
watches, earrings, necklaces, every conceivable kind of jewelry. He
stopped at the watch counter. Out of the corner of his eye, he saw

the saleswoman check him out and approach him slowly, her arms crossed against her chest. He tilted his head slightly in her direction and cracked a half smile. Her face lit up. It worked every time.

"May I help you?" she said.

Pete straightened up. "Sure." He slipped his hands behind him into his back pockets. "I'm looking for a watch for my sister."

"What does she like?"

"Something... trendy."

"How lucky she is to have a brother who pays attention to what she wants. How old is she?"

"She's 20."

The saleswoman took a key from her pocket and opened the door to the back of the glass showcase. She drew out a board lined with blue felt and placed it on the counter. There were about twenty watches, most of them with large round faces and leather straps. She pointed to one with small diamonds around the face. "How about this?"

Pete put his hand on the counter and leaned in. "That looks expensive," he said. "I'm a cop..."

The saleswoman placed her hand over his. "I'll tell you a secret, officer."

"Yeah, what?" he asked and smiled broadly.

She leaned over and whispered, "They're cubic zirconium. Look just like diamonds, she'll never know."

The scent of the saleswoman's perfume was enticing. "I specialize in 'she'll never know,'" he whispered in her ear.

"That's good to know," she said, straightening up. "Why don't you look around the store? Here's my card, you can call me if I'm not at the counter."

"Thanks," Pete said, taking her hand in his, the card slipping into his palm.

Pete looked across the aisle. He wasn't sure at first. Her hair was lighter and she appeared taller than he remembered. She had on sunglasses so it was impossible to see her eyes. He let go of the saleswoman's hand and walked away without another word. He crossed one of the large aisles that dissected Macy's into thirds. For some reason, Latino Christmas music was playing throughout the store. Hard salsa, the kind they had danced to in Santo Domingo. He was sure it was her. As he approached, she lifted her head and tilted it slightly to the right. She took off her glasses. Her eyes were the same, black irises ringed with gold.

"Hola, mi amor," he said.

She hesitated at first, turning her head to the right and putting her sunglasses in the pocket of her bag.

"Mariela?" Pete said.

She smiled weakly and walked toward him. "Sí, soy yo," she said in a low voice. He moved forward to kiss her on the cheek. She pulled back.

"Que pasa?" he asked.

"Let's speak English," she said, her speech almost devoid of any accent.

"OK, English. How are you?"

"I'm well," she replied. "And you?"

"Better now. You look fantastic."

"Thanks," she said, finally smiling. "So do you."

He moved a little closer. "Thanks. No one ever tells me that."

"How's Glynnis? And the kids?"

"They're OK. They're in Santo Domingo with her family for the holidays. I've got four now."

"Wow, four. How come you didn't go with them?"

"I just got a new partner, a Russian guy, he's a trip."

She took the strap of her bag and slung it over her shoulder. "It was nice seeing you, Pete," she said and stuck out her hand.

"No, Mariela, wait. I'm alone. Have dinner with me."

"I couldn't, we shouldn't," she said, withdrawing her hand.

"Please?"

Mariela buttoned her coat, the fur collar framing her face. She walked around Pete and headed toward the exit. Pete stood there staring after her. He tried to keep her in his sight as she pushed through the crowd. Just short of the exit, she stopped. He leaped forward at a trot, pushing through the crowd, reaching her just as she took the final step to the door. "Please, Mariela."

She turned and smiled. He noticed a tear in her eye. "OK, but just dinner and just tonight."

They went to a little Italian place off Ninth Avenue. Pete knew the owner from his days as a beat cop on the Upper West Side. The owner had another restaurant on West 83rd Street off Amsterdam.

They sat in back in a tiny booth for two. Mariela's eyes, those same eyes Pete had fallen in love with ten years earlier, sparkled in the candlelight. After a glass of wine, she let him hold her hand.

"Are you married?" Pete asked.

"No," Mariela replied.

"Boyfriend?"

"I thought we agreed no personal questions."

"Mariela, I have to know. I have to know you're all right."

"I'm all right. No, no boyfriend," she lied. "I go to work and I go home."

"You also go to Macy's."

She laughed. "And sometimes I go shopping. No questions."

"No questions." He paused for a moment. "Then what are we going to talk about?"

"Baseball?"

They both laughed. "You know I never gave a shit for baseball," Pete said.

"Then you're the only Dominican man ever who didn't."

Pete took her free hand in his. "Do you ever miss it?"

"Miss what?"

"Santo Domingo."

Mariela's body tightened. Her smile disappeared. "Miss what? My parents have been dead for over fifteen years. Polito and Henrietta? Yes, I miss Henrietta, but it's too painful to think about. It was like losing my mother twice. Polito? He was a bastard. I don't care what happens to him. He did what he did to save his own skin, not mine and not his daughters. He dragged you into it to use us to get himself out."

"I know that. But why did you run away from us?"

"I had to get away. I had to forget all that pain."

"Will you at least tell me where you live?"

She hesitated for a moment. "No."

"Why?"

"You know why. If you know, you'll try to find me."

"No I won't."

"Yes you will, because if things were good between you and Glynnis, we wouldn't be here right now."

Pete let go of her hands. "It's not like that." He sat back in the booth. "Did you love me?"

Mariela sighed. "There is a price for everything. Each of us has our own destiny."

"But did you love me?"

She weakened. In the dim light, he could see her staring far off into the past. "Amor, it was you, it was always you." She laughed. "It still is."

"We could still be together."

"You know that's not possible. My life is very complicated now and I would never separate you from your family."

The waiter came with the first course and put the plates down on the table. "Would you like another bottle of wine?" he asked.

Pete looked at Mariela. "Sí," she said. The waiter nodded, took the empty bottle and left them.

"Let's just enjoy this evening, Pedrito. Feliz Navidad, mi amor."

Pete touched the rim of his glass to hers. "Feliz Navidad, mi vida."

After dinner, Pete asked her to walk with him for a few blocks to the subway. She took his arm. They strolled like lovers. When they arrived at the subway, he turned to her and put his arm around her waist. "Thank you," he said. He leaned into her to kiss her cheek. She turned her head and kissed him gently on the lips. He lingered there for a moment, then pulled her to him. She kissed him again, only this time harder and deeper with passion. "Don't leave me," he whispered in her ear.

Her breath felt warm and moist against his neck. She whispered back to him, "Take me with you."

He kissed her again, gently, softly. "Is that what you want?"

"Yes," she mumbled. "That's what I've always wanted."

He took her by the hand and led her away from the subway entrance and hailed a cab.

"Where to?" asked the cabby.

"180, between Broadway and Ft. Washington," he said.

"Take the highway?" the cabbie asked.

"Go any way you want, but get there as fast as possible."

He put his arm around Mariela. She sank into him. Her cheek touched his, her flesh cold from the winter air. She turned toward him and kissed him again. "I know this is wrong," she said.

"I don't care," Pete said in between kisses.

"Neither do I."

The next three days were like magic. They made love like teenagers, exploring each other's bodies as if they had never known each other. Pete called in sick. His new partner was pissed off, but hey why not start breaking him in now? This was how Pete operated. Might as well get him used to it.

They stayed in the apartment all day. They made love and watched TV and ordered in some food from Mambí on Broadway and 175th Street. In the afternoon, Pete went to the market on St. Nicholas Avenue. Mariela gave him a list. She would make him a traditional Dominican Christmas meal: pernil, arroz con gandules, maduros. He bought a brazo de gitano at the Dominican bakery.

They talked about Santo Domingo and their childhoods, the people they had known then, the ones who had died and the ones who had gotten away. He filled her in on Imelda and Katarina. She cried a little when she asked about them. That was so hard for her. They had been like her sisters. She had no choice, she had to move on or she would have gone mad.

He asked her about her life more than once, but she would change the subject. In the middle of the night between Christmas Eve and Christmas Day, she told him she was involved, that she had lied to him about being single. "I'm engaged," she said, magnifying the lie to push him away a little further. "I have a fiancé. He's away on business and he'll be back before New Year's."

"Then why aren't you wearing a ring?"

She hesitated and looked away from him. She didn't want to make eye contact, fearing he would see the lie in her eyes. "It's too large. I'm afraid to wear it in the streets."

"What kind of guy goes away at Christmas without his fiancé?"

"One whose god is money."

"Is that what you want? Who you want?" he asked.

"That's who I have," she answered and refused to discuss it further.

"It's not too late for us," he said.

"Yes it is."

Pete got out of the bed and moved toward the window in the darkened room. Mariela came up behind him and put her arms around his waist. She reached up and ran her hands over his chest. He felt an ecstasy he never felt with Glynnis, with any woman he'd made love to. And there had been many, more than he could count. A terrible pang of sadness and guilt overwhelmed him for a moment. He pushed it out of his mind. This was his moment and he was meant to live it. He knew it had always been Mariela. Every other woman was an attempt to replace her, to reach the place he reached with her. He took her hands from him and turned. She wrapped her arms around him again. He felt the cool draft of air through the old windowpane against his back. He said nothing because there was nothing he could say without exploding.

"Please, Pedrito, what we did here was wrong. We both know that. Let's not make it worse. Let's just enjoy each other for tonight and for tomorrow. I'll have to leave tomorrow night."

He nodded in the darkness, too defeated to speak. He picked her up, her body light in his arms, and carried her back to the bed. He laid her on top of the down comforter, bent over her and kissed her. He felt the tears seep out of his closed eyes as they kissed.

"Amor," she said. "Don't cry, make love to me again."

They made love, the act more intense than either had ever known. Afterward, Pete held Mariela in his arms all night as she slept. He fought sleep, kept his eyes open. He wanted to remember every moment of this night for the rest of his life, as he knew it would be the last night he would ever spend with her. Toward morning, he finally gave in and closed his eyes, Mariela's body next to his, her scent intoxicating him as he drifted away, happier than at any moment in his memory.

Chapter
22

WASHINGTON HEIGHTS, NYC
9 JUNE 2010
6:00 P.M.

T OLYA WAS SPEECHLESS FOR A moment. He sped up the
Harlem River Drive. "I'm not sure what to say. I might start with:
Is there anything else you've forgotten to tell me?"

"Yep," Pete replied.

"And what's that?" Tolya said, slowing the car at the light at
Amsterdam Avenue and 179th Street. "Please, tell me now."

"I think her daughter might be mine."

Tolya made the right as the light changed, pulled the car over to the
curb and stopped. "Seriously, Pete."

"I am serious, Tol. Think about the timeline. The kid appears to
be about 6 or 7 in that picture from Disneyworld that we found. I
saw Mariela in December 2002. She would have been born about
September or October 2003."

"Pete, yo. Look, I'm going to have to say this. I'd never hurt you.
You're like a brother to me. I know how much you loved this woman.
But she was a prostitute. There's no telling how many men she slept

with. That child could belong to anyone. And she told you she had a fiancé. The child could be his."

Pete looked at Tolya, then shifted his gaze out the window. The rooftops of the west Bronx stretched into the distance, water towers and TV antennae mimicking little jagged peaks on their summits.

That day in the countryside on their drive back from Samaná flashed before his eyes. That moment, as he looked into Mariela's eyes, the peaks of the Cordillera Central behind her, the sound of the legless bachata guitarist in his ears. He leaned in and kissed her, the sweetness of the coconut flan still on her lips. That was his moment. That was the moment he knew the purest, truest happiness in his life.

He turned back toward Tolya, the tears that had fallen from his eyes now on his cheeks. "I know it, Tol. I just know it. It has to be. It's the only reason she would have lived inside me all these years. Tol, we have to find that child."

Tolya thought his heart would break. He tried to speak but choked up. After Karin and the kids, no one and nothing meant more to him than Pete. Pete saved his life more than a few times, literally and figuratively. He was the brother he had lost in the snows of Siberia thirty-five years earlier. There was nothing he wouldn't do for him. "We will, Pete," he said. "I promise you. But first we have to find Mariela's killer. Before he kills again."

Tolya dropped Pete off at his apartment, put the car back at the station house and headed home. He was disturbed by what Pete had said. Though it was entirely possible that Mariela's child could be Pete's, he doubted it. He was concerned that the case had gotten to Pete, that he wasn't thinking rationally. He didn't want to ask him to step aside but, at the same time, he needed Pete to be at his sharpest and he was beginning to doubt that he was.

Tolya slipped the key into the apartment door. Screams of "Daddy! Daddy!" came immediately from the living room, followed by a stampede of tiny feet. "Hello, sons," he said as they grabbed his legs. "Hop on." The boys wrapped themselves around his legs. Tolya put his arms out in front of him. "Time for the Frankenstein walk," he said, moving slowly down the hallway toward the living room.

As he neared the two steps into the living room, he saw Karin sitting in the corner of the black leather couch. She put the ledger she was reviewing down on the coffee table and looked up at him. "How are you?" she said. "You look tired."

"I am. OK, everybody off. Last stop."

The boys groaned.

"Guys, I'm really tired. Go into your room. I'll be in in a few minutes."

"OK, Dad," Max said, letting go of Tolya's leg. Erno quickly followed suit.

Tolya took the two steps into the living room and sat down at the end of the couch. "I think we need to talk."

Karin sat up straight. She sighed. "Yes, I think we do. Let me start. I'm sorry I didn't pick up your calls today. I was really angry with you. I felt you were getting involved in something that was making me feel small and incompetent. Then you had Pete call and that pissed me off even further."

"But?"

"As is always the case with Pete, his message was so charming, I began to forgive you."

Tolya hesitated a moment. He smiled then chuckled. "I don't know what this power Pete has over women is, but I wish I could bottle it and sell it."

"Amazing, isn't it?" Karin said. "We could all retire."

"Nevertheless, I think we have a big problem."

"With?"

"Your boyfriend."

"Ach, Tolya, don't call him that." Karin got up off the couch. She picked up the throw pillow and threw it onto the club chair. "You see, that's just belittling and it indicates that you don't respect me or my abilities."

"OK, Karin. I'm sorry, that was out of line. It's not at all like that. I respect you, more than you know. I'm also very worried about who this guy might be. We've had a major break in the case and I'm more than a little concerned that your guy is involved."

"What? How?"

"We had some partial prints from the case in Israel that mirrors this one. The name that matched to those prints is Hayat. He was a Russian immigrant to Israel."

"What does that have to do with anything?" Karin interrupted him. "And I might remind you, my contributor is from Germany, East Germany, to be exact. And he's not Jewish. Where is this Israeli now?"

"Well, that's the problem, it appears he's dead."

Karin stopped dead in her tracks. She crossed her arms against her chest.

"Karin, please listen to me. Hayat changed his name from Portnoy when he arrived in Israel. Portnoy means tailor in Russian, Hayat means tailor in Hebrew, Schneider means tailor in Yiddish and German."

She took several deep breaths. Tolya knew this wasn't going to be good.

"You've got to be kidding me. You're out of control over a dead man? Do you think in some way his spirit has taken control of my contributor's mind and body because they share the same name in four different languages?"

"Karin, please, just listen to me. I love you and I'm worried. Something isn't right here. I have a bad feeling about this. People take on new identities all the time. Let me ask you a question. Are both this guy's eyes the same color?"

Karin looked at Tolya dumbfounded. "What?"

"Please, just listen to me. Are his eyes the same color?"

"Honestly, I haven't looked that closely, but I think I would have noticed if they weren't."

"Tomorrow I'll have some photos, hopefully. We'll know for sure if your guy is clear. Just give me a little time. Stay away from him till then please."

Karin closed her eyes to control herself. She took a couple of deep breaths again. "Anatoly Kurchenko," she said, the same way his mother used to when he was a little boy, "this discussion is over. If you want to chase ghosts, you go ahead and do that. But unless you drop this whole thing, don't bother coming to the opening party tomorrow night." She turned and walked out of the room.

Tolya stood up, not quite sure what to do next. He turned to follow her into the bedroom, determined to make her understand. Before he reached the double steps into the foyer, Karin reappeared, his blanket and pillow in hand. "Tonight, you can sleep out here. But first, go into your sons' room and put them to sleep. They've been waiting for you all evening."

She turned and walked back down the hallway, stopping in front of the boys' room. "Good night, my darlings," she said, kissing both of them on their heads. "Mommy has a big day tomorrow so she's going to bed now. Daddy is coming in to read to you, then it's off to sleep for you as well." She continued down the hall and closed the bedroom door a little more loudly than necessary.

Chapter 23

I ADJUSTED TO LIFE IN THE slums. My adjustment was made easier with the resumption of my old hobby. I have to admit, though, that I had been sloppy with that first kill. But then, I was out of practice. I left the body in a plastic body bag in a lot in the no-man's-land where Tel Aviv becomes Jaffa. Some dogs got to the bag, and someone saw them and called the police. I had thrown her clothes into the bag with her, as I wasn't sure where to go to burn them. What I didn't know was that in the rear pocket of her pants was a receipt from a dry cleaner near the hotel where she worked. The owner remembered her. From there, it was only a small step to the hotel and her identity. Apparently, they then began tracing her movements to and from work. They began riding the bus route she took.

To my unluckiness—and as I've mentioned before, I am not a lucky fellow—they found a young man who rode the same route every day who was also a sketch artist. That was how he passed the time of his one-hour commute. He not only remembered her but had surreptitiously sketched us kissing and nuzzling in the back of the bus.

One day in the late afternoon, I received a visit from a detective, a certain Amir ben-Shimon, and his Arab partner, an unusual thing in Israel. The Arab's name was Mustafa Kemal. They reminded me of an American TV program that played on Israeli television, Starsky and Hutch. They were equally as ridiculous.

"How can I help you?" I asked in my still heavily accented, broken Hebrew.

They asked if they could come in. My mother was in the kitchen. My dimwitted brother was watching TV in the living room. I didn't want to take any additional chances. "Officers," I said, "might we go across the street to the little park and talk there?"

"Of course," they said.

As we crossed the street into the park, I spotted the Moroccan kid I had threatened over my sister. He smirked when he saw me sit down at the vacant concrete chess table with the two officers. He must have been the one who told them where I lived. I would take care of him at some future, more opportune time.

The Arab pulled a photo from an envelope. "Do you know this woman?" he said.

My heart raced but I kept my smile on my face. The photo was worn and slightly crumpled. I wondered how they had gotten it. "No," I replied.

"Then how do you account for this?" The Jew said, placing the drawing of us kissing in front of me on the chessboard.

I looked at the drawing. I was surprised to see it, but didn't want to betray my panic. I smiled. "What a lovely drawing."

"Is that you?"

"No."

"People around here seem to think it looks enough like you to have identified you."

"It's not me," I repeated.

"Do you take the bus to work every day?"

"No," I said. "Sadly, I can't work." This was only half a lie. "I have a small disability." I had paid off a low-level employee in the Absorption Ministry to get me a work deferment and disability for two years.

"You don't work?"

"No, so I don't take that bus every day, although I do take it sometimes."

The detectives exchanged a glance. The Jew handed me his card. "We may want to speak with you again."

"At your service." As they walked away, I heard the Jew mumble to the Arab. "Lazy Russian bastards. Who needs them here anyway?"

And it was easy to find my victims. There was no shortage of poor women, Israeli, Arab or foreign, walking the streets of south Tel Aviv. The easiest were the women from my former homeland. Even if they came from the constituent republics, they spoke some Russian. I yearned to hear the sound of it, so gentle and soft as opposed to the harsh, guttural Hebrew. I lost track of the number of women I consumed in my spare time. I did not get sloppy again. I disposed of the bodies well. I had learned from my father how to make a body disappear. No one was looking for these women anyway.

One day, my father came to me in my tiny room in our run-down flat. "Follow me," he said. I did as I was instructed. Even now, all these years later, I had come to accept that it was better to follow his instructions than challenge him. I followed him down the stairs and out of the building.

We walked a few blocks to a small park. There were children playing in the dusty, sandy, grassless soil. He signaled to me to sit down on a nearby bench.

"Nicholai," he said, calling me by my given name. "I have something to discuss with you. This is to be kept to ourselves. Not even your mother knows. Your half-witted brother is to know nothing of this."

I couldn't imagine what nonsense he would bother me with now. In the two years since our arrival, he had become a bit crazy. Or perhaps he always was. He was also receiving disability, so he didn't work. He sat around all day dreaming up schemes to get us out of here. I was sure this was just another one. "Yes, Father," I said.

"I have devised a plan to get us out of here."

I looked away and sighed. "What are you saying, Father?"

"I've hidden a great deal of money, you know."

I'd heard that before.

"It has taken me a couple of years, but I have very quietly put all of my assets in one place."

I was tired. Mostly I was tired of living this life. My patience was wearing thin. "Father, please, what are you talking about?"

My father gritted his teeth. "What do you think I've been doing all these years? You think I like living here among these people? You think this is permanent? I stole millions when I was with the KGB. It was hidden in small accounts in Switzerland and Germany. I stole art, jewelry. I hid it well where no one could find it. It's taken a couple of years and many bribes to dispose of it. There is little an art agent won't do for the right commission. I've got everything in one secure place now. We are going to make another move." He sat back against the broken slats of the bench and smiled broadly.

"Really?" I said. I would do anything to leave this place. "What do you need me to do?"

"We are going to disappear again in much the same way as we did the first time."

His plan was interesting. He spent a lot of time listening to the news on the TV and radio. Luckily for him, with the huge influx of immigrants from my beloved homeland, there was plenty of news in Russian on both.

He determined that we, the family, would be the victims of a terrorist attack. The quickest and least suspicious way to do this required us to move to a settlement in the territories. Chabad, with whom we had registered when we arrived from Russia, was constantly offering him opportunities to join any number of new settlements in Judaea and Samaria. We would join one of these, taking residence in a new house at the edge of a settlement. As we did in Russia, we would obtain bodies to substitute for ours, fake a firebombing of the house and let it burn to the ground.

"What if they try to identify the bodies?" I asked him.

"Not a problem," he said. "These Jews bury their dead the same day. They consider autopsy an abomination. They will assume whoever was found in the house had lived there."

"How will we get these bodies?"

"You and I will do that, right here in the slums of Tel Aviv, just shortly before we need the bodies. We're good at that, you and I," he said and smiled, lifting one eyebrow in a very knowing fashion.

I smiled back and nodded my head. "And what ever do you mean by that?"

He was a very cunning man when it came to himself, my father. He was a scavenger. He knew how to squirrel away a portion of the kill for himself while letting others do the work, like a hyena. What he didn't anticipate was that, while I am a carnivore like him, I am also an attack animal, more like a cheetah. I hunt alone and keep my kill to myself.

My father had spent a lifetime in Russia saving scraps. He made the mistake of telling me how he had skimmed his riches off the unfortunate scum he persecuted, and where he had hid his booty. As an agent in the KGB, he had the ability to travel. He also had access to identities. He used both, primarily to set up small bank accounts in private banks in Switzerland, Lichtenstein, Germany and Austria. He also had access to art dealers in Vienna and Paris and Berlin. He had amassed a fortune.

He had changed, though, since our escape. The hours of mental inactivity, the strange culture, and the warm climate had made him go a bit soft in the head. Now, almost giddy with the idea that he would soon be living the life of a rich Russian émigré in Vienna or Berlin, he told me everything. I now knew where everything was hidden and where he kept the account information. I lay in wait now like a cheetah in the tall grass.

The day after he told me about his plan, we went to see the Chabad Jews in their offices in the center of Tel Aviv. I let him do the talking in his combination of Russian and broken Hebrew.

"The family had taken a decision," he said. "We want to return to the true practice of our faith."

They were only too happy to oblige. "Would you be willing to move to a new settlement in the territories?"

"Of course," he said. "How soon could we move?"

"As soon as you want," they said. "We are filling three settlements now."

A month later, we took up residence in Ramat haDatim in our new house on the edge of the desert hills in our new clothes, also supplied by Chabad. My mother looked ridiculous in that wig.

We settled into life in the settlement. There were a few other Russian families, recent immigrants like ourselves, ha ha, which alleviated the language problem to some extent. My mother had others to talk with. My sister, much to her surprise, did not have to work anymore. Orthodox women stay in the home. She was bored but happy. Even this life was preferable to the factory work she had done in Tel Aviv. The other women occupied her with cooking lessons and meetings with eligible young men. She smiled her way through both.

My brother, father and I attended classes for half a day and spent the other half the day doing construction work around the settlement. This was the price we paid for the house and the opportunity to get out of Tel Aviv. The mornings were excruciating. We rose early to attend the morning service. I cringed with every moment of these people reenacting their theological drama three times a day, every day. It required me to learn their customs and become proficient in their language. They wanted to begin instruction in Yiddish as well. I convinced them that I would eventually learn, to let me master Hebrew first.

The afternoons were a bit of a respite. I was outdoors, moving around in the open air. I could breathe without the stench of their bodies and clothing suffocating me. The evenings were yet another psychological standoff. Rare was the night when I was not first dragged to a study session of their holy books, followed by a strictly supervised meeting with potential wives. I had no choice.

This waking nightmare went on for about six months, until my father whispered to me one morning after prayers that he was ready. He had used his days off wisely. He had secured everything we needed to escape—new passports, new visas, new identities—through criminal connections he had made in Tel Aviv, mostly Russian Mafia types. We would collect bodies on a Thursday night after midnight to substitute for our own. One of his Russian criminals had introduced him to the coroner in Jaffa City, an Israeli Arab. They were more corrupt than even the most corrupt Jews.

Friday night, under the protection of their Sabbath, we would fake an attack and escape in the same van in which we would transport the bodies. By Saturday night, we would be in Eilat. He had secured a safe house there. On Sunday, we would slip across the border to Jordan, then on to Amman by car. From Amman, we would fly to our new life in Berlin, all this under the name Grushkin, my mother's maiden name. While my father thought I was going along with him, I, in fact, had my own plans.

Thursday night went without a hitch. We arrived back with the six bodies just before dawn. We hid the van, loaded with the bodies and a good amount of dry ice to keep them from stinking, in a shallow cave in a ravine just south of the settlement. That morning, we informed the family. They were ecstatic.

Friday night arrived in due time. My brother, my father and I came home from evening prayer. My mother and sister had prepared the Sabbath meal as they did every week. I was always completely dumbfounded by the way my family carried on this charade. We had no choice, really. Though we didn't believe in their ancient superstitions, we had to keep up appearances. We never knew when one of the neighbors or one of the rabbis might stop by on Shabbos for a visit.

My father and brother went upstairs to their bedrooms to discard some of the heavy clothing we wore daily to prayers. My brother and I shared a room. I had created the habit of letting him go first, to have some privacy for a few moments. I went into the kitchen. "What is that wonderful smell?" I asked, kissing my mother, then my sister.

"Wild mushrooms and roast chicken," my mother answered.

"Don't the mushrooms contain cream?" I asked, smiling, knowing full well how she prepared them.

"We'll eat them first," my sister answered. "Before any of the neighbors pop in."

We all laughed.

"Go now and change," my mother said.

I walked out of the kitchen through the dining room, stopping briefly at the table. I also had used my free time in Tel Aviv well. I slipped a tiny capsule of tranquilizer into each of the already filled wine glasses at the seats of my parents and siblings. This would put them to sleep slowly and naturally and very deeply so that I might execute my own plan.

Dinner was as usual. My father dominated the conversation with critical tales of all that had happened during the week, interspersed with recollections of his days in the KGB. Shortly after dessert, one of the neighbors stopped by with a box full of little chocolate pastries. His wife asked him to bring them over. He was from Moscow as well and liked to chat about Friday nights there now and then. By 9:00, my parents and sister and brother were yawning uncontrollably, so our neighbor excused himself. By 9:30, they were retiring to nap before our escape, all of them surprised at how tired they were. My father looked at me through bleary eyes. "I need to sleep a little before we do our business tonight," he said. "Wake me at midnight."

"Of course," I answered.

"I'm so tired," he said. "I don't know why."

"Perhaps it was the wine," I suggested.

"Then why are you not tired?" he asked me. "You drank more than I did."

"Anticipation," I said.

"You must learn to control your emotions," he said and turned, climbing the stairs to the bedrooms.

I waited till I heard the sound of my father snoring deeply. I checked the clock, 11:00 p.m., then stealthily walked to the garage and let myself in. I retrieved the roll of heavy plastic I had left there under a pile of suitcases. I went back into the house to the bathroom. I turned on the light and stared at myself. This would be the last time I would look at this image. I grabbed a scissors and began clipping away at the beard I had been forced to grow over the past six months. When it was short enough, I grabbed for the electric shears I had hidden under the sink and trimmed away the remaining whiskers. Then I did the same to my head, then the sidelocks. Lastly, I shaved. Everything, face, temples, head. For the first time in years, I clearly saw the scar on my ear, the tear from my tussle with Oleg Kurchenko. *Enough of these Jews*, I thought.

I walked into my room. My brother lay asleep in his bed, grunting loudly with each exhaled breath. Who knew what demons were chasing him in his nightmares. I would have preferred to do this with a knife. I always prefer a knife, but that would leave my signature. I picked up the pillow from my bed and placed it tightly over his face. He stirred a bit but didn't wake. He gasped trying to bring in his breath, but the drug did its job. He stayed asleep and, by the looks of it, his arms and legs were pretty much as useless as the drug dealer told me they would be. Slowly, he let go. For a moment, my legs weakened. I took a deep breath and steadied myself. I removed the pillow and checked his pulse. Nothing. He was gone.

I walked into my sister's room, my pillow still in my hand. I looked at her, lying on her back in the narrow bed. For a moment, I felt sad for her. What a waste her life had been. She had been beautiful. Look at her now, pale and fat. She could blame my father for that. She would be better off. This was no life for her, and whatever life my father had planned for her would not have been much better anyway.

I lifted my hand to cover her face with the pillow. I hesitated for a moment. I remembered her as a child, a little girl in a fur-rimmed white parka playing in the deep snow at the dacha. For a moment, I didn't think I could do it. I hated my father and had little use for my brother. But my sister, well, for a moment I almost lost my nerve. Then I looked at myself in the mirror over the dresser in her room and, in the relative darkness, I saw the slightly older version of the man I once was and could be again. I had no choice. It was my freedom, my future at stake. I turned back toward her and placed the pillow firmly over her face. Like my brother, she struggled just a little but not nearly enough to wake and stop me.

My mother. What can one say about killing their own mother? Many of us consider it but few of us do it. While my mother had never protected me against my father, she was still my mother. She was, sadly, incapable of real affection. I would forgive her for that, as she was making a great sacrifice for me right now. I lifted the pillow and placed it over her face. She didn't struggle at all. Her chest rose once, then twice, then heaved a short breath, then collapsed. I checked her pulse. Gone.

That left only my father. I had a slightly different idea for him. I wanted him to know it was me. So I woke him ever so gently. "Papa, Papa," I said. "It's midnight. I'm waking you as you wanted me to."

He groaned slightly and looked up at me, confused. "Nicholai?" he said, staring up at me.

"Yes," I said and realized my clean-shaven face surprised him. "Da. Of course, I shaved. You don't recognize me?"

"But," he began to say, trying to prop himself up on one arm.

I lifted the pillow and placed it on his face, pushing him down and climbing onto the bed, straddling him. He was strong, but I was stronger. Unlike my siblings and my mother, he resisted. Waking him had made that possible. I pushed down harder, the medication I had given him helping me. "You thought you were smarter than everyone," I said to him. "You thought you were smarter than me. Well, not so much. I think I am smarter than you."

He grunted as his body began to give way.

"This is for what you did to me, for stealing my life. Now I'm taking it back and stealing yours from you, as well as everything you have."

On his last breath, I thought I heard my name. Then his body went limp. I lifted the pillow. I checked his pulse then placed the pillow back over his face for a long moment to make sure.

I snuck out of the house and down the path from the settlement to the small car I had hidden in the shallow cave. I grabbed one of the bodies I had in the trunk and carried it back to the house. This body would be me. Later, I would dispose of the other bodies deep in the desert.

I was concerned that someone might see me, so I went very slowly. It took the better part of an hour. I stripped the body, then dressed him in my nightclothes and put him in my bed. I stared at the body of my brother for a moment. I went back to the car and retrieved the bag of things I would need to finish my plan.

When I got back to the house the second time, it was nearly 3 a.m. I changed into the street clothing I had bought in Tel Aviv. Then I took the accelerant and placed it strategically in the bedrooms so that the fire would be more intense there. I went to the dresser in my parents' bedroom and removed the envelope my father had taped to the underside of the bottom drawer and placed it in my bag. It contained everything I would need: passports, visas, money and account information. I slid open the bedroom windows. The flow of air would help fuel the fire.

I walked out of the house one last time. I lobbed Molotov cocktails, the preferred weapon of the Palestinian terrorists, into each window, a low thud and the shimmer of orange light evident moments later. Then I took the last Molotov and crashed it through the living room window. The flames grew quickly. I called out into the night, "Aish! Aish! Fire!" and watched as windows opened in the surrounding houses.

Their lights remained off, as the laws of the Sabbath prohibited them from being turned on. I snuck down the hill toward the ravine and continued watching. Shouts calling for help came from all directions. The neighbors gathered outside our house. They called our names. They watched as the flames grew stronger and higher, backing away as the fire engulfed the whole house. In the distance, I heard a siren. Someone had called for help despite the ban on using phones on the Sabbath.

Several fire trucks appeared, but it was too late. The house was engulfed in flame. The accelerant had done its job well. I quietly slipped away down the ravine and into the car. I started the engine, hoping no one would hear it over the noise of the screaming neighbors and firemen, and drove carefully through the ravine toward the road to Tel Aviv with my lights off. I was on my way to my next life.

Chapter
24

WASHINGTON HEIGHTS, NYC
10 JUNE 2010
9:30 A.M.

TOLYA CLICKED TO DOWNLOAD THE photos ben Shimon had forwarded him the previous night. There were four. Two were taken upon the arrival of the suspect in Israel and the other two when the suspect applied for a driver's license two years later. He also had the printout of a photograph taken at the settlement by the Chabad that Shalom Rothman had provided through his connections to the Orthodox mafia. It was a group shot and was unclear at best. He leaned back in his chair and began reviewing the information sheets ben Shimon had emailed him. The Israeli was a good guy. He'd translated the Hebrew for him, scribbling in English next to or under the Hebrew on the various pages.

Natan Hayat, formerly Portnoy. Born: 1967, Moscow. He was the same age as Tolya. Height: 71 cm, that's just under 6 feet. Weight: 85 kilos, about 200 pounds. He was a big boy, this Portnoy. Hair color: Brown. Eye color: Blue/Brown. Tolya felt a chill down his spine.

According to the summary, the subject had not served in the armed forces. He claimed a Yeshiva exemption. This wasn't unusual in Israel for religious Jews, Shalom Rothman had explained to him once. In the case of the suspect, his family had some connection to Chabad and he agreed to do community service work for two years after his arrival. The government had granted him a waiver.

"What's up?" Pete asked, dropping down at his desk.

"Nice of you to join us," Tolya said, glancing at the clock on the wall over Pete's head.

"I was out late again last night."

Tolya looked at him and smiled. "Liza?"

"No, that's over. Why you busting my ass?"

Tolya put the papers down on the desk. He sat up straight in the chair. "OK, sorry, I was out of line. What happened? When were you gonna tell me?"

"It's OK, I deserved it. I've been late every day this week. I ended it with her a couple of nights ago. You're looking at the new me."

"So where were you last night?"

"Trying to get us some more help."

"Your uncle and his boys again?"

"Yep."

Tolya sighed. "Any luck?"

"Don't know yet."

"Pete, I'm sorry about all this."

"I know you are. What you working on there?"

"The stuff on the suspect in Israel."

"Tolya, that guy is dead. What you wasting time with that for?"

Tolya turned from the screen to Pete. "Maybe he wanted to be dead. This thing with the two different color eyes has me creeped out. I knew a kid once back in Moscow who had eyes like that."

"Tolya, c'mon. I mean, seriously?"

Tolya printed the photos.

Pete got up from the desk and walked around behind Tolya. He examined the black-and-white image on the screen. "So that's the dead man?"

Tolya sat back in the chair. "Yeah, and I gotta tell you, he looks eerily familiar."

Pete laughed. "Man, this whole thing is so weird. How could this guy look familiar?"

"He does."

"Who does he look like?"

"That guy from Moscow I was a kid with. Just, like, thirty-five years later. His name was Nicholai Tserverin."

"Tolya, that's just not possible."

Karin took a deep breath and knocked on the director's door. "Come in," she heard from behind it. The director, Miriam and three board members were sitting at the conference table at the far end of the space. "Welcome," he said and pointed toward the empty chair at the left side of the table.

Karin walked across the room. The director and the two male board members rose. She felt a little awkward as she sat down in the brown leather chair, her pregnancy causing her to contort herself in order to sit.

"When are you due?" the woman asked.

"Three weeks. Not soon enough."

Miriam and the woman laughed. The men smiled awkwardly.

"I think you know everyone here?" the director said.

"Yes," Karin replied. She had met them before. James Shapiro, the civil rights attorney, Madeleine Fuchs, the society matron, and Mark Aretsky, the Wall Street investment banker. It was Aretsky she had to watch out for. He had objected to her appointment to begin with and had thrown a fit when she accepted the donation from Benjamin Schneider. She extended her hand to all three.

"Well," the director began. "It seems tonight is your big night."

"Yes, finally," Karin said. "I hope you will all be attending the pre-opening gala."

"Yes," they responded.

"In particular," added Aretsky, "I'm looking forward to meeting your new benefactor."

Karin smiled at him. "I will make sure to introduce you."

"Karin," Miriam said. "Why don't you quickly run through the series of events we have planned for the opening?"

"Sure." Karin opened a leather portfolio and handed out the five copies of the event schedule she had brought with her. "Tonight we begin with the opening gala at the Hotel Andaz at 5 p.m. We will host a cocktail hour for our invited guests. There will be a Latin jazz trio playing. Sosúa families will receive corsages and boutonnieres. At 6 p.m., we begin our program with a benediction by mixed clergy representing the Dominican and Jewish communities."

"Very nice," said Ms. Fuchs.

"The benediction will be followed by a welcoming statement."

"Given by whom?" Aretsky interrupted.

"Me," Karin answered.

"Is that typical?" Aretsky said, looking to the director.

The director shot a glance toward Miriam. "Completely," she answered.

"Continue," Aretsky said. "My apology for interrupting."

"After I welcome everyone in both English and Spanish…"

"That's perfect, Karin," said Shapiro, the attorney.

"I will introduce the mayor. He will make a short…"

"Is that possible?" said Aretsky.

"…I hope so, statement. Then I will introduce the Dominican Consulate General. He will make a brief statement. That will be followed by the Israeli Consulate General, who will speak briefly about the political situation that faced the Sosúa refugees in 1939."

"So far, this sounds terrific," Madeleine Fuchs said.

"It gets better. After the Israeli Consulate General, we have two more speakers: one of the last surviving original settlers who still lives in Sosúa today, and the president of Sosúa Second Generation. Simon Katz, the representative of Sosúa Second, will also present a short film they made, which is about ten minutes long."

"What time will that bring us to?" the director asked.

"About 7:15. After which, everyone will board buses or other transportation…"

"Yes. Other transportation? Supplied by your friend?" Aretsky said.

Karin swallowed, smiled and closed her portfolio. "No, this was arranged previously, back to the museum for the private showing."

"This is quite impressive," the director said.

"Now let's see how it goes," said Aretsky.

Tolya searched through the Russian newspapers and online archives. Pete had gone to the DA's office to get a warrant to enter the house in Bay Ridge for probable cause. As far as Tolya could determine, Nicholai Tserverin was dead, long dead. Tserverin's father was a KGB agent. He remembered him well. He had supervised their departure from the Soviet Union. He was a mean bastard, just like his son. He remembered how Tserverin's father had confiscated his mother's piano cover out of malice.

According to the Russian papers, Tserverin and his family had died in a fire at the family dacha a couple of hours outside Moscow in early 1990. Later that year, the Portnoy family immigrated to Israel. He'd heard stories like this before, Russians desperate to get out of the Soviet Union posing as Jews and going to Israel. Though usually, Tolya suspected, they weren't vicious anti-Semites the way the Tserverins had been. His mind was racing. The Portnoys had also perished in a fire. This was no coincidence. Tolya picked up the phone and dialed the police lab downtown. "Hello, photo shop please."

The phone rang twice. "Photo shop. Chan."

"TJ?" Tolya said.

"Yeah, who's this?"

"Tolya Kurchenko."

"How are you, man?"

"Well, I'm about to be a father for the third time."

"Congratulations. What can I do for you?"

"I need to age and, I guess you'd say, de-age a photograph. Can you do that, man?"

"You know I can. You wanna send me the images?"

"Yeah, I'm gonna do that now but I wanna be there when you do it. I'll be down to your office in about an hour."

"All right, send them now. See you in about an hour."

Tolya texted Pete, "Meet me at the photo lab downtown 1 hour."

"How old did you say he is here?" Chan asked.

"About 25-26,"

"OK, so we want to see him at about 40?"

"43."

TJ rolled his eyes. "Give me a break, man. Damn, you are specific."

"That's my job." Tolya watched the screen as TJ manipulated the photo of Portnoy from his immigration to Israel. The face filled out a bit, lines appeared around the nose and mouth. The youthful appearance gave way to a more mature look.

"What you got going there?" Tolya heard from behind him.

"Hey, Pete," TJ said. He got up from his workstation and grabbed Pete's hand. "Your perp, I hope."

"The dead man again? We're wasting time here, hermano."

Tolya mouthed "fuck you" at Pete as he stared at the photo. "Can you convert this from black-and-white to color?"

Chan nodded, then started fiddling with the computer, adjusting settings, clicking color wheels, and other tinkering that amounted to magic as far as Pete and Tolya were concerned. After a few minutes, he turned to Tolya. "This should be pretty close."

Tolya stared at the eyes as they stared back at him, one brown and one blue. A chill ran through him. It wasn't possible. It looked like Tserverin's father.

"I know that face."

"Tol, seriously?" Pete asked, dropping into the chair next to Tolya. "How could this be possible?"

Tolya looked at the photo. He felt his stomach turn the same way it did every time he walked by that alley in Moscow with Oleg on the way home from school, knowing Tserverin was waiting there with his brutish friends to torment them or taunt them or, if he was alone, to attack him physically. Tserverin's father was KGB. He was untouchable. "TJ, can you make the image younger now? Like 10 or 12 years old?"

TJ shot a glance at Pete, then at Tolya. "Sure." He clicked on the photo again and typed in a code. The face on the photo changed again, this time growing younger, almost angelic. The eyes stayed the same, staring back at Tolya, vacant and disconcerting, two things that should have been the same yet were malevolently different.

"I can't believe it. It can't be," Tolya mumbled.

"Can't be what?" Pete asked.

"It's Tserverin. I'm sure of it."

"Tolya, he's dead."

"So's Portnoy. We've got to get a picture of him now to confirm this. We've got to get into that house."

"We're in," Pete said. He held up a search warrant. "I'm parked in the lot under the building."

"Let's go."

Benjamin Schneider looked out the bedroom window of his apartment toward New Jersey. The sun was beginning to cast its shadows. During the long days of mid-June, 4 p.m. was far from evening. He turned toward the mirror and slowly, methodically tied the bow tie around the wing-tip collar of his tuxedo shirt. He smiled at himself in the mirror. He was very handsome. She will think he is too. Too bad she is so pregnant. Otherwise he would make love to her before they began his game. Absently, he reached for his ear. He ran his finger into the cleft that had been left as a scar after his encounter with Oleg Kurchenko more than thirty years earlier. How small the world is. He lifted the wig from its stand on the dresser and slipped it on his shaved head. There, she would recognize him now for who she thought he was.

He picked up the phone on the night table and dialed Karin's private number. It rang twice before she picked up. "Karin Martinez-Kurchenko."

"Madame Kurchenko," Schneider said.

"Hello, Benjamin." She laughed. "I thought we agreed you'd stop calling me that."

He laughed. "All right then, Karin, I promise. How are you? Ready for this evening?"

Karin sighed. "I suppose, it's been a long day. I met with the board of directors earlier."

"That same problem you mentioned to me? Mr. Aretsky?"

"Yes."

"Well, perhaps after tonight he will back off?"

"I hope."

"Pick you up in an hour then, 5:00, in front of the main entrance."

"Perfect. Look forward to it."

Tolya and Pete approached the house carefully. They knocked on the door. No answer, same as the day before. They had a warrant. They knocked a second time, still no answer.

"Think we should pick it or just shoot the lock off?" Tolya said.

"How much time you wanna waste?" Pete replied.

"I don't want to alert the neighbors either."

"Good point. Pick it."

Tolya reached into his pocket and slipped the lock pick into the front door. He prayed there wasn't an alarm. "There," he said as the tumblers fell into place. He pushed the door open. They walked slowly through the large foyer, guns drawn. The black-and-gray marble tiled floor was polished to a high gloss. "Police," Tolya shouted to no response and apparently no alarm. They continued down the hallway toward the rear of the house.

"Shit, this is some spread," Pete whispered.

"Yeah, and furnished like a tsar's palace. We should check upstairs." Tolya took the first step up the winding staircase leading to the upper floors. The marble floor gave way to plush carpet. An enormous chandelier hung in the center of the atrium. Its crystals twinkled, refracting the afternoon sun streaming through the skylight at the top.

"Coño," Pete said. "How the hell do you hang something that big?"

"Carefully. Police," Tolya called out again as they reached the landing to the second floor. Again, no answer. The stairway continued upward to the third story. They continued toward the open door at the end of the hall into what appeared to be the master bedroom. The space was a study in white—the furniture, walls, bed, carpet, all in shades and textures of the colorless hue.

"Wow," Pete said, his gun still drawn and held at chest level in front of him. He turned toward the door to guard it.

"It reminds me of Siberia in winter," Tolya said, lowering his weapon. "I hate Siberia, especially in winter." He surveyed the room, then walked toward the dresser. A single framed photograph sat on top of it. He picked it up. "Shit," he mumbled.

"What is it?" Pete said.

Tolya took two steps toward Pete and handed him the photo. He raised his gun as Pete lowered his. Pete looked at the photo. Tolya watched as Pete caught his breath for a long moment, then exhaled.

"It's Mariela and the kid."

"And him," Tolya said.

"Yep."

They continued up to the third story. Three bedrooms, none seemingly lived in. There was no one in the house. They returned to the ground floor and walked through the kitchen to the back of the house into an enormous living space with a two-story ceiling that led to a beautiful Japanese garden.

The room was furnished expensively with low leather couches and glass tables. On the wall opposite the longest couch was a huge wide-screen TV over a mantle and fireplace. On top of the mantle sat several framed photos. The largest, about 11 x 14 inches in a brown suede frame, was of the suspect. Tolya walked toward it and picked it up as Pete continued out toward the garden. He stared at the picture. He felt his stomach turn and his heart rate increase. How could it be? Now he was sure it was Tserverin. But how?

"Tolya, shit, come out here, man. You gotta see this."

Tolya walked out to the garden, the frame still in his hand. Pete stood at the rear of the garden next to a fountain, the sound of the water soothing in the late afternoon light. At the base of the fountain was a small glass case. Tolya dropped the framed photo, the glass shattering on the paving stones. He looked at the contents of the glass case and vomited. It erupted from him the same way it had that day when he was 11 years old in the frozen snows of Siberia, when his father decreed that his twin brother would die to get them out of Russia. Inside the glass box was a head, shrunken, like he'd seen in museums. The head had belonged to someone of Asian descent.

"What does that say?" Pete asked, pointing to the small bronze plaque at the bottom of the case inscribed in Cyrillic letters.

Tolya pulled a tissue from his pocket and wiped his mouth, then composed himself. He looked at the plaque. "It says, 'Here sits the head of the creator of this garden, my escape. Forever will his eyes look out on how I changed it. He should have listened more closely to what I wanted.'"

"What kind of sick fuck does shit like this?" Pete said.

"Nicholai Tserverin."

"Tol, you said he's dead."

"He's not."

"How do you know?"

Tolya picked up the photograph from the ground and pulled out the printed copy of the aged photo TJ had made for them.

"That's remarkable," Pete said.

"And how do I know for sure besides the different color eyes?" Tolya asked.

"Yeah?"

"You see that tear at the top of the right ear in this photograph?"

Pete nodded.

"Oleg put it there. Call for back up."

Part III

Chapter
25

LOWER MANHATTAN, NYC
10 JUNE 2010
4:00 P.M.

TRAVELING IN THE SECURE ELEVATOR to the garage under the building, I recalled my escape from the Promised Land. For all their security, it was quite easy to get out of Israel.

I took my time. I drove back to the old neighborhood in Tel Aviv where we had lived. I junked the van and went to the bus station in Jaffa to clean myself up. I ditched my dirty clothes, changed into fresh clothes I had left in a locker there a few weeks earlier and went in search of a room. I found one in a small building a few blocks from where we had lived. In the months since we had left, the neighborhood had become even worse, now almost exclusively young workers from Eastern Europe and Southeast Asia who could go nowhere else but back to the hellholes from which they had escaped.

I grew restless, and I knew only one thing would satisfy me. Across the street from the rundown apartment building where I took the room was an abandoned house. I broke in late one night and assembled a frame from the debris of furniture I found there. I modeled it after something I had built years earlier in Moscow to dispatch the women who satisfied my hungers. It was crude, but it served my purposes. I found an Arab prostitute working a nearby park, and I lured her into my lair. The kill left me satisfied. I considered another round. But a few days later, I saw a crowd assembled in front of the abandoned house. Those same two detectives who had questioned me about Liya's death were carrying out the body of my latest victim.

Within a couple of weeks, the story of the attack on my family's home died down. The Chabadniks buried us. The right wing used the incident for its benefit and the government used it on the international front as yet another example of Arab intentions. I booked a flight to Berlin. I was smart. I had everything in order. I slid through the gate, boarded Lufthansa and headed for my new life.

I landed in Berlin on a clear, crisp night. I felt clean for the first time in years. I thanked my father silently for insisting I study German. I collected my luggage and headed for a small hotel on the old Communist side. I figured I should ease myself into the West. The room was small and spartan and a bit run-down. But to me, at that moment, it was like a suite at the best hotel in Berlin for one simple reason: I could be myself again, Nicholai Tserverin. Well almost, as that name had disappeared forever. And in the end, I had it all. I had made my father pay for the hell he had put me through. I removed my clothes, showered and went to bed. I slept more soundly than I had in years.

The following day, I put on the suit I had purchased in Tel-Aviv and went directly to the offices of Deutsche Bundesbank. I arrived promptly at 9 a.m. for my appointment. The tall, slim, impeccably dressed banker examined my documents. He smiled and nodded with approval. "Yes, Herr Grushkin, we will be delighted to serve as your financial advisors."

I smiled back. "Danke," I replied. The sound of the German came as a relief to me after the years in Israel assailed by guttural Hebrew.

My father had assembled quite a fortune, 40 million Deutschmarks. The banker was quite impressed. "How much could I reasonably expect in interest per year for my living expenses and still maintain my principal?" I asked.

"At least 1 million Deutschmarks," he replied. "Not a small sum."

"Not at all," I said. "Could you possibly refer me to a good agent to help me to find an apartment?"

"Of course," he said. He excused himself for several minutes. I watched the slim blond secretary as she worked quietly at her desk. How different it was here in Germany from Israel or the Soviet Union. Everyone was quiet and polite. The endless background noise I had lived with all my life was absent. The quiet was seductive.

"Here," the banker said, returning with a slip of paper with three names and phone numbers on it. "Any of these should be able to help you."

"Thank you."

"Think nothing of it."

I rose to leave. The banker extended his hand and held mine for a moment too long. "Call me with whatever questions or needs you might have," he said.

I tipped my head and smiled, released his hand and left.

Within two weeks, I had settled myself into a beautiful flat in the Prenzlauer Berg neighborhood. My neighbors were polite but kept to themselves. When asked what I did, I said I was an investor and art collector. I had kept a few pieces of the works my father had pilfered and displayed them in my apartment. I knew little of art except what I liked, but these artifacts served to underline my cover. With the change in the season, my old urges returned except here it was much easier to satisfy them. There was an anonymous nightlife, the underbelly of Berlin, to prowl through. The freedom and decadence of the West was intoxicating. I could hide in plain sight.

I wandered through the nights dressed in black. I kept my head and beard shaved. I never wanted to feel hair on my face again. I would take a late dinner, usually alone, in the small cafes that surrounded Kollwitzplatz and Kastanienallee. The once heavy cuisine of Germany had evolved in the heady times after reunification. It paired well with the fine white wines I had come to favor. I would watch the groups of young girls, especially on the weekends. When they left, I would follow them stealthily to whatever club they preferred, lagging just far enough behind not to be noticed. Once inside, I would send them Champagne. The Germans are polite, to a fault. They would always turn toward where the bartender had pointed, then smile and tip their heads just slightly, mouthing, "Danke." Then I would make my move, walk out of the shadows, smile, offer my hand and begin the conversation.

"What do you do?" they would always ask.

"I am a collector," I would say.

"Of what?" they would ask.

"Beauty," I would answer. That's how I met Evette. That's also how I met the Albanians.

I saved Evette for later. I practiced on others first. I don't remember their names. They didn't have meaning to me the way Evette did, or later Roberta.

I spent a lot of money at the clubs, so naturally the owners took note, one in particular. About a month after I began frequenting his establishment, he came over and introduced himself. Yusef Leka, an Albanian. He wanted to know everything about me. I told him little. You might say I fed him the party line.

He told me everything about himself though. I am a good listener. I smiled to myself as he chattered away. As if I cared anything for the life of this swarthy Balkan scum. I knew I had an ally though, as long as I kept buying expensive Champagne.

The life of leisure can become full of ennui. Too much time doing nothing. I decided to try something new. For what reason, I don't know. I opened a gallery off the Kollwitzplatz. I made Evette the manager. She knew nothing about art, but together we developed a little following among the newly rich, desperate to fill the vacant walls of their flats. We cultivated a few local artists, held a show now and then.

I took my time setting up a location for my hobby. I found a loft in an old industrial building in the Hackesche Hofe. The walls were thick and the floor strong. The windows faced east so I would have the rising sun behind me if I wanted to complete my creations at dawn.

I considered ways to improve the structure of my killing machine. I wanted the victim to participate more intimately in her own demise. I ordered wooden posts with which to build the frame. I suspended a seat from the posts that ran across the top of the machine, like a swing, and secured it with another post to stabilize it. I added a counter lever with heavy cords and weights. Leather straps would secure the victim's arms to the cords, which would propel the machete across the victim's throat with her own hand as the weight was removed from one side.

On those nights when I couldn't sleep, I would leave Evette and prowl the clubs, especially those owned by the brothers Leka. One time, a couple of years after I arrived, Yusef made a remark to me.

"You're hurting business," he said.

I rotated the bar stool to face him, the leather of the stool squeaking against the tight fabric of my pants. I lifted my glass. "Not buying enough Champagne?"

"To the contrary, your consumption alone could keep us in business. What I have noticed though is that, after you romance a young woman with one or two bottles a night for a few weeks, she disappears from the club. We never see her again. We are beginning to think you are Count Dracula." Leka smiled broadly, then laughed like a hyena.

I laughed as well. "Who knows?" I said. "I am a man of many tastes and pursuits. Perhaps after they encounter me, they retreat to a convent to thank god for the rest of their lives." I smiled broadly and we both laughed madly. I would realize a few days later that the Balkan mentality was like that of a cat, sneaky and curious.

That night I met my next victim, a lovely, tiny blond from one of the former Baltic Republics, Latvia or Estonia, I don't remember. Leka had one of his men follow me. This man had great stealth. I never knew he was there, not till the following month—I always take a month or so off after a creation—when Leka asked me to speak with him privately in his office.

"What is the mystery, Yusef?" I asked him, slipping into the seat in front of his desk. "My bill is paid, I believe."

He looked at me. I could see his arm twitching slightly as he fingered the gun in its holster near his waist. "Yes, it is. I have to ask you not to come here again."

"Why?" I asked him.

He sighed and pulled out a large printed photo and handed it to me. It was taken from the roof of the building across the street from my studio in Hackesche Hofe with a powerful lens. There through the windows was the naked back of my last victim suspended in the machine.

"I don't know what you are," Leka said. "And I don't care. I don't care much about these girls either. I realize you have deep appetites. How many have you consumed?"

I slipped deeper into the chair, staring at the photo in my hand. I didn't answer him. I thought to kill him, but then I would be finished with my life here.

"Nicholai, I care about two things, my business and my family, in that order. How long will it be till you either consume one of my daughters, nieces or cousins, or you bring suspicion on yourself and the police are here ruining my business? Please take your hobbies elsewhere. We will keep this to ourselves."

I knew I had to play this carefully. I had limited options. He had the photo. If I made him disappear, his people would know it was me and come after me. I did the expedient thing. "Thank you, Yusef," I said, "for your discretion and your friendship. Your family is safe. You have my word. And I will not darken your doorway again."

He rose like a gentleman and shook my hand. I turned and walked out the door. As I walked back to my apartment, Evette waiting for me in my bed, I began to sweat. My heart raced. I could get caught.

I didn't see Yusef again till I made my final mistake about a year later. The business was doing poorly. I had had enough of Evette and I dispatched her that night. I would move on, to Paris perhaps. The neighborhood around my studio had continued to grow and this time someone else had seen something through the window into my studio. They had called the police and I was being investigated. I had to get out and fast. I went to Yusef and told him what happened.

"I have a cousin in America," he said. "Prepare what you need. We will get you a passport. And I hope you like an ocean voyage."

It cost me 1 million Deutschemarks.

Chapter
26

FINANCIAL DISTRICT, LOWER MANHATTAN, NYC
10 JUNE 2010
5:15 P.M.

TOLYA TRIED TO REACH KARIN on her cell. No answer. He knew she was pissed off at him, but this was a matter of life or death. "Fuck," he screamed. He hit the speed dial for her office. "Lindsay, where is she?" he screamed.

"Tolya?"

"Yes, where is she?" He felt his accent thickening for the first time in years.

"She left, about fifteen minutes ago. She left for the reception."

"I've been calling her cell, she doesn't answer," Tolya shouted.

"Tol, calm down," Pete said.

"Don't tell me to calm down!" Tolya shouted, slapping Pete's hand off his shoulder. "Who took her to the reception? Did she go with that guy? Schneider?"

"Yes," Lindsay stammered. "He picked her up in a stretch limo about ten minutes ago."

"Are you sure?"

"I saw her get into the limo."

Tolya clicked off the phone. "Fuck," he screamed. The backup crew scouring the living room for evidence turned toward him.

"Tol, calm down," Pete screamed back at him.

"Calm down? Don't fucking tell me to calm down. My wife is in a limo with a serial killer! My pregnant wife!" Tolya crumpled against the wall, crouched on his knees, his head in his hands.

"Hermano, tranqui." Pete knelt against the wall next to Tolya. He put his arm over Tolya's shoulder. "It's gonna be all right. We're gonna find her."

Tolya's breath caught in his throat. He felt like he was choking. "Before he does to her what he did to Mariela?" he whispered.

"I promise," Pete whispered. "I promise."

"You look ravishing," Schneider said.

"Thank you," Karin replied, shifting herself to get comfortable in the rear of the limousine. She let out a sigh.

"Champagne?" he said, glancing toward the bar in the center of the rear seat.

"I really shouldn't."

"I hope you don't mind if I do."

"No. Not at all."

Schneider leaned across the bar to the stemware case in the passenger-side door. "Are you sure?"

"Yes."

He removed one long-stemmed flute and delicately poured the pale yellow liquid into the glass. "Nasdrovia," he said, tipping the glass in Karin's direction then taking a sip.

"Excuse me?" Karin said.

"Nasdrovia," Schneider repeated. "It's a Russian toast. I thought you would recognize it."

"I do. But you're German," Karin said. She shifted uncomfortably in the seat, facing him.

Schneider laughed. "That's rather complicated, Madame Kurchenko."

Karin peered out the tinted windows. "Benjamin, where are we going? This isn't the direction to the Andaz."

"I'm afraid not, Karin."

"Where are you taking me? Stop this car immediately."

Schneider laughed. Karin reached into her bag and took out her phone. She saw that Tolya had called five times. Her heart sank. She pressed Tolya's number to call him back.

"Hand me that phone, now," Schneider said.

Karin looked up and saw the pistol in his hand. Her heart jumped. Her years of training came back to her. She kept the expression on her face neutral. She turned off the phone and handed it to Schneider, then raised her hands over her head. "Benjamin, please put that down."

"I don't think so," he replied. "And then there is the matter of my name. Please don't address me as Benjamin anymore. My name is Tserverin. Nicholai Tserverin." He slipped her phone into his pocket, removed the wig from his head, sat back into the corner of the seat and smiled.

Tolya jumped as his phone rang once, twice, then nothing. He fumbled to grab it out of his pocket. Karin's number. "Damn," he said, dropping his head into his hands again.

"Excuse me, detectives," the uniformed rookie said.

Tolya looked up. "Yes?"

"Which one of you is Detective Kurchenko?"

Pete and Tolya looked at each other. "That should be obvious to anyone," Tolya said.

"We found this envelope with your name on it." The young cop handed it to Tolya.

Tolya stared at the cover, his name neatly written across the middle in heavy block letters. He tore open the top and removed the contents: a single CD. Across the CD, "Tolya" was written in Cyrillic script. He called across the room, "Is there a computer anywhere on this floor?"

"Yes," called out another of the uniformed officers from the other side of the large room. "Looks like it's hooked up to the TV."

"Turn it on." Pete offered Tolya a hand, pulling him up from the floor. He walked across the room, his knees weak, and popped the CD into the side of the Apple laptop open in the cabinet. Almost simultaneously, the screen on the huge TV lightened. A moment later, Tserverin's face appeared. Tolya felt as if he would vomit again.

The other activity in the room stopped as everyone turned toward the screen. Tserverin was smiling. The smiling turned to laughing. The laughing stopped and the invective began in Russian. Tolya listened and translated audibly, mumbling out loud as Tserverin spoke. He realized he no longer thought in Russian.

"Comrade!" Tserverin began. "How many years has it been? Who would have thought we would have come face-to-face again? And how do you like my face? I cannot wait to see yours. In person, I mean. I have seen yours, in newspapers, on the Internet. How busy you've been, solving murders, helping old Spanish ladies. Your father would be so proud. The way mine would be right now of me. Haha! Correct?" The face on the screen began to cackle hysterically. When the laughing stopped, the invective began again.

"I have not had the easy journey you've had. Perhaps I will tell you about it when we meet. And yes, Tolya, we will meet, because I have your wife. Madame Kurchenko. And she is beautiful, in the same way that all Latin women are. How odd that we both would have fallen for them."

Tolya turned away from the screen for a moment and looked at Pete. His hands were in front of him. He thought that if Pete could have reached into the screen and choked Tserverin right there, he would have.

"You have till Saturday, Tolya. I have made the provisions, tovarishch. Saturday, I will dispatch your wife in the same manner as I did mine, only this time, the child will die as well—the setting sun at my back, her silhouette against the wall in front of us, her body slumping as her blood flows out of her, her breast cupped in my hand, my lips on the back of her neck."

The face stopped speaking for a moment. The eyes, one blue and one brown, faded to a place far away, then turned back toward the camera aflame. "Find her first, if you can," Tserverin said calmly. Then the screen went black.

"I'm sorry, I don't know any Nicholai Tserverin," Karin said in the most nonchalant tone she could muster. Her heart pounded. She did everything she could to control herself.

Tserverin slouched into the seat and chuckled. "I'm surprised Tolya never mentioned me. We were boys together in Russia. I don't suppose you would call us friends."

"What do you want from me?" Karin said. Tolya's faced flashed through her thoughts. It was uncanny how he could feel when something was amiss. He always knew. She watched as the car followed an illogical path, turning and re-turning haphazardly. She knew it was meant to confuse her, to disorient her from determining where she was being taken.

"I want to play a little game with you. You will soon see."

"Benjamin…"

"I told you not to call me that," he interrupted her. "My name is Nicholai."

He was angry. She was pleased. She felt herself calm down a bit. Perhaps she could take control of the situation. She wanted him a little off balance. That might distract him, give her an opportunity to plan her next move. "Sorry, yes, Nicholai," she smiled. "You know people will be looking for me. We could just stop this now. Let me out of the car, please."

He chuckled again. "Yes, I know. Why would I do that? This is what I want. It's part of the game now. Your husband has two days to find you. Let's see how good of a policeman he is."

They sat in silence for a long time. Tserverin drank the bottle of Champagne slowly. When he finished it, he began another. Karin tried to watch for landmarks with little success. The windows were darkly tinted and the driver made the trip too chaotic. She spotted the waters around Lower Manhattan and the Statue of Liberty as they pulled into a driveway that led to an underground garage. Despite the long trip, she was still in Lower Manhattan, a stone's throw from the Museum.

The car came to a stop. Tserverin shifted to the seat next to her. "My apologies, Karin, but I can't take any chances at this juncture." He reached under the seat and withdrew a roll of gray electrical tape. He tore off a piece and placed it over her mouth. Then he slipped a black sack over her head.

For a moment, she thought she would lose it. She felt the tears well in her eyes. She saw her children before her standing with Tolya in the street, each holding one of his hands. She was so angry with herself for not listening to him. Tserverin grabbed her by the elbow. She resisted.

"Karin, please, don't make me force you." His accent had changed completely. His lilting Germanic speech now had the hard edges of Slavic vowels. "Come easily, don't make this more difficult."

She resisted again for a moment. He placed a hand under her knee and began to pull. She realized the futility of her efforts and deferred to him, getting out of the car. He led her a few feet. "Stop here," he said. She reached forward with one hand slightly. It met a cold metal surface that she recognized as a door. She withdrew her hand. A moment later she heard a ping. She was standing in front of an elevator. Tserverin put his hand against her back. "Walk a few steps forward, please."

She followed his instructions. When the door closed, he turned her around and removed the sack from her head and the tape from her mouth.

"Soundproof," Tserverin said.

She looked around the elegantly appointed elevator. The button for the 33rd floor was lit. She felt the lift of the high-speed elevator move through her body. They arrived within seconds. The door opened. Tserverin nudged her forward into a dark vestibule. To one side was a washer and dryer, ahead of her was a small hallway. He nudged her further down the hallway. As she reached the end of the hallway, it turned to the left. She followed the turn into a large room. At the far end of the room was a large window. In the darkness, she could tell that the view was of New York Harbor, the lights of Staten Island twinkling beyond. She estimated that it must be around 9 p.m., as night had fallen and it was June. In front of the window was a wooden structure. She had difficulty determining what it was.

"Welcome home, Karin," Tserverin said from behind her.

She turned toward him. "Nicholai, please, it's not too late…"

He smiled and laughed again. "The game has begun. Please walk down that hall to the bedroom at the end."

She knew she had no choice. She sighed and held back her tears. Showing him weakness would only increase his power over her. She walked toward the last room at the end of the hallway and pushed open the door. The room was furnished with a simple but elaborately made bed, a small table and chairs. On the table was a small brown paper bag.

"I'm sure you're hungry," Tserverin said. "I've taken the liberty of bringing you some dinner. Nothing fancy. It's that sandwich you liked so much from your little Vietnamese friend in the park."

Karin sat down on the edge of the bed. She began to shake inside.

Tserverin walked back toward the door. "I'll let you get settled," he said, exiting the room and closing the door. Karin heard the tumbler in the lock as he locked the door from the other side. Her mind raced. Tolya had been right. How would she ever get out of this? She stopped for a moment and focused in her mind on the shadows of the structure she had seen in the living room. Where had she seen that before? She recalled the photos of the crime scene on Wadsworth Avenue that Tolya had shown her. It was the killing machine. She put her hand under her stomach and began to cry.

Chapter
27

BROOKLYN, NYC
1 MARCH 2003
4:00 P.M.

I HAD ARRIVED IN NEW YORK just before the turn of the
millennium. Crossing the ocean as a deckhand on a commercial
vessel was cathartic. It gave me the opportunity to cleanse myself
mentally, prepare myself for my new life and develop a new identity. I
thought about my name. I would have preferred to return to the name
I had been born to but decided against it. The American authorities had
too many files that might include information on my father. I would
use my mother's maiden name, Grushkin, for my business dealings.
For my contact with the world, I would be Taylor, the English version
of the name we had assumed when we left Russia.

Yusef's relatives had been very helpful. They provided me with a
hotel when I arrived. They introduced me to their lawyer. He was a
Jew, of course. But then, they make good lawyers and they will do
anything for money. He helped me to transfer my funds from German
banks to Swiss banks. There the bulk of my capital would stay. He set
up working accounts at a number of small banks in New York for my

more immediate needs.

Then there was the matter of what kind of work I would do. I really wasn't sure. I couldn't, or at least knew I shouldn't, return to the art world. It's a small community and the German police were looking for a murderer, a phantom who had owned a gallery and left a trail of dead bodies, including that of his Baltic girlfriend. Of course, since I never really existed in Germany, I was not too concerned. Nevertheless, I needed to be careful. Perhaps I would become a man of leisure, my money invested in others' ventures.

As it turned out, that wasn't much of a problem. The Albanian's cousin here in America had a thriving business, gentlemen's clubs, like his kin in Germany. And like his kin in Germany, he ran an extensive network to bring girls into the country to work in those clubs. I happily invested. With my investment came a steady flow of young women to entertain me. Despite my urges, I controlled myself. I didn't want to risk getting caught so soon after arriving.

Then came September 11, 2001. I had no love for the Americans, nor did I care much about what had happened. For me it was an opportunity. The real estate market collapsed. I picked up a few pieces at bargain-basement prices. People were terrified. They just wanted to get out.

First, I bought a small apartment on Central Park West for nights when I would prefer not to return to my hotel with its nosy employees. It was also potentially the next spot for my hobby. I was beginning to feel the old urges returning. A week later, I picked up this lovely house in Bay Ridge. There were plenty of Russians in the neighborhood, as well as Scandinavians and Germans and Italians, and the food shops were particularly to my liking, though the bread was a disappointment. It was far enough away from the city to be quiet and private and had good access to New Jersey, where a couple of the gentlemen's clubs were located. And so, after a little remodeling, I moved in. I sipped on my coffee and smiled to myself. How far I had come.

The events of September 11 had created a short-term cash crisis as well. The Albanians needed cash. I invested in more of their clubs. They happily took my money. They also watched me like hawks. No question Yusef had told them of my predilections.

Late one night, I felt the need to get out. I called my driver and told him to bring the limo around. I paid him well. I rented a small apartment for him near my Brooklyn home. He was on 24-hour call.

Andrej held the door to the rear of the limo. "The club on 12th Avenue," I said.

There was virtually no traffic. It was past midnight and a Thursday. We sped up the Brooklyn Queens Expressway to the Brooklyn Battery Tunnel and were in Manhattan in no time at all. Exiting the tunnel, you could still see and smell the destruction those moronic Arabs had wrought. My years in Israel had taught me that the Arabs were even more duplicitous than the Jews, and half as smart. Had they really studied New York, they would have known to fly those planes into Rockefeller Center instead, thereby crippling the entire subway system, not just the end of one line. Instead they went for the symbol. That showed hubris, not creativity.

Andrej pulled the car up in front of the club and opened the rear door. "When would you like me to pick you up, sir?" he asked.

"I'll call you when I'm ready,"

"Of course, sir. I won't go far."

"Thank you, Andrej."

My reception at the club was as usual. The doorman knew me and opened the doors without a word. The hostesses fawned all over me. One of them, a tall Latin girl in a tight red dress that left nothing to the imagination, led me to the VIP area. At the far end was one of my partners, Hassan Leka. He sat at the table with two other men I didn't recognize and some girls who worked at the club. He waved at me. Though I would have preferred my solitude while selecting a girl for the night, I had to respond to his invitation. I approached the table and extended my hand. "Hassan, how nice to see you."

The Albanian stood up. He was short and built like a bull. Perhaps short men lift weights to compensate for their lack of altitude. "Nicholai," he said. "Please sit down, join us for a drink."

I surveyed the banquet, four very beautiful women, three clearly

Slavic. The fourth was much more exotic. I sat down next to her. "Hello," I said. "I'm Nicholai."

The young woman looked at me. Two things stood out about her. The first was her eyes. I still find them hard to describe, black ringed with gold. The other was her face. Her expression was of someone who, while right next to you, was a million miles away in her mind.

"Hello," she replied. "My name is Roberta."

I struggled with Roberta. I became obsessed with her. Night after night, I would go to the club to watch her dance. I had never reacted like this to any woman. I didn't invite her back to my house or my apartment in Manhattan. I would come to the club, watch her dance, buy her a drink. Leka questioned me about it. "If you want her, she is yours," he said. "We own her the way we own all these girls. Just say the word."

The third or fourth time he said this we were alone in the VIP section. She was dancing on the pole. Her body was intoxicating, his crudeness infuriating. I grabbed him by the neck and pushed him back into the seat, pressing against his Adam's apple. I could have killed him right there, but I thought better of it. It would be too costly, too messy. "Don't ever refer to her like that again," I said. I released his neck. He pulled back.

"You fucking crazy, man?" he said, rubbing his neck where my hand had been. "You forget who I am. I could make you disappear tonight."

"But you won't," I said, sipping at my martini. The vodka burned on its way down. "You need my money and therefore me."

"Lunatic," he said and walked away.

Roberta had seen the whole incident. She came over and sat down next to me. She didn't say a word. She touched my hand. I don't know why. It was the first time she touched me, any part of me. I shuddered inside. I wanted this woman so badly. But deep inside, I knew what I wanted her for, and I had promised myself I wouldn't renew my habits. There was really nowhere left to run. I would have preferred to return to Moscow to begin with, but that was impossible given what my father and I had done there. I would be imprisoned and my fortune confiscated if I were found out.

"Are you all right, Nicholai?" she said finally.

"Of course," I said. "He referred to you in a disrespectful way."

She took a deep breath and then smiled slightly. It was the first time I had seen anything approaching a smile on her face. "Thank you, Nicholai."

That night, I brought her to my apartment on Central Park West. I reached a climax too quickly though and was embarrassed. This had never happened before, not even with a knife at their necks. "I'm so sorry," I said.

"For what?" she asked.

"I didn't satisfy you," I said.

"You don't know that," she said.

"It happened too quickly."

"It happened for me at the same moment," she purred in my ear. She moved her mouth over mine and kissed me deeply. I became erect again. She pushed me back against the bed and climbed on top of me, grabbing my member. She lowered herself onto me and began to move slowly and rhythmically. She stretched herself over me and pushed my arms out, holding me down at the wrists. I didn't resist. This was a new feeling for me. Her movements became more rapid. She moaned slowly. She brought me to the edge several times before finally bringing me to climax. As she finished, she stretched herself out on top of me and kept me inside her till I grew soft. All the while, she whispered in my ears. Her words were filthy. It drove me wild. Finally, she lifted herself off of me and walked toward the window.

"What a fantastic view," she said, staring at Central Park to the left in the morning light.

"Can my driver take you home?" I asked.

She laughed. "No need," she said. "I live a few blocks away. I can walk."

My obsession with Roberta was different than any I had had in the past. Yes, of course, I had great sex in the past, but this was different. I had to admit it. I didn't need the blade. Before, with every woman, I would get to that point where I needed the blade, deeper and bloodier each time, till inevitably we would reach the end—the end of her life and the culmination of the experience for me. It was different with Roberta. She was the consummate professional. She knew how to make a man explode.

After a few months, I asked her if she would like to live in my apartment on Central Park West.

"Really, Nicholai?"

"Yes, of course," I replied. "Otherwise, why would I ask?"

She jumped up from the bed, came next to me at the window and put her arms around me. "Thank you, thank you. You're too good to me. Clothes, jewelry, now this." She kissed me sweetly on the lips. A salty tear fell from her eyes onto my tongue.

"Don't cry, my darling."

"I'm sorry," she said. "You don't understand where I've come from and how far."

"You don't have to work at the club anymore either," I said.

"No, no, my darling, I don't want you to keep me. I want to pay my own way. I don't have another job."

"OK then," I said. "As you wish."

"Thank you, darling," she said again, then pulled me back to the bed. We made love. This time I was on top.

I continued to live in Brooklyn in my house. I needed the space and privacy. After all the years with my family in Russia, then Israel and then living with Evette in Berlin, I didn't want constant companionship. At Christmas in 2002, I made a decision. I would go back to Russia to size up the situation. If possible, I would begin arrangements to return. Though New York was tolerable, I hated America. It was filled with the lowest forms of life. Albanians and Jews and blacks and scum from everywhere. I wanted the purity of my own country.

The trip went well. It had been more than ten years and the country had changed. Grown into one of the most exciting places in the world. The grayness of the Moscow I remembered was gone now, it dazzled like Paris or London or New York. I loved the sound of Russian in my ears, in the streets, on the TV. I would find a way to return. Oddly, I found that I missed Roberta. I went to GUM and strolled around a day before Christmas Eve and, on a whim, bought her a ring.

When I returned though, I learned of something that was, to say the least, very disturbing. It seems my darling Roberta was turning tricks in my apartment. One of the doormen, a half-wit named Damien, inadvertently let something slip. I felt a shiver run through me. I kept the anger inside. I would deal with this in my time, at my leisure. I would deal with her the way I had dealt with all the others when I grew tired of them.

I avoided her for a couple of weeks to throw her off balance. Then one night a couple of weeks later, I thought to begin our game. I brought my knife with me hidden in the inside pocket of my great coat. It was a cold, cold night. I entered the apartment. She came to me silently and kissed me. She wore a red lace bustier and six-inch heels. She kissed me deeply, then pulled me toward the bed. She undressed me item by item. When she had me down to my drawers, I pushed her down on the bed and onto her stomach. I tore the bustier from her and entered her roughly. She winced slightly.

"You like that, don't you, whore?"

She winced again as I thrust deep inside her.

"Nicholai, slow down."

"Why, whore? I think you like that," I said, continuing to pound her.

She pulled back and wiggled away from me. My anger nearly overtook me. I turned to take the knife from inside my coat. As I bent to retrieve it, I heard her say something I never would have thought to hear.

"Nicholai," she said. "We have to be more careful. I'm pregnant with your child."

In that moment, everything changed.

Chapter 28

WASHINGTON HEIGHTS, NYC
10 JUNE 2010
10:30 P.M.

"KURCHENKO, CALM DOWN," THE CAPTAIN shouted, slamming his fist against the desk. "You're not helping Karin this way."

Tolya lunged toward the captain. Pete grabbed him from behind, restraining him.

"Stop telling me to calm down. And let go of me." He tried to break from Pete's grasp but couldn't.

"I'm taking you off the case, both of you," said the captain.

"No, no you're not," they both screamed.

"Cap, please," said Pete. "Don't do this, we can handle it."

"I don't think so."

"Tol, you gonna relax?"

Tolya squirmed.

"Tranquillo? Can I let you go?" Pete asked, loosening his hold on Tolya.

"Yes," Tolya said, shaking Pete off of him.

The captain approached him. He put his hands on Tolya's shoulders. "We're doing everything we can. You know that. We've got teams searching for the car everywhere. Reviewing every street cam. You've gotta calm down. We need time."

"We're out of time. I feel like she's slipping away." Tolya's throat tightened again. He fought back the tears. "He's going to kill her."

"We're not going to let that happen. I want the both of you to go home now. I'll be here to monitor the situation all night. If anything comes in, I will call you both immediately. You're too close to this now. Both of you go home, check on your kids."

Tolya was about to protest when he glanced at Pete. Pete raised his left eyebrow and nodded toward the door ever so slightly. He knew what Pete was telling him. "OK," he said to the captain, grabbed his phone off the desk and looked at Pete. "Let's go."

Tolya waited till they had left the station house. "What have you got in mind?" he asked.

"We're not getting anything done here. We can't get the rest of those records on this guy's holdings till tomorrow. Those offices are closed now. This guy is somehow connected to the Albanians. We need to get to the Albanians."

"How do you propose we do that?"

"My uncle."

"That's really crossing the line, Pete. We can't control him or his men. They're not cops, they don't know how to do this. What do we do if they fuck it up? We can't trust the Albanians either. They could tip Tserverin off."

Pete looked at Tolya. "We got no other choice."

"I can't take that risk."

Pete closed his eyes and took a deep breath. "Hermano, you think I don't know the risks? She's your wife, yeah, but she's been like a sister to me. Remember who introduced you to her to begin with. Remember how long I know her."

"I don't know Pete." Tolya fought back tears again.

Pete put a hand on Tolya's shoulder. "You gonna be able to hold yourself together here, pana? Because if you can't, I'm taking you off the case."

"The fuck you are." Tolya took a deep breath. "OK, what we gonna do?"

"First thing we're gonna do is go home and change. You gotta look like you belong in the life for this. I'm gonna pick you up at midnight. Then we're gonna go find my uncle."

Pete walked Tolya to his building and watched as he slid the key into the interior door, then disappeared into the elevator. He turned down Bennett Avenue, then crossed 187th street and turned toward Overlook Terrace. He stopped at a bench on Overlook and pulled out his cell. He tapped Chicho's name in the contact list and waited for a ring.

"Compai!" came the voice at the other end. "Que vaina?"

Pete smiled to himself. Chicho was always Chicho. Siempre feliz, or at least that's what he wanted you to think. "What's the noise?" Pete said, knowing full well what the sound in the background was.

Chicho laughed deeply. "What you think it is? Just getting busy. I don't pick up the phone for everyone when I'm doing this you know, but for you, well…"

"Call me back when you're done." Pete pulled the phone away from his ear ready to disconnect the call.

"Hermano, esperate," he heard from the other end. He put the phone back to his ear. He heard a woman's voice in the background but couldn't make out what she said. He heard Chicho say, "I told you, tranquilo. You gotta wait a minute." Chicho's voice grew louder as he spoke into the phone. "Damn horny bitches. Hermano, what up? Why so serious?"

Pete sighed. "I need to see Polito."

Chicho laughed. "That ain't gonna happen, hermano. Not after the last time. He don't want nothing to do with you no more. You disrespected him too much. He don't understand why you can't forgive him after all these years."

Pete bent over, his head slumped on his chest. His stomach turned as it did every time he had to confront his feelings about his uncle. He didn't know how much more he could take, but he knew he had to help Tolya and he needed Polito to do that. "Chicho, please listen, this isn't about me."

"No, it's about Mariela. Forget about her. She's gone. That was another lifetime. We gotta move on."

"No, Chicho, it's not about Mariela. That's over for me. Mirate, oite, you know how we are, you and me, even after all these years?"

There was silence on the phone for a moment. Chicho told the girl to leave the room. She wasn't happy about it. He heard the door close. "Sí," Chicho finally replied.

"Well that's how it is with my partner and me, like brothers. He's saved my life a couple of times."

"What's this got to do with shit, Pedrito?"

Pete hesitated for a second. He knew how many rules of police conduct he was breaking by having this conversation. "We know who killed Mariela."

There was silence on the other end.

"And he's got my partner's wife."

"Cómo?"

"And she's nine months pregnant."

Tolya slipped the key out of the lock in the front door and walked into the apartment. He walked down the hallway and into the living room. Nilda was sitting on the couch reading.

"Hola," she said. "How was the opening? Where's Karin?"

Tolya sat down on the couch opposite her. He wasn't sure how much to tell her, but he knew he had to tell her something, as he would need her to help him with the children. They would be looking for Karin in the morning. "Something has happened," he said.

Nilda looked at him as if he were crazy. "Where is Karin?" she asked again. "The baby?"

Tolya didn't know if he could continue. His heart was breaking. He had lost too much, his mother, his brother, now Karin and the baby. This was too much to bear. He heard his voice crack as he replied. "She's been abducted." He couldn't believe the words had come out of his mouth.

Nilda fell back onto the couch, one hand over her mouth, the other on her stomach. Tolya felt the wetness of the tears he could no longer hold back.

"How?" Nilda said barely above a whisper.

Tolya wanted to scream, to grab something and break it. He knew he had to keep some control. He didn't want to wake the children. "A madman," was all he could get out of his mouth. Nilda wept silently. He cried with her. "I have to find her," he said.

Karin settled into the bed, her left shoulder against the headboard, her legs curled under her. She stared out of the window into the darkness, the lights in the harbor and across on Staten Island in the distance twinkling. Schneider, or Tserverin or whoever this madman was, had not returned since pointing to her dinner, a sandwich from Tron and Nguyen's food truck. The same sandwich she had been eating a few days ago when she ran into him in the park. She realized now he had been stalking her. How stupid she had been. How she wished she had listened to what Tolya had said. Her pride, as always, had gotten in the way. She was a strong, independent woman and she didn't need anyone, including her husband, questioning anything she did. She hated herself for her hubris.

She had to collect herself, devise a plan. At the very least, she had to find a way to let Tolya know where she was. She thought she heard the madman moving about in the other room. She moved off the bed toward the door, testing the doorknob again, knowing full well it was locked from the outside.

"Benjamin," she called out. There was no response. She waited a moment and called out again, "Benjamin." Still no answer. What was it he had said his first name was? She was confused and anxious. She placed her open palm under her stomach and gently rubbed her hand against it. Oleg was moving around. He always woke at about the same time every night. *It must be around 11:30*, she thought. "Tranquillo, mijo," she whispered, as much to calm herself as him. She breathed deeply. What had he called himself? Concentrate. Nicholai. Yes, Nicholai.

"Nicholai," she called out. The footsteps stopped abruptly.

"Yes, Madame Kurchenko," he called back from the living room after a long pause.

"Nicholai, I need to speak with you."

His footsteps proceeded down the hallway. "Yes," he said from the other side of the door.

"Please open the door, Nicholai, so I can see you."

There was the silence again.

"Nicholai?"

She heard the key slide into the lock and turn. The door opened. There was her nemesis dressed in the suit he had worn the day he had come to her office.

"What can I do for you?" He glanced over at the dresser, the sandwich he had left her still uneaten.

"I need my bag," she answered.

He looked at her, raising one eyebrow. "Madame Kurchenko, whatever for?"

"Nicholai, please. I'm nearly due, I've had some problems with my pregnancy. I don't think you want me going into labor here. I have some pills in my bag that I have to take to prevent that."

"I'll get them for you. They are in the bag?"

She needed to get her hands into her bag. "No, no," she said. "They are loose in one of the compartments. You won't know which one I need."

"Describe it to me."

She felt her stomach tighten. "Nicholai, please, you can trust me. There's nothing in that bag anyway. You took my phone."

He hesitated for a moment, then turned and walked the few feet down the hallway to the small table where he had placed her bag. "Here," he said, returning and handing it to her.

Karin stepped backward toward the bed and sat down on its edge. She figured she had less than two minutes to find something in that small evening bag to help her help herself. She unzipped the inside compartment while surveying the meager contents. "There," she said, withdrawing a white Tylenol tablet from the interior. She knew he would never know. "Could you bring me some water please?"

As he turned toward the dresser to hand her the glass he had left there hours earlier, she slipped two paperclips and her debit card into her right hand and then quickly dropped them to the floor, pushing them under the bed with her bare foot.

"Here," he said. He looked toward the uneaten food again. "You should have more consideration for your unborn child."

Karin placed the Tylenol into her mouth and took a sip of the water. "I'm just not hungry."

He chuckled. "At some point you will be." He picked up her bag and walked out of the room, locking the door behind him.

Karin stared at the sandwich on the dresser. She was too nervous to eat, and the thought of swallowing food was enough to make her gag anyway. She was tired but had to think of the baby. She took the neatly prepared sandwich from the dresser and looked at it. How much care Tron put into every sandwich he made. So much love in such a simple thing each and every time for people he often didn't know and would probably never see again. She took a nibble at the meat and bread. It was cold but delicious as always. The memory that came to her was not of Tron and Nguyen and their sandwiches but rather of the first time she ate Vietnamese food. It was on her first date with Tolya. The firsts, it turned out, were always with Tolya.

Tolya walked down the darkened hallway from the bathroom into the bedroom. He sat down on the bed. The towel fastened about his waist slipped off. He leaned forward and put his head in his hands. He had to maintain his composure, for himself, for Karin and for the kids. He took a deep breath and exhaled slowly, the way Karin had taught him years ago after she had moved in with him. She'd taken a yoga class and considered herself an expert, the same way she did with everything. He smiled. That was one of her most endearing qualities, the way she took everything on with a passion, and how she lived every moment like it would be her last. When he thought of her as he did now in his mind's eye, he saw her exactly as he did that first time. He closed his eyes and remembered.

WASHINGTON HEIGHTS, NYC
OCTOBER 2004

"You wanna eat someplace else?" Pete asked.

"No," Tolya replied.

"What you staring at?"

"Nothing."

"Bullshit."

"I said nothing, I'm not staring at anything."

"OK then, what you gonna have for lunch?"

"That," Tolya mumbled.

Pete followed Tolya's eyes toward the front of the restaurant. Two men and a woman were standing at the front waiting to be seated. He chuckled. "I know her."

Tolya looked at him, his smile half-cocked. "You know you say that shit all the time. You claim you know them all. How could you know her? Then you're gonna tell me you fucked her too."

"Nope, hermano, didn't fuck this one, but I do know her. We went to high school together, a fine Dominicana."

"You're full of shit."

"OK," Pete said, "we shall see."

Tolya watched as the hostess led the woman and the two men across the room, heading directly for them. Pete stood as they arrived at the next table. "Karin Ramirez. Cómo tú ta?"

The woman looked toward Pete, her smile lighting up her face. "Pete

Gonzalvez."

"Sí."

"How are you?"

"Really well. You?"

"Excellent. You're with the department, right?"

"Yep, I'm a detective. This is my partner, Tolya Kurchenko."

Tolya got up from the chair and extended his hand. He could feel himself blush a little. "Nice to meet you."

"And you too. These are my associates, Fred Gilman and Jim Henderson. I've just moved over to this precinct. IA."

"Really," Pete said, sitting down, "so you'll be watching us."

"Only if you do something you shouldn't," Karin replied, flashing her smile again.

The waitress came over, breaking up the conversation. She took Tolya and Pete's orders, then those at Karin's table. The food arrived quickly. Karin was seated facing Tolya a table away. He glanced at her between forkfuls.

"You can't stop looking at that, hermano," Pete whispered, his eyes directed toward Tolya.

"You're embarrassing me," Tolya mumbled.

"That's the whole idea. You wanna go out with her?"

"I suppose you're gonna arrange that too?"

"Hey, anything for my brother," Pete said, scooping the rice and black beans into his mouth. "Coño, I love our food."

"Let's finish up and get out of here. We've got to interview that woman about the break-in on Wadsworth in twenty minutes."

Pete reached into his pocket. He pulled out a $10 bill. "Here, give me a minute, go pay the check."

Tolya stopped drinking his water mid-gulp. "Don't do anything to embarrass me, OK?"

"I would never do that, brotherman." He flashed Tolya his biggest grin.

Tolya got up from the table. "Leave a tip," he said. He slipped through the crowded seats. After passing Karin's table, he stopped and turned. "Nice to meet you. Good luck with your new job."

"Thanks," she replied.

Tolya reached the register and handed the bill and the cash to the hostess. He turned to glance back at Karin again. Pete was bent over whispering something in her ear, that smile that could only mean trouble on his face. He straightened up and sauntered over to Tolya. The hostess handed Tolya the change. "What did you just say to her?"

"I told her you think she's hot and would like to take her on a date."

Tolya felt the warmth rise from his neck into his face.

Pete handed him a card. "She said to call her."

He looked back toward Karin. She smiled at him and waved.

Chapter
29

T HE PULSE OF THE MUSIC echoed through Tolya's body. It was late, later than he was used to. There was a time when this life was normal to him, but now, with a wife and two kids and a third on the way, he rarely stayed up past midnight. Pete stood a few feet away, talking to Chicho. He strained to hear the conversation.

"Coño, why you gotta break my balls all the time?" Chicho said, grabbing himself between his legs for emphasis.

"I'm not trying to break your balls," Pete said, placing one hand on Chicho's shoulder. "You told us to meet you here at 12:30. It's fucking 2:00. I told you, every second counts. We got a potential serial killer here."

Tolya's stomach tightened. The scenario was incomprehensible to him. How could Nicholai Tserverin have risen from the dead, committed murders on three continents, married and killed Pete's ex-girlfriend and now have Karin held hostage? He rose from the chair and stood behind Pete.

Pete took a step toward Chicho while continuing to hold his shoulder, not permitting him to move away from him. "This guy killed Mariela and I'm not gonna let him kill my partner's wife. What part of this don't you understand? You want me to explain this to you again in Spanish?"

Chicho slapped Pete's arm, pushing his hand off his shoulder. "He's your fucking uncle," he said, raising his voice. "Tal vez, you should show him a little respect. You asked me to get him here. I asked him. He said yes. He told me 12:30. He's late. That's not my problem."

Tolya pulled Pete back. "Hermano, leave it."

"Sí, leave it," came a booming voice from behind them. They both turned. Polito stood in the doorway. "You're lucky I showed up at all."

Pete spun around. "You bastard," he screamed. Tolya grabbed Pete as he lunged toward Polito.

"Ay, mijo, you forget who asked who for help here."

Tolya felt Pete's body relax under his hold. "It's OK," he said to Tolya, "I'm OK. This is Uncle Polito."

Tolya extended his hand. Polito took it politely and smiled at them close-lipped. "Rosita," he called out as he slipped into the back of the red leather banquet to the right of where Tolya and Pete were standing. A young woman, perhaps 25, walked through the door at the back of the room. She was about 5'5", but with six-inch stiletto heels appeared much taller. Dressed in a skintight black leather cocktail dress that barely covered her, she had the body of a woman who clearly spent many hours at the gym, tight and lean but with the curviness that defined Dominicanas.

"Sí," she said, leaning over the table in Polito's direction, her breasts nearly falling out of the top of the dress. "Mi amor." She smiled broadly, her red lipstick a sharp contrast against her white teeth. Tolya thought of Karin again, of the way she would entice him with that same tone of voice, that same smile that Rosita played upon Polito. "Qué tú querías?"

"Tú, mi amor, pero first bring me a bottle of whiskey and glasses with ice for our friends, and for Chicho and me as well." At the mention of his name, Chicho slipped past Pete to his left and slid into the banquette, assuming his position next to Polito. Polito raised his hand and pointed to the remaining seats opposite him in the banquette, his fingers heavy with silver rings laden with various stones. "Por favor, siéntate. We'll have a drink and then discuss your problem."

Rosita returned with a bottle of Johnnie Walker Double Black on a silver tray along with a large bucket of ice with glasses. She opened the bottle and poured off a small amount for some long-dead lover into the corner behind the banquette. She then placed ice in each glass and poured the amber liquid into the glasses, including one for herself. When she was done, she slipped into the banquette to the left of Polito. He put his arm around her.

Pete's stomach turned. He remembered how Polito sat in that same position on the sofa in his house in Santo Domingo, his arm over the shoulder of one of his daughters or Mariela or Tia Henrietta, or even himself when he was a small boy after his mother had left and he was alone and lonely. He wondered if Polito remembered those moments or if he had no soul left after all these years. Or if he had ever had one at all.

Polito reached for his glass. He ran it just under his nose, almost touching his lips but not tasting the whiskey, only savoring its scent. That was a signal to the others to take a glass and wait for Polito to make a toast. He lingered over the glass a moment longer.

"Salud," he said finally, the pinky finger of the hand holding his glass extended. Tolya stared at the ornate silver and turquoise ring on it.

"Salud," they all responded and took a sip of the whiskey.

Polito turned toward Rosita. "A ti, mi amor," he said, then smiled and kissed her gently, lingering on her lips. "Now explain to me why you are here, mijo."

Pete closed his eyes and took a deep breath to control himself. "Polito…"

"Tío," Polito shot back. "Show me a little respect."

Pete froze for a moment. He caught a glance of Tolya's face to his right for a brief moment. The pain was evident. "Tío," he choked out.

"That's better," Polito said, easing deeper into the banquet seat.

Pete wanted to grab him. He willed his body to stay seated. Finally, he looked up and spoke. "We know who killed Mariela."

"Who?" Polito asked, taking another sip of the Scotch.

"A serial killer," Pete said.

Polito looked up. The smile disappeared from his face. He put down his glass. "You know this for sure?"

"Yes. And I know him," Tolya said, springing to life.

"You know him?" Polito said, cocking his head to the right and leaning forward over the table.

"Yes, and he's got my wife."

Polito crossed his arms against his chest. "Coño, now this is getting interesting."

Karin sat anxiously on the edge of the bed. Her heart fluttered every time she heard Tserverin's footsteps approach the door that separated them. He checked the lock on the door several times over a period of what felt to her like a half hour, but which she knew could be much less. Finally, she heard the jingle of keys and the sound of a door closing. She waited what seemed to her a long while and then called out for him. "Nicholai."

After a few more minutes, she called out again, still no answer. After the third attempt, she was fairly certain he had left the apartment. She took the two paper clips she had slipped from her evening bag along with the debit card and went to the door. At least her police training had come in handy for something. God knows her police instinct hadn't.

She easily picked the lock and gently, slowly opened the door. "Nicholai," she called out again just to assure herself that he was gone. She walked out into the living room and turned on a lamp to the side of a leather armchair. In front of the window stood an improvised wooden structure. At first she was perplexed by it, then the terror moved from deep within her to her throat, making it almost impossible to breathe. She sank into the leather chair. Now there was no doubt in her mind. It was the same as the frame the killer had used in the apartment on Wadsworth Avenue where Tolya and Pete had found that body, the body of the woman who Pete had known. Now she knew for sure what Nicholai intended, to kill her in the same manner as he had that woman. She had to find a way out and fast.

Polito listened to Pete and Tolya tell their story. His heart broke for both of them. Though he knew Pedrito believed he had no heart and no soul, he knew better. His heart had broken into a million pieces and his soul had been beaten years before. He knew the pain Pedrito felt— to find the one you love dead, to see her lifeless and mutilated before your eyes. It didn't matter how many there were now or had been. The truth was that, for him, there was only one woman, Henrietta, and no one else. It was Henrietta's name he mouthed with the words "duerme bien, mi amor," every night, no matter who might be in his bed. He knew the pain that would pierce Tolya's heart if this madman killed not only his wife but also his child. To lose a child, even one not yet born, only someone who had survived that could know. That was also a pain he was too well acquainted with. The day he had sent his daughters and Mariela away was the day he had buried his children. To them he was dead. They believed he had betrayed them for money and his own skin. "And you think these Albanians know where he is?" Polito said.

"Yes," both Pete and Tolya replied.

"They know where he is. I'm certain of that, they are in business with him," added Tolya.

"Do they know what he is?"

Tolya sighed. "I'm pretty certain of that too."

Chapter
30

BAY RIDGE, BROOKLYN, NYC
14 FEBRUARY 2010
10:00 P.M.

SOMETIMES LIFE TAKES A TURN. I never expected it. I married Roberta and she moved into my house in Brooklyn. A few months later, Luz was born. It took me a long time to get used to the baby. At the beginning I wanted to touch her, to know her, but I was afraid of her. She cried every time I tried to hold her. After a few months it got better and, after about a year, she became someone special for me. I changed. I wasn't so angry anymore. Even my urges subsided. I was, for the first time in my life, calm.

When Luz was about a year and a half old, we went to Moscow. I wanted Roberta to see it. Perhaps if she liked it, we would move there. I had arranged false papers for myself this time and entered on a Russian passport. She applied for citizenship as my wife. She left with a Russian passport. "Would you like to live here?" I asked.

"I don't know," she said. "I think New York would be better for Luz." Nonetheless, I purchased an apartment on Ostozhenka Street. Just in case.

As the years passed, I have to tell the truth, I began to tire of Roberta. I had changed and so had she. The passion had cooled. She became more and more focused on our daughter. She wanted the best of everything for Luz and I did too, so I paid for it. I even agreed to go to Disney World.

I kept myself busy and she didn't seem to care. She turned a blind eye. I went out in the evenings with my business connections. I had as many women as I wanted. I was beginning to feel the old urges again but I continued to control them.

The turning point came in the fall of 2009. It was October. I was sitting in the living room on the leather sofa. Something was underneath the cushion. It was Roberta's cell phone. Someone had just sent her a text, someone named Chicho. The text was a time and place to meet him in Manhattan.

I took a deep breath. Chicho. These Latinos they could never be trusted, neither the women nor the men. She had taken a lover. Shortly thereafter, she came down the stairs and into the great room. "Nicholai, I have to go into Manhattan. I'm meeting one of the mother's from Luz's school to buy decorations for the Halloween party."

"Be careful," I said.

"Of what?" she replied.

"Manhattan can be a dangerous place."

She laughed, took her keys and her phone and left. In a half of a moment. I felt something I hadn't felt in nearly seven years, hate.

I bided my time. I was always very good at that. I waited like a cheetah, as I had in the old days, till I could pounce and catch her. One Friday afternoon, she was about to leave. She had another meeting at the school. "Bye," she said. She turned the knob on the front door, or at least she tried. I had frozen the lock myself a half hour before.

"Nicholai, what's wrong with the door?"

"Who's Chicho?" I asked.

She stiffened.

"Who is Chicho?" I repeated.

She walked back into the great room. She sat down on the edge of
e couch, staring at her hands in her lap.

"Who is Chicho?" I said as calmly as the first two times.

She began to cry. "I can explain."

"OK," I said. "Explain. Who is Chicho?"

"An old friend."

"Is he your lover?"

"No, I said he is an old friend. We grew up together in Santo
omingo."

"How did he find you?"

"I found him."

I catapulted out of the seat. My fist found her eye. She flew backward
f the couch. When she recovered from the shock of the punch, she
mited. I stood over her. "Clean yourself up. Don't ever see him again."

The cancer that was planted now in my soul began to eat away
me. Something, I realized, was not right. It was never right. Luz
oked exactly like Roberta, her color, her features. She should look at
ast something like me if I was her father. I became obsessed with the
ought that I had been raising another man's child. I grew cold to Luz
d even colder to Roberta. She moved into the spare bedroom on the
ird floor. One morning while she took Luz to school, I collected hair
om her brush and from Luz's. I swabbed my own mouth. I took the
NA tests to a lab in Lower Manhattan, and a few weeks later I had
y truth. Luz was not mine. The man I had been for the past seven
ars withered away in an instant. The old Nicholai returned, stronger
d angrier than ever.

A few days later Luz, had a sleepover at her friend's house a few blocks
ay. Roberta took her there, returning alone. When she entered the
use, she attempted to retreat to her room on the third floor.

"Come in here," I shouted.

She stopped at the first step and turned around, walking slowly into the great room.

"Sit down," I said.

She did as I instructed.

"Pick up those papers and read them," I said.

She lifted the papers off the glass coffee table. She read the results of the DNA tests and began to dry heave.

"I could kill you, you know. I could snap your neck in a moment, dispose of the body. No one would ever know. I could do the same to Luz tomorrow."

"Please, please, Nicholai, don't hurt her, please. It was my fault. I deceived you."

"What is it you say in your language? Ten cuidado?"

She nodded her head in the affirmative.

"Be careful," I said. "Protect yourself. I'm going out."

When I got back the next morning, she was gone with her child.

Chapter
31

HEWLETT HARBOR, NEW YORK
12 JUNE 2010
3:45 A.M.

POLITO EVEN ROLLED LIKE A "gansta." Tolya sat on the driver's side behind Chicho in the huge black Escalade. Pete was next to him, tapping his foot nervously against the floor. Tolya had gone along with this, even though he knew it was a bad, no, a terrible idea. There was no calculating how many police regulations they were breaking. If this went bad, they could be thrown off the force and possibly land in jail or, worse, end up dead. But he had to find Karin and the department had nothing but dead ends. He looked at his watch: 3:45. It would be dawn in a little over an hour. He knew how crazy Tserverin was. He said he would end Karin's life today and Tolya knew he meant it. The car was silent except for the occasional directions Pete gave to Chicho. "Get off at this exit."

They pulled up in front of the garish gate with the double-headed eagle. "What the fuck?" Chicho said.

"Albanians," Polito mumbled.

Chicho pulled the Escalade a little farther down the street into the shadows away from the glaring spotlights mounted on either end of the gate. "Wait here," he said.

Pete opened the door to follow him. "I said wait here."

"Pedro, let him do this. It's his job," Polito said. "He knows what he's doing,"

Pete closed the door gently. He leaned back in the seat. "It's getting late."

A few minutes later, Chicho returned. "Tató, vamos, y silencio. You got that or you need me to tell you in English?" Chicho said.

Tolya smiled weakly. "Thanks, I've picked up a few words."

"That's good, gringo."

They followed Chicho through the gate. He was proud of himself now. He hated it when Polito sent him to school in Santo Domingo to learn security systems. He preferred the streets. Now he appreciated what he had learned. He disabled the lock and the security cameras but left the lights on. He didn't want anyone noticing a change in the light level. That might tip someone off that something was going on.

They stood silently inside the gate. Chicho pulled the baseball gloves from the backpack he brought from the car along with the bottle of gauze and chloroform he had packed into the outside compartment. They slipped on the gloves and doused the gauze in the liquid. As expected, the two huge rottweilers appeared. They sniffed the ground and stopped a few feet in front of them, then began growling a low menacing sound. Tolya recalled the dogs behind the fences in the gulag, where they held his father in that frozen wasteland. The dogs would look up at him on the other side of the fence and growl, saliva dripping from their mouths, exactly as these growled now. He wondered why they didn't bark.

Instead they charged. Chicho and Pete slapped the dogs on their noses with the heavy catcher's mitts. The dogs instinctively sank their teeth into the ends of the gloves. The leather was thick enough to prevent their sharp teeth from cutting through. As the dogs attempted to bite their way through the gloves, Tolya and Polito came around them and kicked out their hind legs, forcing them to the ground and twisting them onto their backs. Simultaneously, they covered the dogs' noses with the chloroform-soaked gauze. They went down with a whimper in seconds. Chicho pulled a knife from a sheath on his right ankle and slit their throats.

"Coño, muchacho, that was cold," Pete said. He flashed a memory of Chicho from their childhood crying by the river near the waterfall. He knew at that moment how much had changed, how much they had lost in the long journey that had brought them here together so many years later. How could so much go wrong?

"I don't need those perros waking up and biting my ass, thanks." He wiped off the knife on his pants and sheathed it. "Let's go."

Tolya led the way up the driveway. They stayed just to the side of the tarmac on the inside of the bushes and trees that lined it. When he saw the crenelated outlines of the faux gothic towers on the house, Tolya said, "We wait here. Chicho, you pop the lock."

"OK," Chicho said. He looked around. "Nice digs."

Chicho stealthily approached the front door. A light glared above it. He pressed himself to the wall next to the door and pulled a small black box from his pocket. He placed it against the lock in the door and connected the other end to his smartphone.

"Damn," Tolya whispered. "Unbelievable what you can buy. I'm still picking locks with a credit card and a paper clip." A long moment later, Tolya saw the door crack open silently.

Chicho waved at them. They crossed the driveway quickly and slipped into the enormous marble foyer. The house was dark.

"No alarms?" Pete asked Chicho.

"I disarmed the whole thing."

"Nice," Pete said

Tolya took a deep breath. "Follow me," he said. The four of them proceeded up the stairway to the second floor. He looked down the long hallway toward the double doors at its end. He made an educated guess that those doors led to the master bedroom. They crept down the hall silently, guns cocked.

Tolya breathed deeply again, his heart pounding even harder. He knew that his whole future depended on what happened in the next few moments. He looked at Pete and thought of Oleg. Until recently, with this conversion bullshit, he hadn't thought of his twin brother in a long time. He knew that was because Pete had replaced him. He knew that Pete would do anything, risk anything for him. That was obvious by what they were doing right now. He also knew he would do the same for Pete. He tipped his head and together the four of them kicked in the double doors.

"Get the fuck out of that fucking bed, you bastard," Pete shouted.

Leka jumped up. He was naked. He grabbed the pistol that was lying on its side on the night table next to his bed. A young blond woman was in the bed with him. She too was naked. She grabbed the sheet to cover herself, then screamed.

"What the fuck," Leka shouted, pointing the gun in front of him. Chicho reached over to the left side of the door and found a light switch. He flicked it. The lamps next to the bed went on. Leka said something in Albanian to the girl. She reached over and hit a button on the side of the headboard. An alarm went off.

"Shit," Pete said. "Chicho, I thought you cut all the alarms."

"Guess not."

"We're in it now," Tolya said.

Tolya and Pete came around Leka, their guns cocked. The girl screamed again. Tolya turned his head. Chicho had her from the back, his pistol at the temple. Footsteps echoed from the stairs.

"Drop the gun, asshole," Chicho shouted at Leka, "or I'll blow her brains out right now." The footsteps gained speed and became louder. Three of Leka's henchman entered the room, guns cocked. Pete grabbed Leka and put him between himself and his henchman.

"Let them go or we'll kill you all," one of the henchmen shouted in heavily accented English.

Pete cocked the gun he had next to Leka's head. "Go ahead. I'll kill your boss here first," he said.

Polito stepped out of the shadow near the closet. The henchmen turned their guns on him. He put up his hands, his pistol well hidden in the small of his back as it always was since he began carrying one as a teenager back in Santo Domingo. "Let's all calm down," he said.

Leka struggled against Pete's grasp. The big man was too much for him. He couldn't break free. "What the fuck is this, Guzman?"

"First tell your boys to put down their weapons."

"Fuck you! You break into my house, into my bedroom, and you tell me what to tell my men?"

"Yes, or we can stand here all night with our guns pointed at each other." Then Polito smiled. "And you know what, Hassan, I think you wanna put some clothes on, cover that up."

Leka looked down at himself naked and blushed. He shouted something at the henchmen in Albanian. They lowered their guns. Polito nodded at Pete. He released Leka.

Leka grabbed for the robe on the floor next to the bed and put it on. "Now let her go," he said.

Polito nodded to Chicho. He released the woman. She grabbed at the sheet and fell onto the bed.

"What do you want?" Leka said. "I know you didn't come for my money or my jewelry."

Polito took a step toward him. "Information."

Leka sighed. "I thought I was finished with this shit already."

"Far from it," Polito said.

"Let's discuss this in my study then," Leka said. "I believe you're all familiar with where that is." He walked out of the double door and turned. "You," he pointed toward one of his henchmen. "You stay with her. You other two, follow me."

They proceeded down the hall and the stairs to the rear of the first floor. "You two stay here," Leka said, then mumbled something in Albanian. Tolya, Pete, Polito and Chicho followed Leka into the study. "Close the doors," he said. The henchmen complied.

Leka sat down at his desk, Tolya and the three others in the various chairs facing him. He pulled a cigar out of the box on top of the desk. "Hope you don't mind?" he said.

"Aren't you going to offer us one?" Polito said.

"No," Leka said, clipping the end and lighting the cigar. "What fucking information could you possibly want from me now?" he asked.

"We know about Tserverin," Tolya said.

Leka laughed. "So is that his real name? We weren't sure. He goes by too many. Again, what is it you need to know?"

"Where is he?" Pete said.

"How should I know?" Leka said.

"We believe you know," Polito said.

"You can believe what you want."

"He's got my wife," Tolya blurted out. Pete looked at him. He furrowed his brow. Tolya knew Pete all too well. He knew he was screaming at him silently. He knew he shouldn't have said that but it was too late. "He's going to kill her."

Leka appeared to soften a bit. He exhaled. "I'm sorry to hear that. I knew we never should have brought him here."

Polito sprang out of his chair over the desk. He knocked Leka out of the chair onto the floor. He punched him hard in the face. Tolya, Pete and Chicho jumped up. The doors slammed open and Leka's henchmen joined the fray, guns drawn again.

"You brought this animal here?" Polito screamed at Leka and punched him again. Leka swung up with his left hand and caught Polito on the chin. He didn't budge. Pete and Chicho knew how well Polito could take a punch.

"What the fuck do I care what he does?" Leka screamed. His men moved closer. Tolya and Pete turned, their pistols pointed at the Albanians, another standoff. Chicho cocked his gun and pointed it at the top of Leka's head.

"Because we may be criminals, you and me, Hassan," said Polito, "but we don't slice open the necks of innocent women." Polito raised his fist and struck Leka again. "Now, you're gonna tell me where he takes them."

"I don't know."

"I believe you do," Polito said, punching Leka hard in the nose. Leka's face exploded. Blood was everywhere. "You ready to tell me?"

"No."

It took one more punch. This time Leka coughed and a tooth came flying out of his mouth. He let out a painful groan. Polito bent over him and said again. "You ready to tell me?"

"What do I care what you do to him? He has an apartment," Leka mumbled. "He just bought it. Downtown. Liberty Place. We delivered the wood and other stuff there a few days ago. Thirty-third floor. Private elevators. Now leave me the fuck alone."

Polito bent over Leka close and whispered in his ear, "Thanks." He stumbled as he got up. "Got it. Let's gets out of here."

"Let them go," Leka growled from the floor behind the desk.

They ran down the driveway toward the car. Halfway down, Pete turned. He saw Polito collapse onto the pavement. "Tío," he shouted, "what's wrong?" The three of them ran back to Polito. Pete and Chicho got onto the ground. "He's bleeding," Chicho said.

Pete ran his hand over Polito's stomach. His shirt was soaked with blood. "What happened?" he said.

Polito coughed and blood gurgled out of his mouth. "He stabbed me," Polito mumbled, "when I was straddling him."

Pete got up. "I'm going to kill him."

"No, mijo, no," Polito said, grabbing his ankle. "Go save her. Remember, you're the cop. I'm the murderer. There's no time and I'm done. I can feel it."

Pete sat down on the tarmac and laid Polito's head in his lap.

"Mijo, please, before I die, please forgive me. I am so sorry. I never meant for any of this to happen, ever. Things just went bad."

Pete choked. He didn't know what to say. "Tío, you're gonna be fine. Tolya, call an ambulance."

Tolya was frozen. "Pete, we gotta go."

"Pedrito, you know you can't do that. My time is over. I've lived this hell long enough. Tell me you forgive me, please, and tell my girls how much I loved them."

Pete couldn't speak.

"Pedrito, please tell me. Know this, mijo, when I called you mijo, I meant it, to both of you. From that first moment, you were my sons."

Pete took Polito's hand. "Papá," he said. He felt his throat tighten. He hadn't called Polito that in decades. "I forgive you, please forgive me."

"There is nothing to forgive you for, mijo, you're a good boy. I'm proud of you, of the man you've become. And you, Chicho, the same, I couldn't be prouder of my sons." Polito's body began to tremble. "Mijos, one last thing."

"Anything, Papá" Chicho said.

"Don't let them bury me here. Take me back to Santo Domingo. Bury me next to Henrietta."

"Por supuesto," Pete said.

"Cómo tú querías," Chicho added.

Polito took a deep breath. He shuddered and let the breath go. His head slipped to one side. Pete closed Polito eyes. He held Polito's head in his hands for a few moments, his silent tears falling on Polito's face mixing with the blood that seeped out of his mouth. He turned to Chicho. His face was blank. Pete pulled Chicho's head toward his chest as he used to do when they were kids. Chicho would sneak out to Polito's after his father beat him and wake Pete up. He had that same expression. He was never a child, Chicho. No one ever let him be.

"Hermano," Tolya said, his hand on Pete's shoulder. Pete touched Tolya's hand with his own, Polito's blood smearing onto Tolya's hand. Tolya noticed the sky lightening. It was dawn. "We have to go."

"Yes we do," said Pete.

They rose and lifted Polito's body. They carried him to the Escalade and laid him out in the back, wrapping him with a tarp. Pete found a small cushion in the back and placed it with much care under Polito's head. He looked at Tolya and gave him the keys. "You know, he wasn't always a criminal."

Chapter
32

SANTO DOMINGO, DOMINICAN REPUBLIC
12 FEBRUARY 1984
1:00 P.M.

P ETE HELD HIS UNCLE'S HAND tightly. He fought back the
tears as he watched his mother disappear down the long corridor
on her way to America with his next oldest brother, Yoskar. She had
promised him he would be next. Of course he would be next, he was
the only one left.

"I promise you," his mother had said. "One more year, maybe two."

"But you promised me when you took Zenia that I would be next."

"I know," she said. "But Yoskar, he needs to come now. He got
himself into trouble. I can't trust him here." She put her arms around
him and kissed him. She held him by the shoulders. "You I can trust.
You are my good boy."

"Mama, I miss you. Please, take me now. I don't want to live with
Abuela alone."

She sighed. "You're not going to, mijo. You're going to live with Tío
Polito."

His heart rose when he heard this. What he really wanted to do was to go to America with his mother, but if he couldn't, well, to live with Tío Polito, that was pretty good. Tío Polito was like one of the kids. He wouldn't scream at Pete like his father's mother did. Still, as he watched his older brother and his mother disappear behind the walls at the airport in Santo Domingo, he felt like the tears would burst out of his eyes like the water that came out of the rocks in the hills outside the village where Chicho's grandmother lived.

"Tató sobrino?" Polito asked.

"Sí," Pete said and then the tears came. He couldn't hold them anymore. And he was embarrassed. He was a man, men don't cry like old ladies when someone goes away.

Polito bent down, bringing his big frame to Pete's height. "Ven aca, mijo," he said and wrapped his arms around Pete. "Ven, llora, go ahead, I understand."

First Pete pushed him away, the convulsions of his sobs wracking his body. He didn't know where to look. He had to stop crying, to control himself, to act like a man. But he knew in his heart that he wasn't a man yet, he was a boy and his mother had broken her promise to him. He missed her. One by one, she had taken them, taken everyone, his sisters and his brothers. Now only he was left with no one. No father and now no mother. Polito reached out to him and he collapsed into his arms. "Nobody wants me, Tío."

"That's not true, mijo. I want you."

"She promised," Pete squeaked out through the tears.

"She had to get Yoskar out of here. You don't understand how bad things are here. He would have ended up in jail. Your grandmother was too sick and old to control him."

"Why couldn't she take me too?"

"Money, Pedrito. I know you don't understand that, but that's what makes everything happen, money."

"I have 100 pesos. It's hidden under the floor at Abuela's house."

Polito laughed. "Ay, cabrón. You don't understand anything for your innocence. This is our life in this country. It's very hard. It tears us apart." Polito felt Pete's pain. It was all too close to his own, as they had left him, first his mother, then his sisters and brothers. Then his father died, and then his mother, and there was no one left to bring him. He would have to wait ten years for a visa from one of his brothers or sisters, and that was after they had finished bringing their own children.

He wrapped his big arms around Pete again. "Tío?" Pete said, his crying subsiding, sniffling through his tears.

"Sí?"

"Do you want me?"

"Of course," Polito said, choking back his own tears.

"You won't run away from me like my father and my mother?"

Polito wanted to explain it to him, but he knew this wasn't the moment. "Nunca jamás."

"OK," Pete said, straightening up and wiping his eyes. He took in a deep breath that shook his body. "Then let's go home." He reached up for Polito's hand and pulled him forward out of the airport.

Life with Tío Polito was pretty good. He missed his mother the same way he had for the past five years, but he missed Yoskar more. They had slept in the same bed together. They were together all the time. Yoskar protected him. Taught him how to box, how to play baseball, how to smile at girls.

His mother was receding in his mind. Some days he had trouble remembering her face. He had to look at the photograph on the wall of the kitchen to remember its details. Her voice he had forgotten altogether.

Polito's wife, Tía Henrietta, was very sweet and very beautiful. She would cook for them every day, the best things, the things he liked, mangú with salami and eggs and fish with coconut milk. Now she was going to have a baby in a few months. The baby would be like a brother or sister for Pete. He wouldn't be the youngest anymore.

But the best thing was that Tío Polito took him everywhere with him, to play baseball in the park and to the Plaza to sit with the men and bring them beers from the colmado. They would give him a few pesos for his efforts and he would save them in his secret place. Sometimes Tío would even let him have some beer.

They would have their secrets too, he and Tío, things even Tía Henrietta couldn't know about, Tío's girlfriends and his guapo friends who flashed around a lot of money. Tío was the coolest guy anywhere.

And the other best thing was that he could bring his best friend Chicho along all the time. Chicho lived in the patio just a few houses away. His father was always drunk and would beat Chicho and his mother sometimes when he got really crazy, so Tío Polito said it was OK for Chicho to stay in their house.

It had been a little over a year since Yoskar had left with his mother for New York. It was Pete's birthday today, his second since moving in with Tío. He would be 12 years old. His aunt and uncle were throwing him a party this afternoon. All the kids in the patio would come, they would play games, and Tía Henrietta told him she would make him a big cake. Pedro looked down off the narrow bed at Chicho sleeping on the thin mat on the floor. They had found the mat outside the gym a few blocks away, up the hill past where the new supermarket was being built. The rich people who lived in the new houses behind the high wall went to that gym. His uncle said that land once belonged to his grandfather.

The mat was torn. The rich people, they threw out everything that wasn't perfect. He and Chicho carried it back to the house and Tío Polito had fixed it with some tape. Now when Chicho wanted to sleep over, they didn't have to share the bed. Pedro reached down and touched Chicho on the shoulder. "Hermanito, levántate."

Chicho stirred. He opened his eyes slowly. "Ay, no, tengo sueños."

Pedro pushed him a little harder, then tapped him with his foot. "No, no, mi hermano, today's the day, my birthday. Come on, I want to get up now."

Chicho rolled onto his back. He looked up at Pedro and smiled. "Sí, so you are older than me again today."

"Only for another eleven months."

"Feliz cumpleaños, hermano."

"Gracias," said Pete, jumping out of the bed. He slipped a T-shirt over his wiry frame and pulled back the curtain that separated his room from the living room. He saw his uncle's back to him through the open front door on the porch. He walked toward him to see what he was doing, Chicho following him, rubbing the sleep from his eyes.

Pedro's eyes widened when he walked through the door, despite the bright sunlight that would otherwise have made him squint. There in front of him on the floor were the parts of a new bicycle. He had a bicycle but it was too small for him. His heart raced, he suppressed the smile he felt creeping up around his mouth. "What are you doing?" he asked Polito.

Polito chuckled. "What does it look like I'm doing?"

Pete sat down next to Polito on the rough wooden floor. Chicho dropped to the floor next to him. He touched the shiny red metallic frame, sizing it up. It was too small for Polito himself. "Who is it for?"

Polito continued working on the bicycle. He said nothing, then finally, "I don't know. Who do you think needs this bicycle? You have a bicycle."

"I don't know." Pete said.

"Chicho needs one," Polito said. He smiled afterward.

That was true. Chicho didn't have a bike. Pete had to put him on the handlebars sometimes so they could go where they needed to. He was getting too big to do that and the bike was too small anyway. Pete turned to his left and looked at Chicho. Chicho shrugged.

They watched silently as Polito put the wheels on the bike and locked them into place. They helped Polito as he asked them to, to hold the bike steady or turn a screw as he needed. There was no conversation, only concentration as the parts came together and the bike took shape. Finally, it was time to adjust the seat.

"Hold this here," Polito said, instructing Pedro to stand next to the seat. He measured the height of the seat to Pedro's hip. Pedro said nothing. His heart beat a little harder.

Polito walked the bike off the porch onto the street. He turned and gestured to Pete to come forward. He did as he was asked.

"Get on, mijo. Happy birthday," Polito said. He grabbed Pete and pulled him toward him. Pete wrapped his arms around his uncle's waist. He loved him so much, this man who was everything to him, mother, father and big brother.

"Thank you, Papá," he whispered. He got on the bike. It felt different. It was much larger than the one he had. He felt a little unsure at first as he pedaled out of the patio into the plaza across the street, but then the familiar feeling of moving through the air, of freedom, came to him. It felt so much better. The bike fit. He extended his legs, raised himself from the seat. It was like magic. He took two more laps around the plaza, then back into the patio, Polito and Chicho waiting for him in front of the wood-frame house. He walked up to Polito and embraced him again. "Gracias," he said, then walked quickly to the back of the house. He opened the door to the small storage shed and took out his old bicycle. He jumped on and road it quickly to the front of the house. "Tío," he said, "can we raise the seat a little?"

Polito looked at the bicycle and smiled. "Por supuesto."

Pete put his hand on Chicho's shoulder. "This is yours now, hermanito. Now we can go together."

Chicho looked up at Pete. Pete could see the tears in his eyes. They embraced each other but said nothing. Chicho jumped on the bike and pedaled forward. He disappeared down the alley into the street. Pete looked up at Polito and smiled.

"I am so proud of you, mijo," Polito said. "That was a very nice thing you did. You could have sold that bike."

Pete hugged Polito again. "This will be my best birthday ever."

The bicycles gave them freedom. They could go anywhere they wanted now, together. In the past they had been like brothers, but now they were inseparable. They would ride up the hill into the parts of Altos de Arroyo Hondo where no one lived, where it was still like a jungle. Polito told them to be careful, as it was becoming more and more dangerous because of the drugs. The drugs were everywhere now.

Pete looked back to see where Chicho was as he neared the top of the hill. He stopped and waited for him to catch up. When he was close, he hopped back onto the bike and pedaled forward into the park. He rode a little further to the point where they would turn off the paved road onto the dirt path that led to the little waterfall.

Chicho caught up to him. "Why you so slow?" Pete shouted at Chicho.

"Diablo," Chicho shouted back, then sped in front of Pete before Pete could mount his bike again.

They raced down the dirt path for a few minutes toward the large natural pool that formed at the base of the little waterfall in a bend in a stream that emptied into the Ozama River, which ran through the capital to the sea. Chicho got the better of him and beat Pete to the water by seconds. They pulled off their shirts and jumped in. The water was cool and refreshing in the intense heat of the Caribbean summer. They roughed in the water, tossing each other around and wrestling each other under and behind the waterfall.

The space behind the cascading water between the falls and the stone cliff was cool and calm. Pete loved the feeling of it, the blue-tinged light and the spray from the gently falling water. He took a small rubber ball out of the pocket of his shorts and tossed it to Chicho. The water was shallow here and they could stand, the water pooling up just below their knees.

"Catch for me," Pete said as he wound up, pitching the ball at Chicho.

Chicho crouched slightly and caught it. "Strike," he called out then tossed the ball back to Pete. Pete wound up and pitched the ball again at Chicho. "Bola," Chicho called out.

"No way," Pete said. "Strike."

"No," Chicho repeated and tossed the ball back to Pete.

They continued the game for what seemed to them to be a few innings, alternating between pitching and catching to each other, the spray and the dim light cool and soothing.

"You hungry?" Pete asked Chicho.

"Sí," Chicho said.

"Let's go find some mangoes," Pete said. They waded through the water toward the break in the falls on the right side. "Stop," Pete said, putting his hand back toward Chicho.

"Cómo?"

"Look," Pete said, pointing toward the riverbank.

Three men stood a few feet up from the water at the edge of the forest that led down to the stream. A large wooden crate sat in the dirt a few feet away. Two of the men had shovels. The other was talking on a walkie-talkie. The man on the walkie-talkie was very muscular and bigger than the other two. He gestured to them to start digging.

"We gotta get out of here," Chicho said, shivering. "I'm cold. I gotta get out of the water."

"We can't let them know we're here." Pete surveyed the scene. Their bikes were hidden under some palm branches about fifty feet farther down the riverbank from where the men were digging. "You think you could swim underwater to over there by that tree, then we can run for our bikes and get out of here?"

Chicho looked at the distance. Pete saw the doubt in his eyes. "I guess so," he said.

"OK, take a deep breath. We go on three."

They both breathed deeply, then dove under the falls. Pete listened to the muffled sound of the men talking as he moved silently through the water. He hoped Chicho was OK. Then he heard the shout. He shot up through the water. Chicho was gasping for air in the middle of the pool in front of the waterfall. The big man with the walkie-talkie pulled off his shirt and was headed into the water after Chicho. He had two big X's tattooed on the top of his back.

Pete wasn't sure what to do. He froze for a moment, then turned and swam back to where Chicho was. He reached him just before the big man. The water was too deep for them to stand but not for the big man. He grabbed both of them by the arms and started pulling them toward the shore. They fought back, but the guy was strong and the current was making it difficult for them to fight him off. He dragged them out of the water, the other two men each grabbing one of them and holding them. The big man bent over and breathed heavily.

"Coño, what you little fuckers doing here?"

"Let go," Pete screamed, kicking the man holding him. The man grabbed his shin where Pete had kicked him, letting go of Pete. Pete lunged at the man holding Chicho. "Te mato," he screamed.

Before he could plant his teeth in the man's arm, the big guy with the tattoo grabbed him and lifted him off the ground. "Damn, you a tough one," he said, laughing and holding Pete over his head, Pete's legs swinging wildly. "I'll put you down if you calm down. If you continue this, I'm gonna beat the shit out of you."

"OK, OK," Pete said.

The big man put him down. He squatted near to the ground and massaged his arm where the big man had grabbed him.

"Now, I'm gonna ask you again, muchacho. What you doing here?"

Pete looked up at him. "What the fuck it look like we were doing? Swimming. What the fuck you doing here, maricón?"

The big man took a step toward him and raised his hand. Pete raised his arm to protect his head. Chicho struggled against the man holding him. "Watch your mouth, muchacho, or I will have to shut it for you."

The big man paced back and forth a few times. "Jefe," said the one holding Chicho. "What we gonna do with them?"

"I don't know, I'm thinking."

"I think they've seen too much," said the other guy, the one Pete had kicked.

"What you suggesting, idiota? You wanna kill them? You think maybe somebody is gonna be looking for them? Coño." The big man looked at Pete. "You boys smart?"

Pete looked at Chicho, then back at the big man. He saw the fear in Chicho's eyes. He was terrified himself, sure that these guys could, no, would kill them. He concentrated to remove the fear from his eyes. *Be cool, tranquilo, like Polito.* He took a breath and stared the big man in the eyes for a long second. "Sí, real smart."

"Let him go," the big man with the X tattoos said to the guy holding Chicho. He released Chicho, who fell to the ground. "Pick up the shovels."

"What the..." said Pete.

"Just do as I say. I asked you if you are smart. You said yes. Now pick up the shovels."

Pete and Chicho did as they were told.

"Now, start digging. You see that box? That's gotta go about six feet down, so I'd say you got about eight feet to dig."

Pete and Chicho looked at each other. They started digging. Within minutes they were sweating. Tiny flies that seemed to come out of nowhere swarmed around them. It took the better part of the morning to finish the dig. When the big man said the hole was deep enough, they collapsed inside it. Pete thought he was going to vomit more than once. "Please," he said. "Could we cool off, go in the water?"

The big man hesitated. "Sure, but don't try anything 'cause you know I can catch you."

Pete helped Chicho up. He nearly collapsed. He helped him down to the water. They stepped into the river where the pool in front of the waterfall was calm. The cool water was a shock at first, but then it soothed both of them.

"Pedrito, I can't do any more, I'm gonna pass out," Chicho whispered.

"I know, hermanito. We're almost done, then I'm gonna get us out of here. We just gotta finish up. You gotta push through it. I won't let anything happen to you."

"How you gonna do that?"

"I don't know. I'll figure it out."

Chicho smiled.

"OK, break's over," the big man shouted. "Get back here."

Pete looked at Chicho. He cupped his hands, filled them with the cool water and poured it over Chicho's head. "Hang tough, hermano," he said. He'd heard Polito say that so many times to his buddies when they lifted weights in the courtyard in the patio. It sounded like the right thing to say.

They waded back out of the water and up to where the three men were standing. Two of the men lifted the crate and slowly lowered it into the pit they had dug. Pete looked at the crate. The sunlight breaking through the trees from directly above fell on the tightly wrapped plastic bags inside the crate between the cracks in the wood slats. There was something white inside the plastic. Pete knew instantly what it was. He's seen plenty of cocaina in the streets of Santo Domingo.

"What you staring at?" one of the men lowering the crate shouted at him.

"Your ugly face," Pete said, knowing full well the man couldn't strike out at him, as his hands were occupied with the crate and the ropes. The big man laughed.

"Fuck you, you little scumbag," the ugly man said.

The crate hit the bottom. The men threw the ends of the ropes into the hole along with it. They threw a tarp over it.

"Now, fill it up," Double X tattoo said.

Filling the hole was a lot easier than digging it. They finished quickly. Pete still didn't know what he was going to do to get them away.

"Where do you live?" the big man asked.

Pete didn't answer. He told Chicho with his eyes to say nothing.

"I asked you a question," the big man said.

Pete hesitated. "The small patio on the west side of the Plaza Ecuador," he said finally.

"Tató. Now listen carefully. Remember, I know what you look like and where you live. You never saw nothing here, you never did nothing here, you never saw me or my boys. I ever think you said anything to anyone, I'll find you and kill you."

Pete remained silent. He looked at Chicho, then down at the ground. "We won't say nothing to nobody."

"Stand up straight, both of you," the big man said. He reached into his pocket and pulled out some bank notes. He selected two from the wad. He handed one to each of them. Pete looked down into his hand. It was a 100 peso note. "You both work for me now. My name is Double X. Be back here in one week at the same time, we gotta get that box out of the ground. Get the hell out of here."

Pete said nothing. He looked at Chicho. They pocketed the 100 peso notes and walked quickly to their bikes. As exhausted as they were, they got on their bikes and pedaled up the hill as fast as they could.

Chapter
33

"CAPTAIN, LOOK AT THIS," OFFICER Olivia Peña said, calling to him from her perch at the temporary table they had set up in the hallway. Six officers sat at six laptops scanning the footage from every available street security cam in Lower Manhattan. If people knew how closely they were being watched, there would be a huge public outcry.

"What you got there, young lady?" he said, approaching Peña.

Peña stretched her arms upward and tilted her head toward the frozen screen, then yawned. "I think I've got a partial ID on the plate. It's obscured a little by the pedestrian crossing in front of it, but the last four numbers are correct and it's the right make and model."

The captain scrutinized the frame. "What's the time stamp on that? I can't read it without my glasses."

Peña smiled. "My dad's the same way. Why don't you just wear them around your neck?"

"'Cause I'm not a goddamned librarian, thank you."

"Time stamp says 8:26."

"She was abducted at what, 5:15?"

"About that. Why would they drive around for three hours?"

"To confuse her, and us. What intersection is this cam at?" asked the captain.

"The corner of Water and Maiden Lane."

The captain turned to the officer at the computer next to Peña. "Pull up a map of Lower Manhattan from the department files that shows the locations of all the security cams and then zoom to this location."

"Yes sir."

The captain felt a rush of adrenalin. He had been up for nearly two days now with little more than a couple hours sleep on the cot in the back of his office. He was sore and tired but the possibility of locating the car energized him. "OK," he said, "pull back a little on the zoom. OK, good. Now place a pin at the intersection where Peña located the car."

"Water and Maiden."

"Done," said the other uniform.

"Zoom in just a little bit more," the captain said.

The young officer did as he was instructed. The captain bent over the young officer in the chair, his stomach resting on the chair's arm. "Would you like to sit down, captain?"

The captain looked up. "Um, yeah, sure." He shifted into the swiveling chair as the young officer got up. "Peña."

"Yes, Cap."

"Call up the images from the camera at Water and Broad and look at them from the same time stamp through about the next 10 minutes."

Peña typed a code into the computer and the image on the screen changed.

"Increase the speed to double time," the captain said. The three of them stared at the screen. About two and a half minutes later, the front view of the limo appeared in the screen. "Speed that up till the limo is almost under the cam."

Peña did as instructed.

"Now zoom in on the license plate." And there it was, all seven characters as plain as day. He'd found the car. "Yes," he mumbled. "I'm still pretty good at this." He flipped back to the map screen on the next computer. "OK, where would you go next?" He traced his finger along the screen. There were three possible routes. He looked up at the three young patrolmen seated at the three laptops on the opposite side of the table. They had stopped reviewing the videos and were watching him. "You three come here."

"Yes, captain," they said simultaneously.

"Now, you see these three possible routes the limo might take? Each one of you take one and follow it as far as you can till the limo disappears or stops somewhere."

"Yes, Cap," they replied.

The captain stepped back, leaned against the doorpost and watched as the three young officers each chose a possible route to look for the limo's destination. After about two minutes, two of the officers stopped. They had no sign of the limo on their screen. The third, a young woman, concentrated on her screen. After another two minutes that felt like twenty, with all eyes in that hallway upon her, she shouted, "Got it! They pulled into an underground garage at 2 Liberty Place."

Tolya looked at his watch: 6:30. He looked at Pete and Chicho. They were exhausted and in shock from what had happened. He imagined he looked the same way.

They had driven back from Long Island with Polito's body in the back of the Escalade under a tarp. They had said virtually nothing, any of them. What was there to say? The sound of Tolya's phone pierced the quiet. Tolya looked at the phone. "It's the captain," he said.

Pete said nothing. Chicho stared out the window in the back seat. The phone continued to ring. "It's the captain," he said again.

"Fuck the captain," said Pete. "I know where this guy is and who this guy is and I'm gonna finish him off myself." The ringing stopped, the call went to voicemail.

"Maybe we should tell him what we know," said Tolya.

"We ain't got time," Pete said as they passed under the Brooklyn Bridge. They were almost there. He knew a place he could stash the car with his police sticker, which he'd taken with him earlier from his own car.

The phone rang again. It was the captain. "Pete, maybe we need backup." Tolya's stomach turned. He tried to keep himself calm, for Karin's sake. Nothing else mattered now, only Karin, the baby and their safety, not even his own life or the repercussions of their actions.

"Nope, too much shit has gone down, hermano. No matter what happens here, we're done. They're gonna fry our asses. We going to jail, so who needs them."

The ringing stopped and the call went to voicemail again. Pete pulled into the spot and stuck the police card in the windshield. They got out of the car and began walking toward 2 Liberty Place. He slipped a badge to Chicho. "Put this on the outside of your wallet."

As they crossed the street, Tolya received a text. It was from the captain. It read: "we know where she is."

He texted back, "So do we, and we r there."

The knocking on the door pulled Karin from her dream. She heard Tserverin's voice. It sickened her. "Madame Kurchenko, are you awake?"

Why didn't he just use his key? She didn't answer him. She looked at the clock: 6:30. At this point there was no turning him. He was a psychopath. There was no possibility of a human connection. Tserverin couldn't make one.

"Karin," he said this time. When she didn't answer again, she heard the sound of his key in the lock. The door opened. He stood there in jeans, shirtless. She chuckled to herself. If she wasn't pregnant and out of practice, she could easily take him down. She had a black belt in judo. She couldn't risk anything happening to the baby.

"You're not speaking to me today?" Tserverin said.

"Why should I? Nothing I say seems to change the course of your actions toward me."

"Perhaps you haven't been persuasive enough."

Karin sighed. She weighed the possibilities. If she could knock him down with just one kick, tilt him in the direction of the dresser, perhaps he would hit his head, knocking him out. She could escape. If it went bad she could lose the baby.

"Get up," Tserverin said.

Karin shifted into a sitting position. She had to make a decision now. She knew what was coming. It was only a matter of time until he laced her up into his killing machine. If he succeeded in killing her, Oleg would die with her. If she tried to knock him out she might go into labor. She had no choice. She had to protect Oleg. She thought for a moment of all the conversations she had had over the past months with Shalom and with Tolya about her conversion. She had learned she had faith and she turned now to that faith. *Please help me*, she said in her heart and her head. *I don't care what you call yourself, HaShem or Jesus or Buddha or any other name you want, but if you exist, please help me to save my child.*

"Madame Kurchenko," he said again.

She pushed herself up from the bed.

"Put your hands out in front of you," Tserverin demanded.

She held her arms out, palms up, wrists together. As Tserverin slipped the rope around her wrists, she took a half step, drawing closer to him. He slid one piece of the rope over another. Stealthily and with great speed, as she had been taught, she kicked her left leg slightly out and back nearly losing her balance slamming the inside edge of her foot into Tserverin's ankle, pushing both his legs out from under him. At the same time she slammed her wrists into his chin sending his body in the direction of the bureau. She felt a sharp pain in her lower stomach deep inside. Her heart skipped a beat.

The look of shock on Tserverin's face was enough to satisfy her. His head hit the blunt edge of the dresser and his body turned as he hit the floor face down. Karin noticed the gush of red from the back of his head immediately, as well as the pool of red quickly forming under his face. She felt another sharp quick pain in her stomach and grabbed for it. "Please Oleg, just hold on, Mama's trying," she whispered.

Karin sat at the edge of the bed for a long moment and waited. Tserverin didn't move. She rose from the bed and pushed his body with her foot. As his head turned, she saw that he was bleeding from the nose as well. He was out cold. She felt like crying and laughing at the same time.

She reached under the mattress and grabbed the credit card and the paper clips and headed for the front door. She stopped for a moment in the hallway when she spotted Tserverin's phone. She grabbed it. It asked for the security code. "Coño," she muttered, throwing it down onto the floor. It shattered into several pieces, each flying in a different direction.

Karin bent in front of the door. She placed one hand under her stomach to reassure herself that Oleg was OK. She felt him move and let out her breath. She slipped the credit card into the space between the door and the post, then slipped the opened untwisted paper clip into the lock. She gently searched for the tumbler. She began to sweat, the droplets running into her eyes. Her throat caught as she heard the lock slip open. At that second, she felt her head pull back violently. It was Tserverin. He grabbed her long hair with one hand, jerking her back. She thought he would snap her neck. He lifted her with the other hand, violently.

"You Latina cunt. Now I'm gonna finish you and that Jew filth in your belly for good."

Karin screamed. The pain was too much. Tserverin dragged Karin across the living room and quickly knotted a rope around one wrist, hoisting her into the killing machine. She felt a warm trickle come down her leg. Her water had broken. This was all too much and it was too late. She didn't know it, but she had the same thought as his other victims at the same moment. She remembered all the happiness of her life and none of the pain and was only sad that there wouldn't be more.

"Goddamn it, the both of you!" the captain shouted. "Peña," he continued screaming, "get me a SWAT team and two squad cars down to that address immediately."

"Yes, sir," she answered.

The captain grabbed his gun and his cell phone and headed out to the front of the station. A squad car pulled up. He jumped into the front seat.

Chapter
34

P ETE JUMPED OFF HIS BIKE and left it on the front porch. He ran into the house, waving at Tío Polito as he passed him in his shorts and wifebeater reading the paper. "Qué lo que, muchacho," Polito called out to him as he passed.

Pete flipped open the curtain to his room and pulled it back shut. He pulled off the uniform he wore to school and stuck his hand in the pocket of the pants, pulling out the 20 peso note Double X had given him that morning before school for completing his courier job the evening before. In the two months since they had stumbled upon Double X at the waterfall, he and Chicho had made a considerable amount of money running "errands." Mostly they carried messages and sometimes small amounts of cocaine between Double X and his drug boys. Double X knew when he was being watched, and the less contact he had with his partners in crime, the better for everyone. Pete and Chicho were his courier pigeons.

Pete knelt down at the foot of the bed and lifted the corner of the small rug at its edge. He slipped a small piece of metal between two of the floorboards and pulled up. The board lifted easily. Pete felt as if he had been hit in the gut. The money was gone. He had saved 4,000 pesos in two months. It was gone. He fell back off his haunches and onto the floor, wrapping his arms around his knees.

He heard his uncle's voice from behind him. "Looking for this?" He turned to see Polito holding the wad of bills and waving them in the air.

Pete said nothing. Polito sat down on the edge of the bed. "Where did you get this?"

Pete turned his head. He felt the tears in his eyes. He didn't know what to say. "Please, Papá," was all that came out of his mouth. The tears streamed silently down his cheeks. He couldn't look at Polito. What was it Polito always told him? Do the right thing. Don't get mixed up with thugs like Yoskar did. Be proud of yourself. Act like a man.

"Please Papá what?" Polito said. His voice was calm and even.

Pete remained silent.

"Mijo, turn around."

"I can't," Pete said. "I'm too ashamed."

Polito reached out his hand to Pete's shoulder. He turned him slowly. Pete stared at the floor, trying to hide his tears from Polito. "Mijo, tell me where this came from. I won't be angry."

"Yes you will."

"You have my word. Be a man and tell the truth."

Pete took a deep breath and began recounting the whole awful story from the moment they first saw Double X from behind the curtain of the waterfall. "I was so afraid of him, Papá. I didn't know what he would do to us, to Chicho and me, if we didn't do what he wanted and he was giving us money too. I wanted to give you the money, for Tía Henrietta..." Pete began to sob again. Polito pulled him in and embraced him.

"I understand, don't worry. There is nothing that can change how

I feel about you. You're my son. Now calm down. Tranquillo. We will take care of this."

Pete hugged Polito tightly and cried deeply. They were so poor. He only wanted to help, but how could he have explained this to Polito? They had taken him in when he had no one else and nowhere to go. Even his father hadn't wanted him. Tío was his father now and Pete had failed him, disappointed him. He was only a boy and he was afraid. He breathed in deeply, the scent of Polito in his nose. He knew this man would protect him. He was glad Tío had found the money. He could stop being afraid.

Pete sat at the small table in the living room of the shack with Polito and Chicho. A cool breeze filtered in through the door and windows. It was late in the afternoon and it felt like it would rain soon.

"OK, you understand what we're gonna do?"

Pete and Chicho looked at each other. "Tío, I don't know, this is very dangerous. He's crazy."

"And big," said Chicho.

"Do I look afraid? Or small?" Polito said, standing up from the table.

"Pero Polito, he told us he would kill us if anyone found out."

"Chicho, don't worry, nobody's gonna get killed. He said that to scare you and apparently he did a pretty good job."

Pete and Chicho looked at each other again.

"OK, now tell me the plan."

"Tomorrow afternoon after school, we are gonna ride over to where Double X hangs out," Pete said.

"Sí."

"We're gonna find out if he needs us to do anything like we always do," Chicho said.

"Then we're gonna come back here and tell you what we have to do and where."

"Sí, and where you have to meet him and at what time," reiterated Polito.

"Sí" said Pete. "Then we're gonna do it and you're gonna be there when we go to tell him the job is finished."

"Sí, and I'm gonna finish him."

"Good job, papi," Double X said, rolling the small packets of cocaine over in his hand. He took two 50 peso notes out of his pocket and handed one each to Pete and Chicho. "I'm going to have to consider promoting you two. You both smarter than I thought when I caught you that day. Coño, you made this exchange in the lobby of the Hilton?"

"Sí," Pete said. He saw Polito on the bench in the small park across the street. He tilted his head slightly as Polito had told him to do when the transaction was complete. He watched as Polito rose slowly and walked confidently across the street. Polito was wearing a T-shirt way too small for his muscled frame. All those hours in the patio pressing weights showed. Pete caught Double X's expression as he saw Polito cross the street and walk toward him. X was always suspicious, but in his line of business you had to be, too many enemies ready to take you down and take your place.

"Qué lo que," Polito said, waving from about fifteen feet away.

Double X looked at him. "Quién es?"

Pete had trouble stifling a smile. Chicho stepped back a few feet toward their bikes. "He wants to talk to you. About business." Pete said.

"Coño, papi, you a real businessman now, bringing me a new client."

Pete watched Double X's guard drop. His shoulders relaxed and his hand withdrew from the side of his body near his waist where he kept his pistol hidden, tucked into his jeans.

Polito stepped up onto the sidewalk from the street. He extended his hand to Double X. "Polito," he said.

Double X shook Polito's hand. "Qué lo que, primo. How can I help you?"

"I want to talk to you about these boys," Polito said, nodding his head toward Pete and Chicho.

Double X laughed. "These boys? Why would we be talking about these boys? They work for me. I don't know what you're talking about, brother, but I'm a busy man." Double X stood up from his perch on the three-foot concrete retaining wall he was sitting on. "Coño, why you wasting my time?"

Polito took a step toward him. Double X stiffened. "These are my sons," he said.

Pete watched Double X's hand move back toward the gun. He glanced at Polito. He knew Polito had seen the movement, as Polito's hand went toward the pistol hidden in the small of his back under his shirt.

"These boys are not your sons. They got nobody. They belong to me."

"I said these are my sons. You stay away from them."

As Double X reached to grab his gun, Polito came up from his side fast and grabbed his arm. He twisted X's arm back and pulled X against him. He pulled X's gun from its place at the side of his waist and threw it toward Pete. "Pick that up, put it in your bag." Pete did as he was told.

Polito grabbed his own pistol and placed it against X's right temple. As big as X was, even bigger than Polito, Polito was quicker and stronger. The weights had made him big, but the years in the boxing ring had made him fast and strong, stronger than his size led anyone to believe. He cocked the gun. Pete and Chicho stepped back.

"You come near my sons again and I'll kill you. You understand? I would kill you right now, but I don't want your brains all over them and I want them to learn a good lesson: mercy. You understand?"

Double X struggled slightly. "Sí," he mumbled through gritted teeth.

Polito released him and stepped back. "We understand each other?" Polito said again.

Double X looked at him then lunged toward him. Polito raised his left arm to guard himself, then pulled back his right and hurled his fist into Double X's face. He hit him square in the nose. Double X's face contorted, the blood pouring out. He stumbled back into the waist-high retaining wall, then forward toward Polito. Polito hit him again, this time with a left. X went down completely. Pete looked at Polito. Their eyes met. Pete saw something there that frightened him. It was anger too deep to extinguish. Polito turned back toward Double X, now on the ground. By this time, a crowd had assembled. Polito looked at them. He said nothing. He got down on his knees like a predatory animal proclaiming its victory over its prey, X's body under him. "I warned you, maricón." He spit into X's face and got up.

"Vamos," he said, wiping Double X's blood from his hands onto his shirt.

Chapter
35

LOWER MANHATTAN, NYC
12 JUNE 2010
6:45 A.M.

TOLYA, PETE AND CHICHO WALKED casually through the heavy glass door held open by the doorman. The concierge's head bobbed up, a big smile appearing on his face. "May I help you gentlemen?"

They held up their badges. "NYPD," Pete said. He smiled broadly and walked up to the desk, bringing his grinning face inches from the concierge's. Chicho walked stealthily behind the concierge and placed the nozzle of his gun into his side. Chicho and Pete worked like one unit, as Tolya and Pete did, but Tolya had never seen this menacing side of Pete before, not in all the years he'd known him. He didn't care. He was in the same building as Karin, and no number of laws or regulations or degree of risk mattered now.

"Don't say a word and don't even think of pressing that silent alarm button under the lip of the desk." Pete said.

The concierge withdrew his hand.

"How did you know that?" Chicho asked.

"I watch a lot of cop shows," Pete said, still smiling at the concierge an inch from his face. "Now, straighten up naturally and keep smiling."

The concierge did as he was told.

"Tell the doormen to step outside, clear the lobby of that couple over there, then come back here, lock the exterior door…"

"What if the doormen ask me why?"

"Tell them it's a police emergency. Do it… now."

The concierge walked from behind the desk, Chicho shadowing him. "I'm so sorry," he said. "I'm going to have to ask you to step outside."

"Is something wrong?" the suited, middle-aged man asked.

"Well, actually, it's a police matter."

The man and woman looked at Chicho. He smiled broadly and held up his badge again.

"I hope nothing is wrong."

"No, no, please just step outside."

The couple did as they were told. The concierge followed them and told the doormen to step out as well. He turned back toward Pete and Tolya. Pete smiled broadly again. The doormen stepped out and the concierge stepped back in, returning to his perch behind the desk.

"Now lock the door."

The concierge followed Pete's commands. "You have an electronic tenant notification system?"

"Yes."

"Send out a notice that there is emergency work beginning on the passenger elevators, and for the next two hours, tenants are to use the service elevators. Do not send the notice to 33W"

"Mr. Taylor?"

Pete looked at Tolya.

"Taylor, Schneider, Portnoy, all the same," Tolya said.

"Yep," Pete replied.

The concierge hesitated. Chicho stepped a little closer and pushed the gun into the concierge's back a little deeper. "Don't fuck with me, asshole, 'cause we'll kill you right now and we'll do all this ourselves."

The concierge relented.

"Chicho, you stay here with him till we arrive on the 33rd floor. You can see it on that screen there," Pete said.

"Tató," Chicho answered.

"Cuando llegamos, you tie him down and head up in the service elevator to help us."

Pete and Tolya charged the elevator, open and waiting for passengers. They pressed 33. Though it took only seconds, the ride felt like forever. "How did you know all that shit about the building?" Tolya said.

"It was a crapshoot. Glynnis watches this show on Sunday mornings about luxury real estate and I saw this shit on there. Figured they had the same shit here."

"Coño," Tolya said.

Pete smiled. It was the first time he had ever heard Tolya use that word. "Cuidate, hermano," he said as the elevator slowed and the doors cracked open. "Let's go get your wife."

Tolya and Pete lifted their guns. "On three," Tolya said. "One, two, three…"

The shots slammed directly into the lock over the handle of the door. Pete lifted his leg and kicked at it. It blew off its hinges instantly. "Karin," Tolya screamed as they charged into the apartment. He turned his head to the left and saw her. She was gagged and bound into the machine.

"Freeze," Pete screamed at the figure behind her.

Tserverin stood straight. The insane quality of his smile reminded Tolya of Heath Ledger's portrayal of the Joker. He stared at the face. At first its mouth opened, but for a moment it was as if there were a delay between the film and the sound. Nothing came out of it, then a laugh like a hyena, then a scream. "Kurchenko, you Jew bastard." He held a machete under Karin's neck.

"Don't fire," Tolya said to Pete.

"I see," Pete replied.

Tolya noticed the pinkish fluid that stained Karin's leg and the floor under her. Her water had broken. "Nicholai," Tolya said to him in Russian. "This is between you and me, let her go."

Tserverin stiffened. He brought the machete up a little closer under Karin's chin. Tolya's eyes locked to hers. *Hold on*, he told her through his thoughts. *I love you. I won't let anything happen to you.*

"Don't dare speak to me in my language, zhid," Tserverin replied, his anger rising.

"OK, OK," Tolya said in English.

"That pissed him off," Pete mumbled. His eyes caught Tolya's. He tilted his gaze and his head almost imperceptibly to his right. The non-verbal language between them was so intimate, Tolya caught his meaning immediately. He too shifted his gaze almost imperceptibly to the right. There in the corner of the kitchen in a small hallway leading off to the rear access to the apartment was Chicho, crouched against the wall, his gun drawn, unseen from where Tserverin was standing.

"Nicholai," Tolya called out to him again. "What do you want? I know what you want. Let me give you what you want. You want me, not her."

Tserverin smiled and laughed again. "I have exactly what I want and you know that. When I kill her, it will kill you. I will have my revenge."

Tolya stood up. He dropped his gun to the floor and raised his hands at his sides. "Take me, Nicholai. Go ahead. Take my gun. Kill me with my own gun. Act like a man. Men don't kill defenseless pregnant women."

Tserverin reacted. He pressed the machete a little closer to Karin's neck. She winced in pain, but no blood seeped from the spot under the point of the machete. Tolya knew what was happening. He had seen that before, the arch of her back, and the weakness in her knees. Her labor had begun in earnest. He didn't have much time. Oleg couldn't have picked a worse time to arrive. He spied Chicho moving like a crab along the floor to position himself behind Tserverin.

"Hah, you insult my manhood. You think that will make me charge you, attack you? You Jews, always so devious. You never fight like men, always the tricks. The same way your father tricked mine. He stole his place on the Olympic team. He stole his victories. I will take my revenge now for everything you have stolen from us. I will steal from you the thing you prize most. Your Latina bitch and your half-breed child."

With that, the thinnest stream of blood trickled down from under Karin's neck. She didn't scream, as she felt no pain. The warm trickle alerted her to what had happened. She breathed deeply, both to calm herself and to hide the pain of the next labor pang as it began in her back and spread.

"No," Tolya screamed. He recalled something Erno once told him about revenge sometimes being more important for the soul than forgiveness.

The shots from Pete's gun rang out. The first hit Tserverin in the shoulder. The second hit the window behind them, the weather-proof glass cracking into a pattern of tiny fragments but not shattering, held together only by molecules. Tserverin fell back and, grabbing his shoulder, releasing his hold on the machete, which fell to the floor. Pete charged forward and grabbed Karin, shielding her with his body.

Chicho came up behind Tserverin and grabbed him, holding him up, his chest exposed, and pushed outward. Tserverin screamed in agony as Chicho pulled his shoulders back. Tolya grabbed the machete off of the floor and lunged toward Tserverin.

He had a thousand thoughts in his mind but none came out of his mouth. He was well past words. This man and his family had tried to destroy Tolya's. He had taunted Tolya as a boy, his father had presided over their disgrace, the system and state he worshipped had cost Oleg his life, and he had nearly killed the only woman Tolya had ever loved and his unborn child. He had murdered god knows how many other women, including his best friend's greatest love. He stepped back for a second and spat in Tserverin's face. He lifted the machete with which Tserverin would have cut Karin's throat and plunged it into his chest. Chicho let the body drop to the floor.

Tolya turned toward Pete. "Is she all right?" he said, barely audible.

"I'll be fine," Karin said. "Just get me to a hospital. Your son will be here in no time and this is no place for him to be born."

"Are you all right, hermano?" Pete asked.

"I am now," he said. Tolya caught sight of himself in a long mirror on the wall across the room. He was covered in blood, Tserverin's blood. It had splattered all over him as the machete sliced through Tserverin's heart. He turned his head toward the opening doors of the elevator at the front of the apartment. A SWAT team charged in with guns drawn, shouting. Tolya and Chicho put their hands over their heads. The armed, masked police surrounded them.

"On the floor," the team leader shouted at them. Tolya and Chicho dropped to their knees. Pete remained on the floor, head down, propping up Karin.

A very large man strode into the room. "What the hell is going on here?" he shouted.

Tolya raised his head. "I can explain, captain."

Chapter
36

COLUMBIA-PRESBYTERIAN HOSPITAL, WASHINGTON
HEIGHTS, NYC
15 JUNE 2010
10:30 A.M.

TOLYA SAT IN THE PLEATHER hospital chair in the maternity ward at Columbia-Presbyterian, little Oleg wrapped in a blue blanket in his arms. Karin lay in the bed with Max and Erno. A small white gauze bandage covered the cut in her neck where Tserverin had placed the machete. Pete sat on a folding chair turned backward next to the door, arms leaning on the back of the chair as he always did.

"Uncle Pete?" Max said.

"Yep, buddy?"

"Do you have brothers?"

"Sure do."

"How many?"

"Four, and a couple of sisters too."

"Wow, that's even more than I got. It's hard to be the big brother, you know."

Pete laughed, as did Tolya and Karin. "I wouldn't know," he replied. "I'm the youngest."

"Take my word for it," Max said. "It's a lot of work."

Karin caressed Max's face.

"Oh really?" Tolya said. "You seem to have done well enough with Erno." He moved Oleg's face close to his and kissed him on the forehead. Oleg had one eye open. "I'm sure you'll do fine with Oleg as well. Would you like to hold him?"

"Give him to me," Karin said, shifting onto her elbow to prop herself up. Tolya handed the baby to her. "Come here," she said to Max.

"Me too," said Erno.

"OK, you too. Sit opposite your brother and cross your legs." The boys did as they were instructed. Karin took Oleg and placed him on their laps. "Maxi, put your hand under Oleg's head."

Erno ran his hand lightly over Oleg's silky blond baby hair. "See, I'm a big brother too," he said.

"Yes, you are," Karin whispered to him, stroking Erno's dirty blond hair.

Pete pulled his phone from his pocket. He remembered back some years to a moment in Tolya's apartment when Karin was pregnant with Max. Tolya was frantic. He didn't know how he would ever learn to be a father. Look at him now.

"Smile," Pete said. They all looked up and he snapped a picture. "Finally good for something other than taking pictures of pretty women on the subway when they're not looking. C'mon Tol, we gotta get over to the station. We're meeting with internal affairs in half an hour."

"Yep," Tolya said. He bent over and kissed Karin gently on the lips, lingering for the slightest second. "I love you, all of you." He kissed his children on their heads. "Let's go." He walked around the bed toward the door. He hesitated for a moment at the door, then embraced Pete. "Gracias, hermano," he whispered into Pete's ear.

"For what?" Pete replied.

"When Oleg died, I felt so alone. I felt that way for years. You've made all the difference. You're the brother I lost."

"Igual," said Pete, the tears dropping from his eyes despite his best attempt to stop them. "And you for me. Thank you, man. Thank you for all the years you listened to me without ever judging me. I couldn't have picked a better man to be my brother." He hugged Tolya close, then let him go and walked off toward the elevator rubbing his eyes with his large hands.

Tolya turned toward the bed. There was his family, the woman he loved and the children she had given him. A life he would never have known if she hadn't had the patience to put up with him and all his baggage.

"I think both detectives Kurchenko and Gonzalvez are aware of how many departmental regulations they have broken," the captain said. He was seated at the head of the conference table in the large interrogation room at the rear of the station house. "But they did apprehend and neutralize a serial killer who is responsible for at least one murder in this country, not to mention at least a half-dozen more in at least three countries."

"Nevertheless, there will have to be a hearing. They behaved like criminals," said the investigating officer from IA. "Until that time, I am afraid we will have to suspend both of you. In light of the circumstances, I will recommend that you be suspended with full pay."

"How long?" asked the captain.

"Thirty days at least."

"Guess I'll be shorthanded for a while."

"Take a vacation," the IA officer said. "Off the record, you've both earned it. But we do have to follow regulations. Tolya, please send Karin my regards."

Tolya and Pete sat in the back of the Caridad on 184th and Broadway where Tolya had met Karin so many years before. They sipped on the thick espresso. A sad bachata played in the background.

"Somehow, I think we will survive this," Tolya said.

Pete nodded his head slightly. "Yeah, I think you're right. We might get demoted for some time or something, but we're not getting thrown off the force and we're not going to jail. We eliminated a known serial killer, and your wife worked for IA and she was his next intended victim."

A chill ran through Tolya. It had been that close. A few more minutes and they would have been too late. He always tried to play by the rules, but this time Pete had been right. There was no time. They had to do what they did. What was that ridiculous expression he hated so much? A man's gotta do what a man's gotta do? Well, this time they did. "True. I think we will get off with the minimum."

There was a silence between them for a long moment. That wasn't unusual for them. After all these years, they could nearly read each other's minds. They could communicate with the slightest non-verbal signal: a tip of the head, a wink, or a finger barely pointing at something. "You wanna talk about it, hermano?" Tolya asked finally.

"I gotta bury them."

"I know."

"Both of them."

"I know."

Pete finished the espresso. "Want another?"

"Sure."

He signaled to the waitress. "Dos más, y un tres leches."

"Tató," she called back to him.

"I gotta take them back to Santo Domingo."

The waitress brought the coffees and the cake. She placed the cake with two forks between them.

"You know he hates these plastics," Pete said to the waitress, nodding and smiling in Tolya's direction.

"OK," she said, picking up the forks. She returned with silverware a moment later.

"Why do you always blame everything on me?" Tolya said, smiling and taking a forkful of the white creamy cake.

"Because I can."

They polished it off in minutes.

"Tol," said Pete.

"Yeah, hm... that was delicious."

"I want you to come with me to Santo Domingo."

Tolya hesitated for a moment. "I can't go to Santo Domingo now. We just had a baby. Besides, the bris is in four days and the conversion is tomorrow."

"So you're gonna do it?"

Tolya smiled and chuckled. "Nope, Karin and the kids. As far as I'm concerned, I'm Jewish enough. I don't need anyone's blessing. The moment Tserverin called me a dirty Jew, I knew for sure. I am as pure as I need to be. Nothing to prove."

Pete nodded. "Good for you, brother. I'll wait the four days. The bodies are in the morgue. It's been so long since they died, particularly Mariela, a few more days aren't gonna make a difference. Besides, I gotta make all the arrangements, and what you got to do anyway? You're on vacation, remember?"

"True, I am."

"You'll come with me then?"

"Let me talk to Karin, but yeah, of course. 'Cause I also want you to be Oleg's godfather."

Pete looked away from Tolya. "It's OK? I'm not Jewish."

"Sure," said Tolya. "Technically, neither am I."

Pete smiled. "Hermano, there's one more thing."

"What's that?"

"I want to bring back Mariela's daughter."

Tolya sat up in the chair. "She's alive? You know where she is?"

"Chicho does. He knew all along. He hid her."

"When did he tell you?"

"Last night."

"You really believe she's yours?"

"I think so, but even if she isn't she has no one. I owe Mariela that much."

"And Glynnis? She's OK with this?"

"Yes. She's a good woman, always was. That's why I have to change."

Chapter
37

TOLYA HAD HIS HAND ON Pete's shoulder. "You OK, hermano?"

"Sí. I'm OK, brother. They're at peace," Pete replied, the tips of his fingers touching the closed casket lightly. The deep brown color of the mahogany soothed him. He raised his eyes slightly to the other casket, almost identical, on the far side of this one. How strange, the two people who had touched him the most deeply, side-by-side, gone. There was so much more he would say if he had just five minutes more with either.

"Did you want to be alone with them for a few minutes before everyone comes in?" Tolya asked. His father's funeral flashed in his mind in a nanosecond, then his mother's and then Oleg's, a frozen memory in the white emptiness of Siberia. Here in Santo Domingo, the air warm and heavy even in the air-conditioned viewing room, it felt like another planet, another lifetime. He was alone, an orphan, and then he heard Pete's deep, melodic voice and knew in fact that he wasn't. Fate had provided them with each other to ease the pain of loneliness.

Pete hesitated for a moment. He turned toward Tolya. "No, I've been alone enough. Tell the director to call them in." He grasped Tolya's hand and drew him in. "Gracias, hermano."

"De nada," Tolya said. He walked toward the door and waved at the funeral director. He gave him the sign and the mourners filed into the room.

Pete stood with Imelda and Katarina. He was surprised at how many people had come. He vaguely remembered some of their faces. They had aged. He chuckled to himself, so had he.

Some smiled at him, some asked him if he remembered them. He said yes even when he didn't. He wanted them to believe him, these beleaguered men and women. He knew how important memory and connection were to them.

Finally, toward the end of the line, Chicho entered. He came up to the girls first and took their hands, kissing them gently on their cheeks. Then he stood in front of Pete. He remained silent, then put his arms around Pete and softly began to cry.

"Tranquillo, hermanito," he said.

"Ta demasiado, Pedrito. I don't know who I loved more, him or her. And now I can't tell either of them. They're gone. I'm alone."

"No, little brother. You will never be alone. You will always have me. And they knew, they knew how much you loved them." He hugged Chicho close to him as he did when they were boys, when Chicho, always a little younger and a little smaller, needed his protection and his affection. "Go, sit down, tranquilo." He held onto Chicho's hand and guided Imelda and Katarina toward the front row of chairs. They sat down, Tolya at the end of the row.

A priest entered the room and took to the lectern. He welcomed the family and offered his condolences. He said a short prayer and began to speak briefly of first Polito and then Mariela. At the mention of Polito's name, a high, shrill wail came from behind Pete. He knew it was improper for him to turn and look back. Imelda and Katarina sat to his right weeping silently, handkerchiefs to their noses and eyes. A second wail began from somewhere behind them. He leaned toward Chicho. "Who are these people?" he whispered in English.

"I'll explain later. Your uncle was a very generous guy."

The priest motioned toward Pete to walk to the lectern. He reached into his pocket and took out the notes he had prepared. He looked at them. They were short and too impersonal. He refolded them and put them back.

His uncle had been a very generous person, Chicho had said. It was time for him to make his own peace, with both of them. Who was he to judge? His uncle had done a lot of terrible things, but obviously he had done some good too. And Mariela? Life had driven her to terrible places. He had no right to judge her either.

He looked out over the crowded room. The last pair of eyes he met were Tolya's. Tolya nodded at him with that mischievous grin creeping up in the corners, the same way it did every time they were about to do something clearly unacceptable to the department and its rules. He responded in kind, then began.

"Honored guests, thank you for coming to comfort us in this hour of sadness. I had prepared something to say, but I realize now looking at all of you here that I need to speak from my heart. I want to talk about love, a word that has many meanings.

"There is nothing greater than love and no love greater than first love. There are many kinds of first love. There is the love we have for our parents and the love we have for those who become our parents when our parents cannot be there for us. There is the love we have for our friends, especially those friends who become like our blood, and then there is the love we feel for a woman, the first time we are willing to open our soul to one.

"I have felt all these kinds of love, and the people for whom I have felt that love are all in this room. Sadly, two of them are here behind me. My uncle and I missed many years for very bad reasons, his pride and my shame, but mostly my inability to forgive him. And what is love really about but forgiveness? Forgiving someone for not being who we expect them to be. Tío, for this I am sorry, I ask you to forgive me. You were there for me. You were who I needed you to be when no one else was there for me. You made me the man I am today. I beg you to forgive me. I understand now what you did and why. I only have to look out over this room to understand that.

"And you, Mariela, you were my first true love, my most intense love, and I apologize to you that I wasn't there for you when you needed someone. I had promised you forever and I gave you nothing. I should have understood how difficult it was for you to trust anyone. I should have shown you how to trust me. I know now that you loved me with a passion rare in this world, and I should have returned that passion. Forgive me, please."

Pete looked up. He felt his own tears on his cheeks now. The women at the back of the room who had been wailing stood up. They put their arms around one another's waists and began to sing a hymn, a quiet song he remembered from his childhood. The others in the room stood and began singing with them.

He let himself cry, really cry, for the first time. The man who had been his father was gone, as was the woman who should have been the center of his life. That passion comes along only once in a lifetime. He knew he couldn't change what had happened. He knew now he had to find Mariela's child and make his life with Glynnis work because she loved him, despite him. She loved him the way he had loved Mariela.

Tolya was surprised. They called it a novena. To him, it looked a lot like a shiva. Instead of seven days, it went on for nine. But it was the same. Candles burning, mirrors covered, mourners sitting on low stools, lots of people visiting every night and entirely too much food. These people didn't know it, but Tolya felt it. There were Jews in their past. This was a vestige of hidden Jews who had crept into Dominican history centuries earlier.

Imelda and Katarina observed the custom as they were raised to. In a way, it was more to honor the mother they had lost so many years ago than the father they had had so little contact with in the aftermath of their mother's death. And it was to mourn for a sister they had lost as well. Tolya accompanied Pete every night to the house of a distant cousin where Imelda and Katarina were staying. Then, late in the evening, Pete would call some of his cousins and they would go out. Deep into the barrios where the bars were open all night, filled with people trying to escape the poverty for a few hours by finding a bit of solace in a cold beer and a bachata danced a little too close.

Pete's cousins taught Tolya to dance—salsa, merengue, bachata. He knew a little. Karin had tried to teach him many times. He was always resistant. He never felt right on the dancefloor, somehow clumsy. How could he dance in front of those people in the clubs where Karin took him to meet her old friends from the neighborhood? They moved so naturally. Every step was an effort for him.

But here, somehow, it was different. The music entered his body like a cool breeze on the broad, white beaches they visited during the day. In fact, there was something perfect about the whole place. Everything about it was warm, the way everything about Russia had been cold. He thought of Max Rothman and Erno Hieron. What must this place have been like for them when they came to Sosúa decades ago? When he heard merengue, real merengue, for the first time, he understood that moment when Max met Anabela.

But mostly, he fell in love with the bachata, el alma del pueblo. It had been banned by Trujillo, but in the fifty-plus years since his death, it had become the soul of the people. He mastered the steps, wanting to shock Karin when he came home. Almost always sung by a man, it was almost always about lost love. Its passion betrayed the heart of Dominican men. It stripped them of their macho and bared their souls. These tough guys knew all the words, which they mouthed silently as the music played and the lyrics recalled their own broken hearts.

It touched him as well, though he didn't understand the words. The passion of the music alone was enough. The sweet whine of the guitars and the vocals sparked his Russian soul, the soul he teased about endlessly. It often brought tears to his eyes for its simple emotional honesty. He realized after a week in this warm, close place, where everyone touched everyone all the time, that there was less separating him and them than connecting them to each other. He didn't really need the language. He needed only to respond to a smile with a smile. He was something by birth—Russian, Jewish, an immigrant American who learned to love baseball. He was never sure. But he knew now what he really was. He was Dominican by choice. He would hold this place in his heart forever.

They sat with Chicho on plastic chairs in the late afternoon sun outside a house on a street that consisted mostly of steps. No cars passed here. They couldn't. The patio, the small neighborhood where they were staying, sat on the side of a hill and was accessible only on foot. They sipped at their cold Presidentes. The young girls came by every fifteen minutes or so to bring them fresh ones and food, always something to eat. No one had any money in this country, but no one went hungry either, not a guest anyway.

"You see that retaining wall over there to the left of the church?" Chicho said, taking a long swig on the beer.

"Sí," Pete said.

"It nearly collapsed about five years ago. Those two houses sitting above would have collapsed as well. Your uncle sent the money to fix it."

Chicho had pointed out a dozen examples of Polito's generosity in the past days. After the large turnout at the funeral and the clear affection the people of the patio had for Polito, Chicho began to explain to Pete what Polito had done to make his penance. "Do you understand where we are? Do you remember this place?"

Pete looked around, surveying the hillside cluttered with little houses and broken concrete paths. "Not really."

Chicho sighed. "You were so lucky to get out of here, to go to New York when you did. This is where Mariela was born, where her parents were killed. After they were killed, your uncle protected this place from Double X. After he left, they had no one to protect them. Your uncle contacted me. He told me to check on them and that whatever they needed, he would give them. They had protected Mariela while her parents were murdered and he would always be in their debt. He gave them whatever they needed that he could."

"Why didn't anyone ever tell us?" Pete asked.

"Why didn't you ever ask?"

"How would I have known to ask? And if he was so generous here in the patio, why did he leave his daughters and Mariela to live the way they did?"

Chicho rose from the chair. He turned his back to Pete and swigged back the remainder of the beer. He turned back around. "Coño, it was all so complicated. First of all, you and Imelda and Katarina didn't want anything to do with him. You hurt his pride. He was a man. You couldn't treat him that way. He was desperate to see them, to see you, but the American government was also watching him. Part of his agreement was that he would have no contact with them. It was cruel."

"We all know it's possible to make contact when you want it."

Chicho sat back down on the folding chair, his elbows on his knees. He tipped his head slightly to one side and raised an eyebrow. "You didn't want it and neither did they, and he knew that. They blamed him for their mother's death. They thought he didn't care. He cried for that woman every day. I saw it."

"Yet he had quite a few girlfriends."

"So do you. He was a man. He needed women, but he loved only one woman."

Pete hesitated. His initial reaction was to punch Chicho for that remark, but he stopped himself, recognizing that he and Polito were the same. "I realize I was wrong about him. I only hope somehow he knows that." Pete looked up for a moment, then back at Chicho. "And Mariela?"

It wasn't the first time Pete had asked Chicho about Mariela in the past few days. Chicho kept avoiding the discussion. He sat back, tipping the chair onto its hind legs, and folded his arms over his chest. His forearms were enormous from decades of lifting weights. "I suppose it's time you knew."

"I've been asking you all week and you keep saying you'll tell me later."

"Most of it you already know. She couldn't live the life she was living. She was terrified that the people who killed her parents would somehow find her in the States and kill her. She had seen their faces, and for all those years, Polito had protected her. So she disappeared. She changed everything, from her name to her looks. When we found her in that club, we tried to bring her back to us. But she didn't, wouldn't, go."

"Polito tried to help her?"

Chicho stared at the floor. "And I was so in love with her." He shook his head. "Who didn't fall in love with her? Polito knew the thugs she was involved with. He tried to pay them off to let her go."

"They wouldn't take the money?"

"She told him to leave it alone. She said she was fine. She said she was satisfied with her life. She said she wanted to forget the past and that she was involved with one of the bosses and he could protect her from her past."

"Polito let her go?"

"He had no choice. She came to meet him with the Russian, the same maricón who killed her, who we finished. She came in furs and jewels and said Mariela was dead, that Polito should forget her."

Pete stiffened. He sat upright and stared at Chicho. "You knew she was with this animal?"

"We didn't know he was a murderer."

"And you let her stay with him?" He wanted to choke Chicho. To stand up and strangle him right there. "Why didn't you call me? Why didn't you tell me?"

"And what could you have done? What would you have done?" Chicho replied. They stared at each other for a long moment.

Tolya watched them both, expecting one to jump the other any second. He wanted to defuse the situation. "Pete, there's nothing you could have done. She was a grown woman, free to live her life any way she wanted."

Pete deflated into the chair. He brushed back his hair with his hands. "There's one thing I can still do. Where is the child, Chicho? And don't tell me we can talk about it later."

Chicho stood up from his chair. "With my grandmother."

"Deep in the campo?"

"Sí."

"Why?"

"Because Polito asked me to hide her."

"Polito knew?"

"Yes. When the Russian threatened her, she became terrified for the child. She contacted Polito. He sent me to take the child."

Pete sat shocked. "He knew, he knew all along. Why didn't he tell me the truth?"

"He wanted to save you from more pain."

Pete marveled at the beauty of his country. He had forgotten how green it was. He and Tolya followed Chicho on the highway. Chicho wanted to come in separate cars so that he could stay with his grandmother for a few days.

Tolya rode in the passenger's seat in silence. After a while, the radio reception faded and he turned it off. "How much farther?" he asked.

"Why, you got somewhere you gotta be?" Pete chided him.

"Only thinking about you, hermano. You haven't said a word since we hit the highway."

"I'm concentrating on following Chicho."

"You know these roads like the back of your hand, and besides, there's only one highway."

Pete smiled. "Verdad."

"You wanna talk about it?"

"What's there to talk about?"

"How you're gonna feel when you see her?"

"What's the difference how I'm gonna feel?"

"She might be your child."

"Or she might not."

"Chicho seems pretty sure."

"Chicho says a lot of shit."

"There's one way to find out for sure."

"And Tolya, what difference is it gonna make? I'm gonna bring her back one way or the other. Glynnis is OK with it."

"If she's not yours, how you gonna do that? You know the laws."

"I'll adopt her. Just gonna take a little longer. She's an American citizen anyway."

Tolya saw Chicho's blinker go on just before he turned off the road to the left. "Look,' he said.

"I see it, Tol. Anyway, I know the way."

"Busy following Chicho, my ass."

Pete pulled up about fifty feet from the main highway and pulled over into an unpaved parking lot. He turned to Tolya. "Hermano, you know how I am. I'm a quiet guy, I don't say much. But you always know what I'm thinking."

"I'm thinking you hope she's yours."

"I'm praying, brotherman, I'm praying."

The climb to the village took a little over an hour. The heat and humidity of the valley floor gave way to clean, fresh, supple air at the top. In the clearing, one could see the haze over the capital. In the other direction, the top of Pico Duarte. The simple wood huts and the thick vegetation reminded Tolya a little of the camps in the forests in Ukraine where he would go with his grandparents to pick wild mushrooms in the fall. While it was warmer here, the air had the same fresh feel on his skin, the same scent full of the earth and the sky.

They were met with handshakes and kisses. Chicho led them into a small wooden house at the top of a small hill.

"It hasn't changed in twenty years," Pete said to Tolya as they entered.

In the corner on a wooden rocking chair sat a very old woman. She rose with great effort. She was tiny, no more than five feet and weighing well less than 100 pounds. A small girl of about 7 or 8 helped her up. Pete's head became light. Mariela's daughter, his daughter.

"Ven aca," the old woman commanded Chicho.

He walked to her and embraced her, her entire body disappearing into his. "Hola, Abuela, cómo le va?"

She smiled broadly, her teeth still in her mouth, gleaming white. "Toy bien," she said. "Gracias a dios. Y tú? En Nueva York? Cómo le va?"

"Le va bien, mi madre. Pero es mejor aquí, contigo."

She laughed. He took a small bag from his pocket and gave it to here. She looked inside and laughed again, then slapped Chicho playfully on the head. She put her tiny, bony fingers into the bag and withdrew a handful of candy corn. "Desde Nueva York," she said and laughed again, popping two pieces in her mouth. She offered some to the young girl.

As she stepped out of the shadows, Pete studied her. She was the image of Mariela, her long dark hair hanging slightly over her face, the smile the same as Mariela's, enchanting, intoxicating. Her eyes were deep and dark, intense.

And that was the thing Tolya noticed. They were the same as Pete's eyes, dark as pools at night reaching deep inside. Tolya knew those eyes. They had saved his life more than a couple of times. Being partners was something only cops understood. It was a relationship of trust deeper perhaps than even brothers, even twin brothers. You depended on this man for your life every day, and he on you. You got to know his eyes and everything they said without speaking. At that moment, Tolya knew. He didn't need a DNA test to confirm it, this was Pete's child.

"Luz," Chicho said, turning toward her and bending down to kiss her on the forehead. "How are you doing?" he asked in English.

"Bien, Tío Chicho," she said.

"You're picking up Spanish then?"

"Sí, and I knew a little from before." She looked toward Pete and Tolya.

"These are my friends," Chicho said.

Pete walked forward to greet Chicho's grandmother. "Me recuerdas, Abuela?"

She looked at him, not sure for a long moment. "Pasa mucho años, pero sí, ya recuerdo. Cómo te llamas?"

"Pedrito."

"Por supuesto. Y el gringo?" the grandmother said, pointing her bony finger at Tolya.

"Mi amigo," Pete said. "Mi pana. Mi hermano."

"Bienvenido a mi casa," the old woman said, attempting to rise again from the rocker.

Tolya walked toward her quickly and took her hand, then bowed his head slightly. "Mucho gusto," he said. Pete looked at him and smiled. "Hey, I picked up a few things from Karin's family."

"He has a Dominican wife," Pete said to the old woman.

"Tiene suerte," she said.

Everyone laughed.

Tolya looked at Pete. "She says you're lucky."

Tolya smiled broadly at Chicho's grandmother. "Mucho," he said.

Pete turned toward Luz. "Hello," he said. "I'm Pete. Here everyone calls me Pedrito."

"That's funny," she replied. "You're not little. Actually, you're pretty big. My mom told me she had a cousin once, he was like her big brother. She said his name was Pedrito."

"That would be me," Pete said. "Pedrito."

"She loved you very much," Luz said. "She told me that." Luz tugged at Chicho's hand. "Is my mother coming too? Remember she said she would come with you to get me?"

"She's still in New York," Chicho lied, dropping to one knee and caressing Luz's hair, pushing it back from in front of her face. "We're here to take you home."

Luz looked at Chicho's grandmother, then back at Chicho. "But what about Abuela? Who will help her? I thought Mama would come here and we would take care of her together."

"We'll talk about this later," Abuela said. "Now let's have something to eat. Y tú tambien, gringo."

They walked out of the little house, and on the grassy area in front of it were tables set with plates and platters of food. They helped Abuela to her seat at the head of the table and sat themselves around her. The men began passing around the platters already on the table and the women brought out more courses. Tolya recognized most of it. Karin had been cooking for him for six years. There was rice and beans, two kinds, red and black. There was stewed chicken and rabo and pernil. There was yuca and tostones and maduros and fresh avocado. Then there was the mystery dish that was passed around in bowls. Tolya picked up a spoon and took a taste. It was very rich and flavorful.

"You gonna eat that?" Pete said, mischief in his eyes.

"Don't wanna be rude."

"You know what it is?"

Tolya took another spoonful. "Not sure I want to."

Chicho smiled, took some himself from his bowl. "Hmm mondongo, my favorite."

Tolya nearly choked. Karin had tried to get him to eat this many times. It was her aunt's specialty. But all the same, it was innards and he didn't eat innards.

Chicho laughed out loud. He slapped Pete on the chest. "Now he's a real Dominican."

"Sí," Pete said. He put his arm around Tolya. "Gonna take another spoonful?"

"Fuck you," Tolya said as he swallowed what was already in his mouth.

"Luz, what's your favorite secret spot here?" Pete asked. They sat together on the steps of the house.

"The little house at the top of the mountain. Nobody lives there. You can see everywhere from there."

Pete remembered the little house. The spot where he begged Mariela to become his wife. The spot where she lied to him, told him she was with Chicho so that he would go back to Glynnis. "Would you show it to me?"

"Sure," Luz said, getting up and straightening her skirt.

She did that just the same way he had seen Mariela do it so many times.

They walked slowly up through the dense forest toward the little house, holding hands. After about ten minutes, they reached the top. Luz walked to the edge of the peak, the little house behind them, and pulled back the branch from a bush to expose the view of the valley below. Pete remembered standing in the same spot so many years ago with Mariela. He felt his chest tighten.

"It's very beautiful, isn't it?" Luz said.

"Yes, it is. Do you come here a lot?"

"When I want to think about my mother," she said. "I come here to send my thoughts to her."

Pete's heart broke a little. "Show me the little house, Luz."

"Sure." She led them to the hut. It was tiny, three small rooms, empty now.

They sat down on the steps of the house. "Luz," Pete said. "I have to talk to you about something." He felt himself begin to choke up a little.

"I know," she said, looking up at him, her deep dark eyes reflecting his. "May I call you uncle, Pedrito?"

"Of course," he said. He took her small hand in his.

"Something happened to my mother, didn't it?" Luz said.

"Why do you think that?" Pete asked.

"Because she said she would come for me and she's not here. He hurt her, didn't he?"

"Who?" Pete asked.

"My father. He threatened her, that's why she sent me here. She didn't want to live with him anymore. She didn't want us to live with him anymore. He got very angry."

"How do you know this?" Pete asked her.

Luz looked down at her feet. She released Pete's hand, then folded her hands over her chest. She started to cry a little.

"Luz, please tell me," Pete put his arm over her shoulder.

"I heard them. I heard them fighting at night in their room. Sometimes I would hear things breaking, crashing, something banging into the wall. Then the next day, my mother would have a black and blue mark on her arm or her face. She would say it was nothing, that she fell on the stairs."

"Did this go on for a long time?"

"It started around Christmas last year."

"How often did they fight?"

"At first never. I never remember them fighting. Then my father got this letter or something and he kept screaming at her about a test. A test she failed. I didn't know what he was talking about. That's when he started to treat me badly too. He would scream at me. He wouldn't let me sit on his lap or play with him. I never knew why. What I did."

"Then?" Pete asked. She began to cry more heavily. He pulled her closer to him. "Go ahead, baby, cry. It's all right. Let it out. Then what happened?"

"Then one evening, momma packed my things in two suitcases and took me to meet Uncle Chicho. She said that she couldn't explain it all, but that my father was sick and the sickness made him dangerous and he could hurt me or her, so she was sending me away to someplace safe for a little while but that she would come to get me when everything was OK. She said she would come with Uncle Chicho, but she's not here. I know something terrible happened to her."

Pete held her tightly for a few moments longer.

"Uncle Pedrito, please tell me the truth. Where is my mother?"

Pete opened his mouth to speak. Before the first words came out of his mouth, the tears flowed down his cheeks. "Luz," he said. "My sweet child, I'm so sorry. I don't know how to tell you this other than to just tell you. I can tell you I know how you feel. I loved your mother too. But she's gone. She was killed."

She sobbed. "My father hurt her?"

"It doesn't matter who hurt her now. He's gone too. He can never hurt anybody again. My friend, your new uncle Tolya made sure of that."

"It wasn't my father?"

"No, mi amor, the man who hurt your mother wasn't your father."

"Where's my father?"

"We don't know that right now, Luz."

"Who's going to take care of me?" she said, the sobs shaking her body.

"I will," Pete said.

Mariela's voice rang out in his ears. "Each of us has our own destiny," he heard her say.

He looked into Luz's eyes. "Tío Pedrito will. The same way Tío Polito took care of me and Uncle Chicho and your mother when we were young and alone." Pete looked out over the valley below toward Pico Duarte. He kissed Luz gently on the head. "You will never be alone, Luz. You will always have me. You are my destiny."

THE END

A.J. Sidransky is a longtime resident of Washington Heights, NYC. He travels frequently to the Dominican Republic. He has written several articles and short stories. *Forgiving Mariela Comacho*, his third novel, is the sequel to *Forgiving Maximo Rothman*, which was chosen as a finalist for **Outstanding Debut Novel** by the National Jewish Book Awards. His second novel, *Stealing a Summer's Afternoon*, was chosen as a finalist for **Best Second Novel** by the Indie Book Awards.